MW00623491

The Sound of a Thousand Stars

The Sound of a Thousand Stars

✧ *A Novel* ✧

Rachel Robbins

alcove
press

Published in the United States by Alcove Press, an imprint of The Quick Brown Fox & Company LLC.

Alcove Press and its logo are trademarks of The Quick Brown Fox & Company LLC.

Library of Congress Catalog-in-Publication data available upon request.

ISBN (hardcover): 978-1-63910-896-1
ISBN (ebook): 978-1-63910-897-8

Cover design by Heather VenHuizen

Printed in the United States.

www.alcovepress.com

Alcove Press
34 West 27th St., 10th Floor
New York, NY 10001

First Edition: October 2024

10 9 8 7 6 5 4 3 2 1

In loving memory—
Leon Harold Fisher (1918–2012)
&
Phyllis Kahn Fisher (1919–2009)

For Sadie—
I love you more than the stars.

In the six hundredth year of Noah's life, on the seventeenth day of the second month—on that day all the springs of the great deep burst forth, and the floodgates of the heavens were opened.

—New International Version,
Genesis, 5:32–10:1

God does not play dice with the universe.

—Albert Einstein

Prologue

July 16, 1945
Alice

Alice Katz did not exist. She was a rumor holding a stopwatch. In twelve seconds, she would be lost to all of history, swallowed up by New Mexico. "T-minus twelve. T-minus eleven. T-minus ten." She heard Sam Allison's familiar voice counting down. She surveyed the network of crisscrossed wires entangling her in the cottage, an elaborate spiderweb. She fidgeted with the Geiger counter on the windowsill and adjusted the dial on the shortwave radio, trying to tune away the static.

Alice had passed the witchy hours while New Mexico slept studying the storm through the window, trying to see the empty desert through sheets of rainwater. When the night sky quieted, residual raindrops rolled slowly down the windowpane and her mind recited theories of cohesion and adhesion as she watched the water molecules interact.

"Water is attracted to water," she mumbled. "Water is attracted to other substances."

She thought about how in outer space, raindrops would be perfectly round spheres. But here on earth, gravity weighed down the shapes into teardrops. *Here on earth*, she thought. That phrase might mean something very different soon.

"T-minus nine, T-minus eight, T-minus seven," Sam counted through the radio.

Alice felt like some mythological beast with two beating hearts. The fetus was already the size of a laboratory beaker, and it was growing. She had heard once, somewhere, that pregnant mothers were at once one and also two.

"T-minus six. T-minus five." The radio stuttered into white noise. She braced, knowing that in a matter of seconds, either a second sun would rise on the horizon or it would be the end of the world.

At the edges of her vision, she noticed that the trees were shining gold.

3

T-Minus 20

August 1996
Haruki: A Story Told Backward

Even though Hiroshima Peace Memorial Park was relatively abandoned on weekdays, Haruki Sato hid his face. Overhead, the A-bomb dome exoskeleton loomed. What had once been Hiroshima's busiest downtown district—the place where, at nineteen years old, Haruki had darted between factory workers at rush hour and crammed for exams in the library—was abandoned. Scientists had proclaimed that no vegetation would ever grow from this scorched earth again. As Haruki limped through the field of shrubs in the blaring heat, he marveled at the poisonous red flowers that defied scientific logic. Kyōchikutō, as oleander was called in Japanese, had become the official flower of Hiroshima.

He dragged the wheels of his oxygen tank over the uneven ground, desperate to stand among the toxic roots. Even with tubes in his nose, he could smell the flowers' hazardous perfume wafting. Among the fiery blooms, he couldn't shake the sensation that when they were raked by the wind, the flowers seemed to be breathing.

Haruki knew that ingestion of any part of the beautiful, toxic flower could mean death. He tried to inhale deeply. He placed a blood-red petal in his mouth and it disintegrated on his tongue. It was soft as silk.

1

June 1944
Alice

As she drove through the security checkpoint at the main gate, Alice tried to ignore the warning signs. *Peligroso!* read bold letters in red and black, dappling the barbed wire perimeter. *Prohibida La Entrada* and *No Trespassing. US Government Property.* It felt like the beginning of a horror story.

From so high up on the mesa, she could make out the desert floor combed smooth by the wind. In her rearview mirror, the peaks of the Ildefonso Mountains were drawn like crude animal teeth. The desert sand was redder than she'd thought possible, and the rust-colored silt was everywhere: kicked up in the road and tingeing her windshield. Ahead of her, the red dust whirling in the wind seemed alive.

The gate clinked closed definitively behind her.

Her car jostled and bumped over potholes, and she gripped the steering wheel, terrified of a flat. Laid out before her was a maze of lopsided houses and stairways to nowhere. Everything was painted monotone army green, and the buildings were mirror images of each other. The whole mesa seemed like a mirage, wriggling in waves of heat.

Many of the homes seemed to be facing the wrong direction, their backs to the street, as though they were hiding. Children's toys emerged out of the muddy, red earth like weeds. Crimson dirt lined the side of an abandoned baby stroller fading in the sun. A clothesline sagged near some picnic tables, and colorful laundry flapped like butterflies in the breeze. The trash cans were overflowing, and several were overturned. Parked cars were sinking into the muck, and the license plates were so filthy the numbers were illegible—only a few were discernible with the state motto shimmering through: "New Mexico: Land of Enchantment."

A few young men staggered by like zombies in the heat. Alice was startled to see that even the *people* of the town were coated with a film of red dust, their dirt-caked faces glistening with sweat.

This wasn't what she had expected after her clandestine recruitment—a mysterious phone call around midterms from someone who'd claimed to represent the Office of Scientific Research and Development, seeking under Vannevar Bush to recruit scientists for the Manhattan Engineering District. At first, she had wrongly supposed that meant the research would be located in Manhattan. Now, looking around at the jagged mountain peaks and winding roads to nowhere, Alice keenly felt how far from New York she really was.

She knew she was only there on Dr. Oppenheimer's recommendation as one of his preferred understudies. They were so desperate for help that they were willing to look the other way and hire a woman scientist. Despite her numerous questions, all she had gleaned from her phone call was that she was being sent "somewhere in New Mexico." But she was reassured by the rumors around the Berkeley physics building: whispers of Nobel laureates and the opportunity to test the limits of the known universe. Surely, those legacies were here, too, somewhere, but now, sinking into the sludge, men were dressed in cowboy jeans, their belt buckles flashing in the sunlight.

She hesitated over which of the crisscrossing gravel roads to follow. They all seemed to lead to the same place, Ashley Pond, which was flanked by army barracks and the additional barbed wire perimeter of the laboratory complex. The pond had been named for the town founder, Ashley Pond II, who had built a school for boys on this land—though he was by no means the original inhabitant of this place.

In preparing for her move to the mysterious city, Alice had scoured the Berkeley library. The checkout card on a book about New Mexico had read like a Rolodex of strange, vanished physicists. Alice had read about the indigenous communities Pond had displaced when he constructed school buildings out of horizontally stacked ponderosa pine logs and modeled his curriculum after the Boy Scouts of America: an outdoorsman education complete with uniforms and neckerchiefs. Paying no mind to the history of the site, he encouraged his schoolboys to rearrange remaining pueblo structures to their liking and dismantle holy sites. Alice knew that the homesteaders, mostly of Hispano descent, had been allowed to stay so long as they served food in the mess hall and swept the dormitory floors. But in recent years, they, too, had been removed from their homes to make way for Oppenheimer and his community of scientists. Pond had at least been paid for the land, and it retained much of the ethos of his school for boys who wore shorts year-round to toughen them up, regardless of the plunging temperatures.

It made sense that Oppenheimer had chosen this place. Pond had been a sickly child with bronchial infections and typhoid, and consequently had been prescribed a warmer climate, much like Oppenheimer himself. In this isolated wilderness, Pond had taught boys to ride horses, hunt, and walk with a purpose. Alice wondered fleetingly whether she was one of the first females to cross this threshold.

She braked and stared at the ramshackle laboratory buildings across the pond, the main tech area flanked by a perimeter of barbed wire. Alice had never before stepped foot in a real lab. Most of her research in theoretical physics had taken place in sterile campus buildings, in the company of undergrads vying for a passing grade. As a woman, she'd been barred from innovations like the increasingly larger cyclotrons, or any of the hushed elements housed in the Rad Lab. Now, the slapdash army construction before her on the opposite shore seemed eons beyond her grasp. She couldn't believe she was there at all, and she tried to repress the uncertainty knocking around in the back of her mind that she was only there on Oppenheimer's good word.

She squinted to see through her mud-splattered windshield. She ran the wipers, but they only rubbed the red grime in. The tired station wagon had strained up switchbacks and the steering wheel was still warm, the heat rising up through the dash. She killed the engine.

"Stay here, Pavlov," she said, giving her golden retriever a quick head rub and stepping outside into the glare. Alice had named the furry, yellow dog Pavlov after the scientist of canine reflex fame, but ironically, it was more often Alice who exhibited conditioned responses to the dog's behaviors. She gauged the world through his alarm and joy. She hadn't dared embark on this journey without him. Now, she tried not to feel too unmoored by the worried expression in his storybook eyes as she exited the vehicle.

In keeping with the cowboy aesthetic, Ashley Pond II had constructed a wooden water tower, which rose over the western-style buildings like a second sun. Alice shielded her eyes and admired the structure. It felt like she had driven backward in time. This town built for boys had, until now, seemed mythical, having only existed in her mind as its code name: Site Y.

She watched the reflections of the army buildings sparkle and ripple in the pond.

"Mrs. Katz?" said a voice behind her. She turned to see a young military guard blinking at her. Inside the car, Pavlov exploded into a thunderous growl, rocking the vehicle.

"I told them I had a dog," she offered in explanation. "When I signed the contract." If she was going to agree to sixteen months isolated from the world, bringing Pavlov was nonnegotiable.

"Pets are fine," said the guard, surrendering his hands like she had pointed a gun at him. "Pets don't talk."

The man stepped closer. She could smell the metallic stench of his sweat. His uniform was sticking to him in the heat. His hair was freshly cut and the buckles and badges on his uniform looked very important, but he couldn't have been a day older than seventeen. His face full of freckles and acne gave him away. She relaxed.

"Lieutenant Abrams," he said, saluting her. "Call me Saul." The more he spoke, the more his New York Bronx accent clogged his words. "Welcome to Quantum Land, Mrs. Katz."

She elected not to correct him about her marital status. While she was quite correctly a Katz by birth, she was not yet a Mrs. It would be too hard to explain that she was not married to Warren VanHuff, only engaged while he drifted on a tanker into the port of Le Havre, standing stick straight and saluting in his military fatigues with his chin in the air. Besides, she had only ever agreed to the match to appease her mother. She hated that the pear-shaped diamond she wore on her ring finger was a conversation starter. It rested atop an elaborate art deco setting, engraved with her grandmother's de Young family crest.

As an heiress to the San Francisco de Youngs, Alice bore the elite lineage of both the famous art museum and the most reputable newspaper in the city. While she fingered her ring and Saul hoisted her luggage, it occurred to her that she had not insisted on her correct designation as *Doctor*.

In coming here, she had agreed to trade her penthouse apartment overlooking the Golden Gate Bridge for utter invisibility. Going unnoticed had seemed a welcome change after the high-profile and public drowning of her then fifteen-year-old sister, Abigail, had filled her childhood with the flashbulbs of tabloids and news vans double-parked in their drive. She'd been only eleven years old when it happened, and the tragedy had followed her family in the decade and a half that followed. In the aftermath, her father became a recluse and her mother took to sherry. While her parents secluded themselves in dark rooms and friends delivered casseroles, Alice had watched ferries drift east through her bay window, so slowly they seemed not to be moving at all. She had often dreamed herself onboard, or up onto the blinking airplanes overhead.

Rather than mourn her sister, Alice had vowed to continue where they had left off. Like Alice, Abigail had had a mind for science, and an insatiable drive for professional success. Most nights, they had stayed up late whispering in the dark about Marie Curie. Alice, in particular, was engrossed by Madame Curie's work with uranium salts, even if she had been overlooked, assumed to be merely an assistant to her scientist husband. It broke Alice's heart to think that her name had nearly been forgotten, that she had come so close to being snubbed for the Nobel Prize. But despite the odds, Curie had found invisible rays of energy, an inexplicable additional substance coexisting in the mineral that was more radioactive than anything anyone had ever seen before.

In the wake of Abigail's death, conducting experiments in Alice's high school laboratory had freed her mind from the lonely existence within her penthouse walls. One teacher after another had singled her out, recommended her for scholarships and fellowships, admired her endless curiosity. By day, she exuded academic excellence. But questions of science had kept her up at night.

Alice had accepted this role with no idea how her research would be used, placing all her trust in Dr. Oppenheimer—the same man who held the physics department hostage with his Chesterfields and mood swings. Only last quarter, he had disappeared from class for several weeks and administrators had had to drag him back from the Sanskrit department. But the more he berated his students, the more they imitated him, and Alice was no exception. She had to figure, of course, that her work here was related to national defense and the war effort. Perhaps they were building heat-seeking missiles or lasers. Regardless, she felt certain that Oppenheimer would never be on the wrong side of history. Abigail would have longed for this kind of adventure, this proximity to greatness and scientific discovery. Alice had ached for it all her life. And here she was: she had landed in a faraway land.

Saul dragged her suitcases through the muck, and she slid around behind him in her peep-toe heels, snapping her feet from the goo. Despite the leather ration, she had wedges and espadrilles for every occasion. Usually so proud of her footwear, she was suddenly embarrassed by her extravagance in this dusty, casual town.

Saul jangled a janitor's ring of keys, swinging the door to a small house open and flooding the dark home with light. It was so bright outside Alice had to wait a minute for her eyes to adjust to make out the military-issued chairs and couch. In the bedroom, there was a small cot with a blanket stamped in white letters against that same militant green reading *US Armed Forces*.

"It's no Taj Mahal, but it'll do," Saul said, following a few steps behind her as she opened doors and cabinets and Pavlov ran from room to room sniffing around.

"I've been tasked with reminding you of the operating rules," he said, looking sheepish. He launched into a recitation: "Refrain from calling any of the scientists by their professional titles for any reason," he began. "If you go to town, don't talk to strangers except for in an emergency." He rattled through an exhaustive list he had clearly recited a hundred times over. "If you see an acquaintance," he instructed, "you are allowed a half smile and a partial nod, but nothing more."

While he spoke, Alice watched the layers of her identity blow away like the strands of a cobweb in the wind. It must have shown on her face because he repeated sternly, "A partial nod and nothing more."

He paused, waiting for affirmation. "Right," she agreed.

"And I've been instructed to kindly remind you about the drought," he said. Alice felt her eyebrows react but tried to smooth her expression.

"What does that mean?"

"Showers will be a luxury," he began, nodding in the direction of the claustrophobic shower stall. Seeing her face, he rushed to explain: "Only about five houses are equipped with bathtubs, and those are for the 'special' residents. Dr. Oppenheimer himself is lucky to occupy one of the homes on what the boys are calling Bathtub Row."

Most of the dwellings in Site Y were constructed of plywood or thin wall-board, isolated and sinewy as though they might fly away in a strong gust of wind, their surrounding landscapes barren. Bathtub Row homes, Alice would come to learn, were made from more permanent materials, like logs and stones, and boasted vegetable gardens and trees.

"Cap your showers at thirty seconds," Saul instructed, "like we do in the army." He paused, waiting for a response, but she gave none, so he pressed on. "You need to distinguish between potable and nonpotable water."

"What?" she asked, her voice sounding crosser than she'd intended.

"You'll need to recycle bath water for use in the toilet," he clarified, show-ing her a bucket tucked under the sink for this purpose.

Just then, a whistle hissed outside the window, followed by an enormous boom that made them both jump.

The floor rattled beneath their feet. The army glasses jiggled in the cupboard, clanking against each other. A salad plate toppled from its position on the shelf and crashed to the floor, shattering. Alice covered her head and cowered.

"What in the heavens?" she asked after it stopped, straightening and dusting herself off. "Was that an earthquake?"

Saul grinned. "Dynamite. Keeps ya on your toes. Home sweet home." He saluted, then turned on his heels and left, kicking up red dust on the gravel road until he was out of sight.

This was the most alone she had ever been. Even in the hours after Abigail had been swept away by the undercurrent, Alice had been surrounded by people. She had waited in the pristine Cliff House restaurant with its wall of windows overlooking Ocean Beach while helicopters flashed searchlight beams and boats dragged for the body. Someone had draped Alice's wet hair in a towel. Another had cloaked her in fur. She had still been in her swimsuit. She had been shivering. They had offered her tea, but the cup kept rattling when she raised it to her lips, the tea sloshing around.

In the months and years that followed, her parents developed a habit of turning on the radio to fill the house with conversation. And of course there'd been the noises of the city: the fog horns on the bay, the honking traffic on Geary Street, the exhale of the city buses as they settled at each stop. Now, there were no man-made noises. Alice could only hear the crickets chirping and the cicadas ringing. She fanned herself. The still heat was suffocating, her curls sticking to the nape of her neck.

It was strange that she hadn't told her parents where she was going. She hadn't even told Warren. He had promised her a wedding fit for a queen before being deployed. He was a good man, a brave man, and her parents adored him. He faced rifles, flamethrowers, and grenades in the trenches, and still sent love letters flapping across the ocean, reminding her that to him she was the only girl in the world. Perhaps he said it a little too much, insisted a little too desperately, considering that he had barely taken notice of her change of postal address.

Planning their nuptials had brought her parents joy for the first time she could remember, and her parents deserved a wedding. Since Abigail hadn't lived long enough to do it, she would give them the grandchildren they deserved. Someday, holding their grandchildren's tiny hands, they'd wade into the water without fear.

But first, she would do her part to help end this war. Her children would live in a world free of Nazis and firing squads, shooting prisoners stripped naked into open graves. She had been sick hearing on the evening news about the gas chambers where instead of water, prisoners showered in carbon monoxide. She wasn't sure what, but something had to be done. This was her chance.

She steeled herself and turned the shower tap cautiously. The pipes coughed and spat out chunks of mud before running clear. As soon as the water pooled, two beady-eyed black scorpions darted out of the drain and marched around the tub in a frenzy. Alice shrieked. Sheltering most of her body behind the shower curtain, she strained to turn off the faucet. The insects darted back into the drain and disappeared into the wormhole universe of the pipes beneath her. How many of them lived in there? She had to flush them out.

There were a few basics pre-stocked in the kitchen. She sprinkled the tub with baking soda, the powdery substance snowing out of the cardboard box gently, just like it had when she and her mother baked gingerbread, or she and Abigail instigated a chemical reaction resulting in foam that could fill a balloon. When she dumped the vinegar into the tub, the solution frothed and bubbled, producing carbon dioxide. She had only been there five minutes and already she was using science to kill.

After a few moments, she stepped into the slow trickle of the shower, summoning the courage to wash her face. The chlorine stung. She knew it was a good burn—that the chlorine had been added to disinfect harmful illnesses otherwise prevalent in that slap-shod sewage system of interlocking pipes and tessellations. She pressed her fingers into her eyelids until she saw red, dancing shapes.

Abigail would have wanted this, she reminded herself. Alice had chosen this. She had spent so much of her life faking her way through pleasantries at her mother's dinner parties, and treading softly when the guests departed and there was no one left to put on a brave face for. While their childhood friends had scribbled in *Little Housekeeper* coloring books, Abigail and Alice had stared out their window of stars from their bunk bed and wondered how many light years the helium and hydrogen had traveled to make it to their small corner of the world.

"What's there?" they had asked the night sky. "How does it work? How did it come to be this way?" In Abigail's absence, Alice lay awake at night wondering.

When the news first broke about the mass executions in Germany, Alice was no longer a child. The rumors about soap and candles made from Jewish corpses had launched her into emotional adulthood early, but now she had the lanky body to match her serious affect. A teenager with a "Growing Girl" brassiere and a head of curls swept back in bobby pins and a headband, she had hidden the newspaper from her father. Their family wasn't religious, but they were still Jewish. In light of his grieving over his elder daughter, there was no telling what the news would do to him.

Listening to the radio in the coat closet, Alice learned how the Nazis armed many executioners so that no one man would know for sure whom his bullet had murdered. Even with the anonymity, guards still required psychological counseling as women's and children's arms and legs were dislodged and strategically stashed between torsos to fit in the killing pit. That was why the gas vans, the radio explained, had come along. It was like Schrödinger's cat, she had thought. Sometimes it was difficult to differentiate between science and violence.

The shower water continued to spurt out in uneven bursts, with long pauses when no water came from the faucet at all. When the water did come, it wasn't enough to wash the shampoo from her hair.

She counted to thirty seconds as instructed, limiting herself to an army-style shower, thinking of all the things that came with the number thirty: the atomic number for zinc. The atomic weight of phosphorous: 30.9738. Thirty was the number of eggs in the carton, and the number of upright stones at Stonehenge. The number thirty had everything to do with how humans measured time, she thought, drying herself with an army-issued towel and tying a bandanna around her head to hide her greasy hair. The number of seconds in a minute was divisible by thirty. The average number of days in a month was thirty. Even when Jews sat shiva, mourning their dead for seven days, they abided by the law of thirty where hygiene was concerned. Her own father, Ishmael, had not cut his hair, shaved, or clipped his nails for thirty days after the funeral. At least that was the reason he gave.

Inside the commissary, Alice was underwhelmed by the narrow aisles and the fruit flies buzzing around the spoiling produce. She picked up a basket and strolled the aisles, thumbing the tomato paste and refried beans absentmindedly, scanning the backs of people's heads and observing their purchases. A woman in a purple sundress and large glamour sunglasses was flipping through the glossy pages of a magazine she clearly did not intend to buy. A man was reading the nutrition facts on the back label of a box of Grape Nuts.

She couldn't help but wonder who each of these people were—she was thrilled by the prospect of standing in line behind the same men who had discovered the basic rules of the universe. There'd been rumors in the Berkeley physics department, before her classmates had vanished one by one until the lecture halls were empty, that this place would be chock-full of the world-famous physicists who had written her college textbooks. She knew their words and ideas, but she didn't know their faces. She wondered whether they would look the way their research sounded.

A man with an athletic build and long, wavy hair was lecturing a few young Special Engineer Detachment recruits between the weather-beaten artichokes and the shriveled bell peppers. She recognized their brown uniforms as the same Saul had worn. Saul had mentioned something about being plucked right out of his undergraduate physics class, selected from the other rank and file GIs for his basic knowledge as a machinist. She hoped the SEDs were skilled mechanics and electronics technicians, and they certainly looked important in their gleaming uniforms and military haircuts, but seeing their doe-eyed expressions filled her with doubt. These were boys, not men. They were looking for a hero.

The physicist before them had a long melon face, like a crescent moon. He seemed to have abandoned whatever task had brought him to the commissary in the first place in favor of saying something lofty about nature. He spoke in such a quiet voice that they all leaned toward him. His words strung together, making him nearly impossible to understand. Because of this, all eyes were trained on him, watching his lips intently. "Nobody thought that one could get the basis of biology from the coloring of the wing of a butterfly," he said.

The woman in purple had stopped reading her magazine and lifted her dark glasses for a better look. She nodded at Alice. "Baker's up to it again," she said.

"Who?" she asked.

"Oh, Bohr. He traded his famous name for an American pseudonym. It's all code names these days. Everyone just calls him Uncle Nick." She rolled her eyes and returned to her magazine.

Alice had been taught Niels Bohr's model of the atom all the way back in high school physics. Last she had heard of him, he was fleeing the Nazis in a fishing boat on his way to Sweden. And here he was, in the flesh, shopping for cabbage.

"The trouble is the netting of language," he was saying. "There must be an infinite progression of selves, an entire sequence of *I*'s who must consequently consider each other." He was gazing at the watermelons but didn't seem to see them. "It's like looking down into a bottomless abyss," he said with finality. By now, more scientists and military personnel had stopped to listen. He was drawing a crowd.

"Are you saying we need to divorce science from language?" asked a young military man with a freshly shaved head, framed by a precarious mountain of limes. Behind him, a woman with frizzy hair was pretending to squeeze an eggplant, pausing to listen.

"I try not to speak more clearly than I think," Bohr responded. "But I do think we need to distinguish between physics that seeks to understand what nature *is*, and physics that concerns what we can *say* about nature."

Alice stared. She remembered hearing how Bohr had worked with a chemist to dissolve the golden Nobel Prizes preserved in his institute to save them from the Nazis. The Wehrmacht had goose-stepped right by the liquid gold in a beaker. It was something out of a spy novel. Alice was convinced through and through that whatever side of history Bohr was on had to be the right one.

The bell on the door chimed announcing the entrance of a new customer, and Bohr seemed to snap out of his theoretical reverie and realize where he was. "Oh heavens, Margrethe will be wondering where I've run off to with her tomatoes," he said and sauntered off, leaving the produce aisle mesmerized.

Alice watched him hop effortlessly down the stairs, taking them two at a time, and out of her line of vision. *Niels Bohr eats tomatoes*, she thought.

The basis of biology from the wings of a butterfly. She traced her fingers along the cantaloupe and honeydew, feeling the porous rinds and estimating the radius and linear velocity were she to set them loose, rolling down the aisle like bowling balls. What if the undulating lines on the watermelon had mathematical explanations? Perhaps the meaning of life was hidden in an apple seed. What if humanity was looking in all the wrong places?

Standing there, by the wilting leafy greens, Alice felt closer to Abigail than she had in years. She had done it. She was here.

2

June 1944
Caleb

When Dr. Oppenheimer addressed his squad, Caleb's chest fluttered with nervous energy. It felt a little like falling in love. His thin professor seemed somehow more at home here in this wild terrain than he ever had in a classroom. The sun was unforgiving and, beneath the shadowy halo of his porkpie hat, the normally pale professor had acquired a sun-kissed tan. He strode around the recruits at a fast clip, like he was drawing energy from the earth itself. He seemed to be floating, his heels barely touching the ground. It occurred to Caleb that he was circling them like a predator.

At Berkeley, Dr. Oppenheimer had seemed swallowed up by his clothes, frighteningly skinny, like some sort of alien species in a sports coat. Now, he walked a little bow-legged, and instead of a sweater vest, he wore a large golden belt buckle and Wranglers. Caleb stood perfectly still, staring through waves of heat, refusing the impulse to swat away buzzing insects.

"You are the first Special Engineer Detachment," Dr. Oppenheimer announced, staring over their heads, nodding at the staff sergeant. Behind him, at the barbed wire perimeter, military men spoke code words and numbers into scratchy radios.

"Your work is important and necessary," he went on. "You will usher in a new era." But he still didn't say exactly what they would be working on.

Afterward, like he had been a desert mirage, Oppenheimer vanished before they could get close enough to ask questions.

Caleb was exhausted, but in the adrenaline of this place, he wasn't sure he would ever sleep again. He had ridden in from Berkeley on a specialized Pullman train. When they stopped in Tracy, five more men had ambled onto the car, blinking in the brightness, looking around disoriented by the ornate carvings and beaming brass. Then in Fresno, seven more men had boarded the train. They all wore the same confused expression.

All the passengers had been restless overnight, trying to sleep through the jostling bumps, having been recruited without knowing where to or what for. On the ride, the men made far-out guesses as to what they had been hired to build. They had compared stories about clandestine phone calls and top-secret instructions while they reclined on burgundy upholstery and feasted in the dining car on entrees served on white linen tablecloths. They had sipped ice water from crystal glasses and wiped their faces with napkins folded like clamshells. It was ironic, Caleb had thought, that the train car was one of the most beautiful places he had ever been. The grand interior was finished with oak and lit by amber windows. It was like the inside of a sunset.

Caleb's Orthodox father, Levi, had grown his beard long in accordance with the 613 commandments. Waving him off from the elevated train platform, his beard had blown around like a wind vane. Through his privacy drapes in the sleeper car, Caleb had watched Levi hold onto his yarmulke while his beard wafted in the blowing gale, and the strings of his tzitzith gusted around in elaborate tangles.

It meant a lot that he had come to see him off. Caleb knew his father disagreed with his research on principle, but Caleb had taken this job for the family's sake—surely he had to see that. The only money to their name was tied up in a dilapidated garden unit apartment in the Fillmore, flanked by shuttered dry cleaners and hardware stores that had been owned by Japanese families before the upheaval of Executive Order 9066. Lately, since they couldn't make ends meet with the sales from their family-owned corner grocery, Levi had been dodging phone calls from lenders, lurching with anxiety at every pair of wingtip oxfords that marched by the kitchen window. Even if Caleb hadn't been drawn by curiosity to this mysterious job "somewhere in New Mexico," financially, he had had little choice.

He'd managed to secure a partial scholarship through the National Youth Administration, part of Roosevelt's New Deal. But the program had ended before he could graduate, and he'd had to make up the difference in tuition, an impossible task even with overtime work and work-study. When he took night shifts on the janitorial staff, he had tried not to care when students stepped over his mop or navigated around his cleaning cart without meeting his eyes.

When they'd received the notice of default, it made sense for Caleb to drop out of his PhD cohort. He had already obtained a bachelor's degree, the first in his family, and he could use that for gainful employment. Instead of paying tuition and board, he contributed toward missed mortgage payments. He'd done the math. With his older brother, Asher, enlisted and only earning basic pay, and his mother's arthritis interfering with her ability to do night shifts at their corner store after closing out her day job as a maid in the Marina District, they'd had to hire a replacement. It had made more sense to work the store himself.

Having witnessed his father's shortcomings all his life, Caleb had carefully cultivated his persona to avoid looking Jewish before he departed. He was clean-shaven and kept his curly hair cut close to his scalp, shearing the curls off before they coiled into ringlets. He wore ironed shirts and slacks even on the weekends. He was preoccupied with the illusion of wealth because his family had none. Still, he had stood out like a sore thumb among the truly wealthy on that Pullman train, with their effortless pinstripe-lined coats and designer luggage. You could always tell a fake.

In the heat, orientation felt endless. While military police herded the men slowly like a pack of hunting animals, he concealed his telltale six-pointed star medallion necklace beneath his uniform, but on the inside, Caleb was still a Jew.

Awaiting his assignment, Caleb felt around in his pocket and withdrew his recruitment letter. He'd carried it around like a talisman after someone had slid it under the door of his family's store while he was working the register on the night shift. He turned it over in his hands. *Confidential* was written in alarming capitals. He hadn't disposed of it as instructed. Glancing around at the other recruits to make sure no one was looking, Caleb unfolded it and read the lines he'd already committed to heart:

Dear Caleb Blum, it read. The Commanding General of the Army Service Forces has authorized the establishment of a Special Engineer Detachment, so that essential technical personnel can contribute their expertise to the top-secret project located at Site Y. Your information was obtained through a combing of the National Scientific Roster. If you choose to participate, you will be compensated at a monthly salary of $400 or $4,800/year. In gratuity for your service to your country, all forthcoming tuition fees will be covered by the US government. This fixed-term contract stipulates a sixteen-month enlistment beginning on the first day of June 1944, at the conclusion of which it will automatically renew from month to month beyond the period herein *identified for an additional period of up to three years. To agree to these terms, please board the specialized Pullman train departing from San Francisco's Third and Townsend Station this Saturday, May 31ˢᵗ, at 5:35 PM. Immediately after receiving this notice, this letter must be destroyed by shredding or burning.*

Yours,
Henry Stimson
Undersecretary of War

Careful to fold it along the seams, Caleb slipped the letter back in his pocket. Four-hundred dollars was more money than he had ever had all at once. It added up to eight new suits in a month, or six new cars in a year. Of course, due to the ration on wool, he'd be relegated to single-breasted "victory suits," and with auto manufacturers making munitions for the war, there were no new cars for purchase. But Caleb still couldn't resist doing the math. Beyond that, the letter pledged future tuition. It might be wishful thinking, but there was at least a chance that he could finish his graduate degree. And, he thought, thinking of his father's tight expression and his mother's strained limp, if he sent his paychecks home in time, he could possibly save their home.

When they finally lined them up, Caleb stood a full head and shoulders above the other recruits. He was broad enough to fill a doorframe. His brawny stature made up for the fact that he was a man of few words. Having been a shy child, he'd spent much more time listening than speaking. Words became very precious to him. He'd quietly watched his parents bickering over bills in Yiddish and Asher pressing girls up against walls in alleys strewn with graffiti when he thought no one was looking. He'd watched his mother pretend not to notice the piercing stares when she waited for the bus in her sheitel and scarf, and he'd seen his father's face go white at the sight of a swastika scratched with a key into the brown paint of their front door.

Caleb bided his time. Then, on his tenth birthday, his vision began to fail him, the corners of the room going out of focus like a fishbowl. He got dizzy trying to focus and developed a habit of feeling his way around the room, trying to cover it up. He knew money was tight. He was convincing enough that no one had realized his vision was impaired until he started failing classes in high school.

His glasses had opened his world back up, but they'd also cost them a month of groceries, and he treated them delicately, wiping them clean with a handkerchief obsessively, and double-, triple-checking their placement by the bed before switching off the light. Those lenses were his bridge to the reality of the world in which he lived. Without them, he floated around, his mind full of daydreams and unspoken thoughts.

As an adult, he still wore the same thick-rimmed frames, but now, when he took them off, he was blind as a bat. He still had a shy nature, but he had learned to persevere in the adult world. He spoke up when spoken to, but he would rarely initiate a conversation. He chanted along with the other recruits, "Sir, yes sir!" and there was comfort in the uniformity. He had a strange sensation that while he was blending in, he was also standing out for the first time in his life.

After all, Henry Stimson, the undersecretary of war, had signed his recruitment letter himself. Of course, Caleb wasn't after recognition or fame, or anything so petty. He just wanted to send paychecks home to help his parents fend off the mortgage collectors. For all its flaws, he loved that apartment. Once his vision had been restored with appropriate eyeglasses, he had committed every intricacy of the flat to memory, appreciating every optical detail. He knew every warped floorboard and could make his way in the dark without stumbling. He had patched every hairline crack in the paint and on sleepless nights, he had memorized the knotty pattern of the woodgrain ceiling by heart: a tessellation of stars in space. No matter where he traveled, he had a perfect picture of that flat in his mind's eye. It was the structure by which he measured all other structures in the world. But still, he had to admit, it was nice to feel important in this new place, among these western-style buildings, in this cowboy town. Standing at attention in the heat, he felt certain that this job would make him memorable.

Caleb was assigned to the Critical Assembly Group for something called Project Rufus. He would be working under the renowned Otto Frisch, who worked closely with Niels Bohr himself. When they called Frisch's famous name, the scientist stood up but did not smile. In a harsh Austrian accent, he asked, "Ja?" Frisch had dark hair and close-set eyes. Caleb studied his serious expression. He recognized the resemblance to his equally famous aunt, Lise Meitner. He recalled hearing that she had been invited to Los Alamos but had refused on ethical grounds. He wondered what they could possibly be building that would frighten a woman who had escaped Nazi Germany.

Only after the adrenaline of orientation had subsided did he realize he was starving. He lined up with some of the others outside a small shop, one of only two on the hill.

"Hiya," a soldier said, approaching him. Caleb, having nearly completed his doctorate, was twenty-six years old, which was fairly old by Los Alamos standards. Most of the other SEDs had been recruited right out of their undergraduate classrooms, so they were eighteen or nineteen at most. This particular soldier struck Caleb as being childish, with a face full of baby fat, more like a boy than a man. He was swallowed up by his military fatigues, short and freckle-faced, with a faraway look.

The soldier inched closer and repeated himself. Caleb searched the space behind and around him. It hadn't occurred to him that the young man could be talking to him. At Berkeley, he had always rushed in late to section, a consequence of racing from one odd job to the next trying to pull in extra cash, amplifying the transience of his presence. In his discussion groups, his TA had often called him by the wrong name.

The boy got close enough that Caleb could smell his sun protection cream. "Hiya," Caleb mumbled.

If his affect was less than friendly, the young soldier took no notice. He turned toward the concession stand and whispered conspiratorially, "In Cherbourg, they're burying hand grenades connected by telephone wires and connecting hidden steps to mines." He nodded at the lineup for food. "And we're sittin' here eatin' sammiches."

Caleb immediately recognized the Yiddish in his thick New York accent. Whether he practiced or not, the young man was a Jew.

The soldier shook his head in disgust and spat on the ground, miming the mannerisms of a grown man. It just made him seem even more childish. "I marched with the Young Pioneer League, and somehow I ended up here like everyone else."

At his unashamed reference to communism, Caleb glanced nervously at the guards. "It's only a sixteen-month enlistment," Caleb said. "Blink and you'll miss it." He was lying. Sixteen months was a lifetime. Only sixteen months ago, his older brother, Asher, had joined the air force. He could still hear his father mumbling the words of the Tefilat Haderech, the Traveler's Prayer, under his breath when Asher had suited up. He had mumbled the words all over the flat in different octaves like a tuning orchestra: in the lofted bedroom, staring at the herringbone linoleum in the kitchen, thumbing through the moth-eaten winter coats in the coat closet, and opening and closing the pantry endlessly, searching the corn meal and bread flour for something he could not find.

"Sure," the soldier grumbled. "And after that it's month to month. They try to make it feel like a choice. But it's still a bunch of gobbledygook." He lit a cigarette and tried to shake out the match, but it nearly burned him. He flicked it onto the dirt and stomped it out.

"We would have been drafted anyway," Caleb justified. It was true—they likely would have ended up on the front, and he didn't want to kill anyone. He imagined Asher piloting his fighter plane above the clouds. From above, the trenches below would look like anthills. He wondered whether Asher would write him at PO Box 1663—the secret address he had been given for correspondence. Asher was stationed with the Royal Air Force in Britain, maintaining fleets of aircraft, far from the Nazis. At least, that was the last Caleb had heard of him; he hadn't responded when they asked for help paying off the mortgage collectors.

The soldier was staring at him hard like he was trying to place him. He stood squarely in front of him although he was dwarfed by Caleb's size. He offered his hand with brazen confidence. "Private Saul Abrams," he said. "Just down from NYU." He wore several golden rings. When they shook hands, the rings pinched Caleb's fingers. Despite his petite build, Saul had a surprising handshake.

"Private Caleb Blum," he said, trying not to wince. "Took the train over from Berkeley."

"Ah, so you know the director from before he was the director."

The admiration on the faces of the other SEDs at orientation had not been lost on Caleb. Oppenheimer was the messiah of science. There were feverish rumors about the lecture he had given in Dutch in the Netherlands, despite not speaking the language, which had led to the acquisition of his beloved nickname: Oppie. Men and women alike swooned in his presence. Caleb deduced that by proximity to Oppenheimer, there was hope he could become the sort of man who left an impression. Saul was staring up at him with intrigue. Caleb didn't see any harm in letting him think he knew the famous professor better than he did.

"He took a shine to a few of us," Caleb said, averting his eyes. "Always wanted to talk shop."

Truth be told, Caleb had never spoken to Oppenheimer directly. He had never even dared to raise his hand in lecture. The crippling shyness Caleb had worked so hard to overcome from his childhood seemed to come flooding back in that domineering man's presence. When Oppenheimer asked a question, his eyes seemed to go bluer as he searched the room, reminding Caleb of the way a shark's eyes roll over into white right before the attack. Then, inevitably disappointed, Oppenheimer would turn his back to the stadium-style seats and mutter more to himself than to the students, a cigarette dangling from his lips and bobbing with each syllable. He'd scratch out incomprehensible ramblings on the chalkboard, and act as though the class wasn't there at all. It was him alone, confronting the cosmos, speaking a strange dialect made up of physics and poetry and prayer.

Occasionally, Oppie stopped scribbling, pausing in heroic poses. Even with his pleated trousers and muted vest and sports jacket, Caleb remembered thinking that no one had ever looked more like a cowboy. He was enchanted, but he never once said a word. Instead, he had leaned in close and tried to smell up all of Oppenheimer's smoke.

What harm could come of pretending he had been in his inner circle? It was just a gentle lie. Being associated with Oppenheimer was currency in this place, and the more success he garnered, the more money he could send home. "'Course," he continued, relishing in the way Saul's eyes sparkled, "Berkeley's a small town."

"Is it true what they say? That his physics are good but his arithmetic is awful?"

Caleb smirked. "You should see the scratch-outs in his gradebook. He's a genius all right, but he couldn't run a hamburger stand."

He turned away to avoid further questions and selected a warm Coca-Cola and a limp deli sandwich from a rack with a sneeze guard. He unwrapped the sandwich, but he only stared at it. The combination of honey turkey and swiss cheese wasn't kosher. Faced with his first opportunity to break the rules, he couldn't bring himself to take a bite.

"How do you eat this stuff?" he muttered.

"Don't ya figure God's got better things to worry about than whether I eat bacon or get laid on Yom Kippur?" Saul said through a mouthful of food.

"It's more than that," Caleb said. "It matters who we are. What gets me"—he paused, staring hard at his turkey on rye—"is the way everyone flocked to the Berlin Olympics with all the rumors of murdered Jews being turned into lampshades."

Saul's face turned. "Listen," he said. "That's why we're here. Somebody's gotta do somethin'. It ain't perfect, but when they write about it in history books, you and me will be heroes." He thumped his chest.

Caleb looked around the room at all the young men who had traded their lives, chewing deli sandwiches and potato salad. It gave him hope to think about it. They had done as they were told and promised their futures to the army. "I guess that's something," he said. "Blind faith. They could have sent us to the moon. Or overseas as spies. And here we are."

"Oh, but ain't it worth it," Saul said. "They're going to let us look behind the magic curtain." Saul was referring of course to *The Wizard of Oz*, but Caleb pictured the embroidered curtain in front of the ark veiling the Torah scrolls, shielding the word of God.

Suddenly, the lights buzzed off and the room went dark. Caleb startled, repressing a horrified sensation that God had read his thoughts. He was no longer a believer, but the traditions and superstitions that had governed his life still had a hold on him. The soldiers stopped eating and looked around confused.

"It happens all the time." Saul shrugged. "Blackouts, I mean. Just means they're up to something exciting in the lab." In the darkness, Saul's eyes seemed to glow, making him look like an animal. "Just you wait," he said. "Our lives are about to become science fiction."

T-Minus 19

August 1996

Haruki: A Story Told Backward

Haruki sensed something moving. He realized he was not alone with the oleander. He turned and tried to clear his foggy vision. He couldn't quite see the cenotaph, but he could make out the arc of it blocking the sky. Standing before it, at the center of the abandoned Peace Memorial Park, stood a figure who looked about to blow away in the wind.

Rolling his oxygen tank, he drew close enough to see that it was an older woman in a housedress. She was too tall to be Japanese. With one hand, she clutched a bonnet with a flapping veil, fighting off the summer breeze. On her other side, she squeezed the arm of a middle-aged man with night-black hair. She seemed to be leaning on him for support.

Haruki stared at the man. He was old enough that his eyes gave him away, but young enough that he still stood straight as a rod. He thought of the buried child beneath their feet, or what was left of her. If Junko were still alive today, she would be about the same age, perhaps a little older. It wasn't fair that she'd never grown old, that he had only ever known her as a child. He suddenly felt lightheaded, holding his oxygen tank for support. The woman didn't hear him over the wind. She looked both ways furtively, her gray curls billowing up in the air, then she dug through her purse and removed something. The thing seemed to shudder in her trembling, wrinkled hand, and it took Haruki a moment to realize it was only a stone.

She gingerly positioned the stone at the base of the memorial beside a spray of yellow chrysanthemums rattling in the breeze. When she stepped back, it seemed to glow.

Haruki recognized the tradition. In all his peace talks and travels coping with the aftermath of the war, he had acquired many Jewish friends. He was familiar with Hebrew prayers for the dead and the tradition of sitting shiva. He knew the placing of stones on gravesites was not a biblical commandment, but more of a superstition. It had to do with the ephemerality of flowers, like humans, as organisms that wither and die. A stone, on the other hand, would live forever.

3

June 1944
Alice

"I told you, I can't say where I am," Alice hissed into the rotary telephone. She could hear her mother, Mabel, grimacing across the line. Mabel had spent years warning her that if she wasn't careful, academics would intimidate Warren away from marrying her, and now her worst fears were coming to fruition. In the background, her father, Ishmael, sounded frantic.

Ishmael was always telling Alice she was shaped like a scientist. "Your height was designed for daydreaming," he'd say, laughing that she was taller than any of the men who courted her, and she suspected he was thrilled when she showed no interest in any of them. "Your head belongs in the clouds." He, too, was full of dreams, but she often thought he was too fragile for the world.

Now, he sounded terrified over the phone, rattling off talking points and headlines. He sounded like the world was closing in.

Her mother ignored him and sighed through the receiver. "I'm trying to understand, dear, but you're not making it easy." Alice was being shorter than she'd intended. She hadn't slept a wink that first night in her army-issued cot, trying to tune out the chirping insects and roaring desert noise. It was early, and Alice wondered whether her mother was already wrapped in the formality of a silk scarf. She always draped herself in linens like a set table. Mabel took up a lot of space in the world. Everywhere she went, people watched her. She couldn't fathom her daughter actually wanting to go unnoticed in a crowd.

"This is about *him*, isn't it?" her mother sneered, meaning Dr. Oppenheimer. "You would follow that man to the ends of the earth."

Alice denied it, but secretly, she wondered if it was true.

She wondered it again that afternoon when she had to still her heart, flashing her white badge on her way through the barbed wire into the laboratory complex for the very first time. The building itself was less than impressive; it resembled an animal barn, made of galvanized steel that no one had bothered to paint. She grunted, straining to open the heavy sliding door. The wheel was off its track. She jiggled the handle and hurled her body against it to no avail. Finally, someone took pity on her and slid it open from inside. He was wearing a grease-stained shirt and coveralls and he stared at her for a beat before stepping aside to reveal a labyrinth of hallways and corridors. Alice supposed he hadn't expected a woman on the other side of that wall.

"Can you point me toward the theoretical offices?" she asked, smoothing an escaped curl behind her ear and dusting off her skirt, attempting to compose herself.

"This here's mostly chemical and metallurgy," he grunted. "That's why so much is under construction. Bethe's group is on the north side. Don't need so much equipment for theoretics."

He meant Hans Bethe, Alice realized, starstruck—quite literally. Dr. Bethe had published groundbreaking work on the theory of energy production in stars. He was the reason she'd gone into astrophysics. In 1938, at twenty, she'd been enamored by his research on the fusion of hydrogen into helium that released energy and ultimately, light. Now, she tried to maintain her composure, wrapping her mind around working with him.

She thanked the man for his assistance and rushed down the indicated hallway with a flickering emergency light that would certainly fizzle out within the hour. She hadn't made it ten steps when she smelled the familiar aroma of cigarette smoke. It could only be *him*. The fumes were intoxicating, snaking down the hallway. Following close behind, Oppenheimer nearly drifted by her without looking up, his hands in his pockets, his lips rattling silently through some equation or possibly a Hindu prayer. His mind was elsewhere, beyond the barbed wire that encircled them in the tech building, far across the desert horizon.

She was always surprised when she got up close to him that despite his larger-than-life reputation, he seemed frail. She studied his bony, nicotine-stained fingers, and the tightness of his belt buckle that made his waist seem impossibly narrow, almost concave. Below his belt, his pants hung limply like there was no body beneath.

As a student, she had visited him frequently in his upholstered office, talking heatedly about indefinitely collapsing thermonuclear energy sources beneath a halo of lamplight. She'd been trying to make up for the fact that her feminine name stuck out like a sore thumb in class. Still, being alone with him had made her nervous. She knew she needed to be careful. The rumors about his affairs were prevalent; in his small office, they had always sat very close, their knees almost touching. At dinner, in his favorite steak house in Berkeley, he had once folded his napkin with expert precision, shrinking it down from a rectangle to a square and finally a smaller rectangle, before stretching his arm around the back of her chair and whispering in her ear about displacement and velocity.

Now, she cleared her throat.

"Dr. Katz," he said, the clouds in his light blue eyes clearing with recognition. "When I added your name to the list of preferred understudies, I hoped you'd join us. But I never thought in a million years you'd actually step foot in New Mexico." He glanced at her slingback heels, indicating her fancy footwear. She took in his mud-spattered cowboy boots and tattered seams, then raised her gaze to meet his. She shrugged. "Heels or not, I can do anything a man can do with a Bunsen burner."

He smiled, but there was caution in his eyes. "In all my years, you were the only student brave enough to write about the single perpetual freefall that undermines the basic rules of the universe."

She swallowed, remembering the research he had warned her away from in the weeks before her presentation to the committee. It had been his own research before it was ever hers. He had discovered a tear in the fabric of the universe, then ran in the other direction, publishing his findings then never mentioning it again.

"I had to know where it led," she said, meaning his abandoned research on collapsed stars and neutron cores. "It remains to be seen whether physicists are more frightened of Hitler or what you uncovered." She knew the research made him nervous. Hitler had marched on Poland the very day he had published it, and the scientific community had looked the other way.

"It was a bunch of superstition," he said, exhaling two plumes of smoke through his nostrils like a bull.

"Forgive me, Professor," she said. "But just because you don't look at it, doesn't make it go away." She swallowed the lump in her throat and held his gaze.

He humphed and tapped out his cigarette on the lab table that was meant to remain sterile. "The optimist thinks this is the best of all possible worlds, Dr. Katz," he said, staring past her while the smoke danced between them. "The pessimist fears it is true."

Back in Berkeley, none of the male scientists had dared to challenge Oppenheimer's authority. They'd be the first to talk about him if he wasn't in the room, but nobody would dare say it to his face. Now, in the haunted laboratory lighting, he had the ice-blue eyes of the undead. He was terrified—and she was not. She suddenly felt her power.

"You always called me Alice," she said. "I see no reason for formality now, here of all places." She gestured at the windowless wall of galvanized steel, indicating the desert horizon beyond it.

He nodded and indicated a man who shuffled up eagerly to join them. "Robert here will show you around, Alice," he said, clapping him on the back. Alice recognized Robert Serber, Oppie's favorite understudy. He had a reputation on campus as Oppie's lieutenant, his alter ego, always standing slightly left and behind him, mimicking his mannerisms. She had frequently seen Serber around the physics complex at Berkeley, but he showed no sign of recognizing her now. It was unsettling.

Her family was always being written up in the society papers. She was regularly photographed at galas and fundraisers, and she had learned to always pin up her hair and paint on her lipstick even just to go to brunch. "You never know who is looking," her mother was fond of saying. But here in these halls of science, she was wallpaper. Sure, they had all agreed to invisibility in this top-secret town. But some were more invisible than others.

"It's not much to look at," Oppenheimer boasted, gesturing at the labs. "But for our intents and purposes, it might as well be the Vatican."

Reality couldn't have been more at odds with Oppenheimer's grandiose statement. To Alice, the labs seemed primitive. Robert Serber toured her around sheepishly, flashing his badge at the guards in a fleeting gesture as they moved between buildings. He was small and spoke with a lisp, but everyone nodded to him deferentially. He hardly looked at her behind his boxy glasses. She wondered whether he resented her being there, a woman scientist. He opened creaky doors, revealing chalkboards filled with scribbled equations. There were wires in intricate tangles on the floor in every room, and discarded electrical equipment littered the hallways. It had to be a fire hazard.

"Why are there army cots?" Alice asked. They were in nearly every room.

"We work such late hours, most of us don't make it home 'cept to shower and change," he said grimly.

Alice stared at the ramshackle extension cords and shoddy equipment strewn about with no rhyme or reason. How could they conduct the level of research necessary in this mess? Yet, there was an undeniable electric excitement and a buzzing frantic energy in the lab. People whispered in urgent voices. Everyone seemed jittery. They were constantly teetering on the brink of discovery. It was infectious.

Robert passed her off to a man wearing a greasy undershirt. A golden dog tag flashed around his neck. "This is Fred," said Robert. "He'll get you set up."

"Secretaries aren't my jurisdiction." Fred thumped a dismissive thumb over his shoulder like a hitchhiker, pointing her toward the stock room. "Belinda will show her the ropes."

"Oh gosh, Fred," Robert said, tugging at his collar and avoiding Alice's eyes. "She's actually in metallurgy."

"I specialize in spectroscopy," she corrected flatly. "But magnetic fields are magnetic fields."

"No kidding?" Fred circled her like a cowboy inspecting a horse at auction. She became very aware of her body beneath her dress. His glossy eyes reminded her of an undercooked egg and his gaze lingered on her chest instead of her face. "Follow me," he barked. The lines left behind by the comb were still visible in his slicked-back hair, which didn't move with the rest of him when he sped down the hall in front of her. She trotted to keep up in her heels as he led her down a long, poorly lit corridor to a room filled with typewriters.

"First is a typing test," he said coldly.

"But I have a PhD in physics," Alice protested.

By way of answer, he pulled out her chair like he was seating her at a fine restaurant and handed her a page of copy like it was a menu. He hovered over her, clicking a stopwatch, instructing her to start and stop at intervals. *RESTRICTED SECURITY HANDBOOK RESTRICTED*, she typed. It was curious that the authors of this document had deemed it necessary to repeat the word "restricted." A bare lightbulb flickered, suspended from a wire overhead, making it hard to see the page.

Examples of facts considered as classified information are included in Appendix I, Paragraph D. A principle affecting handling of all classified information is that it shall be made available only to those persons requiring it for proper performance of their official duties. This obviously means that all persons employed on the Project are not entitled to the same amount of information, and further indicates that no employee may transmit classified information that is made available to him in the course of his duties, to friends or members of his family.

Fred struck up a cigarette and exhaled a puff of smoke in her hair. She resisted the urge to swat it away. He was standing very close to her. His shadow fell across the page of copy, exaggerated by the dangling overhead light.

"What is this document?" she asked, pausing with her fingers still poised on the keys. He clicked off his stopwatch in annoyance.

"Security Guidebook," he said, not bothering with a predicate. "We need three hundred copies by Monday." He clicked his stopwatch again, and taking his cue, she rushed back to typing:

Members of the Project must be responsible for avoiding revelations about the nature of this post, its size, the technical background of the Project personnel, the names of key Project personnel, and the relations of this Project to subcontractors or other branches.

There was an entire section outlawing photographs of the secret city. Alice typed up regulations on phone calls, telegrams, and many, many rules about what could not be mentioned in letters. She had, of course, already agreed to these terms when she accepted the position, but it was jolting seeing them in print, and now that she was here, faced with a life mandated by these limitations, the clacking letter stamps made her skin crawl.

She felt Fred's eyes burning into her and willed herself to focus on the page. She paused, slowing her pace as she digested the ominous closing words: *Do not leave work classified or classifiable as confidential or secret unattended. Erase blackboards, conceal papers in a locked file or vault, or burn.*

She was still picturing secret documents blazing in the desert horizon when Fred clicked the stopwatch with finality. He raised an eyebrow, seeming impressed, and shoved the watch back in his pocket, keeping his hands concealed down near his crotch. "We ran out of security pamphlets to greet the new recruits at orientation. Those boys need to be taken down a notch. Anyhow," he said, grinning and flashing yellow teeth, "that's one down, two hundred and ninety-nine more to go."

She typed up the regulations for secrecy so many times over, she committed the rules to memory. With each letter stamp pressed into the permanence of black type, she felt herself growing more distant from Abigail's dream.

How could she change the world and shift the paradigms preventing women from fulfilling careers in the sciences if she couldn't escape this claustrophobic room? Although she'd never before worked in a functioning laboratory, she had known that the handful of women who worked in labs across the country served mostly as computers, despite their advanced degrees in mathematics, performing calculations by hand or the occasional mechanical calculator. They solved equations without asking what they meant. Somehow, foolishly, she had gotten her hopes up over Oppenheimer's recommendation and thought it would be different for her.

Alice dreaded returning to the lab the next morning. She flashed her badge, avoiding the guard's probing eyes, and hurled her body weight around to shimmy open the shed door. She tried to keep her chin up as she trudged down the dimly lit hallway, making her way to the Olivetti typewriter, back to the pages of copy. She was three pages into her second pamphlet when Hans Bethe casually strolled into the room.

She leaped out of her chair.

"Hallo," he said in his thick German accent. "Dr. Katz, I presume?"

He had a plume of curly chestnut hair that stuck straight up and a prematurely receding hairline. The effect made his forehead look enormous, like he had evolved into a true egghead genius. "Dr. Bethe," she managed, her heart flapping in her chest. "It's a pleasure to meet you."

He approached a chalkboard on the side wall, and, retrieving a rag from his jeans pocket, wiped away a scrawled equation until all that remained was an amorphous cloud of residue. Using the same dirty rag, he wiped the sweat from his brow, smearing a white film of chalk across his wide forehead. "Oppie warned me about you." He broke into a charming smile. He had deep-set dimples, and his whole face changed with the grin. He took on the affect of a schoolboy. He thumbed through her security pamphlets, fanning himself with the pages. "If this is what we're doing with minds as sharp as yours, this place will be duller than coal by Christmas."

Alice tried to steady her voice. She did not want to come across too eager. "What did you have in mind?"

He paused, arching an eyebrow as though he hadn't considered the question until that very moment.

"I heard you can read figures like the chapters in a book," he said, rubbing his chin. "I've got a new batch of SEDs setting off explosions by the

blast walls. I need someone with an eye for detail to interpret every spark."
Alice stiffened, recalling the dynamite blast jolting her windowpanes and
rattling her kitchen. As an astrophysicist by specialty, much of her disser-
tation had focused on burning hydrogen. It was a leap to move from celes-
tial bodies to dynamite, although one way or another, energy would still be
transformed. It wasn't light produced by a galaxy, and it certainly wasn't the
whole electromagnetic spectrum, but optical light beat out security pamphlets any day. She could do it.

She nodded, wordlessly accepting his offer.

She vowed to search every column for its story structure, its rising action,
and its climax. Numbers and charts always did have a way of coming alive
for her: prime numbers glowing a bit like dwarf stars and remainders trailing
away like the tails of comets.

The matter resolved, Bethe turned to leave, but she couldn't help herself.

"Dr. Bethe, why sparks?"

His face hardened and once again, she found him intimidating. "Every
spark is an opportunity if you think small enough," he said. Her stomach
dropped.

Over the next few days, Oppenheimer sent scientists out to bars and cafés
in Santa Fe to talk loudly about electric rockets in an attempt to misdirect
locals. The joke in town was that they were building windshield wipers for
submarines. But now that she was to work with dynamite, Alice had her
fears that they were actually building an explosive, possibly a heat-seeking
missile, but she couldn't be certain exactly how her research would be used.
She didn't dare ask.

She justified her decision to proceed blindly with the German scientists'
twenty-nine Nobel Prizes from 1901 through 1932. In that same time, the
United States had only won six. Everyone was afraid Heisenberg would build
it first, and yet nobody knew what *it* was. Her father was so terrified of what
was coming, he'd screwed double-bolt locks to the front door.

Whatever the work was, it felt necessary.

Residents had been instructed to refer to Los Alamos by code name, of
which it had several. Known as Site Y by the military, most just referred to it
cryptically as the "hill." Some called it Shangri-La after James Hilton's novel,
Lost Horizon: a magical mountain community where time stood still. Others
called it Lost Almost, feeling suspended in a national amnesia. The town

seemed a shifting mirage, and the fluidity of names describing it was fitting. It was more than one thing. It was also nothing.

When the lights switched off across the mesa, Alice let the night in through the open window in her bedroom. The hum of insects was deafening. She tried to pick out the bleating of crickets and the occasional warbler from the cacophony. She thought of her father conducting the violins in his record player. All over the hill, primrose and phlox were still in bloom, but there was an overwhelming medical smell in the air from some native plant she couldn't pinpoint. The scent reminded her of camphor, and she feared if she fell asleep she would dream of morticians.

She stared up into the dimensionless darkness. Physically speaking, dark did not exist, she rationalized. Not as a physical entity, at least. Dark was simply the absence of light. Regular people tended to think of light as a physical thing, but scientists had to consider the full range of the spectrum. An object might appear dark, but it might emit a bright frequency that humans just couldn't perceive.

She couldn't sleep after that.

She pulled on her boots, clipped on Pavlov's leash, and stepped out into the wilderness. She had meant to clear her head and just go for a short walk on the gravel road along her drive, but there were no streetlamps, something to do with security measures. It was blindingly dark. The landscape she was accustomed to in the daylight looked strange. She held her hands out to find her way, waiting for her eyes to adjust. In the blackness, the mountainside seemed even more like a mirage. Pavlov pulled her into the woods near Bathtub Row. She hesitated, then followed his glowing eyes down one of the paths that flickered in the darkness, rearranging in the shadows like the tail of a snake. She kept approaching phantom figures in the dimness but when she got close, it was only cottonwood trees.

When Pavlov started barking in alarm, she searched the landscape with illogical terror. On a porch, a lantern was throwing strange shadows. She approached slowly, startled to find the blanched face of a woman staring through the window like an apparition. She did not respond to the racket of Alice's barking dog. She stood so still, she appeared to not be breathing.

"Do you need an escort, miss?"

Alice shrieked and spun around, coming face-to-face with an armed guard. She stared at his rifle glinting in the moonlight. He had been so quiet and still, he seemed to have morphed out of the trees. Behind him, she recognized the gleam of rifle barrels dappling the forest, and slowly her eyes pinpointed the silhouettes of an entire fleet of guards flanking the woman's house.

"No, thank you, sir," she said. "Just out for a walk. Couldn't sleep."

"No one goes for a casual stroll around the director's house," he said. So that was Oppenheimer's cobblestone house, along the coveted stretch of Bathtub Row. And the skeletal woman with the blanched face? That must be his wife, Kitty. That explained the vegetable garden. She had heard that Kitty was a botanist with a green thumb.

"I'm going to ask you one more time what you're doing out here, miss." Behind him, there was movement—the troop of guards was closing in.

"Let her be, Private." She heard him before she saw him, a phantom on horseback swooping between the trees, the sound of hooves, a flash of chestnut tail.

She wondered what it was about sleep and scientists. In Berkeley, Oppenheimer had often complained of trouble sleeping at night. He told tales in class about riding his chestnut mare, whom he had aptly named Crisis, around the New Mexico trails in the dark. Alice had often pictured him nodding to greet people who crossed his path, then disappearing for days at a time into the desert wilderness. When he peered into the infinite scribbles in his gradebook, he seemed to be squinting into the brightness like a cowboy. And now, here he was, on one of his triumphant returns, and the desert stars seemed to smolder in his presence.

"Fancy meeting a girl like you in a place like this." Oppenheimer grinned and tipped his hat. Pavlov barked and charged at the horse, his fur up on end before Alice could yank him off. Crisis pawed and snorted, jigging in place. "Easy girl," Oppenheimer said, stroking the horse's neck. The mare's muscles shifted beneath its silky fur, tightening and flinching. "Gotta love redheads," he said. "Wouldn't have a mare any other way."

"Dr. Oppenheimer," she said, summoning the courage of her sister. She thought of Janet Taylor, who designed nautical instruments and worked in compass adjusting, despite the controversy surrounding magnetic deviation and distortion on iron ships. She had been awarded a patent for her Mariner's Calculator, along with gold medals from the kings of Holland and Prussia, and even one from the Pope. She thought of Helen Gwynne Vaughan, who had been barred from the unladylike field of zoology, instead dedicating herself to botany, becoming renowned for her study of fungi genetics. Then there was Mary Anning, "Princess of Paleontology." She had uncovered what at first seemed to be the bones of a crocodile, but later was classified as an

Ichthyosaurus, the first complete fossil of a dinosaur. She went on to discover the Plesiosaurus and the Pterodactylus buried in the Jurassic Coast, single-handedly launching the field of paleontology and disproving the Bible.

Alice sighed. "I've come all this way. I've been assigned the analysis of sparks, but to what end? It would aid my research to know what we're looking for."

"I'm no more a fan of compartmentalization than military drills," Oppie replied, "but they've got me in a chokehold."

"Please," she said, surprising herself with the strength in her voice. She approached his horse and stared up at him with her hands clasped as though in prayer. "I'm not afraid."

A long moment passed between them. A cicada rattled, concealed somewhere overhead in the trees.

"You should be," he said finally, the muscles in his jaw grinding away at something.

She watched him ride away into the mountains, the moon glowing down on him like a spotlight.

T-Minus 18

May 1995
Haruki: A Story Told Backward

Haruki was homesick for a place that no longer existed. That spotlit plane was all he had left.

His doctors had warned him not to travel, but he had to see the *Enola Gay* himself. He needed to confront it up close, face-to-face. That plane had outlived everyone he loved. He needed to understand why he had survived.

Initially, he joined the protest at the Steven F. Udvar-Hazy Center, an annex of the National Air and Space Museum in Chantilly, Virginia. The display had restored the *Enola Gay* and celebrated the role of its engines, vertical stabilizer, aileron, propellers, and the forward fuselage in "securing Japanese surrender." The exhibit was careless. It celebrated the victory of the technology without addressing its horror.

After picketing in the heat, Haruki entered the air-conditioned exhibit, wheeling his portable oxygen tank behind him—a second shadow. When he saw the plane, glowing beneath the gallery lights, he had to hold tightly to the protective railing to prop himself up. It was smaller than he had imagined. He saw his reflection mirrored in the silvery metal, and with its gridded windows, the *Enola Gay* looked a little like it was looking back at him. It might have just been his impaired vision; his cataracts progressively made details blurry, but when he looked closer, his reflection shifted. Instead of his own likeness in the windshield, he saw a small girl, a toddler with pigtails that stuck up like horns.

He rubbed his eyes and looked again. This time, the girl's reflection was slightly older. Maybe seven years old. She wore a backpack and grinned. "Banzai!" she said.

All around him, museum visitors circled the exbibits. They walked right by the girl in the reflection without seeing her, chattering dreamily about satellites, space flight, and aviation. In the ruckus and commotion of the room, Haruki was the only one standing still. He and the girl stared at each other. He had the sensation that if he leaned in close and listened, even over all the noise in the room, he could hear screaming.

4

July 1944
Caleb

At night, dovetailing explosions shook the rocks loose in the canyons. They detonated around the clock. The sounds made Caleb jump. The blasts interrupted conversation and kept them awake at night in the barracks. In the dark, the men sat around a card table, acting tough, sipping lab-made spirits—which they dubbed "memory erasers"—from vials pinched from the labs. With every blast, the liquor sloshed in their cups. They turned their backs to the windows and resisted the impulse to look. No one would admit that they couldn't sleep with the world blowing up in their backyard.

The SEDs were mostly absent-minded academics, not military men, but since they hadn't yet acquired degrees, they were used mostly for manpower: working cleaning shifts in the top-secret labs, computing, and keeping records in addition to contributing full-time to their assigned areas of research. Overwhelmed with responsibilities and ill-accustomed to such an all-consuming lifestyle, they failed at military precision. They slouched and forgot to tie their shoes. They were slow-moving and sloppy, leaving discarded clothes scattered around their bunks and failing to make their beds prior to morning bed checks. Most were too bony to fill out their fatigues. They were a sorry sight marching out of step behind the MPs.

But after only a few weeks, the military had rubbed off on them. At night, when the explosions rattled the pictures on the walls and sent their combat boots skipping across the room, they loaded and unloaded the magazines of their pistols endlessly, polishing the barrels until they gleamed. They kissed the muzzles of their guns the way they'd seen it done in the movies.

Although he towered over the other recruits and was too tall for his combat pants, Caleb's laconic tendencies convinced most of them that he was either aloof or arrogant. In matching uniforms, there was no evidence of the depths of his family's poverty, so his brevity went misconstrued for snobbery. All of them, that is, except for Saul, who seemed to have taken a shine to him, clapping him on the back and telling exaggerated tales of his adventures and tomfoolery in New York City nightclubs.

Caleb sensed the recruits stiffening when he approached and consequently receded into himself. His peers had no way of knowing that much of his personality had been cultivated in direct response to his sheer size combined with his limited vision. Being both farsighted and brawny, he was careful never to trample flowers or step on insects. Until he spoke or shuffled around with his hands in his pockets, it was possible to find him intimidating. But after a moment or two in his meek, silent presence, he was easily forgotten. In this new mysterious city, he was determined to break the cycle.

He had never had a drink before in his life, unless he counted the occasional sweet sip of Manischewitz at religious ceremonies. In his family, alcohol had been an untold luxury. He longed to be accepted, for the conversations and the friendships to flow, so he swallowed the clear, odorless liquid.

"Attaboy," one of the recruits across the table cheered him on.

"L'Chaim!" toasted Saul, tossing back his third.

It was his first Shabbat away from his family, so even though he was no longer a believer, Caleb silently recited the kiddush, unable to break away from tradition. It was a silly thing to do, given that he had given up on God as a child. On a grade school field trip to Ocean Beach, he had felt the sinking sensation of his feet in the wet sand as the water pulled away. Even then, he had known it was a combination of the earth's gravity and the gravitational pull of the moon that shifted the tides, not a bearded man in the sky, pulling invisible strings. He had always been a man of science. He had only just recently admitted it out loud to his father. Still, staring into his glass, he recited that silent prayer beginning to end.

The liquor had an acidic bite and a fiery aftertaste. It burned his throat and stung his eyes, but he choked the spirit down like medicine. He welcomed the warmth of the drink sliding down his chest, heating his insides while the men played cards. After a while, he experienced a sensation like seasickness. He clutched his chair like it was dry land.

A *tap*, *tap*, *tap* against the window made Caleb turn his head, but he didn't see anything.

One by one, the recruits who weren't playing cards switched off their lamps and retired to bed. After a while, it got so dark they could barely see each other's faces, and the whites of the cards seemed bright in his hands.

Around the table, the white undershirts glowed too. It was like playing poker with ghosts.

A sudden explosion knocked a picture off the wall. Caleb jumped, and a few of the men flinched, but they just stared at their cards. Caleb stooped to pick up the picture frame. He wiped the smudges from the glass with his shirtsleeve, studying the photo of FDR cruising in a convertible coupe in a bowler hat, flanked by his woolly Scottish Terrier, Fala.

"That man right there's the funding and the brains behind this whole project," Saul crooned. "Better put him back on his pedestal."

"He is?" Caleb asked.

"He invested five hundred mil into us back in '42. Set up corporate assistance to construct and maintain all our facilities." Saul knocked on the table. "Like this one you're squattin' in. Say what you will, but he believes in us." Saul looked at him cockeyed. "Sometimes I think you scientists get so wrapped up in your textbooks, you forget to read the news."

Caleb hung the picture and straightened it, unable to shake the sensation of being watched. It was like the president was staring back at him.

Back at the table, Caleb tried to focus on his cards, but again, there was that knocking on the window.

Finally, he folded his hand and followed the sound. A moth with concentric circles as big as human eyes etched on its wings was flapping against the glass, throwing its body repeatedly against the pane. It froze, seeming to feel his gaze, and folded its wings. He teetered toward it, then sprung, cupping it in his palm. He tried to be delicate with the fragile wings, fearing that between the effects of the alcohol and his size, a wrong move could extinguish the small life in his hands. He cracked the window and reached out blindly into the darkness. But instead of flapping away, the creature rested on his palm, feeling him with its antennae. Its furry abdomen tickled his skin.

As far back as Caleb could remember, his brother, Asher, had longed to fly. Long after they'd passed the tennis balls soaring on the courts along their route, Asher kept talking about their curved flight paths. They couldn't afford train sets or building blocks, so Asher's physics experiments had been stand-ins for toys. While other kids played baseball in the park, he had made Caleb calculate the force of lift complicated by the thrust needed for forward motion. After he was deployed, Caleb had often imagined their small apartment in the Fillmore from his brother's airborne vantage point, shrinking until it was only a speck. Now, in his hand was a creature with wings, content to walk among men on the ground.

A cool breeze swept the mesa, and the moth shuddered up into the air. It floated over Caleb's head like it was reading his thoughts, then flapped away into the night. It was gone without a trace, but he kept trying to track its movements. He saw glimmers of things shifting in the dark woods, but on closer inspection, there was nothing there.

Then he caught his breath.

Beneath the field of stars, a lone woman was wandering the desert. There was an animal by her side with glowing eyes—maybe a coyote. Her shock of hair bounced as she walked, glistening in the moonlight. She was tall and dignified. As she approached, he realized what he had first taken for a coyote was just a golden retriever, following closely at her heels.

From the twists in her hair to her pointed bust, he could see that she was elegant: a city girl. He felt a strange fluttering in his chest, an awakening urge inside him. A girl like that would never even look at him twice, so why did he feel a sudden need to go to her, to help her across the puddles, to let his hand linger on the pale exposed skin of her moonlit wrists? It wasn't until she turned in his direction that he recognized her long Roman nose and heavy eyebrows. He had met her once before.

The first time he had seen her, she had been wearing a sky-blue dress with shoulder pads that puffed up like clouds. She had been seated across from him, at the end of a long table, beside Oppenheimer himself. Oppie made a tradition of treating all the doctoral candidates to a meal at the end of the term, and the lot of them had taken up nearly the entire steakhouse, Oppenheimer's favorite in town. At dinner, the students gossiped about notable Jews in the scientific community, but they kept their voices low, mindful of the Jewish quota.

"One Jew on the faculty is enough," a student near him had grumbled. But nobody could touch Oppenheimer. He might have been Jewish, but he could not be mined by ordinary laws.

Occasionally, Oppenheimer had wrapped his arm around the sky-blue woman's chair, animating a story or reacting to something being said with an expressive shift nearer to her. When he did, she seemed to stiffen. Occasionally, she would smooth the wrinkles from her dress. He imagined that later that evening, when she removed the dress, it would look like a blue heap of sky on the floor.

He had been mesmerized by her, the only woman at the table of physicists. She must be someone very important to be invited to that table of men. Perhaps she was one of Oppenheimer's notorious flames, a secretary or a clerical assistant turned lover. But then, never before had one of Oppie's romantic flings joined the boys in the steakhouse to talk shop. A black flower clipped back her curls and matched the black gloves that she removed discreetly and folded neatly beside her dinner plate. She clasped her long, narrow fingers into a canopy and tapped out her thoughts while the men around the table spoke theirs. Her fingernails were ruby red, and her arms were milky white. He imagined what it would be like to touch the velvet-soft skin of her forearm. She was not traditionally beautiful; she had a long nose that caught the light and sad, deep-set eyes. It seemed to pain her to smile. She did not speak other than to agree and tightly nod along. Unlike himself, she seemed accustomed to the rows of gleaming silverware and the waitstaff pulling out her chair, but like him, she was hiding something.

Suddenly, sensing his eyes on her, she'd turned and glared at him. He averted his eyes, staring hard at his plate, and felt himself turning beet red.

She scanned him up and down, from his raggedy saddle shoes to his moth-eaten trench coat, the only one he wore all winter. She arched an eyebrow. "Stop staring," she huffed. "You can't afford me."

"I beg your pardon?" He feigned innocence, but his heart sank like a stone.

She rolled her eyes in disgust and made a face at a gentleman seated across from her. "They're letting anyone in here these days," she muttered, laughing at his expense. "Might as well set the table in the alley with the pigeons."

He receded into silence while across the table, she knitted her eyebrows together, feigning interest in something someone nearby was saying. He could see the charade of her interactions plainly. She was the sort of woman who only spoke to those who benefited her, those who were deserving of her own social station. Perhaps if he had won a Fields Medal, she would bother to learn his name. If he was the heir to the fortune of a cotton tycoon, or an eligible bachelor with a penthouse suite, she'd turn back his way.

In desperate moments, Caleb fancied that disappearing was something he chose, rather than something that was forced upon him—more like a superpower than a consequence of his inhibited nature, but now, in her utter disregard, he knew that to women like her, even when he was seated beside her, he wasn't even in the room.

After that night, he hadn't seen her again. But he did not let go of his anger.

So now that she was there in his window, the woman in the sky-blue dress, drifting across the mesa, he heard his heart pounding in his ears and realized he had clenched his hands into fists. Out there, she seemed unaffected by his world: She began to recede into the darkness. Her long, unbuttoned trench coat flapped in the breeze behind her, beating like wings.

If he didn't do it now, he might miss his chance. He had to tell her who he was, and all the ways she was wrong about him before she was swallowed back up by the night. He left the room in a flurry, ignoring the men's extended hands and opened mouths, calling after him. He raced down the dimly lit hallway and through the barbed wire periphery out into the open, until he was panting beside the lapping shores of Ashley Pond. Where had she gone? He spun in circles, squinting in each direction, tracing and retracing the path she had taken. The wind gusted, bending the wheatgrass and drawing a thousand tiny pinpricks on the mirrored surface of the water. The stars wiggled around in the reflection. He waited for his eyes to adjust fully. Seeing nothing but the unobstructed sky of stars that overwhelmed the landscape, he hung his head in despair.

Suddenly, a chilly hand on his shoulder. He spun around to see her large dark eyes squinting with suspicion, sparkling in the moonlight. Startled, he tripped over a loose stone and reached out to steady his balance, unintentionally grabbing the arm of her coat. He stared at her pursed red lips. Why had she bothered to paint on makeup at this hour, to walk alone? Why dress up for the cottonwood trees?

She was so close to him he could smell her overwhelming confectionery perfume. She smelled like a bakery.

"Why are you following me?" she said with a mischievous smirk, like this was some sort of game.

"I wasn't," he started to explain, but there was nothing he could say to counter this point.

He stared helplessly into her heart-shaped face, her passionate, smoldering glare, willing his thoughts to form coherent words. From her trench coat to what up close he realized was a sheer shirtwaist bodice, she oozed wealth and a life of silver spoons. He thought her utterly beautiful but horridly spoiled. She wouldn't last a minute in the Fillmore District, he thought, getting leered at by vagrants around a trash can fire or stepping over the shards of glass in her alligator heels. He was still thinking this when she barked, "Kindly release me, Private."

Caleb followed her stare down to his hand on her arm. He hadn't realized he was still clutching her coat sleeve.

He let her go and dropped his arms awkwardly to his sides, not sure what to do with his hands, as though he had never before had such appendages.

She recoiled, swatting faux dirt from her coat in the places his fingers had touched.

"You know, tailing someone is a crime in California," she said. Was it just his imagination, or had the edges of her lips curved up into a smile? There was something coy in the way she acted appalled yet leaned closer, seeming in no rush to remove herself from the situation.

"Well, lucky for me," he snorted, "we're in New Mexico."

"Next time, I'll send Pavlov after you. Don't think I won't." She indicated the overweight golden retriever panting at her side. At the sound of his name, the animal wagged his tail so vigorously his whole hind end wobbled. His tongue lolled out of his mouth in a toothy grin. She meant it as a threat, albeit a playful one, but nothing could have been more comical than the thought of that fluffy canine fending off an attacker. Despite himself, Caleb chuckled.

Her small smile faded. "It won't be funny," she huffed, "when he bares his teeth." As she said it, her own teeth flashed white in the night.

"Good boy," Caleb said, scratching the dog between the ears. The canine rubbed up against his legs and looked adoringly up at him with glittering, beady eyes.

He could feel her studying him curiously and felt himself blush. "What?" He shrugged. "Dogs like me."

"Pavlov is usually a better judge of character." But as she said it, Caleb fished something out of his pocket and Pavlov lopped it out of his hand.

"Oh," he said, noting her furrowed brow. "I carry jerky in my pockets," he explained. "It's kosher, and well, I can't always trust the food they dish out in the commissary."

"A drifter carrying old, processed meat in his trousers," she huffed. "Why am I not surprised? I suppose you stash dinner rolls in your coat pockets for safekeeping too." She stalked away and the dog good-naturedly trotted after her.

Caleb stepped into her path. "Wait."

She moved to pass him, stepping into the tall grass. Again, he blocked her way. Her eyes flicked over his chest, his strapping arms, his extended hands, and, for just a heartbeat, settled on his face. Then she set her sights over his head, intent on making her escape.

"I said *wait*." His voice came out louder than he had intended.

"I'm not in your platoon. I don't take orders." She bustled up her full skirt to step across a log and surpass him. For a fleeting second, he saw the tender hollow of her anklebone, the defined outline of a silky calf. Having caught his lingering gaze, her expression hardened. She dropped her skirt back down like a curtain around her legs and a defensive blind flicked closed across her features.

"Please move out of my way." Her lower lip stiffened. Where there had been a playful spark before, now there was a warning in her eyes.

He realized with a lump in his throat that she did not recognize him. What had been a monumental, unhinging moment for him had not even registered for her. He felt the anger of the last year heat his chest and pulse through his veins. He considered the tatters in his mother's shawls hanging in the linen closet, the empty canisters of dried goods in the larder, the colony of ants that had taken up residence beneath the broken toaster, the cockroaches that skittered out of sight when he flipped the light switch by the front entry beside the cracked window, a shape like a streak of lightning. He recalled the underground view of the alley from their garden-unit kitchen window: an endless parade of strangers' shoes passing him by, loafers and strappy sandals, making their way out of the Fillmore and onto better lives. Standing before him was a woman who would consort her way to the top, keeping company between the bedsheets with the most brilliant minds in the academy and the most powerful men in the government.

He gathered himself to tell her off once and for all, to say what needed to be said, what he wished he had said a year ago, something he was certain no one else in her life would dare say to her. The words came out of his mouth like gravel: "There's a name for women like you, draped in diamond tennis bracelets and cashmere," he said. "If I ever saw you again, I promised myself I would say it." He paused, for a second losing his nerve. He avoided her eyes, staring down at her peep-toe crocodile heels. "JAP," he spat out. It was a word they saw everywhere, spray painted on looted Japanese businesses, in newspaper headlines, and on signs barring entry. It took a second for the recognition of its secondary meaning, as an acronym for Jewish American Princess, to settle across her features.

She shrank away from him. Any trace of a smile vanished and her posture buckled. Perhaps the term had been used on her before. He hadn't thought it would cut her so deeply. He felt something drop in his stomach seeing how she cracked open. He had waited so long to avenge himself. Now that he finally had, he wished desperately he could take it back.

"Partner! You OK out there?" Saul's voice pierced the darkness. His flashlight flicked back and forth across the path.

Like a frightened animal, she turned and fled. As she vanished into the night, the pressure of her touch still lingered on his shoulder.

His ears were ringing. Occasional bullfrogs called from the water, sounding almost human. Overhead, the moon was fuzzy. He stood there staring into the expanse where she had disappeared, and the desert looked back at him with its vastness, its army of insect eyes all trained on him.

"Man, what is eating you?" asked Saul, trotting up from the darkness and clapping him on the back. Caleb spooked at his touch. "You look like you saw a ghost." Saul kept his hand planted and searched his eyes. Caleb tried to concentrate on Saul's freckled and pock-marked face. He was wearing his glasses; this blurriness was different. He realized, perhaps belatedly, that for the first time in his life, he was drunk. Saul exhaled a plume of smoke and searched the empty desert that occupied his friend's attention, arching a concerned eyebrow. "You feeling all right, Private?"

"Sure," Caleb lied. He ran his hand through his hair. His heart was still beating in his ears. Now he could make out the shadowy forms of the other men, having wandered out of the barracks to see what the commotion was about. They were silhouetted against the floodlight of the periphery fence, standing in contrapposto like Greek sculptures. Their cigarette butts glowed red in the dark. "I needed some fresh air," Caleb said, trying to sound casual.

"You'll feel better if you ralph," one of the men called over, clearly enjoying the spectacle.

Another shouted, cupping his hands to project his voice: "Ain't my first rodeo!"

"I think I need to sit down," said Caleb. He buckled over in the dirt, crossing his legs and holding his pounding head in his hands.

"Attaboy," cheered the men. They took turns tilting their heads back to nurse from a flask.

"Quit doggin' me," said Caleb, waving Saul away. "I'm just beat. I'll catch up."

"I never leave an airman behind," said Saul quietly, a soldier's creed. It was a predictable thing for him to say, being both a private and a communist. He assessed the pond with reverence. "Safety in numbers."

In the brightness of morning, making his way up the dusty trail to the blast walls, Caleb tried to block out the memory of the way she had shuffled off through the desert with the conduct of a duchess. But he couldn't stop picturing her entitled, lilting walk. Overhead, even the desert sky seemed to be a never-ending A-line gown. As he climbed higher through the canyons, the air got thinner and it became hard to breathe.

He'd been rattled by nerves anticipating the dynamite. A cautious man through and through, he'd never fired a gun or even set off a flare. And now, he and Saul had been assigned to ignite sticks of dynamite stacked like logs on a fire. It was a subset of G Division, short for "Gadget": a clandestine group assigned to set off explosives and chemical reactions to assess unknowns and record whatever happened. Saul hadn't batted an eye at the assignment. He'd snored soundly in his bunk then been up and at 'em, whistling while he buttoned his fatigues. Caleb had tossed and turned all night. He was incredibly nervous. On the walk up, he was so furious about his exchange with the mystery woman, he'd forgotten his nerves, but it all came flooding back to him now when he spotted Saul crouched by a blast wall, flanked by barbed wire and a series of signs that read *Danger Hazardous Area* and *Explosives Keep Out.*

The heat steamed visibly on the sand, and the two spent the morning meticulously laying out the sticks of dynamite, setting them out gingerly, then dashing back. They positioned camera lenses at every thinkable angle, circling the elaborate tangle of wires.

Saul smoked cigarettes down to butts and rattled off stories while they worked. He spoke endlessly of Manhattan—he told tales of doughnuts good enough to marry, and the way the Statue of Liberty had once been brown and shiny as a penny and now glowed green against the fog.

"It's oxidation," Caleb said quietly, his first words in a while. "A chemical reaction. Copper reacts with the air to form a patina."

"You don't say," said Saul, clapping the dust from his hands. "All right, partner, here goes nothing."

He fastidiously wired the explosives and stared hard at his wristwatch. "Ten, nine, eight, seven," he began counting down. They scurried behind the blast wall, lay down on their bellies, and plugged their ears. Saul positioned his thumb over the camera lens trigger. Caleb was paralyzed with fear, his extremities tingling. "Three, two, one," Saul continued, but when he said, "zero," his voice was muted by the force of an explosion that seemed to trigger an earthquake, shaking the rocks loose across the canyon. Saul eagerly tapped the camera trigger over and over. Behind his clenched eyelids, Caleb saw an eruption of sparks, the birth of a galaxy.

Caleb still had his belly to the ground and his eyes shut when Saul slapped his back. "Hoo whee!" he exclaimed. "I've a feeling we're not in Manhattan anymore." He circled the steaming, blackened pit, investigating the cameras.

Caleb slowly opened his eyes to the brightness. "Do we have to change up the variables and run it again?" he managed, his mouth feeling dry. "Before we head to the darkroom?" He prayed they didn't have to keep going, that they'd captured what they needed in that first round—that later, in the dark-room, they'd shake the shimmering droplets from the soggy photo paper and find simultaneous shutter captures as evidence of simultaneous sparks.

"No need." Saul shrugged. "That technical mumbo jumbo is too classi-fied for the likes of us. Word is whoever is inputting the data wants to do it himself. A real control freak over at Project Rufus."

"What's Project Rufus?"

"Got me." He gently picked up the still-steaming camera lenses and piled them in the truck bed. "All they said was drive 'up' 'til you can't go up anymore."

Fifteen minutes later, Saul's pickup was struggling up a grueling trail of switchbacks and hairpin curves. Like he was seasick, Caleb tried to keep the horizon centered in the window. Finally, the road leveled off. Saul ran his fingers through his hair, taking in the view. "Sometimes I feel like Alice in Quantumland," he said.

When they arrived at the Project Rufus compound, four cars were parked in the lot with doors swung wide and motors humming. Puffs of smoke coiled from the tailpipes like the exhalations of large animals. Why would their owners have left in such a hurry?

It was curious, too, that the door to the top-secret facility was wide open. The two could just walk right in. Caleb squinted, waiting for his eyes to adjust. Inside, there were slide rules and clamps and all sorts of measuring devices at the ready spread around the laboratory. A team of ten men was flanked by security guards. When they entered, everyone stopped talking and turned to look at them. Caleb cleaned his glasses on his shirt and replaced them for a better look. Otto Frisch's scowl came into focus, as did a thin wisp of a man with round glasses and bouncy hair.

"We have a delivery," Saul offered, breaking the tension. "From G Division."

"We've been expecting you boys. Name's Louis," the man said, offering his hand to Caleb first. "Slotin."

"Caleb," he replied. "Blum."

"Are you of the Oak Park Blums?"

If only, he thought. To save money, his mother had hung paper towels to dry for reuse. It had always embarrassed him that whenever anyone opened their door, the breeze caught the clothesline of paper towels, and they flapped overhead, looking like flying seabirds.

"No, sir, I'm afraid that's a different Blum. My family's out of San Francisco." Blum wasn't truly his family's surname, but he elected not to explain that the original name had been lost to history and he couldn't claim it if he tried, that Blum, German for *flower*, was just something an immigration officer who was fond of gardening had bestowed on his father at the Austrian border.

"Ah," said Louis. "The Marina District is beautiful this time of year. Or are you from one of those scenic châteaus over in Sea Cliff?"

Caleb had never been to either the Marina District or Sea Cliff. As a child, he had learned to sleep through the beeping truck working the night shift in the shipyard. "Something like that." He winced.

When Slotin turned to Saul, Frisch pointed at Caleb and barked, "No fatigues." It sounded harsh, but it might have just been his accent. "Around here, we wear civilian clothes."

"Yes, sir," said Caleb, saluting and then regretting it. But Frisch wasn't looking. Caleb followed his stony gaze. He was staring at a silver sphere wedged in an intricate casing of geometric bricks in the center of the room. It was at least the size of a small child. He could feel the heat emanating from the metal and warming the room. He'd never seen a substance like it before. It seemed to glow with its own internal light like a fallen star. From one angle, it appeared to have misshapen growths, like moles and warts the size of baseballs, but up close it was smooth as icing. He drew closer for a better look. Caleb scrolled through the elements in the Periodic Table in his mind, trying to identify it.

"She weighs 13.7 pounds," boasted a stocky man who wore a tight-fitting V-neck and cowboy jeans held up by suspenders, disregarding the safety guidelines requiring lab coats. He stunk of ammonia and cleaning chemicals.

"What is it?" Caleb managed.

Harry motioned at the metal core with pride. "This old thing? If I told ya, I'd have to kill ya." He laughed heartily, then removed his rubber gloves and stepped forward to offer his hand to Caleb. "Welcome to the cave." He flashed a gray-toothed grin. His off-the-cuff manner in proximity to the strange orb churning before them agitated Caleb. Surely, whatever this was, it warranted caution.

"This here's Harry," said Louis, clapping the young man on the back. "Don't let his graduate-student status fool ya. He's worth every penny."

Caleb hesitated, wondering if he should volunteer his own lack of terminal degree.

"Come on, I suppose we should introduce the whole team."

Caleb repeated each new name as he made his way around the room, attempting to offer a firm handshake and look each scientist in the eye. He met two photographers, three security guards, and a rotating Rolodex of scientists who popped in and out of the lair throughout the day to check in on timetables and sign in for shifts. Caleb tried to keep everyone straight, but after a moment, he had forgotten them all. He didn't like turning his back on the metal core. It seemed like something from outer space, or something that had lived in another time and had been resurrected by foolhardy men trying to play God.

He was staring at the contraption, wondering what on earth he had gotten into, when he heard the clicking of heels striding across the floor. It couldn't be. But, somehow, he knew it was her.

"Ah, Caleb," Louis said. "You'll be passing your negatives to Mrs. Katz here. She'll develop them and interpret the data, then you'll do the whole song and dance all over again tomorrow. We need to pair SEDs with PhDs. Liability, you see. She'll be your supervisor—well, the supervisor for the lot of you." He indicated Saul and several other SEDs in the room. "Don't take it personal that we've placed you recruits with a woman scientist. You'll work your way up to the big leagues."

In all his racing thoughts about the woman in blue, Caleb had never pegged her for a scientist. A female companion to Oppenheimer, sure, even someone who kept books in the lab and was privy to secrets, but it had never dawned on him that she could have a mind for numbers. His mind flashed back to the steakhouse in Berkeley, the way she'd batted her lashes and dabbed at her lipstick with the corner of her linen napkin. He hadn't figured her for the sort of girl who could mentally tabulate the bill at the table while the men around her tapped it out on their fingers. And not only was she a scientist, but she outranked him. He stared at her, dumbfounded.

"It's a pleasure, Miss Katz," Caleb croaked, not recognizing his own voice.

"It's Dr. Katz," she corrected flatly. "Not Miss." Her eyes flicked over Caleb's heavy figure with a tight expression; she scanned his face fleetingly, then darted her eyes away. So that was how she would play it—like he hadn't made an indent. Her lipstick was comically bright in this relaxed environment. Between her buttoned-up blouse, her parasol, and her makeup, among all those men in cowboy jeans, she looked ludicrously out of place.

He nodded, and a flush of heat rushed to his cheeks. He stared down at her peep-toe heels on the floor.

"I told you, I can take it from here," she said to Slotin tightly, no longer paying any mind to Caleb's presence.

"These boys gave their lives to this project," Slotin grunted. "They've got nothing to fill their days, no warm meal waitin' for them at home. Least you could do is flash them a smile now and then."

The darkroom was narrow enough that they had to turn sideways to fit all ten recruits Slotin had appointed to the job inside. Caleb was distinctly aware of the mere inches between their bodies as he squeezed past Dr. Katz. Wordlessly, she tampered with the focus finder on the enlarger. Behind her, trays of chemical baths glimmered in the red light. In the nightmarish ruby glow, Caleb had no sense of the time. It could have been the middle of the night.

As Dr. Katz worked briskly, dipping photo papers into the wash bath with a pair of silver tongs, then clothespinning them up to dry, Caleb stole glances at her. She worked with lightning speed while he, Saul, and the other eight SEDs crammed in the small, dark space fumbled with their negatives or chewed on their pencils, trying to look busy.

"I wouldn't do that if I were you," she said, laying a safety-gloved hand on Saul's arm when he started snacking on some pretzels he'd stashed in the pocket of his military cargo pants. "That's a bath of Monomethyl-p-amino-phenol sulfate and hydroquinone."

Saul blinked at her.

"It's highly toxic by ingestion. Didn't anyone warn you not to eat around the developing agents?"

The men disregarded her instructions about intensifiers, reducers, and toner, shrugging off her warnings regarding hydrochloric acid and potassium dichromate, calling her "baby doll" and "toots," and telling her to "chill out." One of the recruits pretended to drop his notebook and made a big show of looking up her skirt. Others made lewd gestures behind her back. One unruly recruit quipped, "She must have gotten her degree at Berkeley by sucking more than just the air out of the cylindrical vacuum of the cyclotron, if you know what I mean."

Watching her sigh and brush it off, Caleb began once again to regret what he had said to her. It had to be difficult to be a woman in this place. He got it in his head that perhaps he should apologize.

He approached her when they'd finished and there was nothing left to do but wait for the photos to fully develop so they could record the data. After so many hours in the darkroom, the bright open air of the lab was blinding. The sun sent vivid red streaks through the window. When he was within arm's length, close enough to smell her sugary perfume, she stiffened and scrambled away, muttering something about needing a C clamp and a slide rule. The rest of the afternoon, all he could do was watch her bustle around while the unspoken words in his head collided and rearranged. Behind her, outside the propped door, the sky went to watercolors.

That night, Caleb slept hard in his military bunk. Pillow lines still dented his face when he made his way back to the Project Rufus lab. He consumed contemptible amounts of coffee—"battery acid," the guys called it.

In the small darkroom, he found Dr. Katz staring intently at the photo prints, her dark hair swept up and pinned into place with a pencil, looking red in the glow of the safe light.

"Did you find what you were looking for?" he asked.

She took a while before answering, considering the question. She spoke without turning toward him, hands on her hips, studying the pinned photographs. "In astrophysics, we study things as large as planets, all the way down to tiny particles. Stars have their own life cycles, anywhere from a few million to trillions of years. But these sparks were birthed and deceased in a matter of milliseconds."

"Is that a *no*, then?"

"What I'm looking for can't be found in a single detonation, no matter how well documented. At this rate, we'll be at this for a year."

Caleb shrank. The thought of returning to the canyon and setting off more cartridges, blasting cubic meters out of hard rock in the canyon, or throwing a volume of water and sand up with each detonation horrified him. He could still hear the blast ringing in his ears.

"I'll need to subject the dynamite itself to chemical analysis, extract the nitroglycerin, and investigate the silica and mixtures of lime, iron oxide, and alumina," she said, "to assess the danger of simultaneous explosions. And of course, we can't rule out spontaneous combustion."

Caleb gulped, recalling the heft and consistency of the dynamite. He had swaddled it delicately in his arms like a newborn baby. "What," he managed, "do you think they'll do with this data on simultaneous explosions?" He couldn't help wondering how the work would be used, and who might be on the receiving end. He kept thinking of that blackened sand pit, the crater in the ground where he had stood only seconds before the detonation, positioning the lenses. Everything in his body was screaming for him to stop this work. It was toxic and dangerous and would only lead to more toxicity and danger. But Dr. Katz was working diligently, seeming lovestruck with curiosity about the world.

She turned to face him. "You can't stop asking why things happen because you're afraid of how the information will be used. Science is science. It can be used for evil or for good. It's not the research that we should fear, it's the men who wield it."

"Do you mean Oppenheimer?"

"With stars," she said, ignoring his question and barreling onward, "we're looking for an aperture of twenty seconds, trying to capture the spectrum. At first, I didn't know what to do with detonations. It's apples and oranges. But then I thought of Cecilia Payne-Gaposchkin."

"Cecilia who?"

"The botanist turned astrophysicist who turned her jeweler's loupe down at the earth rather than looking up through telescopes to determine what made up the stars. Instead of plotting hydrogen and helium in space, we're splitting light into its constituent wavelengths right here in the canyon. This work is bringing the stars down from the sky and right into my hands."

She turned back to the photographs, pulled the pencil from her hair, shaking her locks loose, and began jotting notes. Caleb took her cue and turned to leave.

Before he could get out the door and make his way back to the blast walls, Frisch burst into the lab fresh-faced, eager to get to work on his mysterious research with the metal core, whatever it was. He rattled through check-ins and orienting the new recruits. He pulled Caleb aside for paperwork and informed him that in addition to photographing the detonations, delivering film negatives for G Division, and assisting in the darkroom, he'd be directly helping Slotin with Project Rufus. He was saying something about clocking in and out, but Caleb wasn't entirely listening. While Frisch droned on in his harsh accent, Caleb couldn't help marveling that Dr. Katz had emerged from the darkroom wearing what he could now see in the brightness of the lab was a ruffled, beige blouse tucked into a mauve pencil skirt and seamed stockings. She was still writing furiously in her notebook. He got a whiff of her perfume and wondered if she was freshly showered. She had brought her enormous golden dog to the lab, and the canine cocked an ear when she reappeared, then watched her lazily from an army cot, resting his head on his folded paws. He ran through movies in his head, replacing her as the romantic lead. She was Ingrid Bergman in a trench coat in a nightclub in *Casablanca*; she was Katharine Hepburn falling in love while proofreading the news; she was Betty Grable watching the moon.

"Are you listening?" Frisch asked.

Caleb snapped out of it, realizing his focus had wandered. He tried to look confident. "Yes, sir," he said.

Frisch was staring at him, and seemed to be frowning although, granted, it was hard to tell. He had the sort of face that rarely smiled. "I said you'll need biweekly medical examinations of your fingertips." He waggled his pinkie demonstrably. "Fingertips are the first place to show changes." He didn't say what sort of changes, or what caused them, and Caleb knew he wasn't supposed to ask.

He racked his mind, trying to figure what substance could require such hyperfocused medical attention. His eyes flitted back momentarily to Dr. Katz, who had been measuring out a liquid in an eye dropper and holding the vial up to the light. She had overheard and looked up from her work in alarm. The dog looked up, too, and cocked his head.

Frisch followed Caleb's gaze over to Dr. Katz. He lowered his voice and cupped his mouth so she wouldn't hear. "There's no knowing what it might do to the female reproductive system, so naturally we'll get her out of your hair in a fortnight or so."

"Sir?"

"After the next shipment comes in, that is."

Shipment of what? Caleb wondered. He doubted it was possible to say no, to refuse this next assignment. If he could, he'd reject all of it: the dynamite, the research, and whatever they were planning to do with it. "Yes, sir," he parroted, gritting his teeth.

"Anyhow," he said, "if you do notice any discoloration"—he faced his palms forward and splayed his fingers—"be sure to alert us. The next step is a blood test. After that, you might as well try your luck with prayer."

T-Minus 17

April 1969
Haruki: A Story Told Backward

Blinded by the bright lights, Haruki recited an old kamikaze song to calm himself. "We load fuel for a one-way trip / while crying. / Our destination is Ryukyu, our journey to the other side." Sometimes, when his fear of making public appearances got the better of him, he recited the song like it was a prayer.

When he took the stage, Haruki feared that everyone was staring at his scars. Never having fully grown back, his eyebrows were penciled in. His left ear was missing and only the helix of his ear canal remained, so strangers could peer into the cavity of his head like a seashell. The keloid scars that marred his chest had always reminded him of the scrawled cursive of some alien language. Consequently, he wore his shirt collar buttoned all the way up, concealing further overgrowths of scar tissue and protrusions on his skin. He had combed his hair aggressively, streaks of silver and strands so white they looked blue. His eyes were milky from cataracts; his vision was misty. He couldn't make out the faces in the audience at the International Atomic Energy Agency Conference, but he could sense that there were many bodies in that packed lecture hall.

Outside, the boats drifted by on the brackish water of the Chicago River, hundreds of feet below. He got dizzy, walking the platform to the stage. He couldn't back out now. Not with the Treaty on the Non-Proliferation of Nuclear Weapons on the line.

When he finally spoke into the microphone, he used lots of gesticulations. He insisted on standing despite his health—he suffered from chronic aplastic anemia, angina, cancer of the large intestine, and prostate cancer, all directly linked to his radiation exposure twenty-four years earlier. He was on a vitamin B complex and vitamin B12 IV drip every fortnight for fatigue,

57

metabolism, and neurological function, as well as blood-forming medicine and nitroglycerine.

He stared out at the sea of faces beyond the blinding edges of the spotlight. "After the bomb fell," he began in faltering English, nodding at the startled interpreter who slowly found a seat, "I spent forty days lying unconscious, then a year of immobility with bedsores. Three times, I was pronounced . . . what is the term . . . medically dead." He laughed softly but in the audience, nobody stirred. "To this day, doctors are shocked that I am alive."

When the atomic bomb fell on Hiroshima, a new word was needed in Japanese to describe the people who'd survived. There was no sufficient label for the half-dead population that was doomed to spend the rest of their lives suffering from radiation poisoning, living on borrowed time. They were waiting out the clock, doomed to join their loved ones who had died at ground zero. The word "hibakusha" was given to these ghosts, meaning *explosion-affected people*. Haruki was among the last of them.

"I fear that too many hibakusha are dying," Haruki said, looking right into the clicking camera lens.

He had lived twenty-four years longer than he was meant to, and he was trying not to let his fatigue show on his face.

5

July 1944
Alice

"We just got a new shipment in from Hanford, Washington. Next week we're expecting one from Oak Ridge too. Right now, it's sealed in fuel slugs. Have the boys cast them into spheres," Louis Slotin ordered, "carefully." He seemed to be trying and failing to contain a nervous twitch in his lips. "Tell them I said to monitor its temperature overnight like it's their sick mother."

"Doctor." Alice felt her heart pounding in her ears as she mustered the courage. "What is it a shipment of?"

Slotin already had one foot out the door, but he paused. The silence between them was palpable. It was the same silence that filled the previously boisterous lab every time she walked into the room to delegate the SEDs at their stations. They thought she couldn't see their lewd gestures behind her back, that she was unaware of their eyes burning through her, that their dismissive pet names for her were terms of endearment rather than degrading slurs. It wasn't entirely their fault; Slotin himself was laid-back. He allowed the men to smoke and tell jokes while they worked, two things she despised, and though she tried to measure her expressions, she swatted the smoke out of her path and stiffened at the toilet humor.

And now here she was leading the project without an inkling of an idea what the project was.

"I do think it's important from a metallurgy standpoint," she said, losing bravado when Slotin broke eye contact to check his wristwatch, "for us to know why you need spheres."

Slotin rolled his eyes. He had not tried to hide his frustration at having her under his employ at Bethe's insistence, only interacting with her to bark orders and always whispering with Frisch in corners of the room, his eyes tracing her movements between the beakers and the defibrillators. To make matters worse, Alice was buttoned up and did everything by the book, following the scientific method and referencing safety protocols. Meanwhile, Slotin disregarded the safety shims when he was working on the core, preferring to do things with ungloved, naked hands. He liked fast cars and wild horses; he had been an amateur boxer in a past life, and he used sports metaphors to describe all the goings-on in the lab.

Now, he looked at her in her tea dress and knit hat and said cryptically, "It's not exactly in your wheelhouse, Dr. Katz."

With no exterior lights, no streetlamps of any sort, and blackout curtains pulled in every home, at sundown the city was erased into the mountainside. Since no interior lights were switched on in the lab, it felt like a dark, one-dimensional cave. Alice held her hands out, feeling her way through the flat darkness. It was eerie and expansive, and the shadows threw strange shapes. Pavlov disappeared into the obscurity, unafraid, finding his way to the army cot and hopping up to watch over their progress like a gargoyle with glowing eyes.

She made her way through the cold, cavernous laboratory, waiting for her eyes to adjust. Overhead a ceiling fan turned wobbling circles, whirring time through the air. It emanated a soft breeze that rearranged Alice's curls. She caught herself thinking about the air currents, how hot air rises and fans travel counterclockwise in the summer months. This fan was traveling clockwise, preventing it from pushing the cooler air down. In this secret world of precision and men of science, this was a telltale oversight.

"Why didn't anyone switch on the lights?" she muttered, feeling her way through the room.

"They told us to leave 'em off," someone answered from the blackness, "if we wanted to see it glow."

She realized, with a pit in her stomach, that she recognized the gentle, husky voice. It seemed she was unable to escape Caleb, either in her work or in her thoughts. She had played their exchange by Ashley Pond over and over. She'd been furious with him, and then unmoored by his quiet intensity in the darkroom. Afterward, she'd been trying to parse his rude insult with his nervous questions about what her research was being used for.

If she was being honest, she had thought him handsome, with his broad chest and boyish smile, but the same force that had pulled her toward him had also driven her to flee. Perhaps it was guilt over Warren, or discomfort with the nervous, fluttering pulse she felt in her chest when she met his watery, sensitive eyes. There'd been something vulnerable in his demeanor yesterday and it had softened her toward him, despite herself. She gathered herself now. It was unforgiveable what he had said to her. Jews were the first to hurt other Jews. And those words mattered.

She followed the path of flickering emergency lights to the back of the room, searching for his broad shoulders and shorn curls. The recruits were lined up and awaiting her orders, their faces fading into the shadows behind their safety goggles. Untouched on the counter stood two enormous wooden boxes.

"I suppose we have to open them," she said, snapping her glove and stepping forward. She hesitated, waiting for her eyes to adjust.

She pried open one of the boxes with a crowbar, revealing a carton of twenty metal fuel slug containers within a water-filled cask. She went to work dissolving the aluminum with hydrofluoric acid, and around her the room burst to life, the SEDs following suit. She set up a siphon station for the liquid waste that would ultimately be funneled into an underground storage tank.

It was only a matter of moments before the fuel slugs had disintegrated and the room flickered with the dim glow of a substance that seemed to be from outer space. On the counter in front of them, metallic cylinders glowed with their own radiant light like fallen stars. The recruits seemed mesmerized by the lustrous substance, reduced by its enchantment from men to children. The samples flickered, lighting their cheekbones in the dark, making their faces look like skulls.

She donned safety goggles and gloves, but despite all the protective gear, she held her breath as she admired it. She recognized the silver element. It was plutonium. Atomic number 94, on the very bottom row, an afterthought on the Periodic Table. Mass number 244. It glowed in the dark, not because it was radioactive, but because it was pyrophoric—that is, it burned reddish orange when exposed to the air. The cylinders were roughly the size and shape of crayons, bright and silvery at first, oxidizing rapidly in a firework of yellow, green, and gray. This was its alpha form, she realized, hard and brittle as cast iron. It wouldn't be possible to mold it into a sphere unless it was alloyed with another material to make it soft and malleable. Or perhaps she could change it to the plasticity of its beta phase at a higher temperature.

While she charted her options, her mind tried to solve the puzzle of what they were helping to build. There were the obvious fissile properties, but then plutonium could also be a source of thermoelectric power. It could enable the exploration of the solar system. But why a sphere? What did it mean? What was Oppenheimer's plan?

Caleb was standing no nearer than the others, but she could hear the rustle of his double-pleated trousers and see the glimmer of the buckles on his suspender straps flashing, reflecting the dim red glow in her peripheral vision. Even with the fans rattling it was hot in there, and he wiped the sweat from his brow with the sleeve of his coat.

As they worked through the night, heating the cylinders with aluminum to create an alloy, they peeled off their lab coats. Underneath, the men were unforgivably casual in their Hawaiian shirts and sweat-stained undershirts, but Caleb maintained formality even out of uniform in his pinstriped shirt. Standing so close, she could smell the wafting cedarwood in his aftershave. She thought he smelled a little like the path out to the ocean, the one she had always taken as a kid, where the treetops touched to form a canopy.

"God missed this at creation," Saul marveled across the table. It dawned on her that these men, some pulled right out of undergraduate courses in the middle of the semester, with their limited understanding of the laws of physics, had been told more about the substance they were handling than she had. "I prefer to just call it element 49, if you have to call it anything." Saul had flipped the numbers, Alice realized—a subtle proxy to use the inverse of the element with the atomic number 94. "Or rich man's copper." He whistled in admiration like he was catcalling a beautiful woman in traffic.

"You got it on the nose, Saul," Caleb replied, keeping soft eyes locked on Alice. Why was he looking at her? "It's a metal, but it doesn't act like any metal on earth. It's missing magnetism."

Magnetism, she thought. And then that was all she could think about— the electric charge that resulted in attractive forces pulling two objects together.

At one point, they reached for the laboratory tongs at the same time, and their safety-gloved hands touched. She drew back like she had been burned. "I'm sorry," he said, letting her take them, looking sheepish. That threw her. It didn't line up with the narrative she had written in her head about his arrogance.

"Here," she said, handing them over when she was finished, a peace offering. "I'm through." For just an instant as he took them, their fingers lingered. It was still just two gloves touching, but she felt the warmth of his hand through the latex.

They failed. The sun rose in the window, and the alloy was malleable enough to mold into spheres, but it would emit neutrons when bombarded with alpha particles. She should have realized sooner. She decided to call it and send the recruits home.

They scrubbed in the sink, their skin going pink from the hot water. Caleb waited behind her while she soaped, and she was aware of the quiet heft of his body. "It's important to be thorough," she instructed the room, without turning to face him. "Check under your fingernails."

"Don't get your pantyhose in a twist. We wore gloves," one of the recruits protested. Alice pretended she hadn't heard. Pavlov made a big to-do of stretching and extending his limbs and yawning, then walked a circle and sank back down into his cot.

"Report back here at fifteen hundred hours," she instructed, as the recruits ducked out the door.

Caleb lingered. "Dr. Katz," he said in a shaky voice. He pulled off his safety goggles, and it might have just been the irritation of the dry air, or the exposure to chemicals, but his fragile eyes were glossy like river pebbles.

She wiped her hands dry on a dishtowel and folded it in on itself, once, twice, three times, afraid to look directly at him.

"I want to apologize for my behavior the other night," he said. "You being my team leader, and all. It was ungentlemanly. And these recruits, they're just boys being boys. You should ignore them." He dropped his eyes to the floor and his face went scarlet.

Alice didn't think boys being boys was much of an excuse, and ignoring their behavior was next to impossible, but she only nodded. She could smell him again—redwood trees and ocean air, the canopy closing in. It was hard to breathe. She stared a hole through his chest, afraid to meet his eyes and let him see the things that lingered on her mind. She shook the sensation away and straightened.

She wasn't one of those girls who sat around with curlers in her hair, reading *Ladies' Home Journal*. What was this desert existence doing to her? She was suddenly homesick for San Francisco, for her father's dusty library books, for Abigail's bedroom, untouched, just the way she had left it. She reminded herself that she was a professional, a team leader, and he was a mere understudy.

She straightened and took on a no-nonsense tone. It was the same voice she had used at Abigail's funeral, forcing out the words. "Call me Alice," she ordered.

6

August 1944
Caleb

In Caleb's gloved fingers, the plutonium was soft as cheese. He pressed indents into the malleable surface that remembered every touch. The impressed places glowed back at him before finally fading. Even through his protective gloves, it was warm in his hands. He should have grown accustomed to it by now, but still the metal was surprisingly heavy and warm to the touch, like a living thing. It reminded him of the baby bird he had once found at the base of a eucalyptus tree while he was waiting at the bus stop—you didn't want to jostle the stuff around. Who knew what could happen.

He recalled learning that before its reinvention at Berkeley, plutonium was an element that had never existed in the universe before, except perhaps for a very short while at the beginning. Others thought it only existed in outer space, or that it had vanished altogether, until man resurrected it a few years prior in the sixty-inch cyclotron on the Berkeley campus. At its discovery, plutonium had been named for the small planet at the edge of the solar system, Pluto. This name fittingly also summoned the ancient Greek god of the underworld whose mythology was often conflated with Hades's. Plutonium, in other words, was named for the god of the dead.

There were a million possible uses for the stuff. Certainly, there were applications in energy, other ways to help the war effort besides its fissionable properties. Caleb couldn't stop sweating. It wasn't just the mystery of what it was all for that had his pulse racing—it was the way Alice kept chewing on the end of her pencil, deep in thought, and taking small sips from her canteen, leaving lipstick imprints, perfect blush butterflies dappled along the rim.

They had been at it for a week now, heating the plutonium, experimenting with different alloys, casting molds at different temperatures. This assignment had taken precedence over the detonations in the canyon, and he was thankful for that, although he knew he hadn't escaped the dynamite for good. He and Saul would be back there soon enough.

Harry, who spent most of his time assisting Slotin in the Rufus lair, had been assigned occasional shifts alongside the recruits, and he and Saul kept up a casual banter that made it hard to think, ranging from conspiracy theories to femme fatales. Every time Caleb started to relax, sinking into the work, he recalled that enormous orb in the main laboratory, the one Slotin was always tampering with, and Harry was always going on about, his eyes sparkling. "It's the closest thing he's got to a girlfriend," Harry had said just that morning, elbowing him as Slotin polished the orb with a sterilizing cloth.

It was quite possible setting off dynamite by the blast walls was safer than standing in that laboratory in full protective gear. They couldn't know the effects of the plutonium at their fingertips in all its different states as they heated it to its unusually low melting point at 1,184 degrees Fahrenheit, then fired it to a boil at 5,842 degrees. On account of that low melting point, there was a large range of temperatures at which the plutonium was a liquid, sloshing on their clothes, and Caleb worried over cuts and scrapes on his exposed forearms, any avenue for it to enter the body. At the rate it oxidized, they were likely inhaling it too. It could already be in their intestinal tract, glowing in the center of their bodies. The only way to know would be a urine test, and Caleb wasn't one to make waves.

"You worry too much," Harry had said when Caleb brought it up. Then he snorted. "Just hold yer breath."

For the sixth time that week, they had failed to successfully craft an alloy that would allow for moldable spheres, and Alice sent them home. "That's a wrap," she called to the room of exhausted men. While the recruits scrubbed at the safety station, she cradled one of the cylinders in her hand and held it very near her face. *Too* near, Caleb thought. The glow lit her cheekbones and sparkled in her eyes, making them reflect a dazzling aurora borealis. She was charmingly disheveled by the research, several curls having escaped her updo, sweeping down into curled ringlets at the base of her neck. He wondered whether the heat he felt in his chest was from the radioactivity or from her.

Behind Alice, the last of the recruits floated out the door. "Allow me," Caleb said, ushering a tray of vials out of her way.

She whisked past him, almost touching his arm. "No need," she said dismissively. "I'll just lock up."

She pawed through her purse, then dug out a jewelry box, sliding a diamond ring up her finger. *Was she married?* Caleb's heart sank.

She must remove the ring for work, he reasoned. Given all the toxic substances, it made perfect sense. Now, she seemed to be fastening it back on before venturing back into the world of cowboys, like it was some sort of armor.

She noticed him staring and straightened her posture, folding her hands elegantly into each other, her tea rose–colored manicure quietly asserting her class.

"All right," he said, closing and locking a cabinet of gleaming lab instruments, overcome with a sudden need to flee. "I'll get out of your hair."

"It's late and it's a hike," she said, leading the way outside into the expanse of starlit sky. Pavlov slipped out past her knees and vanished into the shadows. Something in the weak, breathy way she spoke seemed to transgress what she knew he had just learned about her. "I'd appreciate an escort."

It was just a walk, Caleb reasoned. And she, after all, was a lady venturing out into the southwestern wilderness.

He would never get used to the depth of darkness, a consequence of security concerns, without streetlamps. It felt scandalous to be in such utter darkness so near to her. Thankfully, the moon was bright enough to light their way through the trees. They stepped gingerly through the mud, hopping from unstable rocks to fallen branches. Pavlov trotted ahead, disappearing into the darkness, then circling back to round them up every few minutes, bounding through the bushes with burrs stuck in his fur. Caleb offered his hand a few times to help her across the rickety logs, and though initially she waved him off, eventually she took his arm.

She slid her hand up his wrist and wrapped her fingers around his bicep for support. Responding to her touch, he flexed. He felt immensely important, helping her across the mud and deep sand. Even through the fabric of his shirt, he was aware of the indentation of the massive gem she wore on her finger, but he tried to dull the sensation of it, and focus instead on carefully placing his feet in the moonlight while they carried on a forced conversation about shift procedures and time clocks.

They paused at the steps to her front door.

"It's a sorry excuse for a squad," she was saying, meaning the untied shoes, slouched posture, and tardiness of the SEDs.

He wanted to defend the men who snored beside him, dreaming up at the stars, but he knew she was right.

"There's something else I've been meaning to address," she said.

"Oh?" he asked. He met her gaze and then shrank a little. Up close, her eyes had two narrow rings of green outlining her pupils—it wasn't the rich sheen of emerald green; it was more like the cloudy, tinted green of chlorine gas. His mind scoured the periodic table trying to pinpoint that color—he knew he had seen it somewhere before. When copper sheeting is exposed to the atmosphere and oxidizes into verdigris, perhaps. That was it. Her brown eyes were viridescent. They weren't fully brown and they weren't yet green, but they were shifting greenish. They were in the process of transitioning. He longed to see them more clearly in the daylight.

"By the pond, the night we met, you said something about swearing if you ever saw me again . . .?"

His breath caught in his chest and he choked out the words. "That's because it wasn't the first time we met."

7

August 1944
Alice

"I'm sorry, when did we meet?" she asked.

There was something about the way he looked at her, like she might be the only thing tethering him to this day, this place, this year. She had the sense that if not for the thick glasses he wore, shielding the nakedness of their looks with a protective barrier, he could read her mind.

"We met last year," he said. "In Berkeley."

"Oh, dear, I'm afraid I can't remember. I've been trying to place it." He had such a heartbroken look, she wished she had lied.

"It's quite all right," he said, shuffling his feet. "I wouldn't expect you to. I know I'm forgettable." And because of his insistence on his own insubstantiality, he suddenly became the most memorable person she had ever met.

None of the men in Alice's life were self-deprecating. Her father, Ishmael, had been named after the narrator of *Moby-Dick*, and like his namesake, he had spent his life wandering. But unlike the Ishmael of Genesis who is banished to the desert, or Melville's Ishmael who sails the endless seas, Alice's father wandered in his memory. He was chasing the past tense, a time before, when Abigail was still poring over her chemistry homework and filling balloons with corn syrup, oil, and water to see what would sink. Instead of white whales vanishing to specks beneath ocean swells, the tide of his memory was brimming with her textbooks and hair bows floating like buoys in the surf.

Then there was Warren, too busy fluffing his feathers and fancying his reflection in the hallway mirror to take any notice of the content of her sentences. She had tried not to be bothered by the way his eyes wandered to other women, their hosiery peeping out from beneath their skirts in every color of the rainbow. He had thought it was cute, or an endearing quirk the few times she had dared mention that she had earned a PhD. He had assumed it was a phase, and she would grow out of it into the wife and mother he had been promised. Physics was not an appropriate hobby for a wife. If he ever learned what she'd been up to as he was facing rifles, flame-throwers, and grenades in the trenches, he would certainly call the marriage off. Even long after this was over, someday when everything was declassi-fied, he wouldn't want a woman who could analyze wavelengths or calculate kinetic energy. By contrast, Caleb seemed to be memorizing her every word. He was not planning what he would say next while she spoke; he was truly listening to her. Perhaps he was even afraid to speak.

Pavlov was waiting for them on the porch, contentedly gnawing on a stick that he sandwiched between his paws. They climbed the rickety steps up to her small home, approaching the dim lantern swaying from the overhang. She turned to see Caleb's face in the light, but he avoided her eyes, investi-gating her ramshackle windows and lopsided roofing. He knocked on the wooden siding, feigning a knowledge in carpentry. He ran his hand along the hinge of the screen and the jutting windowpane. "These houses look like they were drawn by someone trying to remember their childhood home," he said. His expression cracked as he studied the humble siding. What child-hood home was he trying to remember? "Blueprints made from nostalgia."

"I'm not married," she said, unprompted, catching her breath. "Yet." She watched his features rearrange. Her chest fluttered, beating with hundreds of frantic wings. She tried to hold steady. "My fiancé is somewhere in the northeast of France. 38th Infantry Regiment."

Caleb still had his hand on the windowpane, and he seemed afraid to move it, to break the spell of whatever was happening between them. "I'm sorry," he said.

"Don't be. It's easier for him to have a relationship with a pen and paper than a woman who talks back."

"I never liked the phrase 'talking back,'" he said carefully. "Maybe you were just talking forward."

Alice felt something tighten in her chest at the suggestion that her words might mean something more. "I shouldn't be so hard on him," she said in a rehearsed voice. "He's fighting to save us." She tried to mean it.

She fingered the diamond with her thumb. Warren was a kind man. He didn't deserve her coldness, even if he did talk over her. She pictured him in his fatigues, in a cloud of yellow gas like a swarm of bees. She imagined him clawing at his throat while overhead, birds fell stiff from the sky. She shud-dered and blinked the thought away.

Alice and Caleb stood there for a minute beneath the pale halo of light. The wind blew the lantern slightly and the outline of the circle of light rocked back and forth, moving the shadows on Caleb's face around, making him look young and aged and then young again. It felt like time travel, like they had suddenly lived a lifetime together. The night seemed to thicken around them. Nothing else existed in the darkness. They were the only two people in the world.

He leaned in to kiss her, and she did the only thing she could to stop herself from herself. She pushed him away with words.

"You think I'm a floozy," she said.

"I don't," he said. "I wouldn't."

"All the work I've done, everything I've fought for, it will be for nothing tomorrow morning if you go blabbing to the barracks. And you'll be a king."

"I'm no king," he said, a flash of something crossing his face.

"You can't know what it's like to be a woman in this place," she said.

"No," he allowed.

"And the bunch of you in your undershirts and dog tags. None of you should be near those samples without degrees in the first place."

"I'm sorry, how do you figure?" He stepped back.

"Don't you get it? Your lack of formal education in a place like this is dangerous. You're charity cases, the lot of you."

His face hardened. She had struck a nerve.

"You don't know anything about my degree or my reasons for being here," he said flatly. "All you had to do was ask."

He ducked away and swept out of the light into the darkness, taking the three steps from the porch in a single hop. Then he turned back. "I knew it was too good to be true," he said, running an exasperated hand through his curls, making his hair stand up on end like a field of wildflowers. "A girl like you and a schmuck like me. Your palace walls are too high in Pacific Heights. You think you love your maid and your nurse and your housekeeper. You think they're part of your family, but they have their own families to feed and children they leave behind to plait your hair and drive you to piano recitals. I know. I'm one of them."

A cool breeze swept them, making goose bumps erupt on her skin. She had only wanted to keep him at an arm's length while still spending more time with him. She suddenly knew that if she let him storm off into the darkness, it would be the ending to whatever had only just begun. The momentum of the wind drove her to him.

She raced out of the light, pulled him to her, and kissed him. She pressed her mouth hard against his, like she was famished, desperate for something she needed to survive. Her eyes hadn't adjusted, and she was blinded from the porchlight, so she felt his body with her body, found her way around him and into him.

He kissed her back. Together they stumbled back up the steps, up against her door. With feverish intensity, she lined up their hips and braided her fingers through his. The interior of his palm and the tips of his fingers were calloused, and his knuckles were cut and bruised. They were the hands of someone who had scrubbed and polished and lifted. Her own small hands were untouched by the world. She wanted to touch all the places he had been.

Pavlov barked, breaking Alice's trance. She was overcome with a sudden panic, but she wasn't quite sure of what. Was she afraid they would be caught? Or was she more afraid of what she might do?

She pressed him off and smoothed her hair behind her ear, composing herself. On her finger, her ring divided the lantern light like a prism. Hot-faced, with shaking fingers, she unlocked her door. Without bidding him goodnight, she ushered Pavlov inside and slammed it closed. She slid down the other side; she could still feel the heat of him through the door.

She had locked herself inside her house, but she was still right beside him.

T-Minus 16

March 1967
Haruki: A Story Told Backward

Haruki could feel the heat of the doctor's stare. "You may want to contact a minister about last rites," he said, eyeing Haruki quizzically as he awaited a response. The doctor was young and sharply dressed, with a fresh haircut. He had his whole life before him. "Usually, when I tell someone they're dying, they have a few questions."

"I've been told I was terminal three times," muttered Haruki.

"What I'm saying is it's a good idea to get your affairs in order. It's time to make final arrangements. Gather a last will and testament, power of attorney."

Although he sat perfectly still on the crinkly brown hospital paper, Haruki had the sensation of wind running through his hair. He imagined himself on the hill of blowing purple azaleas where he had buried Shinju. They had come there to die once before.

"Death can be a burden on the living," the doctor was saying.

But Haruki wasn't listening. He was distracted by the smell of salt in the air. In his mind's eye, he could make out the red spires of the Ondo Bridge. Shinju's final resting place overlooked Ondo-no-seto, in the Seto Inland Sea, which connects the main island of Japan and Kurahashi Island. It was a tourist trap down there in the hustle and bustle of honking taxis and drifting ferries, but from so high up, he was alone with the wind. He could see the whole strait; the spring flowers had bloomed in fallen clouds of pink and purple.

He realized the doctor was waiting for him to say something.

"I died on August 6th, 1945," he said. "I may have left Hiroshima, but I will never leave Hiroshima."

He might have still been breathing, but he was already buried beside her.

8

September 1944
Caleb

Growing up, Caleb had been forbidden to touch any girls before marriage. Once, he'd brushed hands with a neighbor in the building during a game of pick-up-sticks, a ten-year-old named Phoebe with a long braid that hung down her back and wagged in the wind like a tail when she ran. He'd been so ashamed of his behavior that he dug his fingernails into his palm at dinner, terrified his parents would find out. That same year, a first grader fell from a swing set in the park and sobbed unconsolably. No one had come to help her. He'd repressed the urge to pick up the child and comfort her. Physical touch with the opposite sex, in any circumstance, was unseemly. He didn't believe, like his parents did, that God was always watching, but he couldn't bring himself to act on that hunch. Rules were rules.

As a teenager he kept his hands to himself. He had once rubbed elbows with a girl on the bus on the way home from yeshiva, and he could still remember the nervous swaying of their bodies as the bus climbed the hills and lurched forward from the stoplights. And of course, there was the way Alanna Greenfield had made eyes at him across the mechitzah during high holiday services.

Caleb thought of Alice constantly, but he was terrified of actually seeing her. He didn't know whether to be devastated or grateful that, now that Alice had struck upon a gallium alloy to mold the cylinders into spheres, he'd been sent back out to the canyons to photograph dynamite and sparks, and he wouldn't have to work with her until he reported to the lab next with negatives. Until then, it was a matter of chance and ratios. They were in the same orbit; at some point, they would cross the same axis.

Until then, he didn't know how to act when he spotted her in the commissary, sitting poised with her silverware. He knew she sensed him from the way she tensed when he passed her table to sit by the far wall. Later, watching a movie in the common room that stunk of sun cream and burned popcorn, he studied the back of her head, her curls frizzing out of her fishtail braid in the heat.

When their paychecks arrived at the end of each pay period, something changed in Caleb. Four hundred dollars was more money than he had ever had. That monthly amount added up to eight new suits in a month, or six new cars in a year. It was three new houses: one for his father, one for his mother, and one for Asher. Suddenly, he had something worth protecting. Suddenly, he had something to offer a woman like her. The other recruits had the polar opposite reaction, immediately upping their bets and playing their wages away at poker and hearts.

"Pennies from heaven." Saul jingled the coins, shaming Caleb over to the folding table. "Everyone likes a little gravy. Come now, don't be a drip." He shuffled the cards like a magician about to perform a trick. But no amount of peer pressure could change Caleb's mind. Each time he turned the men down, the wedge between him and the other SEDs grew deeper.

Saul kept trying to gloss over it. He pulled up a chair for Caleb at the card table and poured him a drink. But when he finally took a seat, one of the men groaned and another rolled his eyes.

"He wants to sleep on a pillow of greenbacks," griped the first recruit, waving him away. He had a shiny bald knob of a head and a malformed skull. Caleb had never learned his given name. Everyone in the barracks just referred to him as Bruiser, and Bruiser seemed bent on living up to this title. He had a cigar clenched in his teeth and was flipping through a wad of bills. He held the money up to his nose and sniffed deeply. "I say let sleepin' dogs lie."

"Don't mind him," interjected another, a man with one brown eye and one green. Caleb had heard the guys call him Two Face. "He don't like immigrants."

"He means Jews," huffed a man who looked too old to be a SED. He went by Ghost among the men, a play on the notion that he already had one foot in the grave. He was losing his hair and he had brushed it forward, where it lay lifeless across his forehead. He stood all the way up, not taking his eyes off Caleb. "Personally, I worry about Jews hovering over the samples. Anything that glitters is liable to go missing."

In unison, all the sets of eyes swept over Caleb and Saul; a trick of the light made Two Face's one green eye seem to be hovering closer than the rest.

Caleb and Saul weren't wearing prayer shawls or yarmulkes, but they were clear as day. Saul stared hard at his cards. His face went red, but he didn't say a word.

"What's the difference between a Jew and a pizza?" Ghost went on, emboldened to have an audience. He looked around the circle, anticipating the punchline. "A pizza doesn't scream when you put it in the oven!" Nobody laughed except for Ghost himself, who cackled at his own joke long and hard. Then he stopped laughing.

He placed a hand on Caleb's tense shoulder. Caleb flinched. "I don't mean to bust your chops," he said. "If we stamped out all the Jews on this hill, there'd be nobody left." He smiled, but it wasn't friendly.

After that, Caleb made a point of getting out of there on payday.

He never told anyone that he was sending away his money, mailing it home to their underground flat in a neighborhood so poverty stricken, there wasn't a bank. He still hadn't heard back from his father about the mortgage and their second thirty-day grace period, but he sent the money home like clockwork. He was terrified it had perhaps been stolen, or worse, it was too late, and they'd already been served. But folding up and sending away his paycheck was the only prayer he had left in him. The green bills felt like rice paper in his hands, like the pages of a holy book.

It was better to let the guys think he was a tough guy hoarding it all, just another bank-hungry Jew, than the alternative—a pushover aiming to pay off a house that would be worth more demolished and sold as a lot.

When Alice unexpectedly crossed his path, he was sitting in his civilian clothes, dangling his feet from the barracks porch, smoking a cigarette and watching the smoke clear. He'd never been a smoker, but he figured he'd better get used to it.

Alice sped past the army homes and the skeletal barracks, trailed by her furry golden dog. She wore faded denim blue jeans and hiking boots and her hair was swept up. But she still seemed to be wearing the sky. The faster she walked, the more the clouds seemed to billow, the horizon draped around her shoulders.

Still unsure what he could possibly say to smooth things over, some force awakened inside him, and he jumped up and ran after her, grabbing her by the arm. She swung around to face him, and in that moment the wind caught and brushed back her hair. She looked so enchantingly lovely that he forgot to breathe. Her skin was sun-kissed and glowing. The sun glinted on her dark hair, giving it a polished sheen. He would have kissed her right there if it weren't for the burning flames flickering in her dark eyes. Her breathing was shaky and erratic.

"What do you want?"

The pond lapped the shore behind them, making it hard to think. He wasn't sure what he wanted other than to be near to her. He was still clutching her arm, and although she seemed to be breathing fire, she let him hold onto her, softening into his grip. "There's a seminar," he said, trying to sound nonchalant. "Tonight."

When she didn't offer a response, he rushed to explain. "It's the inaugural lecture—Richard Feynman." He paused, assessing her reaction to the famous name. Her eyes sparkled and her mouth fell slightly open. She was intrigued.

Feynman was a prodigy. Caleb's own brother, Asher, had heard him give a lecture once and came home in hysterics. There had been a debate about art, science, and beauty. Someone had made the harebrained claim that art celebrated beauty, but science took it apart at a cellular level and made even flowers dull. But Richard Feynman had spun logical circles around the near-sighted assertion. "It's not just beautiful at this dimension," he had said. "At one centimeter, there's also beauty at smaller dimensions, the inner structure, the processes." After that, Asher had marveled at the intricate workings of small and secret undulating worlds: a universe embedded on the head of a pin, a spiraling galaxy in the fingernail of a child. By Feynman's logic, the barrier between the earth's atmosphere and outer space wasn't out of Asher's reach. It was right there in the kitchen, in the cracked molding on the sink and the spilled particles of sugar scavenged by the colony of ants behind the stove.

Arguably, Feynman had changed the course of Asher's entire life. Asher had made the strategic choice to enlist when they expanded the draft from eighteen to forty-five; it had made more sense to pick his branch of service. He was always going on about the barrier between the sky and the beginning of outer space. So, he picked propeller mechanics and learned to fly. To Asher, Feynman was more miraculous than an entire airfield of propellers at rest, waiting to take flight. Now, he had flown away, and Caleb wasn't certain he'd ever fly home.

He hadn't heard from Asher in the three months since he had been reassigned from the Royal Air Force and deployed to the Marianas. It wasn't like him not to write. It was terrifying to think what he had encountered in those tropical waters. He might be conducting airstrikes in Saipan or Guam, for all Caleb knew. He wondered whether his brother had found heaven through the plane window. Meanwhile, Caleb still hadn't been able to bring himself to taste the shrimp in the salad bar, or to try the bacon at breakfast. A nervous pressure built inside him each morning when they called out the mail by last name and skipped right from Abrams to Campbell.

Attending Feynman's lecture was something he could do. It was better than waiting around. It was a way to commune with the brother he hoped was still breathing.

Of course, he said none of this. Instead, he released Alice's arm and gestured across the pond in the direction of Fuller Lodge, where the lecture would be held. "You know Feynman." He forced the corners of his mouth into what he hoped was a whimsical smile. "Supposedly he has a pictorial mind, rather than an analytical one. That's why he doesn't use equations."

She nodded. "I know," she said, sounding irritated, "who Richard Feynman is." Now that he had released her arm, she placed her hand emphatically on her hip. "I would go, but they don't let women go to those things." She sounded defeated. "White badge or not, there's no security clearance that accounts for being female."

"I didn't know," he said, but it came out in a whimper. It didn't matter anyway. She had already turned and stalked away.

Caleb arrived early with his white badge pinned to his collar and his notebook in hand. He checked his watch. The lecture was already ten minutes delayed past schedule. He picked up a program on the folding chair beside him and leafed through it, scanning the room for famous faces. Alice was right. There was not a single woman in the room.

Even with the sun down, it was still sweltering hot. In front of him, a few young men fanned themselves with their programs, keeping their eyes locked on Oppenheimer's sweat-stained hat in the front row.

The young scientist who finally took the stage had sparkling eyes, deep dimples, and a shock of wavy hair. He spoke with a heavy Brooklyn accent, which surprised Caleb. He sounded like a street bum, which triggered something vile inside him. How could Asher not have mentioned it?

"Please excuse my Brooklynese." Dr. Feynman grinned, eschewing a formal introduction.

Instead of talking about ignition or sparks, he bragged about cracking the safes of distinguished scientists. "Dollars to doughnuts the numbers

27–18–28 will crack most locks on this mesa," he said, casually implicating the digits for the base of natural logarithms, e = 2.71828. "This one belongs to Mr. Farmer," he boasted, demonstrating with a slide of an unhinged padlock.

Caleb noticed Enrico Fermi, who sat near the front, had reddened at the sound of his code name. He wore a fully buttoned vest despite the heat and his balding forehead glimmered with sweat. He was so short that from behind he might be mistaken for a child.

"I cracked it on the first try, Ace," Feynman announced triumphantly, winking at Fermi.

At this jubilant declaration, Oppenheimer shifted from his relaxed posture and sat up rigidly. Nearby, Neils Bohr, his long face like a crescent moon, broke into a grin. He raised his hand and said something, but he spoke in such a soft, mushy voice, no one could make out a word.

"I'm sorry, Uncle Nick, couldya repeat yerself?" Caleb winced that Feynman had not used Bohr's designated code name, Baker, but had called him this casual euphemism frequently used on the hill, referencing Bohr's Christmastime arrival on the mesa despite his Jewish heritage. Feynman, being Jewish himself, seemed oblivious to the trouble with furnishing a Jew who had escaped Nazi-occupied Denmark with this nickname derived from Santa Claus. Being in proximity to Bohr still enchanted Caleb, and it was undignified to treat him so informally. Bohr was a hero. He had argued for asylum for thousands of Danish Jews in Sweden, and, working alongside him, Caleb felt assured that they would save thousands more. Looking around the room, Caleb marveled for the first time at how many of his heroes were Jews. They weren't the kind of Jew he was, but a Jew was a Jew.

Bohr repeated his question about sparks, and Feynman launched back into science, a language Caleb could digest. He soon found himself leaning forward, enraptured. Sure, the young prodigy spoke like a bum, but this man was evidence that the streets of Brooklyn, and the Jews who lived there, could find their way into the realm of physics.

At the cocktails that followed, Caleb did something he never did—he approached him. "Fascinating lecture, Dr. Feynman," he said. He half expected the celebrity scientist to brush him off and look right past him, but instead he flashed a charming smile.

"I learned very early on the difference between knowing the name of something and knowing something. These blowhards sometimes need to be reminded."

Caleb scanned the room. He counted three Nobel laureates. "You think even the best of us get caught up in semantics, Dr. Feynman?"

Up close, the young prodigy seemed an even wilder character. He had the smile of a practical joker and the glossy eyes of an artist. Despite the heat, he wore the mesa uniform of long pants and cowboy boots. He was equally tall, so the two met eyes above a sea of cowboy hats and hairlines. "Call me Dick," he said.

Despite Caleb's lowly status as an SED, his awkward hands, and his sheepish demeanor, Dick didn't seem to be looking past him to see who else was in the room. He didn't nod along when Caleb spoke, searching for a way to end the conversation. Instead, his playful copper eyes flickered. He seemed young, naive to the world. Caleb had the sense that he wore his heart on his sleeve, that this was the sort of man who was often in love.

Dick inched closer and put a hand on his shoulder. He got so close that Caleb could see the individual pores on his nose. He whispered conspiratorially: "If you think you understand quantum mechanics, you don't understand quantum mechanics."

"My brother is a fan of yours," Caleb blurted out. "He's in the air force now."

"You don't say."

"He says he heard you give a lecture once about flying, that the barriers between earth and outer space are at our fingertips."

"In our fingertips is more like it," said Dick. When Caleb furrowed his brow, he elaborated, "The most remarkable discovery in all of astronomy is that the stars are made of atoms of the same kind as those on earth, those already inside us. People are all pretty much the same at the cellular level."

"Right," Caleb said, nodding. "Atoms are atoms."

"You got it," Dick said, tapping his nose. "That's why love and soulmates don't make any scientific sense, but here we are, falling all over dames like spring chickens."

Despite himself, Caleb pictured the way Alice had cradled the plutonium. She'd had a maternal way of holding it, almost like the element was an extension of herself. The glow had flushed gradually across her face, like watching the sunrise.

He realized Dick was staring at him curiously. "Oof. You got it bad. Who's the whistle bait's got you flippin' your wig?" he asked, his eyes glittering playfully.

"No one," Caleb said, but he could see her so clearly it was like he was still standing at the shore of Ashley Pond beside her, the wind whipping her hair. He forced himself to meet Dick's gaze. "What about you? Any spring chickens in particular, Dick?"

A dark cloud swept Dick's features. Caleb immediately regretted asking. For a moment, they stood there while everyone in the room hustled and bustled around them. Someone squeaked a chair across the floor. Several people broke into laughter behind them.

"My wife is dying," Dick said finally, flicking a piece of lint from his shirtsleeve. He said it flatly, like he was commenting on the weather. "In Albuquerque of all places. She wanted to die in Brooklyn."

"Oh, I'm so sorry," said Caleb. He measured Dick's expression, trying to figure what to say next.

In response, Dick cracked a smile and smacked him on the back. He seemed to have the emotional capacity to run marathons between joy and pain, traveling at breakneck speed. "My high school sweetheart," he said. He broke into a grin, making him look very young, like he was just a schoolboy passing notes and sticking gum in his crush's hair. "You never get over your first love." A few tufts of chest hair peeked out of his collar and the hint of a silver chain sparkled in the light. Was there a Jewish star tucked under his shirt?

They were standing very close. Caleb took a step back. Dick took another step forward and leaned into him. "Arline was diagnosed with tuberculosis and given two years to live when we were just kids. Before we were even married." He said this with the same intonation with which he had moments ago discussed logarithms.

"That's just awful," said Caleb. Despite himself, he wondered why on earth Dick had gone through with it. He had had the whole world in front of him—why marry someone with a death sentence? Then he was ashamed of himself for having the thought. If love was to logic what fission was to the future, who was he to split hairs?

"I married her in Staten Island," Dick said. "The forgotten borough." He stared for a minute out the window.

There was something inspiring about this brilliant man beside Caleb. He had left his heart in Albuquerque. It gave him hope. Dick's romantic Hail Mary, this star-crossed romance, was a foreign thing to him. Under his father's roof, everything had always been routine and practical. Levi ate the same food every day. He wore the same clothes. He even insisted on praying toward Jerusalem morning, afternoon, and evening, no matter how many times Caleb argued that from the perspective of mathematics and cartography, there is not just one scientific answer for standing in one point on a globe and facing another. The reality of compass direction on a round earth was problematic. But tradition was tradition.

Dick seemed to feel Caleb's eyes on him and came back to himself from wherever he had gone. He turned from the window and his face had changed, softened. "Watch out or you'll end up with a ball and chain before you know it." He winked. "Cupid only comes for ya when you're not lookin', Ace."

"I don't think he'd make it past the guards in this place," Caleb quipped.

It was supposed to be a joke, but Dick didn't laugh. He scanned the room and wrapped his arm around Caleb, making sure no one was listening. "Arline writes me letters," he whispered.

Caleb tried to pull away without looking like he was trying to pull away. "Letters?"

"Once, she put a hair in one as an experiment. When it reached me, it had gone missing." His copper eyes flickered like Shabbat candles. "They claim they don't read our incoming mail," he said. "But you can't trust anyone around here." He scanned the room. "Listen, Ace, if you knew the half of what they're building, what they cut out of the letters, and what's inside those safes, you'd run for the hills. My wife might be dying, but we're all as good as dead, the lot of us."

T-Minus 15

April 1966
Haruki: A Story Told Backward

Shinju had been the love of his life, and now she slept peacefully while outside her room the hospital whirred with life. Visitors were arguing with the staff by the reception desk. Nurses wheeled carts up and down the hallway, their medical instruments rattling as they passed. Every so often, the violent crash of the ice machine made Haruki jump.

When a doctor in a white coat came in to consult with him about her condition, he was in a stupor. It was his eldest daughter, Junko, named for his sister, who had to field the questions.

"No, she isn't allergic to sulfa drugs," Junko responded. "Yes, she is already on a blood thinner. Yes, she takes beta blockers."

Through it all, Haruki held Shinju's pruned hand. It was hard for him to comprehend that she was sick. To him, she still looked like the girl he had met at twenty-three.

They had always assumed he would die first. A few years prior, his mysterious bleeding and bruises had been diagnosed as leukemia, a consequence of his radiation exposure. He had no ability to resist infection and had to wear a face mask in public. He was always sick and he had lost his hair to chemotherapy. But he hadn't been able to die fast enough. He wondered whether it was his curse to outlive the people he loved.

"We tried to warn you," said Junko when they were alone again. By *we*, she meant his three adult children. They'd seen the changes. Haruki, with his opaque eyes, had been blind to the signs. He couldn't see that when Shinju smiled, her lip drooped. He didn't notice the unevenness in her expression.

"We spent more of our life together than apart," he said. He stroked his wife's hair. It had fallen out in uneven clumps and was streaked with silver tufts, like cobwebs.

He turned to Junko, struggling to see the details of her face. He touched her cheek, trying instead to see her with his hands. Sometimes, he wondered whether, if given the chance to grow up, his sister would have looked just like his daughter.

And he knew then that it was time.

"Listen to my story," he said. "I promised your mother I would tell it."

9

November 1944
Alice

Alice blamed this place. It had to be the desert. The mesa had a way of enchanting people. It had a way of making rational people do irrational and passionate things, especially at night, when the trees disappeared one by one as the light faded. For months, she was overcome with guilt over what she had done with Caleb. She thought of Warren's letters, the cursive written in pristine slants and tendrils, spelling out the promise of a future. She had to behave better.

When the sun went down, Oppenheimer's parties were lifelines propping the town up against the dark, endless mountainside. His house on Bathtub Row became a revolving door. When dusk made the sky glow, the whole community filtered in: weary scientists looking to forget the things they knew, their wives in strappy sandals desperate for the moxie to ask their husbands questions, single women employed as school teachers and calculators in the computing room, and lonely SEDs in their civilian clothing looking for companionship. They swallowed lab-made cocktails like medicine. They tried to snuff out their fears for their loved ones storming the beaches in Normandy, their husbands stationed in Northern Ireland waiting for their turn to fight, or their brothers staving off seasickness on the bloody ocean swells of the Mariana Islands.

With the salad bar's array of wilting vegetables and spoiled fruit that had been hauled up the switchbacks in a flatbed, and the acidic coffee in the mess hall, the young population functioned mainly on adrenaline and cigarettes. Their watering hole was Oppenheimer's standing bar beside the large, latticed window. The alcohol flowed while the light faded, painting hatched shadows across their faces and dramatizing their dark circles and clenched jaws. The gossip intensified when darkness fell and the woods outside the

84

kitchen window came alive. Postures began to slouch, collars unbuttoned. Touching began as a shy meeting of eyes, a slip of the wrist, a brush of a hip in passing through the crowd.

Even when it was still light out, the wives drank like it was the middle of the night. They stood posed with elbows cocked like mannequins in the Macy's window display. Because of their impractical pumps, they leaned tired hips up against the kitchen island. Oppie's martinis were famously strong enough to knock out a horse, and appetizers were sparse at best, so the intoxication made everyone nearsighted. Young wannabe scientists stumbled through the room, squinting up at the high vaulted ceiling, tripping over chair legs and their own feet. They clasped the exposed beams and inched their way through the crowd, holding their hands out in front of them like they had gone blind.

During one such evening, Alice wanted desperately to talk shop with the men in the smoky study, but after one look at her, in her plaid, A-line skirt, she was filtered into the dining room with the wives. Her next-door neighbor, Bonnie, waved her over to the loveseat. Alice was used to hearing Bonnie's voice in indistinct murmurs through the wall, and the low baritone of her husband droning back in response. During lonely meals and long, sleepless nights, she had committed hours to trying to decipher their words. She had relished in Bonnie's gifts of oatmeal raisin cookies and artisan loaves of bread left in baskets at her front door, but the two hadn't ever formally introduced themselves.

"We wives got to stick together out here." Bonnie smiled, patting the floral cushion beside her.

"Oh," said Alice, casting nervous glances around the room of sun hats and scarves and sinking onto the seat beside Bonnie. "I'm not a wife."

"Heavens! You're out here alone?" asked Bonnie. Alice admired her blonde ringlets up in elaborate twists. Bonnie was wearing an apron cinched tightly around her housedress.

"Well, I'm engaged," Alice said quickly. "Warren, my fiancé, is serving in Belgium. In the meantime, I'm on theoretics, and filling in as needed at Project Rufus." She hated herself for making her career out like it was a lighthearted hobby while her fiancé was out of town. She flashed the white badge pinned to her collar. "Under Frisch."

When she said it, one of the wives, a stout middle-aged woman named Rose, looked up at her over a sparse cheese board and shimmering cutlery. "My husband stopped talking about his work," she said bitterly. "And then we just stopped talking." She had a bob of dark curls and wide-set, worried eyes. There was something unsettling about her look. When she smiled, she was almost pretty, but when she gazed at Alice head on, something felt awry.

Bonnie didn't flinch. "I want to get a job while I'm here," she continued. Perhaps she said it out of pity. "With my husband, Vic, of course. I could do something. You know, like Rosie the Riveter."

Alice listened politely. She was thankful to no longer be hovering awkwardly in the dining area, but she kept straining her ears to make out what was being said in the study. Oppenheimer was in there; she could tell from the nervous energy and the careful way men kept elbowing their way through the cracked door, balancing overflowing martinis. She wondered fleetingly whether Caleb might be in that room somewhere, just through the wall. She tried to invest in the conversation with the women, but she could hear Abigail in her mind, urging her to get inside that room where the secrets were being kept.

"I was thinking maybe I could teach at the public school, work with children," Bonnie said, meaning the army green outpost set up for the gifted offspring of scientists.

Now, Alice was certain she could make out Oppenheimer's muffled voice in the study, but only a few words here and there were distinct. He was saying something about magnetism, followed by a heated debate. The men were shouting over each other. And then it got quiet again.

Suddenly, Oppenheimer swaggered out of a cloud of smoke and made his way to the bar for a refill. He flashed a grin at the ladies, who had gone quiet and were staring at him. He shook the cocktail shaker and held it up to his ear playfully with the manner of a man who was about to roll the dice. "Remember," he said, giving the ladies a mock military salute, "if anyone asks, they have us out here sewing parachutes and invisibility cloaks." He winked and swaggered back toward the study at a snail's pace, taking his time. He was loving every minute of this. He'd finally been given a leading role in a real-life Western, and he was playing his heart out. Then he vanished back into the cloud of smoke.

Alice must have been staring because a woman seated nearby nodded in the direction of the study. Her frizzy hair hovered over her head like a halo. "It's a form of torture," she said. She was sitting cross-legged in trousers on the floor like a kid. She had kicked off her shoes and they were belly-up beside her. She stared at her feet and wiggled her bare toes. Her square glasses took up most of her small face. "Being so close to where the ideas are born, yet so far."

Alice glanced back at Bonnie nervously and saw that she was consumed in gossip. She joined the young woman on the floor, smoothing her skirt neatly across her knees like a tablecloth.

"If I hear one more recipe, I'm liable to explode," said Alice, quickly regretting the unintentional pun. In her right mind, she would never make light of explosions in a town where dynamite interrupted the flow of conversation. The woman smiled faintly, forgiving the slip.

"Name's Elizabeth," she said, offering her hand. "Everyone calls me Diz. I'm on theoretics too."

"Alice," she said. She could barely get her name out in her excitement over befriending another female scientist.

"Al's in there," Diz said, jumping to her feet to exhale a puff of smoke through the open window. It drifted away into the night. "My husband. He'll fill me in later."

"Is it always like this?" Alice asked.

Diz smiled and put a hand on her shoulder. Alice noticed that she did not wear any nail polish, and dirt was caked under her nails. It was like the hand of a man. "It's all downhill from here," she said.

They both turned to look at Kitty Oppenheimer, who had entered with a tray of cocktails. "I'm practically royalty," she was saying, meaning her bloodline connections to Queen Victoria, certainly not her Nazi relatives that everyone wondered about but nobody dared ask. She set down the tray like an offering. "And that makes you ladies my courtiers."

When her husband left the room, Kitty was the queen of the mesa, and it went straight to her head. She reigned over female gossip with an imperial air. Like her famous husband, she was skeletal, with pale skin. She was nearly translucent, more jellyfish than woman, and intricate blue veins showed through her wrists when she lit a match and then shook it out.

"And royals don't tolerate armed guards lurking about," she continued, balancing both cocktail and cigarette in a single hand. "So I put them in charge of watching Peter, and it took all of three days for him to chase them off." Her smile deepened at the recollection of her toddler chasing off the military. The wrinkles around her eyes folded up like crepe paper. Around her, the wives nodded in admiration and nursed their drinks obediently. Like with her husband, women found themselves drawn to her, but Kitty eventually tired of them, or grew jealous of them, whichever came first.

"I don't trust any woman with no female friends," Diz whispered, her eyes locked on Kitty. "She has as hard a time with friendships as she does with love affairs." Alice must have looked confused because she elaborated: "She was married to someone else when Oppenheimer got her pregnant."

Alice gasped. As much as it would have outraged her mother, the idea of their secret affair excited her. She knew his reputation with women, had heard the gossip about his affairs. In all the years she'd worked with him, how could she not have known the truth about him and Kitty? Suddenly, he was reduced from a messiah to a mere mortal.

When the talk turned to linoleum patterns, Diz rolled her eyes. "That's my cue."

"Oh, you're leaving?" Alice had only just found her.

"It was a pleasure." Diz nodded, giving an adieu that seemed masculine in its informality.

Alice wanted to chase after her, but instead she settled back into her seat beside Bonnie on the upholstered couch.

"Just a pinch of salt," Bonnie was saying, like the secret ingredient was the most top-secret intelligence on the hill. "You can't eat just one."

"One egg makes it like cake," responded Judith, who lived down the way with her two screaming children. "Two and they melt in your mouth." She sank deeper into the cushion with each sip of her martini.

The women's talk shifted to school curriculum while the light waned and stars unfurled across the sky. Before long, Kitty's canary-yellow scarf was the brightest thing in the room, but no one made a move to turn on the light. Looking to Kitty for guidance, they stayed put and drank themselves under the table.

They refilled their drinks, reapplied their lipstick, and worried over their children's education in this strange, lost country. One of the women removed a hatch-mark scarf and draped it over the back of a chair where it billowed around in the breeze from the opened window, like wind in the trees.

Alice tried to focus on what Bonnie was saying, but she kept staring at the hatch-mark pattern on that scarf. It was a trompe l'oeil. Some of the design seemed miles away, like cottonwood on the horizon, while other shapes popped forward into her airspace, making her dizzy. She put down her drink and tried to clear her head.

Alice recalled something Warren had said about an entire wilderness of trees imprinted inside a single seed. He hadn't really been talking about trees. He'd meant that in the army, a single soldier could change the future. But Alice had pictured the genetic imprints unfolding exponentially in her mind. "Just think," he had said when he stooped to kiss her goodbye before being deployed. "A thousand birch trees in the wind."

"They're barely teaching them letters, let alone cursive," Judith was saying beside her. "They're letting Milo write with his left hand!"

"I'm a lefty," Alice blurted out, then immediately regretted it. Judith and Bonnie snapped around to look at her like a single animal with two heads. "I mean, I write with my right, otherwise it gets smudgy," she lied, quickly realizing her error. Handwriting was often conflated with intelligence, but her father had insisted that that was hogwash.

"Write the way you think," he had said when she came home from grade school in tears. "If that's gobbledygook, then so be it." Ever after, her handwriting had been a drivel that smudged into complete illegibility. Miraculously, it hadn't kept her out of the universities, but it was a shameful secret.

She took a pull of her martini. All the women had looked so pristine in their ironed blouses and head scarves, but now they were coming undone. Alice smoothed the wrinkles from her shirtsleeves. She mentally cursed the mangle: a monstrous contraption in the common room that was meant to dry and de-wrinkle clothing. She was used to looking elegant, but she was afraid that she, too, was coming undone. In more than one way, this town had already stripped her of who she had been.

Around midnight, the men retreated from the study and the women crossed their legs toward them and fingered their hair. Someone put on a record, and several kicked off their heels and wiggled their sore toes through stiff hosiery, then found dance partners.

That was when Fred staggered toward Alice. She hadn't spoken to him since he had shown her around the labs and administered her typing test. But she had seen him every morning, perched on his high-backed chair like a pigeon on a telephone wire watching over the theoretical group. Evenings, he strode around the labs with an inflated sense of importance and jangled a large janitor's ring of keys on his belt loop. He made it known that he had access to all the private offices. There was no secret too classified for his level of clearance. He rarely buttoned his shirt and he was often scratching—his chest, his protruding belly, his crotch. She was acutely aware of his glossy eyes on her whenever she passed him in the hall.

Now, he was headed right for her with an eager bounce in his gait. Despite this bounding motion, his gelled hair was immobile. His golden dog tag bounced against his chest as he walked. She could see tufts of thick, curly chest hair peeking out from the pink, sunburnt skin at the collar of his sweat-stained undershirt. He'd clearly been overserved.

"Well," said Fred. "What have we here?" He flashed a sinister grin, revealing sharp, yellow canines. It wasn't a smile so much as a smirk—the expression of having caught her at something. A cigarette twitched in his mouth. He plopped down beside her on the couch, leaning close. The weight of his body jolted her seat cushion up into the air. He spread his legs and jiggled his ankles like he was wearing imaginary spurs. She tried not to retch at the stench of his stale, dried sweat masked by an overwhelming cologne as he leaned closer. "Join me for a jitterbug, baby doll?"

She didn't have a chance to refuse. He grabbed her wrist and pulled her from her seat, pressing against her. She could feel the eyes of the wives in the room tracing their movements. She didn't want to cause a scene in front of the entire town. He grasped tightly around her hips. The skin of his knuckles was brittle and cracked. She twisted away, but he clutched tighter, the places he pressed his fingers into her skin going white, blanching from prevented blood flow.

"Easy does it, kitten."

She tensed but acquiesced, following his lead. "You're too pretty to be a scientist," he whispered, his breath hot in her ear. He got so close his stubble roughed her cheek. "Looker like you should be bakin' bread with the other dames. Not wastin' away in the lab with the men."

"Respectfully, sir, I have every right to work in the lab. I have the same white badge as everyone else."

His face blanched. "You're foolin' yourself, thinkin' what you do out here matters. Your job is to give us scientists something nice to look at."

He leaned in and kissed her hard on the lips. She arched away and shoved him off, but he locked his arms around her hips and pulled her in. She felt Bonnie's eyes burning into her. From her perch on the loveseat, Rose clutched her chest.

He slid his hand down the front of her skirt, underneath the fabric. She shoved him again, with more force this time. His eyes had gone feral. He pressed harder against her. She could feel his erection against her thigh.

"Get off!" she yelled, but he only clenched tighter.

"Oh, come, now," he cooed. "You're no fun."

"I'll report you!"

He laughed. "I'm the grievance department. Are you going to report me to me?" He pushed his fingers up her skirt, inside the seams of her panties. Everything went blurry.

Somebody had switched off the music, though Fred took no notice. Everyone was staring at them, but nobody moved to help her.

Suddenly, Caleb was there, dragging him off. He shoved him with an inordinate amount of force, and Fred was just drunk enough that he crumpled to the floor, his still-lit cigarette spinning like a top across the room. "Get your mitts off her," Caleb growled.

Fred felt around for the fallen cigarette. He found it on the ground and puffed right there, splayed out on the floor, eyeing Alice up and down provocatively, undressing her with his eyes. "She couldn't wait to spread her legs for me. A girl like that is looking to sleep her way to a Nobel Prize." He flung the cigarette at Alice's feet and she jumped back. He strained to lift himself and stepped it out with the heel of his boot right in the middle of the floor. Then he marched proudly out the door. The cigarette died slowly, curled up like a bug on its back.

The room slowly came back to life. Someone turned the music back up. "Are you all right?" Caleb's eyes were magnified through his lenses, blinking with concern.

"Sure," she said flatly, searching the crowd. People were dancing and activity had resumed. No one was gawking anymore. "Just embarrassed." She brushed her hair back from her face. She pushed out the words through clenched teeth, still shaky: "They saw the whole thing. All these respected scientists." She couldn't shake the alarm ringing in her head, the horror of nobody lifting a finger to help her. Did they agree with what Fred had said, that she was the kind of girl who slept her way to the top? She was furious about the double standard, that tomorrow Fred would just go back to doing his job, no questions asked.

Caleb gave her a pitiful smile. "I wouldn't worry over it. I'm unaware as yet of Nobel Prizes being given out for bedroom performances." He offered his hand, inviting her to dance. "Best thing you can do is show 'em you don't care."

They glided across the floor. She was startled by the heat and presence of him even through his shirt, and she was overwhelmed by a breathless swiveling sensation as he leaned closer. She could feel the defined muscles on his shoulders. She wondered if they were the result of physical labor, night shifts, working with his hands. He rested his cheek against hers in the manner of a child, making her dizzy. Again, she breathed in the scent of him— redwood trees leading to the ocean. He pulled away and they wove their fingers together. She met his eyes and found they were already fixed on her, a look so direct it was more like being touched than being looked at.

"Just be more careful next time, with who you choose to flirt with," he said.

For a second, she thought she had misheard. "What did you say?"

"Be more careful," he repeated. She flung his hand off and stepped back. He looked shocked and frightened—his eyes flashed with alarm, seeming to change color behind his specs, going lighter blue. "What did I say?"

"I didn't *flirt* with him." She felt her mouth clench and fiery heat coursed through her veins.

"All I'm sayin' is you just can't smile at a man like that. He gets the wrong idea."

"I see." She tried to maintain her composure, to finish out the dance holding her chin up, but the walls were coming down around her. Her eyes filled with tears. She had done nothing but try to repel Fred from the moment she met him.

Forgetting her coat, she turned and ran out into the chilly weather, which had begun to plummet after sundown now that the seasons were turning. She could hear him chasing after her. "Alice!" he called. "Alice, wait!"

Her arms stung in the cold and she tripped in a divot, losing a heel. She limped on one shoe, still trying to outrun him. But his legs were longer and he was already beside her. He wasn't wearing his coat either. "I'm sorry. Listen to me." He grabbed her hand. "I'm so sorry. I didn't mean it like—" He broke off, shaking his head. "Please, try to understand. Where I come from, dresses reach past the knee. My own mother won't leave the house without her sheitel. I'm reeling in this world of fitted waists and va-va-voom. I'm just trying to play catch-up. But you . . ." He ran a tentative finger through her curls. "Please believe me when I say you are perfect."

Maybe it was the cold, but his touch, even just in her hair, made her soften. She knew there was much he didn't know about the world, her world. That same innocence was a large part of his appeal. She studied him, breathing out puffs of cold air beside her, his face braced with concern. She thought of the way Warren's eyes always drifted past her when she spoke. She had never known this kind of focused attention and kindness.

She wanted Caleb's hands on her. In the aftermath of what Fred had just done, it was hard to imagine touching anyone else in that way. But Caleb's eyes on her made her stomach knot. His gaze traveled down her neck to the hollow of her throat.

Over the course of their yearlong engagement, making love had been a task to be completed when Warren felt inclined—always in the evening, always in the dark. And it was all always about his pleasure.

Now, she struggled to resist the overwhelming need to be close to this man. She felt herself buckling. She found his shirt with her fingers, sensing his tensed abdomen beneath, and pulled him close. Without thinking, she kissed him. Again and again, she kissed him, her eyelashes fluttering, grabbing his arms, wrapping them around her like a coat. They kissed until her mouth tingled, and she could barely stand, bumbling on legs that wouldn't bend. She wanted more of him. In his arms, she felt weightless.

"Holy mackerel," someone said in a heavy Brooklyn accent. They jumped away from each other and both turned, guiltily straightening their clothes and hair. It was Saul, looking wide-eyed at the pair of them in the darkness, holding his cap over his heart. "So the schmuck gets the girl."

T-Minus 14

July 1950
Haruki: A Story Told Backward

They boarded the ferry by moonlight. Haruki hesitated at the gangboard. Shinju's black hair tossed in the wind, covering half of her face, erasing part of her in the darkness. "I never thought I would leave Hiroshima," Haruki said.

"It's me or Hiroshima. You can't have us both," she said, leveling him with her dark eyes. It was true, of course—her family wouldn't allow them to be together if they stayed. Her hair whipped with the drama of the wind. Then she softened. "We'll still be in Hiroshima Prefecture, just not in the city itself."

Haruki stepped onboard, thinking of the oyster beds and sprawling beaches waiting for them. The life he knew was over, but their life together was only beginning.

It was a three-hour journey. The water was low and flat. Behind them, the boat left a wide wake that unzipped the water, which was brimming with reflected stars. By the time the ferry drifted beneath the looming spires of the bright red Ondo-no-seto bridge, the sun was rising. Haruki gazed off the stern, watching the mirrored reflection of the sunrise in the rippling water, a perfect twinning, a second sun.

An hour later, on solid ground, they washed their hands and mouths at the temizuya before entering the shrine. Haruki looked up at the gabled roof, and the fitted joints of cypress roots. He felt the presence of the kami as he entered.

Inside, a priest in formal vestments, an eboshi hat and balloon pants, announced the beginning of the san-san-kudo ceremony, filling the first, smallest cup of sake and passing it to Haruki. He drank from it before offering it to Shinju, who had draped herself in a white kimono and Tsunokakushi.

She was the most beautiful bride he had ever seen. Her feet hidden by the length of her kimono, she seemed to have floated up the aisle, and beside her, he felt weightless.

"When we were hopeless, we spoke of being Ohatsu and Tokubei, but we were wrong. We are Orihime and Hikoboshi," he said, referencing the deities represented by the stars Vega and Altair. Legend had it that once a year on the seventh day of the seventh lunar month, the Milky Way separated so they could meet. "We sailed through the Milky Way to get here," he said, meaning the reflected stars on the water's surface.

He wrapped her fingers in his. She looked small and delicate, swimming in the large kimono and white silk paper hat. He promised himself he would spend what he had left of his life protecting her.

10

"Attaboy," said one of the recruits the next morning with a grin as they scrambled to prepare for bed checks. He smacked Caleb on the back so hard he nearly spat out his cigarette.

This man had slept near him for weeks and Caleb didn't even know his first name. Since the soldiers just went by surnames or nicknames, he still only knew this soldier by his epithet, Cyclops. He had earned the term of endearment for having an unsightly mole like a third eye.

"That dame's got a pair of headlights if I've ever seen 'em." He smirked, waiting for affirmation. Caleb was still hung over and it was early. He hadn't left Oppenheimer's house until it was light out. After Saul had interrupted them kissing in the snow, Alice had given Caleb a desperate look and slipped away. He'd wanted so badly to chase after her; to stop himself, he'd drank until he couldn't see straight. But he had a sinking feeling that Cyclops meant Alice—which meant everyone knew. Word traveled fast in the barracks where they slept and snored head to toe, close enough to smell the feet of the man in the next cot. "She's too rich for my blood, you know, but I think I'd make an exception for those gams."

Caleb smiled tightly, aiming to disengage.

"They might be skinny, but they're nice and long like popsicle sticks," Bruiser joined in, turning from his bunk. "I'd like to give 'em a lick."

"Quit flappin' your lips," Caleb said, avoiding both men's shining eyes. The thought of these men and their grimy hands on Alice made him flush with anger. And after what happened with Fred last night, he couldn't dismiss their words as idle threats. He stood rigidly by his unmade bunk.

"What's got his panties in a twist?" asked Two Face, nodding at Caleb, his different- colored eyes sparkling provocatively. He was chewing sunflower seeds with his mouth open and spitting the shells into a paper cup.

"Bergensteinowitz caught him and the lady scientist necking last night." On account of his Yiddish accent, in the barracks, they all referred to Saul as Bergensteinowitz, never mind that his last name, Abrams, was already Jewish.

"He wants to see what's under her blitzies." Two Face laughed, slapping his knee.

"It ain't so hard to believe," chimed in Bruiser. "Caleb ain't no dog-face."

"I'm just sayin' he also ain't a dreamboat," said Cyclops, sizing Caleb up. "What's he got I don't?"

"Nah, it's less about him and more about sleepin' her way to a higher security clearance." Bruiser was talking loudly. Everyone in the barracks could hear.

Caleb was thankful when Sergeant Moony stalked into the room with a stiff salute, interrupting them. Moony had little patience for the slapdash SEDs and resented being placed in their charge. He had a storm cloud over his head. From his hair buzzed close to his scalp to his polished tall boots, he oozed precision and confidence.

Caleb took the opportunity to duck out of there as soon as they were put at ease.

"Don't let these buggers get under your skin," Saul said, still out of breath from chasing after him.

Caleb watched Ashley Pond glisten. He tried to unclench his jaw. Saul put a hand on him and he jumped, a reflex like someone was trying to hurt him.

"I'm sorry," Saul said, looking genuinely forlorn. "Truly. I only told one person. I never took Dave for a gossip," he said, implicating David Greenglass, the crude-talking recruit from the Lower East Side who slept beside them in the next bunk over. "He didn't even seem all that interested." Greenglass was an outspoken communist. It figured Saul had trusted him.

"The work we're doin' out here," Caleb said, meeting Saul's eyes by way of accepting his apology, "it will get done the same whether I'm there or not today."

They'd been back at the dynamite for weeks now, photographing sparks by the blast walls, and leaving negatives in the darkroom for Alice to develop. Caleb was starting to worry more and more about what they were learning from their experiments, what those sparks might look like on a larger scale, but he put stock in Alice's notion that the science wasn't the thing to fear, but the men who wielded it. Over the weekend, a new truckload of explosives had made its way up the treacherous, winding road, bouncing over potholes loaded with dynamite intentionally mislabeled as cinderblocks to deter suspicion. It needed to be unloaded, stored cautiously, then detonated in the weeks to come.

Saul nodded, acknowledging both the things he had said and the things he hadn't. "We can make do with one less pair of pipes if you got somewhere you gotta be."

With the drop in the weather, yellow and red fallen leaves had carpeted the mesa floor and the scent of sagebrush filled the air, smelling medicinal, like camphor. In the trampled leaves at his feet, Caleb saw the indentations of horseshoes. He knew Oppenheimer regularly led scientists on rides astride his emotional and high-strung quarter horse, Crisis, who mirrored his own countenance. To Caleb, horseback riding was almost as terrifying as the dynamite in the canyon. But he had to do something to keep busy, to keep from showing up at Alice's doorstep. He decided to join Oppenheimer's excursion, taking his place in the lineup of fourteen men.

He'd never liked horses. He respected them with their velvet muzzles and silky coats, flashing chestnut and gold in the sunlit fields of the mesa. But when he approached, they always snorted and stomped their hooves. His anxiety transcended the species barrier, and it was clear that his mount could sense his fear from yards away.

Oppenheimer handed him the reins of an enormous bay who refused to budge from his bale of hay. The draft mix had humorously been named Tiny despite his mammoth proportions. Caleb had cursed his height the second he saw the animal. He was always getting into these situations. His temperate personality didn't match his stature. He feared the gargantuan horse was no gentle giant like himself.

When he tried to pick Tiny's feet, the gelding slammed his enormous hoof down on his toes. He hopped in circles on one foot, reverting to Yiddish in his anguish. When he took too long to select a carrot from the saddle bag, Tiny bared his square teeth and sunk them into the soft flesh of his belly, pinching him until he had a bruise the color of a rainbow, plum purple at its center and orange, yellow, and green around the edges.

Up close, the horse's whiskers were coarse and wiry. He couldn't help thinking of the tangled curls of his father's beard. That motivated him. He took a deep breath and stepped into the stirrup. When the saddle slid under his weight, he felt airborne for an instant, and for the second time since leaving his father's house, he said a silent prayer. He clumsily swung his right leg over the saddle and settled into the tack, feeling the horse's swayed back sink beneath his weight. The gelding pinned his ears.

"You had better hold on tight." Robert Serber, who was not only Oppie's understudy in the lab, but apparently also his equestrian's assistant, laughed. "He knows his job. Just let him alone."

If I live through this, Caleb promised himself, *I will write another letter to my father.* He was desperate to know if they still had the house, or whether everything he had done was for nothing. A foreclosure was the sort of thing his father would let slip and just not tell him. He knew his mother, Sarah, would be the first to confide in him, but she couldn't write him—she didn't know how. He would call her, he decided, if he made it back in one piece.

Caleb was not alone in needing to be assured on the trail. In addition to the equine element, there was the risk of scorpions and snakebites in the mountains. Many of the city-dwelling scientists who had been lured onto horses that morning were terrified. "Is it poisonous?" Caleb whispered under his breath when a snake twitched in the center of the narrow path. No one responded. He knew the physicist riding in front of him heard, but, like every other danger in that secret city, they weren't supposed to ask.

Caleb gulped and urged Tiny on, praying the gelding would refuse. They rode onward, Caleb nursing his nasty hangover headache as they meandered up seemingly endless mountain paths. Red-orange flowers bloomed from the claret cup cactus, and yellow blooms sprouted from prickly pears; spikes and thorns threatened them around every corner. The sounds of the calling bullfrogs and rattling insects were amplified in his ears. But, like an addict, he trailed Oppenheimer and Crisis under increasingly ominous skies.

It was Friday and the sky was darkening into Shabbat. This strenuous activity would have been blasphemous back home. The clouds sank low, hovering just barely above the treetops. If he didn't know better, he would have been certain God was punishing him. Wind rattled the branches, and occasional flashes of lightning lit the atmosphere like flashbulbs. The temperature plummeted. He considered breaking off from the group and turning back. There was still time.

Then he saw Alice trotting up on a small pinto, with Pavlov galloping alongside her.

His breath caught in his chest. His headache vanished. A cloud shifted from in front of the sun and the whole desert seemed to brighten by a shade. Alice was fresh-faced and her horse was shiny and clean. She must have just finished a shift and opted for an evening ride.

"Evenin', cowboy." She saluted him playfully, sitting stick-straight in her tack, bouncing a little stiffly as the horse hopped over brush and bramble to take her spot in the lineup in front of him.

His heart somersaulted in his chest. He shoved his specs up his nose and waved back, too breathless at the sight of her to respond.

He followed her as though in a trance, watching her horse—whose name, he learned, was Apricot—swish its copper tail at flies. Caleb tried to shift his weight on Tiny's swaying back and the horse pinned his ears in response. He desperately needed to hold it together.

The brightness was only temporary. Thunder crackled.

Alice reined Apricot effortlessly along the path. Every so often, a gust of wind threatened her cowgirl hat, and she held onto it with her free hand, laughing about the ominous weather. He could see her rose-petal fingernails on the white hat brim even from the back of the lineup. She rode the animal effortlessly, like the gelding was an extension of her body. Meanwhile, Tiny kept dragging him off the trail and chewing the tall grass with no sense of urgency while the sky rumbled, causing Caleb to fall farther and farther behind.

When Alice trotted back to rescue him, he wasn't sure whether to be grateful or mortified. Pavlov chased her, barking and trying to herd Tiny, which only angered the horse and added to the untenable chaos.

"Shorten your reins," she instructed. "Look where you want him to go. It's about confidence." He realized she was trying not to laugh.

"I don't want to hurt him," he said.

She gave him a pitying look. "Like this," she said, nudging her horse with the spur rest of her boot.

He summoned his courage and kicked the animal with his heels. Tiny's head shot up and he took off running, nearly knocking Caleb's head into a branch on his rampage back to the lineup. Caleb lost his stirrups and dropped his reins, and he held the horn with all his might while the animal moved like lightning beneath him.

He heard Alice calling from behind. "Pick up your reins!"

He grabbed the knotted end and skidded to a stop just before colliding with an angry-looking buckskin who turned sideways and bared his teeth.

"You can see it in their eyes," Alice said later, when his horse had fallen back into line. A soft drizzle had started by then and the raindrops sparkled on the horses' coats.

In total, Oppie guided them along the Frijoles Creek for fourteen miles before arriving at the frothing rapids of the Rio Grande. Caleb's seat ached in the saddle. So suddenly that it startled their horses, the drizzle turned to a downpour, and Oppenheimer paused at a fork in the road. The men skidded to a stop behind him. Water pooled in the brim of Oppie's porkpie hat and cascaded from the corners when he turned his head to consider the trails.

With the sound of beating hooves silenced momentarily, Caleb could hear a snake rattling in the bushes beside him. The noise startled him all the way back to Fillmore Street. It was the same sound his father had made in the sukkah when he rattled the lulav: "Baruch atah Adonai, eloheinu melech haolam," he would recite, as he turned to face the four corners of the planet, then implore up at the heavens and down at the earth.

Caleb watched Oppie contemplate a sign that read in all caps: *US GOV-ERNMENT PROPERTY. DANGER! PELIGOROSO! KEEP OUT.* Crisis pranced nervously, foaming at the bit, her chestnut coat drenched dark by the downpour, and Oppie suggested lightheartedly between echoing thunder strikes, "That way it's seven miles home, but this way"—he gestured toward the forbidden terrain—"it's only a little longer, and it's much more beautiful."

Caleb felt Alice look at him. It was the first instance of hesitation he had seen in her yet. He wondered whether she feared for herself or for him. Oppie took a pull from his flask and disappeared into the fog.

Back at the stable grounds, they huddled around the campfire, cooking hot dogs on sticks and passing lab-made memory eraser liquor back and forth. Oppenheimer had packed plenty of oats for the horses, but no provisions for the hungry riders, so Caleb tore into his hot dog before he remembered to inquire whether it was kosher. Oppie reclined by the fire, his hands folded behind his head, quietly watching his cigarette smoke twist overhead and mingle with the stars. Everyone's clothes were rain-soaked and Caleb couldn't help admiring the way Alice's blouse clung flatteringly to her long-limbed shape as she braided her wet hair beside him. There was something decidedly birdlike about her movements. She bobbed her head when she spoke, and she had a way of shaking loose the excess water from her hair, like a sparrow in a bird bath.

He wasn't sure how to act around her. He folded and refolded his hands. She sensed his eyes on her and turned to look at him. For the first time, instead of looking away nervously, he held her gaze.

"Available to be my escort this evening?" She nodded toward the dark expanse beyond glow of the fire. It was only a half mile back, but in the pitch-black darkness, it seemed farther. He forgot entirely about his exhaustion and his aching backside. Adrenaline swept through him at the prospect of being near her. He was wary of what might be lurking out there in the shadows, but he wiped the dirt from his palms on his soaked jeans and followed her like a man under a spell. Pavlov, who had been sleeping contentedly by the fire, popped up with alert ears the instant Alice stood. He bounded out in front, leading the way, disappearing into the tall grass.

They pressed through the knee-high growth, leaving indented trails behind them like the wakes of small boats. Everything was still wet from the rain, and leaves shimmered in the moonlight. It smelled green and wild. It seemed they could feel the vegetation growing. Insects that he couldn't see buzzed in the darkness. They came to a clearing and she paused.

"That ridge over there is Truchas Peak," she said, pointing into the night sky. He couldn't see anything, but he nodded. "I hiked it not long ago."

From somewhere overhead, an owl hooted. Caleb was out of his element in this desert expanse. He was surprised by Alice's passion for the 360-degree views and steep cliffs.

"I would expect a woman like you to prefer the skyscraper cliffs of 42nd Street." He smiled. He'd meant it as a compliment, but she looked upset. Or perhaps she was bothered by something else that he couldn't pinpoint.

As they walked, their bodies occasionally grazed each other. Through her soaked cotton blouse, rubbing up against her felt like the intimacy of naked skin. There was nothing left between the sheer fabric and her body, no dignifying fashion or formality of shapewear. The path was narrow, and they brushed against each other more frequently as they vanished into the empty night. He could feel her breathing. She scratched at a mosquito bite on her arm and paused, staring in the direction of Truchas Peak. Now, he could make out the silhouette of the jagged summit in the darkness.

"I prefer the parts of the world without sidewalks," she said, finally. She gestured around at the expanse. "Without the light pollution, you can see the stars." It was halfhearted at best. He noticed she wasn't wearing her ring. He wondered then if perhaps she was running from something too.

Nearby, a salamander slithered along a rock, pausing in rigid poses, its scales glinting in the moonlight. They watched it breathe for a while, doing its push-ups. It was like they were the only two people in the world out there.

They both craned their necks to look at the cosmos spiraling overhead. The desert sky was endless.

"Does studying the stars make it harder to enjoy them?"

She laughed, swatting the question away. "Quite the opposite, actually."

"What is it that's so fascinating about them to you?"

She shifted a bit, mulling it over. "Early on, I was interested in dark stars."

"Dark stars?"

"That's when a sufficiently massive star runs out of thermonuclear fuel. You can see it in the wavelengths. When an object is moving toward us, it blueshifts, and when it's moving away from us, it redshifts. But when I was working under Oppie, studying the cores of neutron stars, we found things you wouldn't believe if I told you."

"Try me."

Her eyebrows lifted. She glanced around the dark expanse, making certain they were alone. When she finally spoke, it was almost a whisper. "Well, for starters, it seems dark stars contract indefinitely."

"Indefinitely?"

"Not even light can escape."

Caleb turned to look at her. Her eyes had filled with a contemplative gleam.

"Oppenheimer denied the research shortly after it came out. And anyway, his publication was overshadowed by Hitler's invasion of Poland. But I guess I haven't stopped looking for that missing light."

"Is that what led you here?"

"Some people spend their lives trying to sail around the world or fly faster than the speed of sound. I guess I'm no different."

Caleb removed his specs and rubbed his eyes. Sometimes, he preferred the world without his glasses. The details vanished, of course—he was practically blind without them. But in the blurriness, he felt the energy and essence of things. Wearing those clarifying lenses kept daydreams at bay, and without them, there was possibility in the unknown. He took off his glasses now and as the stars turned to blurry streaks, he said, "My brother was like that. He always wanted to fly. That's why he enlisted. He wanted to work in aeronautics, not explosives. But these days it's one and the same."

"Warren's somewhere in the Ardennes Forest," she commiserated, "polishing his rifle beneath the fir trees." She flinched. "Without all that glare, I'll bet he can see the North Star," she said. "But he'd never tell me if he did. He doesn't want to encourage my 'eccentricities.'"

Caleb hesitated at her bitter tone but decided to brush past it. "I wanted to fly every bit as much as my brother did. But I didn't follow him. I didn't want it badly enough to pilot a gunner or a bomber that kills people."

She nodded. "Wings come with a catch."

Suddenly, in the dark, Asher was a dimensionless blur beside him. Caleb stared at his shadowy form. He tried to fill in the details of his face. In his mind, Asher's features rippled as though afloat in water. Every memory of his brother seemed like something from someone else's life, like a dream vanished upon waking.

Alice shifted almost imperceptibly closer. He held perfectly still. "Where did you go just now?" she asked.

The shadowy image of his brother beside him returned to a patch of tall grass beneath the night sky. He apologized and put his glasses back on, watching the blurry stars shrink down to pinpoints. He longed to tell her all the things he feared most, from his father's blind faith to the mortgage, but he didn't want to scare her away.

"My father stopped sleeping altogether after my brother shipped out. He would just pace around the house rambling in Yiddish about the noise of the stars keeping him up at night."

"There's no noise."

He looked at her. "What do you mean?"

"The stars. They don't make any sound. By definition, sound is a pressure wave, but in space there's no air, so there's nothing to carry a pressure wave to our ears. So, hard as it is to believe, if we could hear outer space, it would be entirely, utterly silent."

"And here I always imagined stars sounding like the dynamite in the canyon."

"That's why those negatives fascinate me. That data, those simultaneous sparks, seeing it all mapped out in waves—that might be the closest I'll ever get to hearing the sound of the stars."

"Sure." He nodded. "But I've got a hunch Groves and his military are planning to do more with that research than listen to it. Stars might come with a catch too."

"I've been stuck on that lately," she admitted solemnly, "now that we've collected so much data."

"What do you think they aim to do with it?"

She sprung to her feet and turned her back on him, staring up at the sky. Pavlov leaped into action. "I'm afraid I have lots of questions and no answers."

Later, when they ascended her steps to the front door, he was desperate to keep talking to her. He didn't want the night to end.

"Let's say you found that missing light, the light that was swallowed by those dark stars. What would you wanna know?"

"By the time we see light, it has already touched and moved on. Everything we see in our present is in fact already in the past. So, instead of an aerial view, I guess I'm looking at history."

"So it's time travel you're after."

She seemed to buckle at his suggestion. What was she trying to change from her past?

"At its base, every particle of matter is exactly the same," she said. She leaned closer and reached past him to unlock her front door. His pounding heart, he thought. Surely, she could hear it. "Pine cones, bullfrogs, the moon, strands of hair. The past is right here in the present."

Slowly, like he was moving in reverse, like he had done it many times before and was cycling through a behavior from years before, he reached out and took her hand. Her fingers froze around the key. The door swung open on its hinges, but she didn't go inside.

"I've been holding my breath since yesterday," he said.

"I'm engaged," she said in a strangled voice, as though they didn't both already know it, as though they didn't both think of it constantly. But she was leaning closer.

"Then why aren't you wearing your ring?" he huffed.

He felt faint waiting for her response.

But instead of answering, she kissed him—softly at first, and then harder. He wrapped his arms around her and pulled her in. He'd have to make this brief moment last a lifetime.

As soon as they were in the privacy of her dark entry, he surrendered into her. She closed and bolted the door, pressing him up against it. He pulled at her blouse in a frenzy, tugging at the buttons, desperate to remove the silk slip glinting like silver against her panting chest. His fingers slid across the smooth fabric. She grabbed him by the collar and pulled him close, pressing her hips up against his.

Someone rapped on the door. They startled and leaped back. The knock came again.

"Caleb! I know you're in there! I saw you go in. Open up!"

They buttoned up and straightened their clothes with numb fingers. He swung the door wide to reveal Dick Feynman, the prodigy scientist himself, with his boyish grin. He was windblown and out of breath. His mouth fell open, studying Alice over Caleb's shoulder in her disheveled state. He stared for a moment, then his eyes flashed with purpose. "Come quick," he said. "Sergeant Moony came lookin' for you, thought you might be at the seminar series. There's been an accident."

T-Minus 13

July 1950
Haruki: A Story Told Backward

Haruki took a swig of water to chase down the overdose of sleeping pills and passed the canteen to Shinju. He could read the determination and fear on her face. Her skin was smooth, unmarked by the world. Her eyes sparkled with emotion.

"We'll be like Romeo and Juliet," she said. "Like Ohatsu and Tokubei." She was shaking. Perhaps, it occurred to him, she referenced the three-hundred-year-old Japanese play to convince herself. With the looming death sentence of Haruki's radiation exposure, her parents were still refusing their marriage despite their repeated appeals. If they couldn't be together in this life, they would be united in the next. In Ohatsu and Tokubei, she found strength. They wouldn't be the first to die for love, and they wouldn't be the last.

"I'll meet you at Ohatsu Tenjin Shrine," he said.

They lay back in the grass and watched the clouds shift. They grew heavy and sank into the hill of blowing purple azaleas, overlooking Ondo-no-seto and the red bridge that blossomed up from the hillside. He felt the warmth of Shinju's hand in his and waited for the sensation to dull away. He drifted into a dreamless void. He believed himself to be dead.

A long period of darkness passed before he felt the grass itching his arms and came to. He looked over at Shinju beside him. Her hair was the only thing moving, blowing in the wind. He was filled with dread. He panicked. In this most important way, he had failed the woman he loved. He reached for the sleeping pills. He was about to take more when Shinju gasped and opened her eyes. She looked at him like she couldn't place him for a moment. She had just returned from someplace very far away. They held each other and wept.

It seemed to be all over for them. They couldn't be together in this world *or* the next.

11

November 1944
Alice

Alice composed herself. A thirty-second army shower could never make her feel clean after what she had done. Thank God they'd been interrupted. She'd lost control of herself, of everything, around him. She had to do better. She couldn't stop thinking about the way he left—without a word of explanation or a look of acknowledgment. He didn't even glance back over his shoulder when he trotted down her steps.

She draped her hair in a towel and flipped it over her head like a turban. She stared into the mirror and hardly recognized her reflection. Without her makeup, her eyes were dark and empty. She picked up a bottle of lotion and dabbed a little on her skin, smoothing it over the smattering of freckles on her nose and the dark depressions under her eyes, massaging the worry of the last few months. Absently, she flicked an eyeshadow case open and closed while her mind traveled across the ocean. She pictured Warren, crouched in a foxhole, bandaging swollen fingers. Behind him, explosions lit the sky.

She opened a book and tried to read, but there Warren was again, bleeding on a sandy beach. Behind him fish were rolling belly-up in the waves, shining like silver coins. She closed her eyes and shook the thought away, but even through her closed lids, she saw the silvery flashes of dead fish, clear as day. Just beyond them, drifting like a log, posed like Ophelia draped in pansies and rosemary, was Abigail, waterlogged and rocking in the current.

She couldn't stop replaying it. She'd recognized Feynman immediately from his photographs, but she had been alarmed by the grim expression on his face. What emergency could have made Caleb race out the door into the night?

Alice lay in bed wondering, staring up into the darkness, flicking the eyeshadow case endlessly. She jumped when the phone chirped. She half expected it to be Caleb.

"Ma?" Alice asked, recognizing the careful voice on the other end. "It's the middle of the night." She didn't try to mask her irritation.

"Alice," her mother said in a voice like glass. "Warren is dead."

The eyeshadow case slipped from Alice's hand and cracked in half on the floor, a single cell divided into two. The spilled powder snowed down slowly around the room.

"What do you mean?" Her hand covered her mouth.

"It's better not to ask, dear," Mabel said. Alice could picture her mother trying to steady her quivering chin. It was infuriating that Mabel felt the need to quiet her in that moment, but it wasn't surprising.

Mabel had always been practical and desperate to maintain control. When Abigail died, she locked herself in her room and cried for three days; after that, she got back to work and never shed another tear. When Ishmael neglected to change his bedsheets and began spouting conspiracy theories in the wake of the funeral, Mabel smoothed it over among their acquaintances. "Migraines," she explained his ailment away. "Tomorrow, he'll feel right as rain."

"He had you listed as next of kin," she said, "but your PO box was top-secret, so they came here. It was over in a matter of minutes. A uniformed officer knocked on the door, interrupted dinner. What was I to do? When the war knocks on your door, you answer."

"How did it happen?" Alice tried to steady her voice.

"It's nothing you wouldn't expect. The US military deeply regrets to inform you, and so on."

"Ma. Read it to me."

Mabel sighed. "I don't know why you do this to yourself. Honestly." She heard the sound of crinkled paper and her mother cleared her throat. "Let's see . . . Deeply regret to inform you that Private Warren VanHuff was killed in action in the performance of his duty and in the service of his country. The Department extends to you its sincerest sympathy in your great loss. On account of existing conditions the body, if recovered, cannot be returned at present. To prevent possible aid to our enemies please do not divulge the name of his station. Signed Rear Admiral Jacobs, Chief of Military Personnel."

"So he died in Ardennes? In the snow?"

"You know there were seventy thousand casualties. Germans broke through the American front, seizing bridges, cutting communication lines. It's all over the news."

"I heard about the Belgians putting up their swastikas. And the curfews in Paris. I knew soldiers were catching frostbite in the knee-high snow drifts. But I never thought he would be one of those people you read about."

Her mother's tone stiffened. "You're no stranger to death, Alice. You didn't want to marry him, anyhow. You got your wish."

"You don't know what I want," Alice said through clenched teeth.

"Sure I do."

"I never wanted him to die."

"No one did, dear." She paused for a moment. "I'm sorry, honey." This was the best her mother could do.

"Warren," Alice repeated quietly. She pictured his lifeless body submerged in a snowbank, his blood pooling out into the freezing weather.

"Indeed. The funeral is in twenty-four hours if they'll let you leave that godforsaken place."

From the window of the New War building's fifth-floor office, the desert was muted. The only noise inside the room came from the oscillating heater, which rustled a stack of papers with each swivel.

Alice sat primly on the edge of her folding chair, pretending not to notice General Groves's private secretary, Jean O'Leary, sizing her up. Alice felt too numb to care. Her eyes were swollen and she was certain Jean could tell she had been crying.

Alice admired Jean's chestnut hair that was parted down the middle and swept up and back in a glamorous twist. She wore golden stud earrings that reminded her, wincingly, of her mother, and a silk blouse with a slit neckline that struck her as far too formal for the desert. Alice, too, had worn such things when she first arrived, but lately, she'd found trousers and hiking boots more practical: stockings and long skirts snagged on the cottonwood trees and the desert mud ruined her shoes in a single outing. She was always rushing around. She never had time to do her hair and often forgot to look in the mirror before leaving the house.

The reality of Warren's death had kept her awake, sobbing, most of the night. She had finally drifted into a dream and woken to chattering birds, having forgotten momentarily that her mother had ever called. For two full minutes, everything had been normal. Then, it all came flooding back.

Jean's desk was so polished and clean that the whole room reflected on the surface in miniature. Alice tried to cultivate a similar no-nonsense attitude as she prepared herself to confront Groves. When Jean finally called her name, she forgot everything she had planned to say.

Groves snapped at her the moment she stepped foot in his office. "These scientists are a godless bunch." He scowled. She hesitated, unsure whether or not she was implicated in the criticism. It was true that there was a lacuna of religion among the scientists on the hill. Most of the physicists, like herself, had given up on God long ago. They had been mere children when they first uncovered the covenant of laws governing the forces of nature. Their worlds circumscribed to a mathematical set of rules rather than some fiction about a burning bush and a stone tablet handed down on Mount Sinai. Of course, this wasn't true of the wives. They regularly organized church services in a movie theater on the base. But it was true of the Jews. Even the faithful ones were simply too inundated with work and too fearful of Hitler to bother with religious tradition. But Groves, for all his boorish behaviors and curt words, was a God-fearing man.

"Sir?" she asked, opting for meekness. She decided that her vulnerability could serve as an asset. This military man would see her not as a scientist, but as a woman.

"I don't tolerate the pipe-smoking academic pace," he said. He gestured for her to be seated without looking up from the paperwork on his desk.

"Neither do I, sir," she agreed nervously. She perched in the small folding chair that placed her far beneath him. She already felt small beside Groves's enormous stature, but this lower altitude made her feel nearly invisible.

"I would like to request a leave," she said, "for my fiancé's funeral." She was horrified hearing the words out loud.

Groves rocked back in his chair and made a church steeple with his fingertips. She stared at him with an intensity that her mother would have called unbecoming. She had no qualms. She wanted to make him uncomfortable. "His body was lost in Belgium. I have nothing left," she pressed, clinging to the shift she saw in his features.

He rolled up his shirt sleeves and poured himself a drink. The ice cubes clinked and rose to the surface and Alice caught herself thinking about displacement. After it melts, ice occupies the exact same volume. It was a fascinating equilibrium, but it was doubtful this man who nursed the beverage thoughtlessly had ever given a second thought to the complexities at his fingertips. She watched him fold his shirt cuffs into perfect rolls on his weather-roughened forearms while she waited for him to respond. "I'm truly sorry," he said finally in a voice she hadn't heard before. "But we need you to remain here. This operation is time sensitive."

"What do you mean?" In the five months she'd been here, through the work on Project Rufus and the endless data collection, she still had no idea what the project was. She had no knowledge of any timeline or any concrete plans. She thought again of the look on Feynman's face last night, of Caleb racing out the door. What dangers were at their fingertips? What had this military man drinking to calm his nerves?

Groves cleared his throat and inspected his drink. He took a small sip and closed his eyes. When he finally opened them again, she watched his pupils shrink in the light. His eyes had cleared, returning to stasis. Whatever softness had come over him had been fleeting.

"That information is classified," he huffed. "Your clearance is limited. You knew that signing up."

"Forgive me, sir, but, I can't be a security risk if I don't know the secret I'm supposed to conceal, can I?"

"Security is not your concern. You've spent too much time with Oppenheimer, fraternizing with his inferiors. I give the orders; your job is to follow them."

Alice bristled. She felt her old life slipping away, the barbed wire closing in. "What harm can come of letting a widow attend a funeral?"

His jaw clenched. He swirled the drink in the glass, watching it fizz. "All these academics with their noses up in the air think I've gone soft. They think they can beat around the bush with me like one of their university students." He balled his plump hand into a fist and slammed it on the table, making his drink splash. "We are fighting a war," he said with disgust and outrage. "You scientists and your moral debates." Alice wasn't certain what moral debates he was referring to, but her mind raced through the plutonium samples and the negatives in the darkroom. She recalled Caleb worrying over the research. "It's in the hands of the military," Groves spewed. "Where it belongs."

She turned to leave and had one foot out the door when he called her back.

"Dr. Katz," he said, his face pinched. "I'm not the villain here."

12

November 1944
Caleb

"Did ya bring the other fingers?" asked the doctor who was stitching the tip of Saul's ring finger back on while a younger physician held him down. The younger man had to take a broad stance to keep a steady grip on the frantic patient, and he looked about to faint at the sight of Saul's melted skin.

Saul couldn't focus. He kept asking what had happened. Caleb had to remind him over and over that the boxes he'd been stacking had been mislabeled—intentionally, for security purposes—as cinderblocks. Saul had known the cargo was dynamite; he wouldn't have hoisted it carelessly, like bricks. But then, the stuff was so finicky, especially stacked precariously and jolting around in a bouncing truck, the weight of a feather could set it off. Because he was an expendable SED, put to use for manpower with limited security clearance, he'd likely unloaded far more dangerous materials many times over. A betting man through and through, the odds had finally caught up with him, and he hadn't realized it was too late until the coil was snickering on the ground.

The squad of men in the desert had concocted a bloodstained tourniquet from a blasted jacket. What was left of Saul's hand was inflamed and bulbous, the size of a baseball mitt. Saul's forefinger and middle finger had been blown clean off. The remaining fingers were hanging by threads. His thumb was sliced open. It looked like a flap had been peeled back and they could see all the tendons and ligaments, the inner workings of the hand. They had to pin him down while he thrashed and screamed. His pinky finger was bent ninety degrees in the wrong direction, and his ring finger curled in toward his palm like a claw. They called it swan neck deformity: the tendon that flexes the middle joint had torn.

The doctor paused, needle driver and tissue forceps in hand to glance up at the blood-splattered men. "If the fingers are on ice, we might be able to . . ."

"No," said Caleb sullenly, cutting him off. They would do what they could to avoid amputation. They would need to graft new skin onto his palm and thumb. But without his missing fingers, they couldn't possibly save the whole hand. The rest of the squad shuffled behind him. "Didn't see them out there."

After leaving Alice, Caleb had searched every inch of the blackened pit with his headlamp and flashlight. There was still an indentation in the sand where Saul had rocked back and forth in the fetal position. Caleb had found two of his silver rings glinting in the dark. The sand had recorded all the frantic footprints, even the aimless rolled circles of the rings circling the pit like loose tires. Blood had been everywhere: a nearby cactus, the truck, the boxes, and the spilled electrical wires. No fingers anywhere.

"He'll need a constant rotation of medications." The doctor moved on without lingering on the fingers that had, in so few words, been swallowed up by New Mexico. The doctor looked old by Los Alamos standards—he was probably in his forties. His hair was still mostly dark, but his beard had gone gray. "Opiates and antibiotics, concomitantly. He'll be prone to bacterial infection in the tendon sheath."

Once his hand had been stitched, splinted, and cast, Saul rocked and muttered to himself. He kept complaining of unbearable pain in the fingers that weren't there anymore—something about dragging the wound through gravel. His flannel shirt had been disintegrated and his abdomen was covered in lacerations and blisters. His cowboy boots, too, were stained red. They had been placed in a plastic bag and handed back to him, and he gripped them in his left fist, like a prize goldfish at a carnival.

The doctors congregated behind a closed door, talking in low voices like tuning guitars. They did injury intakes on the other men who had been present and observed them closely for head trauma. Eventually, the squad was told they could go home, but Caleb couldn't bring himself to leave. It should have been him lying there. He had taken paid leave to nurse a hangover and abandoned his friend to trot up a trail on a horse he didn't know how to ride. If he'd been there, he might have noticed the discordant weight of the boxes; he might have acted with more caution. If he had been standing close enough to Saul, perhaps he would have noticed the snickering coil a heartbeat sooner. He could have pulled him to safety.

Sitting there at Saul's bedside, Caleb still had Alice's lipstick on his mouth. He wiped it with the back of his hand. He could still taste her. He pictured her jet-black hair curled into springing coils at the nape of her neck, and her silver slip glinting beneath her clothes. "I shoulda been there," he whispered while Saul finally slept, blissfully numb on painkillers and opioids.

Saul slipped in and out of consciousness for several days. He had several surgeries and was groggy and incoherent—either from the anesthesia or the shock. When he awoke at last, and the two were finally alone together, the only noise in the room was the swoosh of a bellows pumping liquid into a tube that ran into his arm.

Saul forced a hollow smile. "It really is the Wild West out here, isn't it?"

"Cowboys and Indians," Caleb replied, monotone. They searched each other's eyes.

Caleb had said the word "Indians" without thinking directly of the Hopituh sun temples built right into the mountainside, or the homes on the mesa decorated with rugs and pottery purchased in the pueblos. But the colonial guilt certainly loomed in his psyche. In his time here, he'd learned that in the name of science, the indigenous and Hispano residents of this desert terrain had been given forty-eight hours to abandon their homes to make way for the "project." The young, mostly white scientists had taken so many inconsiderate photographs and trampled through so many holy sites. He often thought of his father when he came across abandoned sun temples on the mountain trails.

Saul tried to shift in bed and yelped in pain. Caleb scrambled to his knees and clasped Saul's remaining hand. "I'm sorry I wasn't there," he said.

"Tell me you at least got lucky." Saul managed a groggy smile before drifting back to sleep.

13

November 1944

Alice

Alice nursed her martini covertly in the middle of Oppenheimer's crowded kitchen. She refilled her glass with a cheap red wine, not bothering to rinse between pours. So what if the Syrah mixed with the vodka?

She was convinced that on some cosmic level, her infidelity had precipitated Warren's death. As a scientist, she knew that was hogwash, but she couldn't shake her guilt. She rubbed away the smudges from her lipstick along the rim of her glass and increased her dose by three fingers, a miracle elixir for tragedy. She receded into herself, trying to repress the image of Warren's remains going blue in the snow. The Ardennes Forest haunted her every time she closed her eyes—men hanging from sagging branches, corpses staring up at the shaking treetops without seeing them. Since it had happened, she had been afraid to go to sleep. She was terrified of the wilderness behind her eyes. Now, she held onto the counter in Oppenheimer's swirling kitchen, forcing a frozen smile but trying not to show her teeth for fear they were stained grayish purple from the drink.

Across the room, Kitty refreshed her gin sour and reapplied her lipstick poorly, making her frown look crooked. She had given birth to her second baby, a girl, only a few weeks prior and seemed to be drinking away any recollection of it. She had kept the pregnancy secret so long and she had such a small frame that her delivery had taken much of the town by surprise.

Now, she looked pale and bone thin. Her lips were pressed into a thin line and her hair was swept up severely, tugging at the worried creases of her forehead. Her movements were jumpy and erratic like she was a marionette on a string. She seemed to have no interest in the baby, leaving the infant alone with the maid and throwing these parties.

"Maybe I should have an affair," Kitty said to her audience of admirers. "To even things out." Oppie's previous mistress, Jean Tatlock, had died by suicide almost a year ago, but now that there were rumors swirling about her communist ideology, her autopsy, and the possibility that it hadn't been a suicide at all, the news story had been resurrected and Kitty seemed especially fraught.

Alice winced. She knew Kitty didn't know about her infidelity, but the fine hairs on her forearms stood on end and the nape of her neck tingled. She kept thinking someone was looking at her.

Kitty tried to make light of the tabloids among her drinking companions, but the more she drank the more bitter she sounded. "I can't wrap my mind around why these women make such a fuss over him in the first place. He's worthless in the bedroom." She smirked. She always had loose lips when she drank, and regularly shared too much about their sex life. But tonight, she seemed in rare form. "Robert doesn't bother with foreplay," she announced. Around the room, women found nearby objects suddenly fascinating, averting their eyes. "I had to teach him that sex should be fun and not necessarily a religious experience."

All around her, the wives were whispering. "Did you know that Oppie tried to murder his tutor in high school?" a woman said conspiratorially in the corner.

A nearby housewife in a headscarf nodded. "Made a poison apple, just like the fairy tale."

"I smelled liquor on his breath at the commissary," responded Judith, eyeing Kitty's turned back. Her heavy eyebrows arched with feigned concern. "It wasn't even noon."

"I hear Oppie has enough gas in his tank to get to Taos and back," whispered Bonnie over her bourbon. She wore a skintight floral dress that gathered in rolls around her hips and knee-high boots with a faux fur coat that had slipped down around her shoulders, revealing the angular gleam of her collarbone and the cleft of her bosom. She still wore her cooking apron, but she had uncinched the bow behind her back, and it hung from her neck like a decorative scarf.

Alice watched Kitty absently stirring the ice in her drink with her pointer finger. The guilt washed over her. Kitty and Warren were one and the same.

Oppenheimer launched out of the smoky study then and opened the front door, revealing three dolled-up ladies in feathered hats. "Welcome to Bourbon Manor." He grinned. When they entered, a gush of cold air blew into the room from the open door, sending the drapes flapping and every-one's hair blowing in their faces. Oppie fought the door closed with the force of his thin body like the wind was a wild animal he was desperate to hold back. He had been losing weight, drawing in his silver belt buckle by sev-eral notches. Alice estimated her thin professor weighing in at merely 120 pounds.

Oppenheimer seemed entirely blind to his wife's agitations from his van-tage point in the foyer. He shook up martinis and placed skewered olives in glasses. The three new women were young, bright-eyed schoolteachers—Madge, Barbara, and Belle. They wore their hair in matching bobs and each had a slightly different shade of nude nylon peeking out from beneath their tea-length skirts. Unwrapping their scarves and unzipping their coats, they revealed sweetheart necklines and keyhole backs. They peeled off layers of winter clothing, leaving their feathered hats and mittens discarded haphaz-ardly between the entryway and the kitchen table: a breadcrumb trail of debauchery. They shrank smaller with each item removed, like Russian dolls.

Alice looked down at her practical trousers. Her elegant wardrobe was collecting dust in her closet. With the restrictions of the war, the abundance of wool and rayon grafted onto her pleated skirts had come to embarrass her. She realized, seeing herself more clearly in juxtaposition to these ladies who had dressed to the nines, how the desert had changed her.

"Join me on the patio for a toast," Oppenheimer said, tipping his hat at the three young ladies, his eyes flickering.

"You must be crazy," Madge retorted.

"We've just come in from the weather!" agreed Belle, checking her face in her compact. The tiny mirror reflected a glowing rectangle of light on her forehead.

Oppenheimer knocked his head back and belly laughed heartily. He turned his gaze on Alice. "This one's tough enough for a frozen cocktail," he said loud enough for everyone to hear. Alice braced. Oppie's blue eyes traveled her body, adding up the poison oak on her arms and multiplying her frizzed hair, long since freed of its rolled curls. He offered her the crook of his elbow, but she didn't want to go with him. She was conflicted by the bouts of attention he lavished on her. She wanted to be his equal, one of the guys, not an ornament paraded on his arm. But everyone was staring. She took his offered arm and he escorted her out the back door. She glanced back at Kitty, staring out the window. She longed to turn him away, to send him back inside to his depressed wife, but she did not protest.

Outside, the balcony was dark, making the white snow seem to glow all around them. She was having trouble keeping his face in focus. She held the railing to stop the stars from spinning.

He handed her a glass and she inspected the drink. "To the free world," he said, downing his flask and nodding at her. She watched him stagger back and forth, tapping a cigarette out of the carton, sheltering the flame and sucking it in. He swaggered, walking a little bowlegged in his cowboy jeans as he stepped closer to her.

"Don't fret, dear," he said, chewing on the cigarette, "although the world is full of cruel and bitter things." She realized her distress must be showing on her face and she tried to pull herself together. Oppie coughed into his fist, the hacking cough of a seasoned smoker. On the backside of his coughing fit, he looked up at her with sensitive eyes. "You know, I need physics more than friends."

"Is Kitty OK?" She eyed Kitty's rigid back, visible through the sliding glass door. She hadn't moved. Inside, someone flipped on the patio light, and the brightness erased the faces inside the house, making them the only two people at the party. They both squinted, willing their eyes to adjust. Moths excited by the brightness danced in the light between them.

"She's a drunk," he said. Alice stopped herself from pointing out the obvious irony. "Ever since Katherine was born, she's been falling asleep smoking, setting our linens on fire."

He dropped his cigarette and stepped it out with the heel of his boot. It steamed in the snow.

"Not to worry. I placed a trusty fire extinguisher by the bedside," he said, responding to the alarm in her look. Alice pictured the duvet filled with cigarette burns, a constellation of fever dreams. She worried about the infant, sleeping helplessly in a bassinette by the crackling flames. "You see, motherhood never suited Kitty," he said. "She wants to talk big talk." He looked at Alice, searching her face. "She's like you."

"It's a pretty name," she said, trying to keep the conversation lighthearted. She sensed something dangerous turning in his mood. "Katherine."

He had been looking at her this whole time, studying her eyes, her curls, the geometry of her blouse, but now, he looked away, shame-faced, down at his hands. Even in his drunken state, he spoke such elegant words. That's why it surprised her that he seemed to have trouble forming the next sentence. Finally, he asked, "Do you want to adopt her?"

Alice startled. This man who carried the weight of the world was running from a newborn. Her voice came out more cross than she intended.

"Of course not. Why on earth would I do that? She has two perfectly good parents."

"Because I can't love her," he said. His eyes on hers were hypnotic. A rush of wind swept around them, making her shudder. It lifted her hair. He held onto his hat.

Wasn't it strange, she thought, *that he wore his hat even at night*. It must be meant to shield him from something more than the sun. The cigarette and hat were props that set him apart from the others, that made him instantly recognizable and iconic in a crowd. But when he removed them, he was mortal like everyone else.

Perhaps she could take advantage of his intoxication, charm him into telling her what they were building. She could see the years all the secrecy had already added to his face.

"Penny for your thoughts?" She stared down at her hands on the railing, trying to appear aloof.

He laughed and snorted, exhaling a plume of smoke. Then he sobered. "We're the good guys, right? But I suppose the bad guys think they're the good guys too." He stared past her with glossy eyes. "We're like two scorpions in a bottle. Each capable of killing the other, but only at the risk of his own life."

Alice's mind raced back to her first day in the desert, the scorpions in her drainpipe. Her chest tightened and it was suddenly hard to breathe.

They were standing very close. She realized for the first time that those famous blue eyes seemed too light for his face, like they were too delicate for the things they had seen. She was suddenly afraid to leave him alone with himself. They all needed this man in one way or another.

"Let's get you back inside," she said. "You'll catch a cold out here, and then where will we be?"

He smirked. "The only woman on the hill who will never love me back."

"I think love is a choice," she said, feeling somewhat sobered by the cold now and trying to talk reason into this broken man. She didn't believe it, of course. She would have loved Warren if only she could have. She tried not to think of Caleb. He hadn't made any effort to see her or to explain his mysterious disappearance the other night.

"Beautiful women are always so hung up on free will," Oppie said. His eyes were fiery now. "We're all just butterflies caught in a net."

"There's no net," she said defiantly, "unless you believe there's a net."

"I love my wife, you know," he said, turning suddenly defensive. "The problem is, I love too much. I love too easily, you see."

Belle slid open the patio door and poked her head out. "You two will turn into snowmen out there." The laughter of the party escaped through the open door and Oppenheimer seemed to snap out of his trance. She watched his whole face contort into a grinning mask of showmanship. He straightened the brim of his hat and staggered back into the room. Alice followed him back into the chaos.

All night, everyone had been stepping on the cat. Over and over, it had hissed and hopped sideways, then darted through the room. Now, a tall man had stooped to pet it, and the animal was purring, arching, and lifting its head to graze and nudge his hand. Alice tensed, recognizing Caleb's brushed-back curls. The chemistry of his presence overrode the sobering effect of the cold.

She snatched a martini from a nearby tray. It was filled to the brim and she nearly spilled it bringing it to her lips. When had he arrived? She was still furious that he hadn't called on her—that he'd been absent from Project Rufus and hadn't shown up to drop off negatives in the darkroom. Now, days later, he had yet to apologize for hightailing it away from her under the full moon. More than anything, she was nervous. Her heartbeat drummed in her ears. In light of Warren's death, she wasn't sure how to face him. She had to put a stop to whatever they had become.

Caleb nodded at her, freshly shaven, baby-faced. He looked boyish that way, despite his size. "He's going to kill us all," he said, cozying up near her in the breakfast nook and trying for nonchalance, "with these martinis."

Alice forced a smile. The cat was still rubbing up against Caleb's legs and prancing figure eights around him "He's self-medicating," she said tightly, keeping her eyes locked on Oppenheimer. "He's deciding the fate of the world every day with the flip of a coin. And he has to pay the price."

"We all pay that price," Caleb said. Meeting his eyes, she realized he had dark circles.

"Can't imagine the pressure he's under," she said. "Playing God."

"A strange pursuit for an avowed atheist." He smirked.

"People need a leader." Her voice came out forceful. She was surprised that she said it—she had never been more uncertain of Oppenheimer's lead.

Caleb was acting strange. He still hadn't apologized or addressed his disappearance. She decided to press him. She lifted her chin, a gesture learned from her mother. "Warren's dead," she blurted.

He turned to look at her head on. His eyes widened behind his lenses.

"My mother received a telegram."

"Oh, Alice." He reached for her, but his hand fell short.

"Where have you been?" She was determined not to cry. She blamed him for everything, but she also longed for him to hold her, to envelop her in his enormous arms, to move her hair around with his breath.

"Saul." He rubbed his neck. "There was an accident."

Something inside her jolted at the word. "An accident?"

"An accident," he repeated.

"When you two went missing at work, they just said it was shift changes."

Caleb shrugged. "Siloes are siloes," he said. "It only concerned the recruits involved. Other than that, they kept it quiet. Didn't want a panic."

"Is he OK?"

"He'll live," Caleb said, his face setting. His lip twitched at the corner like there were more words trying to get out. "The fool is lucky he didn't croak." As soon as he said it, he seemed to realize his error, speaking crudely of a near-death escape to one who just lost her betrothed. His eyes filled with alarm and his palm covered the gasp that escaped his mouth. "Oh, I'm so sorry, I didn't mean to . . ."

It was no use. She was crying. He reached for her again, this time his hands finding her shaking shoulders. "I didn't mean it," he whispered. "Alice, Alice," he tried again. He seemed convinced that if he repeated her name, he could knock the words out of the air between them.

At his touch, her heart somersaulted. She couldn't take the concern in his eyes. The longer she stood there with his hands tingling on her shoulders, her skin smoldering for him, the harder she would shake and heave and cry. She knew that any moment now, she would embrace him in front of everyone, take solace in his arms.

Alice turned and ran from the room. She felt his eyes burn into the back of her head as he chased her through the crowd, following her outside into the weather.

She crunched through the knee-high snow, escaping the swirling lights of Oppenheimer's house, fading into the dark landscape of the garden. Groves still hadn't allowed streetlights for fear of giving away the location of the secret city, so as she descended into the dark landscape, the stars splashed brightly across the sky. She tore through the snowdrifts until the snow scattered like glitter in her peripheral vision and her trousers were wet up to the knees. She paused at the edge of the property to catch her breath, consumed in the darkness and the quiet. Caleb trotted up and paused a step behind her.

She could see the plumes of his breath floating in the cold—small globes of the past excised from the curve of time. Without a word, he removed his coat and wrapped it around her, pulling her to him.

The second he touched her, Warren's war-torn body and his platoon of soldiers crouching in foxholes vanished from her mind. The party behind them disappeared into the night. She could only see Caleb.

He looked at her like he was starving. It was nothing like the way Warren had looked at her. It had nothing to do with her fine dresses or her notable mentions in the society pages. It was not about her lipstick, which she still painted on out of habit even when her outfits derailed into trousers and hiking boots. For the most part, she had shed her frills as remnants of her past life, but she couldn't go out, even to get the mail, without that lipstick. In that respect, she couldn't shake her mother. A lady never left the house without her face painted on. But Caleb saw past that. In what he saw, she felt possibility take hold.

Maybe it was his Orthodoxy that set him apart. He never stared at other women the way Warren had. He never looked her up and down like the other men here did. He didn't rest his palm on the small of her back, copping a feel of her hips when he passed by. Instead, he lit up when she spoke, looking deeply into her eyes. It made her nervous to be listened to with such close attention, but it also excited her. In his presence, the horror of Warren's death and her overactive imagination quieted. Shadows shrank down to appropriate sizes. Some of the darkness lifted.

He pulled her close. He smelled like cigars and campfire.

Like she was bewitched, Alice took Caleb's hand and guided him to the edge of the property. They scraped the snow from the handle of her Dodge. He rushed to open the door for her, but she opened it first. He grinned sheepishly. She suspected he liked a woman who could open doors for herself.

She shook the powder from her boots and settled into the driver's seat. When she turned the key, the engine coughed before turning over. He walked all the way around the back of the car, his tall, thin body glowing red in the taillights. As they drove, soft cowboy music came on the radio. Almost immediately, the windshield fogged over, and she blasted the heater. It ran cold for a few minutes before it warmed.

14

November 1944
Caleb

When Alice pulled into her drive and killed the headlights, something primal inside him flared. As they walked side by side up to her front door, she jangled her key ring and his pulse rattled. Everything hung in the air between them.

"This is the part where you say good night," she said, hesitating on her porch. She seemed cold, hugging her midriff with her arms. They stood against the wind. Her unraveled hair flapped like moths.

"Good night," he said. But neither of them budged.

Her hair whipped in her face, and she pried it out of her eyes with her free hand while with the other, she swung the door wide, allowing him in.

They kissed heavily in the windless entry, pressing each other up against the door, breathing each other's air. It started slowly, then everything got frantic. He felt he had to undress her with an urgency that could not be explained. If he didn't do it now, he might never again muster the courage. She broke away to hang up his coat still wrapped around her, so large she was swimming in it. In her absence, he couldn't breathe. He was terrified by the sheer intensity of the passion he felt for her, a magnetic force pulling him home.

His hands were shaking. He worked at unbuttoning her scalloped neckline with fingers that refused to bend. It would take the lightest pressure to push the untethered fabric down over the swell of her breast. He covered his eyes, like he did when reciting the Shema, and nudged the fabric loose. Beneath her clothes, her skin was shining. She stood naked before him in full light. He stared at her clothes on the floor instead of her nude body; he was afraid to look right at her, as if she was the sun. Her trousers and blouse on the floor looked just the way he had imagined her sky-blue dress once, a heap of fallen firmament.

Instead of kissing her gently, politely, he kissed her like he was starving. His hands found the soft curve of her buttocks and he pulled her close. She ran her fingers down his waist. Under her fingertips, even the weather-beaten skin of his forearm felt exceedingly intimate. In all his years, no one had ever seen his midriff, save himself in the shower and a few other campers at the public pool. He could swear there was an earthquake rattling the desert when she ran her hand up his thigh. In the kitchen, dishes were falling from the shelves. Glassware shattered. *God help me*, he thought when she unbuttoned his jeans.

It was a funny thing to think at a time like that. He no longer believed in God's dominion. He had abandoned that world when he left for Los Alamos. No, scratch that. He abandoned it when he went to Berkeley. No. Further back. He had left his father's world behind long before, as a child watching the tide roll out at Ocean Beach. He had felt the sinking sensation of his feet in the wet sand as the water pulled away. He knew it was a combination of the earth's gravity and the gravitational pull of the moon that shifted the tides, not a bearded man in the sky, pulling invisible strings. He had always been a man of science. He had only ever pretended to believe in God.

So why did he feel God's presence when her breasts pressed flat against his chest like challah dough? She removed his glasses, and he could no longer see where she ended and he began. He pawed around for her. The heat of her naked body shot off eruptions through his nerves and vascular system that smacked of the miraculous.

He tried to think of anything else to make it last, but he could think of nothing but her skin and the curtain of her hair flapping against his face, filling his nostrils with lavender. He found her slender hands and wove his fingers through hers—her nails were neat, perfectly trimmed, but she wore no polish. That was the first she had let her bare nails show since arriving on the mesa. He gazed at the moons of her fingernails with wonder. He tried to hold on. If he could, he would have lived in that instant forever.

Her naked skin against his own was a sort of intimacy he had never imagined possible. His own parents had carefully timed their sex life around his mother's cycle, and she had disappeared like clockwork to the mikvah every month to immerse herself and recite blessings, returning home clean and sanitized. When they did have sex, the sound of it was unabashed and mechanical—a series of grunts in the middle of the night while he and Asher lay perfectly still on their cots, pretending to sleep. The whole production was a banal and unremarkable part of their routine, an act of baseness and evacuation of bodily fluids rather than an act of passion. It was nothing like this.

Beneath him, beads of sweat clung to Alice's forehead. She rocked her head back and her teeth flashed as she moaned.

They melted into each other.

She pulled the bedsheet around their naked bodies and they sank into parallel dreams. Lying exposed beside her, for the first time in his life, Caleb was filled with the potential of his own worth.

Caleb opened his eyes and felt around for his glasses. Alice's bedroom came into focus. Streaks of light filtered in through the blinds, slicing the room into bar graphs of varying value. Alice was sleeping in his arms. She sighed softly. Her eyelashes fluttered, still in a dream. He kissed them, waking her gently, and they kissed sleepily. Holding her to him, he was filled with a joy he hadn't known existed.

"I want to know everything about you," he said.

She opened her eyes. A shadow spread across her features. When she finally spoke, her voice was weak. "What is there to know? I was engaged and now I'm not." She turned from him. Of course, he realized, deflated. He was so filled with joy, he had nearly forgotten that she was in mourning.

He caressed her temple with a touch that he hoped would both affirm her guilty feelings and allow them credence, then banish them into the ether.

"Start earlier. When did you decide you wanted to be a physicist?"

She bit her lip. "Instead of playing house, my sister and I played chemistry."

"Is your sister a scientist?"

She pulled away from him, taking the bedsheets with her. He kissed her exposed shoulder patiently, willing her, encouraging her back.

She shook her head. "Abigail drowned when I was eleven," she said.

"Oh no," he said. "I'm so sorry, I didn't know."

She shrugged, saying it casually like it was just a thing people said, like it happened to everyone. "At Ocean Beach. A rip current, or undertow, or whatever they call it now." Her face was pinched and for a moment, she looked like somebody else, a stranger in bed beside him. "She was bigger than me and so much stronger; it seemed impossible."

"She was older?"

Alice nodded. "Fifteen," she said, her voice flat. "She was teaching me about salinity. That's why she was in the water."

He looked at her blankly, afraid to ask but eager to know. She looked so fragile, perched beside him, her eyes brimming. Instead of speaking, he pulled her to him and lay her head on his chest. She fanned her hair out across him. They breathed up and down together and were quiet for a moment, staring up at the cracks in the ceiling.

And then she started talking. "We'd been doing it all summer, collecting vials from freshwater habitats and estuaries. She didn't have to get in the water; we could have just collected at the shore. But you know, that was Abigail. Increased sample size and such. She figured swimming out and diving down might at least vary our samples in terms of parts per thousand. Anyway, we had all these samples in glass canning jars with labels detailing the date, weight, and location, and we'd been setting them out on a cookie sheet in the sun all summer, waiting for them to evaporate. It was our last one, Ocean Beach. It was August. We figured it would be our last chance at the shore for the season."

He stroked her hair and waited.

"There wasn't much difference between the samples," she reasoned. "What with the salinity-raising factors of the ocean water evaporating and the formation of sea ice. It was all pretty homogenous."

"You still completed the experiment? After she died?"

"It was what Abigail would have wanted."

He chewed on that for a moment. It was hard to picture an eleven-year-old learning to mourn through science. And that child, he realized with a heavy sensation in his chest, had never stopped. He peered down at the top of her head, the parted hair and wispy curls. She had always seemed unflappable in her work. It had never occurred to him to wonder why.

"Anyway." Alice shrugged. "Abigail dove down and never came back up."

"I can't imagine," he said, and then with nothing further to add, he repeated himself. "Truly, I can't."

"It was windy, or maybe it was the Doppler effect as she got dragged away. The decrease in frequency as she drifted out. You know, the way a wailing siren fades away after it has passed and everyone goes back to driving and comes back to life. She must have been calling to me from the water, but I didn't hear. I saw her go down and I figured she must have just dived down again somewhere else when I didn't see her come back up. I didn't say anything. I didn't want to worry my mother when she was probably just goofing.

My mother was reading a book in a beach chair. It was a nice moment. I didn't want to wreck it."

She swallowed, bracing for what she was about to say. "I watched it happen without saying a word."

She stopped talking. He couldn't see her face, so he swept his fingers through her dark hair, which blanketed his naked body like a bedsheet.

"It seems to me," he said, "that you were just a child."

She pushed off his chest and sat up to look at him. She looked so vulnerable, her brown eyes flashing, the green circles flaring, her cheeks flushed. He wished he hadn't made her say any of it. It clearly pained her.

"I've never told anyone," she said. "Until now." She tucked her hair behind her ear. "What about you?" She still looked raw. It broke his heart, watching that private part of her retreat back behind the dimples that worried her cheeks. Her lipstick had worn off and her nude mouth was salmon pink, the upturned corners of her lips faded to peach. She looked achingly beautiful and lonely.

"What about me?"

"What's your family like?"

He suddenly got nervous thinking what might change between them if he told her the truth about his family—the piles of bills, the calls from collection agencies, the skepticism about science. His heart thumped in his chest while he tried to figure what he could say that wouldn't frighten her away. He stared up at the knotty ceiling, picturing the orange notice taped to the scratched-up paint of their front door. He considered his mother's sheitel, limp and hanging from the coat rack like a dead animal. He thought of the way his father had grunted feverish prayers when Caleb told him he was traveling far away but couldn't tell him where.

"With every door I pass through without kissing a mezuzah and with every spoonful heaped on my plate of unkosher meat, I think of my father," he said. "'Treif,' he would call it."

"Treif?"

He gave her what he hoped was a charming sideways smile. "The meat."

"But you have to eat. What can you do?"

"He thought I was a coward. That it was safer for me to leave than to stay."

"How do you mean?"

He hesitated. She had just bared her heart for him, but she was still an heiress. His world was a side of the city she had only heard of in headlines about crime. Alice could never understand what it was like in his neighborhood. She would never dare set a pedicured toe in his flat even if he managed to save it. She was staring at him curiously. The longer he took to answer, the more she furrowed her brow.

"It was a bunch of nonsense," he said, "from an old Jew who believes animals actually boarded the ark two by two."

She seemed to accept this. "Once the war is over, and you finish your degree, do you want a job at the university?"

There was no money left. It was a pipe dream. Even with the promise of tuition he'd garnered by working here, the very silver lining that had drawn him here in the first place, he knew his family would lose the house if he went back to school and stopped contributing paychecks. The reality of what they were facing had hardened him. He'd let go of his dream for his future, at least for the present, worrying about his parents being cast out on the streets in their prayer shawls. If he was being honest with himself, he'd never really believed he'd go back to school, even when he'd first folded up the recruitment letter and stowed it in his breast pocket. But he couldn't let Alice give up on him. She was looking at him so delicately, like everything hinged on him being the man she imagined, the man her sister might have dreamed up. "I don't see why not," he said.

"You'll need a new suit for your commencement," she said, "and a pair of oxfords. We'll go to dinner to celebrate." She was making plans. That much felt good. In so few words, she had just willed a future for them into existence.

Still, he smiled tightly, calculating the expenses. She was blinking up at him, her face so close to his that her eyelashes brushed his cheek. He turned and kissed her.

They tangled the bedsheets into an elaborate and wonderful twist. He slid his hands up and down the curves of her body and fell asleep that way for a while, cupping her to him. He had never felt so perfectly aligned. He could leap out of his skin.

Nothing else mattered. In the barracks, Caleb floated through drill and hardly heard Sergeant Moony shouting. He hadn't slept, but he was wide awake and dreaming. He couldn't feel his feet, but they went through the motions, taking him through his day. He seemed to be hovering above the ground. He could still smell her perfume on his skin. He was in such a daze that he was the last one in the room to notice the cold air seeping in from the open door, and Dick Feynman brooding in the doorway.

Dick wasn't at all dressed for the weather. He looked to have just rolled out of bed in his slippers and he clutched a half liter of bourbon. Everyone took notice of the young prodigy, wondering what he wanted with the SEDs. Dick ran a hand through his mop of curls and his eyes flashed. He clearly relished the attention. "How ya doin'." He nodded when his gaze landed on Caleb. "Came to sniff you out."

Caleb hadn't spoken to the young scientist since the night of Saul's accident. Once, he'd caught his eye and nodded at him in the mess hall. But otherwise, they had gone back to their respective social circles, Dick among the Nobel laureates, and Caleb with the nobody SEDs, helping the freshly disabled Saul scoop his food and change his pants. Now, here Dick was, the celebrity scientist in the flesh, asking for him by name.

They set up at the folding table, Dick pouring the bourbon into disposable cups while Caleb shuffled the deck. Dick stared at him morosely, then slammed his drink. Caleb dealt slowly, keeping his eyes on the young scientist. He was hedging his bets—and not only about the cards. They played a few hands in silence. Finally, Dick started in, launching into the story as though he was picking up the conversation right where they'd left off, ignoring the fact that the two barely knew each other.

"We summered at the beach in Far Rockaway," he said, leaning back in his chair recklessly. He meant him and his young wife.

Caleb shot glances at him between hands. They had to be about the same age, but their lives couldn't have been more different. Staring at his cards, Dick looked immeasurably lonely. He could talk ignition and sparks with the most famous men on the mesa, and he could swap stories with Nobel laureates, but when it came to his personal heartache, Caleb realized, Dick had nowhere else to turn. He just wanted someone to listen to him.

"She was really something back then. I knew I'd marry her the first time I saw her—holdin' onto her hat by the waves."

"Musta been quite a sight," offered Caleb, feeling it out. "To propose so young."

"Junior year," he said. "We were babes." He threw his hand down. "Fold," he said. Caleb swept up the deck and began shuffling, flexing the stiff backs of the cards and letting them cascade back into place.

"We thought typhoid," he said. "At first." He looked up at Caleb and his dimples faded. His eyes gave him away. "I was sure back then that science could save her."

Dick didn't pick up his hand. He just stared at the symmetrical pattern of red-and-white curled plants and coils on the backside of the cards. "Everyone, the doctors, her family, they wanted to keep it from her that she was terminal. My own sister said it was cruel and heartless to tell her, so I lied. I lied to her."

"Seems to me," said Caleb, surprised that he felt certain, "if it was me, I'd wanna know."

"It was when she figured it out that I asked her to get hitched," he said. He drained his cup and refilled it. He rocked back again in his chair, losing his balance for a second, then catching himself. "My parents were furious. Said I was marrying her out of pity instead of love."

"Were you?"

"Was I what?"

"Marrying her for love?"

He picked up his hand and inspected the cards. "Goddamn it," he said. "These cards ain't shuffled for shit." He snatched the deck and began to shuffle roughly. "I love her the way you love your kidney. Or your gall bladder. She's my white blood cells. We fight off the world together." He slammed the cards down for Caleb to cut the deck. He took a long, slow sip while he waited, swishing the whiskey around in his mouth like mouthwash.

Caleb gingerly split the deck in two. Dick scooped it up and tried to shuffle again, but a few cards caught an edge and the entire deck spilled across the floor. Caleb looked at the scattered numbers—the seven of hearts, the four of diamonds, the queen of spades, and the ace of clubs—a massacre of logic. He crouched down and started collecting them, cataloging primes and composites in his hands.

Dick stared past him. He was looking somewhere miles away. "I couldn't kiss her," he said. "Woulda killed us both."

"At the wedding?"

"Wasn't a wedding. Got hitched in a city office in front of strangers. The Staten Island Ferry was our honeymoon ship."

Caleb offered him the fallen cards, but Dick swatted his hand away. "Listen to me, Private," he said. "The accolades and medals, the lectures and journals, it don't count for nothin' at the end of the day." He looked up at him and the light snuffed out behind his green eyes. "You find a bird like that, you hold onto her." He meant Alice, Caleb realized. "We may live in four dimensions, but love is the final frontier."

Out of the corner of his eye, Caleb caught Saul watching him from across the room. He was seated on the edge of his cot, his bandaged arm sticking straight up in the air like a flagpole.

Dick followed his gaze and Saul, caught spying, darted his eyes away. Dick leaned close to whisper, "If you knew what we were up against, Private, you'd love like there's no tomorrow."

Caleb searched Dick's eyes. Breaking the stare, Dick launched upright, knocking over his folding chair and teetering on unstable limbs. They had polished off the bottle. "Meet me in the heart at noon Friday," he said, sliding a red badge across the table. "Don't say I didn't warn you."

T-Minus 12

April 1950
Haruki: A Story Told Backward

"I'd like to marry your daughter," Haruki said. He could feel the energy radiating off Shinju beside him. He knew she longed to say yes. They were only a few feet apart, seated on the tatami mat, but rather than look at him, Shinju's father stared into his sake.

Her mother was worse. She wouldn't stop gaping at him. Her eyes traced his scars over her dinner plate. When she met his gaze, she searched for the glossed-over pearls of cataracts setting in. She fixated on the bruises on his arms, combing for evidence of blood disease. When he turned to pass the miso soup, she recoiled in terror at the sight of his absent ear: a spiral galaxy, a pine cone, a hurricane in her living room.

No one ate anything. Outside the window, cherry blossoms were blooming across the prefecture. The blooms seemed just out of reach. Shinju was trying to sit still, but the cap sleeves on her dress were quaking.

"You're a good man," her father said finally. "You're even a hero. But you won't live long." He meant his radiation exposure. "I can't marry my daughter to a man perpetually about to die."

15

December 1944

Caleb

The temperature plummeted overnight. It got dark early and the wind howled, whistling through the barren trees. In the morning, it was still dark overhead. They cranked up area heaters in the tech area, which by now they were just referring to as the "T." Caleb had never set foot in the secluded conference room at the building's center, the one they simply called the heart. The door was always bolted, only a thin line of light in the gap at the baseboard implying activity within. No noise could be heard in the hallway. It was secluded by design. Now, the door was cracked. Inside, Caleb could make out men huddled around blowing on their fingers. He flashed Dick's blood-red badge and kept his head down.

Only top security clearances were ever allowed in the room. But today, the large room was flooded with scientists, eager to leave their thumbprints on history. They were all talking over each other, nervously weighing the danger of Nazis occupying Paris, dining on French wines and cheeses, shipping home paintings and jewelry stolen from forgotten Jews. All the seats were taken by those who'd arrived early, and others stood, hands on hips, or squatted on the floor. All around Caleb, a field of red badges glimmered in the harsh lab lighting. He stood quietly, calibrating the room. He didn't dare take up a chair in this meeting of important men with cigars. He was thankful to spot Harry, seeming equally out of sorts removed from his Project Rufus cohort, standing against a back wall.

"Hiya." Harry grinned broadly as he approached. "Nice to see a familiar mug."

"It's my first time at one of these things," Caleb hedged. "I'm just tryin' to keep a low profile."

"No one is thinkin' about you 'cept you, Scout's honor." Harry saluted. Then he said softly, "It's been nice havin' you and Saul back at Rufus. That cave starts feeling lonely when the temperature drops. How's Saul holdin' up?"

"I'm not sure he is." Caleb grimaced. Truthfully, he hadn't checked in on his friend enough lately, being preoccupied with Alice. The guilt was consuming him.

Harry nodded. "Can't imagine how he manages, tryin' to stack dynamite with one paw."

"We're all afraid to sneeze when he's at it. But no one has the heart to stop him."

"We're all missing something," Harry said, surprisingly morose. "Saul's is just on the outside."

Just then Dick burst through the door in a frenzy. Caleb caught his glittering eyes from across the room and nodded.

Dick elbowed his way through the crowd and set up beside Caleb, taking no notice of Harry. "A lot of pomp and circumstance," Dick said. His hair was mussed, like he'd just gotten out of bed. "I bet it reminds you of a bris on Nob Hill." He winked.

"I'm just excited to see how the sausage is made." Caleb tried to sound casual, but his heart was racing. Any second he could be recognized and tossed out.

Dick grinned. "Sorry to keep you waitin', sweetheart. I've seen more oralloy this morning than I wanted to see in my lifetime."

"Oralloy?" Caleb asked. He knew it was a code word, but he had no idea what it meant.

"It's an honor to meet you," Harry cut in, eager to shake hands with the celebrity scientist.

But Dick was focused on Oppenheimer, who had silenced the chatter in the room momentarily when he appeared in a cloud of smoke in the hallway. Dick leaned close to whisper, "U-235. I'm swimming in it."

"235?" He knew that naturally occurring uranium was composed of three major isotopes: U-238, U-235, and U-234. The isotopes could theoretically be separated by gaseous diffusion or thermal diffusion, although to his knowledge this had never been done. It would require a series of progressive stages. Each stage would pass a slightly more concentrated product to the next stage and return a slightly less concentrated residue to the previous one. But, he thought, something heavy settling on his chest, while 238 was naturally more abundant, it was nonfissile. 235 was far more potent. Those "shipments" delivered to the labs, many of which he had handled and manipulated, were not naturally existing elements; they were man-made.

"Right," said Dick, watching the realization take hold. "They discard what's depleted carefully since it is still hazardous even in its granulated form. The rest," he smiled weakly, "comes to us. 'Oralloy' is code for Oak Ridge Alloy."

Caleb stared, the severity of their undertaking dawning on him for the first time. If what Dick said was true, the saturation of the 235 would be fissile enough to support a self-sustaining chain reaction. Which meant . . .

They were building an explosion with a life of its own.

He had already known, he realized. He had been holding back, not allowing himself to admit it. He might be just a military cog, but he was working in defense. What else could it be? Obviously, the photographs and numbers they charted would not be without consequence for the world. The presence of plutonium samples had terrified him, but he had justified their purpose. Plutonium had other possible uses to support the war effort. But not enriched uranium.

Before he could ask more, Oppenheimer waved his hat in the air to quiet the room. "We need a name," Oppenheimer said. "Something more sophisticated than 'gadget.'" The heated debates took a long time to fizzle out.

"Let's name it after a boat," said a young scientist, evoking the code word for *bomb*.

Linking the gadget's name to the existing code language made sense. A whole alphabet of code words fit the bill: atoms were called "tops," and chemists were called "stinkers." Everyone in that room was a "fizzler," according to code since the word "physicist" was especially off-limits. But, thought Caleb, his head still swimming with the new realization, this was no ordinary bomb.

"We felt we should name it for the president," Oppie retorted, "since he was the first to support this project. His vision is the reason we're all here, heaven help us." He spoke with resolve, and as always, both young and old scientists looked to him for direction in a rapidly spinning world.

"What, name it 'Franklin'?" asked one, his inflection reflecting his doubt.

"What about 'Delano'? Has a nice ring to it," said another.

Oppenheimer waited for the room to quiet, mounting a tangible excitement before speaking. He stubbed out his cigarette on the table. "We will call it 'Thin Man,'" he said, his eyes flickering. "Like Dashiell Hammett's detective novels. Robert here suggested it." Oppie gestured at his beloved and constant follower, Robert Serber, and the room cheered. Without being too heavy-handed, it seemed the perfect macabre nod to the nation's thin and crippled, yet fearless president.

But, Caleb knew, they had everything to fear, far more than the president could possibly imagine. An atomic bomb might ignite the atmosphere, setting the hydrogen in the ocean and the nitrogen in the sky on fire. In the middle of that crowded room, he thought of Alice, endlessly brushing her hair, oblivious to the rolling storm clouds outside her window of a post-atomic world. He was still picturing the heavy black rain and the fingers of gas seeping through the seam of her windowsill when a question from across the room made him catch his breath.

"And what of the implosion prototype?" If he had still had any doubts, any pipe dream that the plutonium had held a more innocent purpose, his hopes were dashed.

He caught Dick's eye beside him and the two traded looks. "Implosion" was a forbidden word in Los Alamos, along with "atomic," "fission," and "nuclear." The whole crowd hushed momentarily, alarmed by the breach in protocol.

Ernest Rutherford's famous words rang in Caleb's head: "Some fool in a laboratory might blow up the universe unawares."

During the pause in the commotion, the raucous "Hut! Hut! Attention!" of the parading militia beyond the T echoed across the room. Saul had agreed to cover for Caleb, but it wouldn't be long before someone realized he was missing. But none of that mattered now. A countdown had started in his head.

"The implosion prototype is a rotund shape," Oppenheimer responded coolly, playing to the crowd. He never was much for rules. "So, we have chosen the alias of Sydney Greenstreet," he explained, referencing the British actor who co-starred in the film interpretation of Hammett's *The Maltese Falcon*. He paused, then annunciated, "Fat Man," letting his words land. Finally, he explained, "For Churchill's . . . rotund stature."

The room burst into laughter. "Hurrah!" they cheered, toasting with Styrofoam cups of coffee and sparking up cigarettes. Referencing the film, they shouted: "The Fat Man is in San Francisco!"

Caleb, Dick, and Harry seemed to be the only ones not talking or laughing.

Outside, Caleb's vision blurred and he keeled over. He tore off his glasses and propped himself up against the exterior wall. The side of the building and the tall grass at his feet went hazy.

Someone tapped his shoulder and he turned to see Alice, clutching a bouquet of orange flowers to her chest. In his fuzzy vision, he couldn't make out
the stems; it looked like a bouquet of drifting stars.

"What's got under your skin?" She smiled, her eyes glittering. She had no
idea the world was about to end.

His first impulse was to tell her immediately. But then, she had been so
downcast lately about Warren. Her research was the only thing she truly had
left. "I've just been thinking of the Nazis in Belgium and Luxembourg," he lied.

"Did you know Hitler claims the smell of Jews makes him sick to his
stomach?"

He raised an eyebrow, not sure how to respond. She was still wrapped up
in the theater of war across the sea. She had no idea what was happening at
her fingertips. "It's right there in *Mein Kampf*," she pressed on. "The Führer
thinks we have poison fangs and hidden horns."

His palms were damp. It would be so easy to tell her everything—she
deserved to know what he had just learned. But he didn't want to be the one
to tell her, to be the person to ruin everything she thought she was working
for. He couldn't be the one to destroy her whole world.

"Who are the flowers for?" He tested the water. "Should I be jealous?"

"Oh, these," she said, suddenly shy.

He put his glasses on and waited. The spray of orange chrysanthemums
seemed to bloom and enlarge with the clarity of his specs. He studied the
worried dent between her eyebrows, still trying to figure how to put it all in
words.

"I missed the funeral. I can't bring flowers to his grave. I figure the least
I can do is a makeshift memorial, a marker and some flowers—a place to sit
and think."

She looked at him brazenly, unguarded. They leaned closer. Soon, he
decided. He'd wait to tell her another day—when she felt stronger.

"I'm sure you're familiar with sitting shiva?" he asked.

"I may be Jewish, but . . ." She shrugged. "I mean, my parents said prayers,
you know, when we had to." She blanched. "It wouldn't hurt to remind me."

Caleb nodded. "Well, there's a tradition of placing stones on gravesites.
It's not a biblical commandment, but more of a superstition. It has to do with
the ephemerality of flowers, like humans, as organisms that wither and die."

"Ah," she said, not missing a beat. "And a stone, on the other hand, lives
forever."

16

December 1944–January 1945
Alice

On Christmas Eve, snow fell silently. The whole hill glittered with fresh powder, leaving the town eerily quiet. The military homes transformed into a Christmas card, the little green roofs iced with amnesia. It was almost peaceful.

Being Jewish, although of very different sorts, neither Alice nor Caleb had any Christmas Eve traditions. They congregated in the common room to sip hot chocolate and warm their wet mittens on the radiator. Someone had strewn up green wreaths with red bows in the frosted windows, and a spray of mistletoe draped the doorway. A sad fake bough adorned with white Christmas lights tangled with wires from the solitary outlet in the room, and it blinked shifting patterns. It was a bold move, Alice thought, stringing lights across a military town that experienced frequent blackouts since complex experiments in the tech area regularly zapped the power. But no force on earth could stop people from celebrating.

There were a handful of other Jews with nowhere to go, so they all gathered around the television. Alice inched closer to Caleb, making a show of trying to hear, but secretly she wanted to feel his thigh against her own. A hush fell over the room as Roosevelt's voice emanated:

"In fixing the time for this broadcast, we took into consideration that at this moment here in the United States, and in the Caribbean and on the northeast coast of South America, it is afternoon. In Alaska and in Hawaii and the mid-Pacific, it is still morning. In Iceland, in Great Britain, in North Africa, in Italy and the Middle East, it is now evening. In the southwest Pacific, in Australia, in China and Burma and India, it is already Christmas Day. So we can correctly say that at this moment, in those Far Eastern parts where Americans are fighting, today is tomorrow."

Alice glanced at Caleb. He was sitting stick-straight in his uniform with his hair slicked back. He looked so handsome in his military getup that she caught her breath. An aching part of her was reminded of the way Warren had looked polishing his boots and straightening his coat in the mirror right before he shipped off. She searched Caleb's eyes, glittering in the twinkle lights, assuring herself it was still him. She inched closer.

Lately, he'd been despondent and quiet. There was something on his mind. She wished she could let him all the way in; she wanted to so badly.

"He makes everything sound so majestic." She nodded at the television set. "Speechwriters and poets dress it up for him, but he's mined by the same laws of nature as you and me."

"So you'd rather he let us see him in his wheelchair? Told us not to have hope?"

"I just worry about his misguided faith in science."

Caleb raised an eyebrow. "You, of all people, who believe in research more than your own eyes?"

"Lately, I'm not so sure." He stared at her evenly. Something was on the tip of his tongue, she could tell. He was struggling, so she spoke first, filling the silence between them. "I've not been myself lately. You know that better than anyone. And we work such crazy hours. What if I made a mistake somewhere? Miscalculated something? What if I mess up the whole operation?"

"Ah." He swatted the thought away. "Most of these eggheads put together can't hold a candle next to you and your slide rule." He grinned, then quieted to a whisper, breathing right in her ear. The heat of his breath made a tingle run up her neck and all the way down her back. "They can describe the way water molecules vibrate and escape into the air, but have they ever really watched water turn to mist? They speak of visible electromagnetic radiation, but can they wrap their minds around the way stars burn in the past and present all at once?"

"You have me pegged for a romantic rather than a physicist." She shrugged it off, but she was happy with the compliment.

"God knows what we need is a romantic," he said. "We're kidding ourselves if we think we can control the natural world."

On New Year's Eve, Alice and Caleb left Oppenheimer's party together just before midnight. As they made their way through the snow-blanketed garden, there was a sea of party hats still visible through Oppie's kitchen window and a steady chorus of noisemakers only slightly muted by the whistling wind. A light snow misted their vision while they walked, heads bowed in the weather. Her fingers stung, and the cold killed her buzz.

By the time they shook ice from their boots on her steps, she felt sober. They peeled off their jackets, mittens, and windbreakers, layer after layer, leaving a trail of discarded clothes like shed skins. Underneath everything, she wore a sky-blue party dress with puffed up sleeves and shoulder pads. When she unzipped her coat, Caleb looked at her as if in that dress she had the power to melt the cold weather.

She stoked the coals in her Black Beauty stove to heat the room and put on the kettle for tea. When she turned back, Pavlov had his head in Caleb's lap, pawing at him for belly rubs.

"Oh, stop it." She addressed the dog but meant both of them. "He's here to see me, not you."

Up close she could see the stubble of Caleb's five o'clock shadow, and the shorn curls of his overgrown army haircut springing back into ringlets. She made him nervous, she knew, even after all the time they'd spent together. He always seemed uncomfortable, smoothing the fabric of the couch or fluffing her pillows. But it was good for him, she told herself. She was pushing him outside his comfort zone, into the unknown.

She thought of Warren, slinking between the fir trees, training his rifle on shaking leaves in the distance. He had been more comfortable risking his life than in her arms. In his last letter before he died, he had practically begged her to love him back. "Some women wear their hearts on their sleeves, but you my dear, wear yours in the soles of your shoes. I deserve a true love, not a love that's just a closing word to a letter." After reading it, she had stopped wearing her ring for good, tucking it away along with his letters in a linen napkin in her dresser.

Behind Caleb, through the window, the sparkle of a Roman candle shimmered. People were lighting off fireworks in the street.

"Must be midnight," she said, running her hand up his inner thigh. Several other explosions followed, lighting up the room in flashes. It was funny. They were so used to the rocketing dynamite blasts, the constant explosions knocking books off the shelf, that these puny fireworks seemed banal.

"Happy New Year," he said, patting her hand on his inseam, lingering on her bare fingers. She could feel the electric surge of his energy, the restrained power of his thick forearms.

She slowly removed his glasses, placing them on the wooden coffee table just out of his reach. She knew that without them, he only saw streaks of color and pulsing lights. But his eyes were beautiful when they were not shielded by those thick frames. She studied the light playing on his face and thought of all the chemicals she had left behind in vials in the lab that reached flashpoints at low temperatures and could illuminate like fireworks at any instant: acetone, petroleum ether, titanium. Of all the colorful theatrics—magnesium burning up in a shock of white bright enough to temporarily blind you, or barium making the Bunsen burner flame shudder into pale green—she preferred the quiet elegance of radium. In daylight, it could be mistaken for water. It was always being overlooked. Only in the darkness, when no one was looking, it came alive.

That was it—he had radium inside him, this nervous man beside her. And she alone could set it loose.

Caleb was still in her bed when Bonnie rang the bell in the morning. Alice held Pavlov back with one arm and propped the front door with her hip, keeping the screen closed like a veil between them.

Bonnie had painted on a full face of makeup. Her blonde curls were pinned up, and her kitchen apron was tied too snugly around her waist, creating an uncomfortable-looking bulge around her hips.

"It's a New Year's Day tradition," Bonnie said, brandishing a pie. She peered past her, through the screen door, down the hallway. "It's blueberry, like Oppenheimer's eyes." She seemed to be trying to glimpse around the corner where Caleb's naked thigh could almost be seen motionless, tangled in her sheets. Alice pivoted to block her.

The pie was a beautiful thing with a woven crust and grains of sugar that sparkled in the sunlight. "Oh, my," said Alice, placing her hand over her heart. Pavlov immediately quieted, admiring the dessert and sniffing the air with his wide, triangular nose.

"May I come in? Or am I interrupting something?" A smirk crossed Bonnie's face ever so subtly, like the shadow of a bird flapping across the sun.

Alice thought of the couch pillows, thrown to the floor in a fit of passion, the empty champagne glasses on the coffee table, one smudged with lipstick, and the slingback heels discarded haphazardly in the kitchen.

"Another time," she said. "I've actually got to get going to the lab."

"Surely you don't have to go to that godforsaken place on the holiday?"

"Well, New Year's or not, the Nazis are still in France," Alice said. "Hitler doesn't take days off, I imagine."

"My New Year's resolution," began Bonnie, ignoring her plea for privacy, "is to spend more time with Vic. It's like we're just roommates these days. No spark." She glanced around Alice into the house once more. "Once, we were hot and heavy as Roman candles. Now, I'd give anything for a struck match."

"It's the war to blame," said Alice, cringing as a cough sounded from her bedroom. "Hard to feel romantic with the world breaking in two."

"Oh, bless it," Bonnie said, covering her mouth with her palm. "I'm about as insensitive as a butter knife, going on about my marital woes when you've lost your man."

Everything crumpled inside Alice. Poor sweet Warren. If he had lived, he would have crossed German-occupied bridges and rivers and enemy lines to make his way home to her, only for her to break his heart. She would have refused him and insisted proudly, as she had never dared before in his company, that there *was* room for women in physics.

Bonnie was studying her expression with a nosy eyebrow. Alice had to say something, and quick. "Oh, you know," she said. "Better to have loved and lost."

She wasn't sure she meant it, though. Her heart was on the other side of the wall, where Caleb was dreaming and oblivious, naked in her bed. She loved him; she was certain of that now. But it wasn't that she was planning a life with him in Warren's place. It was her *own* story arc she longed to tell.

"Well, you're wrong about one thing," Bonnie said. "It's not the war that made Vic into a stranger." She swatted flour residue from her hands on her apron, sending puffs of small snow flurries in the air. "Just look around. All these scientists are having babies like spring rabbits. War might as well be an aphrodisiac. I think the guilt of this work, whatever it is, is eating him up."

Her words hung on the air. She was waiting for Alice to respond, and the suggestion of guilt lingered. Alice still had no idea what they were building, or what precisely they should feel guilty about. But she knew enough to piece together that it was something deadly. And aside from the project itself, Alice was immeasurably guilty for loving Caleb. It was destroying her. Bonnie must be able to see it on her. They stood there for a moment, the motes of flour dust drifting aimlessly between them.

Bonnie forced a tightly creased smile. "Well then, put it in the oven for fifteen minutes, 'til it turns golden brown."

"Thank you," Alice said. "Happy New Year."

"Listen," said Bonnie, taking her hand as she turned to leave. "It's lonely out here. If you let it, this place will drive you crazy. If you need anything, anything at all, I'm right next door. Just call for me. These walls are thin." She knocked on the wall to demonstrate, and there was a trace of that knowing smile again. "Easy to overhear things you don't wanna know."

17

January–March 1945
Caleb

Caleb waited for Bonnie to leave before getting out of bed. He didn't want to risk creaking the floorboards and being discovered. As much as he ached for a public display, to kiss Alice in front of all the scientists who undressed her with their eyes or rushed to carry her grocery bags at the commissary, he would truly do anything for her. If patience was what she required, he could keep quiet, hide in the bedroom when she had company. It was a small price to pay.

When he heard the door clink and the bolt slide closed, he pulled on his briefs and made to swoop into the kitchen. He wanted to dance with her to the cowboy music on the radio and spend a little more time feeling airborne. They'd make coffee and eggs, and for a few more hours, do this whole song and dance like the world wasn't ending. It was the only thing that gave him hope.

He found her with her back to him, standing by the sink, but she wasn't washing dishes. She was just staring aimlessly out the window. Outside, they were setting off dynamite in the canyon despite the holiday. The sudden blasts rattled the piled plates in the drying rack. A dark cloud had bloomed over the blast walls. Alice had knotted a bathrobe over her nightgown and swept her hair up in a hasty twist. He watched her rigid back as she flinched at each blast.

He knew he needed to tell her what they were building. It was getting harder to bear. Last night, he'd almost done it. But then she had rested her head on his lap while he ran his fingers through her hair, and it had been perfect. He hadn't had the heart to puncture her worldview.

He knew that for her, everything hinged on honesty, and that she'd find out sooner or later, but he selfishly wanted to wait. Maybe he would tell her tomorrow. But, he knew, watching the smoke coil through the window, after enough tomorrows, they'd run out of time.

He summoned the courage. He'd drink a coffee and tell her that the world was ending, that they were to blame. He took a deep breath, filling with resolve, but before he could clear his throat and make his presence known, the phone rang.

Alice picked it up after the first ring, not noticing him hovering in the doorway. "Ma," she said, sighing heavily into the receiver. "Happy New Year." She did not sound happy.

He slunk back to the bedroom to wait it out. He'd tell her when she was through.

He nearly drifted back to sleep while they talked through outfits for fundraisers and table settings. This could take a while. Then, suddenly, he sat up straight in bed.

"No, Ma, I told you, I'm not seeing anyone important. I promise."

He held his breath, trying to make out what was being said in muffled tones across the line. "I don't care what you heard from Sally Greenberg. No, it doesn't matter that she's dating a scientist. She should mind her own business." She paused and he could make out the buzz of a frantic voice on the other end.

"I told you, he's nobody," she hissed. "Can you imagine me, going to the mikvah? Wearing a headscarf? Don't worry. You raised me better than that. Now, if you don't mind, I have a pie to bake."

Caleb's heart splintered.

As far back as he could remember, he had thought of love as being exempt from gravity. In their small seafoam-green kitchenette, his father had hung a Chagall print over a hole in the wall. In it, a man kissing a woman seemed to drift away on the wind, his spinal anatomy turned to clouds. Tangled in Alice's bedsheets, Caleb always felt just like that—weightless and dizzy— like he was seeing his life from an aerial perspective. But now, it had all been wrenched away in a matter of seconds. He had come crashing back to earth. She was Jewish, too, of course, but Jewish wasn't always Jewish. Especially when money was concerned.

"How do you stomach it?" Caleb asked. Dick was bent over scribbled calculations in the computing room with his back turned. He was only half listening. "Bohr, Bethe, Teller, Rabi. We're all Jews. Nobody wants us." Even

Oppenheimer himself downplayed his Jewish heritage—although he would never admit it, J. Robert Oppenheimer had been named for his Jewish father, Julius.

"I'm not a Jew," Dick said, chewing a pencil in the corner of his mouth, "any more than a tiger is a house cat."

"Saul's been assigned to work with those scumbags in explosives. You know he's not good for much with one arm. They won't even look at him."

"You don't need to look at someone to work with them."

Caleb shot out of his chair and paced around the room. "I just don't get it. Aren't we all on the same side?"

"Listen, Ace, if you think we're all fightin' for the same thing, you've got a screw loose." Dick had started scribbling again, and he glanced up at him over his notes. "You always forget, religion is a culture of faith. Science is a culture of doubt." He turned back to his work. "Sometimes when you get to believin' in things, I wonder whether you're really a scientist or just a rabbi in a lab coat."

Dick got absorbed again in the page in front of him, mumbling about separating isotopes, limited by the total amount of current you could get in an ion beam. He'd been working at a breakneck pace lately, under the pressure of Hans Bethe, who he reported to in theoretics, same as Alice. Over the last few months, Bethe had acquired the nickname "The Battleship" for the way he navigated straight ahead despite danger. By his side, Feynman was known as "The Mosquito," reflecting his inability to sit still.

His feverish work ethic grated on Caleb in light of what he now knew about the project. How could Dick knowingly contribute to the creation of a weapon with such horrific consequences?

"Listen," Caleb said, his tone hardening, "I'm glad you brought me to that meeting and told me what the secret was. And, cross my heart, I won't tell a soul, but I'm not going to keep doing the work. I can't."

"Suit yourself, Ace." He went back to his notes.

Again, Caleb paced the floor.

With his back turned, Dick said, "What we do know is Hitler's probably workin' on developing an atomic bomb of his own. I had the same reaction as you when I first found out. But that thought gave me a fright."

Caleb stiffened at the implications for Jews. He'd read about tiled shower capsules where instead of water, German prisoners bathed in hydrogen cyanide. "They've got Heisenberg," Caleb said slowly. He thought of his parents. When his mother had waved him off at the train station, the silky synthetic hairs of her wig had billowed around her head in the wind like an angel halo.

Dick nodded solemnly. "If you change your mind, I could use a second pair of hands in here tomorrow tonight. Ten o'clock."

Caleb thought about it overnight and through the next day, then showed up promptly at ten o'clock.

Dick didn't seem surprised in the least to see him. "I can't wait on the technician," he said. He had received a shipment of IBM punched-card accounting machines, and was working at assembling them using only a set of wiring blueprints. Instructions and machine parts were splayed out across the floor. "It's not so much physics as engineering."

"What do they do?"

"Once we get these babies up and running, we can program them to hammer out anything from popular music to refining the implosion simulation."

Caleb stared at Dick, squatting on the floor in his wrinkled white shirt and brown wool pants rolled up, tangled up in gadgets and wires like a mad genius. "Someday, when they make a moving picture about this," Caleb said, "you'll be the hero behind the bomb, and they'll have you dressed in a suit, carrying a briefcase. No one would dream of you in your dirty shirtsleeves with your hair sticking up."

After that, they stayed up nights, working the PCAMs, Feynman taking occasional breaks to drum or make an impromptu xylophone by filling water glasses. Caleb avoided Alice. A few times, she came to the barracks looking for him and he ducked out the back door, telling Saul to say he was on assignment. It was like refusing air. He thought of her every few minutes on an endless loop, his mind circling back from sorting C clamps and electrical cords to the clasps of her bra and the coils of her hair.

Mostly, though, he and Dick stayed up nights, hiding out in the theoretics lab. Under those bright lights, it was always morning. Dick could escape the loneliness of his empty bed where Arline should have been, and Caleb could escape, or at least fend off, Alice's impending rejection. They were both heartbroken, but in starkly different ways. Caleb stayed up with Dick as late as he could, the light going to streaks in his vision. Fighting off sleep, he would take off his glasses and press his thumbs into his eyelids, watching the splashes of color jiggle. As soon as he removed his specs, his imagination flooded him. He was suddenly overcome with the aroma of lavender and the intimacy of Alice's velvet skin. The cold draft seeping in through the windowsill became her breath, beckoning him back to her bed. He had to fight it off. He had to stay strong.

Sometimes Dick used careless expressions that brought Asher, rather than Alice, to the forefront of Caleb's mind. "I'm flying by the seat of my pants," Dick said, mixing flammable liquids with bags under his eyes and nervous fingers, and Caleb pictured his brother so vividly, it was like he was right beside him, piloting his plane up into the ether. "Time is flying by," Dick said, winding the second hand of his watch to align with the clock on the wall, seeming afraid of what was coming.

On several occasions, Dick interrupted their work to take phone calls from Arline's father on the rotary telephone in the computing room. Caleb wondered how he'd even gotten the number for that top-secret room to give out. Mostly Dick nodded and agreed. "Yeah, sure," he said, and "You betcha," on an endless loop, braiding his fingers through the curly telephone wire. He spent hours on the line with her doctors. He wanted to know exactly what was shutting down in her body in what order. Caleb understood. Dick was a scientist through and through. He had never felt that way himself, but he imagined he would behave the same way, given the same scenario.

On a Sunday evening, after one of those phone calls, something snapped in Dick. Caleb couldn't hear what was being said on the other end, but Dick's eyes welled and his lip quivered. Caleb removed his glasses, willing the room into a blur. The act was a semblance of privacy for his friend, a gesture of respect and shared heartache. But instead of hanging up when the conversation ended, Dick slammed the receiver against the counter over and over, then stormed out into the lab, smashing beakers and vials, sending shards of glass flying. To Caleb's naked eyes, it looked like he was smashing flashes of colors and shapes, and they broke into smaller flecks of color that rained down around the room. When he was done, Caleb realized the trickling waterfall beside him was methanol and acetone dripping from the table corner.

Dick heaved over and sobbed with his head in his hands. He had knocked over his chair in the commotion and it lay with its legs up in the air, looking to Caleb like some sort of helpless animal.

Eventually, Dick composed himself and started mopping up the mess. "It shouldn't matter so much to me," he said in a broken voice, bending over to sweep the slivers of glass into a dustpan, "if Arline dies a little earlier than the rest of us. What's tuberculosis when we're facing the end of the world?"

Caleb put on his glasses and immediately his vision was so clear he could make out the woodgrain on the doorframe across the room, the squiggles in the Formica countertop beneath his fingertips.

"Makes tuberculosis seem like a holiday when you realize what's coming, don't it?"

April 1945

It set Caleb apart from the other recruits, knowing what they were building. Around him, the men chewed salami and played cards, blissfully unaware. Now, without the reprieve of Alice's bed, he had no escape from his thoughts, or from the mounting tension inside his head.

"Blum," Sergeant Moony barked, interrupting his thoughts. Caleb jumped to attention and saluted, a cigarette still dangling from his mouth. Sergeant Moony plucked it from his quivering lips, took a puff, then stubbed it out with the heel of his boot. "Phone call."

The barracks office was a narrow, elevated offshoot, overlooking the men's sleeping quarters through full-length windows. It made Caleb think of a panopticon. They were always being observed. What other reason could there be for constructing the building with this view, he wondered, looking down at the tops of people's heads while they reclined in their cots. The sergeant handed him the receiver and he eyed the folding chair in front of the desk, wondering whether he dared sit in this important room. He elected to stand while Sergeant Moony reclined behind a stack of important-looking papers and rocked back in his office chair with cushions and wheels. Caleb wondered if he knew. From his hair buzzed close to his scalp to his polished tall boots, he oozed precision and confidence. He doubted this man had an inkling of the Faustian attempt to harness the forces of the universe that was going on right beneath his nose. He would never be able to feign such virility if he had the faintest idea what he was up against.

He pressed the phone to his ear.

"Bruder," said Asher's voice, traveling over mountain ranges and ocean tides, zapping through telephone poles, loud enough in his ear that he could have been standing right next to him in Sergeant Moony's office. Caleb choked back a sudden gush of emotion at hearing the Yiddish word for *brother*. He kept his eyes locked on the sergeant's stern face.

Every week that no mail had arrived from Asher, he slowly accepted that Asher had forgotten him like everyone else. Asher was busy saving the world, one propeller blade at a time. What did he need with a little brother who didn't have the stomach to shoot anyone in the army? Aside from the money he sent home to Fillmore Street, Caleb's life before this place had been all but erased. Now, there it was on the phone line.

Asher's voice transported him across the globe to the turquoise waters of the Mariana Islands. His boots were still planted firmly on the barracks floor, but his mind soared—from above, as seen through the plane window, he could make out the drifting seagrass and the bony spines of coral reefs in the crashing waves. His brother repeated "Bruder," but in the word Caleb heard the rustling feathers of great egrets.

"Asher," Caleb said finally, awakening.

Asher cleared his throat. Neither seemed sure what to say across the void.

"Are you stationed in Saipan?"

"Tinian. Haven't been in Saipan since Hirohito issued an imperial order for thirty thousand suicides. There's no one left."

Caleb felt his chest clench. That number, a tragedy on that scale, it didn't seem possible. "Why on earth would he do that?"

"He was afraid they'd defect to us. I watched with my own eyes. Some things you can't unsee."

Caleb inhaled sharply. He tried to steady himself before responding. "What do you mean you *watched*?"

"We tried to save them." He paused, gathering the words. "So many women jumped with their children, they're calling it 'Suicide Cliff.'"

Caleb hesitated. He was frightened by the detached tone in his brother's voice. He tried to revive him. "Remember the Thanksgiving we barely had anything to eat and you had me write secret messages in baking soda and water?"

"With a paintbrush in cranberry juice." He could hear the hint of a smile in Asher's voice.

"And the candy canes I got at school for a holiday I didn't celebrate, and you had me time how long it took them to dissolve in various jugs?"

"Hot water, vinegar, and oil."

Caleb nodded. "Your science was my childhood."

Asher was silent. It was a stupid thing to say, sentimental and naive after the horrors Asher must have seen.

"I'll be honorably discharged," Asher said stoically, "in six months."

Caleb jolted. He had figured his brother would be gone for the duration. It had impacted his decision to agree to this place, and frankly every choice he'd made since. "You're getting out early? Why?"

"Hard to say. Sergeant says I am taking it harder than most, that I have a thousand-yard stare. Whatever that means." His voice was dull and monotone, like there was nobody behind the words.

"Well, that's good news. You're coming home."

"Good news for some means bad for most."

"How do you mean?"

"They're sending me packing while my comrades die. One of our engineers stepped on an improvised explosive device last week."

Caleb was nervous. No matter what he said, it seemed wrong. "How are they treating you?" he asked.

"At night, I end up sleeping on my floor instead of in my cot. We have nice enough quarters, but I wake up to my ceiling fan and catch my breath, thinking it's a helicopter."

"Once upon a time," he hedged, "that would have thrilled you."

"Well," Asher said. "People change."

The detachment in his brother's voice filled Caleb with renewed resolve. At worst, an atomic bomb might destroy the world. But, he thought for the first time, what if it worked? It might just end the war. "Asher," he tried, desperate to break through. "Whatever you've been through, you can tell me."

There was some shouting and commotion on the other end. Asher raised his voice to be heard. "You know, normal people move from one moment to the next, sunrise to sunset. I think I'm stuck."

"Bruder, listen to me," Caleb said, very slowly like he was reasoning with a child. He suddenly had the sensation of being watched, and he looked up to find that Sergeant Moony's eyes were flickering, studying him intently. He cupped his hand around the receiver as though hiding it from the sergeant's view would afford him some privacy. "You always told me that science wasn't about rules. It was a way of thinking. That men were not in control of it but part of the experiment."

"I was wrong," Asher said dryly. "About everything." And he hung up.

Caleb stared at the receiver. He hadn't recognized that stranger on the phone.

When he made it back to his bunk, Alice was waiting for him in the doorway.

T-Minus 11

August 1949
Haruki: A Story Told Backward

"You have to tell them about what you've been through," Shinju pleaded. She meant the kids at Ondo-Cho Junior High School. Haruki had picked up a second mathematics teaching gig to help scrape together a living. "You can teach more than math."

He studied her earnest face. Inside, she was still a child. He felt so much older than her even though he was young for a teacher, only twenty-three. His pain had aged him dramatically. He was slow to make friends, and he had never spoken openly about the bomb. Something about Shinju's ambition was unsettling to him. He was troubled by her optimism as much as her beautiful name. Shinju had been named for a pearl, but it only required a haunting shift of accent to elicit the Japanese word for *double suicide*.

Now, they were seated in chairs at a mutual friend's house and she placed a warm hand on his thigh.

"Students lost their families. They don't want to talk about the bomb," he protested.

"I thought you said they asked about your ear?" She didn't use the word "deformed" although they both thought it. He traced the twisted helix self-consciously. The corkscrew of his ear canal was a spiral staircase into his private thoughts.

"They call me Mr. Flash-bang. They don't really see me."

"Then make them see you."

Later, she flitted about the party, making small talk. He pretended to participate in what was being said around him, but his mind traced her movements. Occasionally, they locked eyes across the room. She glanced away, seeming flustered, her cheeks ripening.

So many times, he thought, he'd made plans to leave Hiroshima. The month of August was always particularly painful for him. Somehow, he always managed to have car trouble or miss his train. He had started to feel there was some magnetic force drawing him back, closing him in. And he wasn't the only one. Rather than leave, officials had tried to rebuild the city. These days, they even had a baseball team. But despite the new construction, tragedy hung in the air.

When Shinju finally returned to sit beside him, he found it difficult to breathe. She smelled of rice straw and ginkgo trees. He felt weighed down. His tongue was lead in his mouth. He was afraid to look at her directly, like whatever was happening between them might swallow him whole. Maybe it was her all along, he thought, keeping him prisoner in Hiroshima.

18

April 1945
Alice

"Can we talk?" she asked. He wouldn't even look at her. "Caleb," she said, frustrated that her voice came out brittle. "You owe me that much."

He hung his head and followed her outside onto the deck. As though her mental state had willed it, overhead, dark skies prevailed. Last week, a premature burst of sunshine had urged the cactus flowers to bloom too early, unraveling toward fleeting light. For a few days, jackrabbits had scurried and then froze, breathing visibly, their ears and whiskers quivering, while heavy-footed scientists plodded the muddy paths. But then, like someone had shaken a snow globe, spring storms descended again, glittering and severe. An inch of fresh powder erased all the tire marks and footprints. It iced roofs and blanketed cars. Beside her, Caleb was shivering in his undershirt.

"I don't know what I've done," she said. "But I aim to fix it." She stared at him, framed by the white weather. Snowflakes landed lightly on her lashes and she blinked them away. She longed to hold him close and make promises. She wanted to let him kiss her in front of all those soldiers, propriety be damned. It might be inappropriate behavior for a woman in mourning, an utter disregard for her war-hero fiancé. But watching him quaking beside her in the frozen landscape, she was almost certain that he loved her too. He loved her so much he couldn't look at her.

"If you end up with me," he said finally, turning to search the snowy horizon, "they'll never publish your writing in scientific journals or consider you for conferences."

"How do you mean?"

"You'd never get a teaching post."

"That's my concern, not yours." She watched him watch the gently falling snow, trying to measure his temper. There was so much he was leaving unsaid.

"The thing is . . . I think that's exactly what you think. You're afraid that, with me, you'll be sitting on the other side of the mechitzah at services. That you'd have to cover up." He thumbed at her blouse and she shooed his hand away, her chest flashing with heat. "Sew up the slits in your skirts. You're terrified you'd have to use the mikvah, wash soiled linens with the other Orthodox wives."

Her hand flew to her mouth with the crushing realization. "My mother," she said. "You heard."

He gave her a sardonic smile. "I take it she doesn't want you in a long skirt and sheitel?"

She reached for him. "Caleb," she began, but then she caught Saul's eyes, flickering on her from the doorway, and let her hand fall limp. "Of course I know that you would never be like that. That that's not who you are. Listen, you have to understand. I don't mean a word of what I say to her."

He sighed. "Then why say it?"

If only she could make him understand. In every way, he represented the same dead-end waiting for her if she had married Warren: cooking, cleaning, childcare, tending a garden. There was truth at the heart of it. Orthodox family or not, she dreaded being someone's wife.

"You know," he said gently, "I'd want to live any sort of life you want, so long as it's with you."

"I know," she whispered.

"All I'm sayin' is I'm someone worth calling home about. Even if, all my life, people have told me otherwise."

She clenched, feeling the heat rush to her cheeks and tears flood her eyes. "I'm not a floozie," she said stiffly. "I don't just do this!" She gestured at the length of him erratically, surprised by the emotion in her voice. She always spoke in a mannerly, refined tone. She measured her responses and maintained gracious composure. It was the intonation of elite society, branded into her through an endless barrage of afternoon teas and charity events. This was someone she didn't recognize taking her over, animating her limbs, squeezing her chest. And yet, she felt fully herself and oddly powerful. She realized they were attracting stares from the barracks.

"I never said you were," he retorted.

"You didn't have to."

She considered the implications. In the short term, there were the judgmental eyebrows of the other SEDs to consider, congregating to watch them. As it was, they barely let her get a word in while they were all at work in the labs, regardless of her status as their superior. After this display, she'd have no authority left.

It was snowing harder now, and behind Caleb, the whole town was being erased. She could hear her pulse thundering in her ears. They were standing very close. He was only asking her to see him. That was all. Everything else melted away. *Just kiss him.*

An explosion of voices startled them out of the moment. Frightened, they jumped away from each other. She watched in real time as her dream dissipated.

Men were shouting in the barracks, huddled around a radio. Caleb whipped around to look. He glanced back at her one last time, his ice-blue eyes bright with worry, and he sped away to join the men. Behind her, Bonnie was trotting up the drive with a pale face, her blonde curls bouncing in the wet snow. She gripped Alice's forearm, tugging her away from the military housing. She could feel Bonnie's sharp, manicured nails through her wool coat sleeve.

"Come quick!" Bonnie ordered, dragging her away. Alice let herself be led stiffly away from Caleb. She was leaving her heart behind in that ramshackle barrack.

"What's happened now?" Alice inquired as Bonnie dragged her toward the common room. She figured it was more news of kamikazes. Attacks had hit an all-time high with Operation Kikusui, which translated as "Floating Chrysanthemums," a name that made her think of drifting flowers. She hated to romanticize murder, but she couldn't help herself.

"You wouldn't believe me if I told you," Bonnie said, nodding toward the radio and shoving her down onto the sofa.

"The president is dead," Judith whimpered, sniffling into a kerchief and waving it haphazardly at the radio. "May he rest in peace." Alice was out of breath and her head was spinning from their race through the chill. It took her a moment to process the words.

She hadn't noticed right away that Bonnie had been crying. Now, it was clear that she had streaks of mascara running down her cheeks.

It didn't make any sense. Roosevelt was their fearless leader. He was the brains and the funding behind their whole operation and he was the guiding principle behind not only constructing the gadget, whatever it was, but using it ethically. When Oppenheimer himself hesitated, it was to Roosevelt's vision that he turned. If he'd died, what came next? Did Truman even know their town existed? What would become of all of them now?

They hovered around the radio until sundown. FDR's sudden death from a cerebral hemorrhage in Warm Springs, Georgia, filled the airwaves. Though rumors were rampant due to changes in the president's appearance, his declining health had been relatively unknown by the American public. Now, it was all anyone could talk about over bourbon or around tables in the mess halls. In Bonnie's living room that evening, the women chattered about the president's rumored affair with Lucy Mercer. Alice wondered whether Caleb was siloed in a similar room with similar gossip. She ached to go to him, to chase away the distance between them, to assure him that he was somebody, so much of a somebody that she would consider going up against her mother, San Francisco, all of California, and its golden hills for him.

"He tried to repress his love for her," Bonnie said dreamily to a captive audience of women in shining, wet raincoats. She meant the president. "His mistress." She blinked her heavily mascaraed lashes, signifying emotional distress. Bonnie's gaze bore into Alice until she felt herself blush. Judith was leaning close, eating up the sordid details. "Of course their affair is only speculation, ladies will talk, but she was there with him when he was at death's door. What else could it have been?" Alice watched the others swoon and wondered as she often did, whether something was broken inside her. There was nothing romantic about falling in love on one's deathbed. Could you even really call that love?

"I have to say, I feel just awful for Eleanor," Judith said. "She's sure in hot water now."

"They'll be issuing Truman's presidential oath any moment now," said Bonnie, tuning the radio. Her red fingernails gleamed like rubies. "If anyone's in hot water, it's him."

"You know, he was already dying at Yalta," said Diz, waddling into the room, holding her enormous, swollen belly. Alice swiveled around and did a double-take. She had not seen Diz since Christmas.

Diz pushed her square glasses up the bridge of her nose. The castoff frizz of her curls billowed around in the breath of the open door behind her.

Several of the women hopped up, offering Diz their seats. Diz eased down into a chair, holding her belly like a bowling ball. All the glossy eyes turned to Diz expectantly. Her eyes scanned the faces in the room through her square glasses. She paused, allowing the tension to mount. "Al says that even Churchill's physician called Roosevelt a 'dying man.'"

"Isn't that something?" asked Judith, agog. "Just the other day in his fireside chat, he apologized to the American people for sitting."

"Keeping up the ruse," said Diz knowingly.

Alice couldn't stop staring at Diz's belly. She had always assumed that one day she would be a mother, but it had never been her priority. While other girls had played with baby dolls and set tables for tea, she and Abigail had been conducting experiments with salt crystals and magnifying glasses. And Diz, the one female scientist she had befriended in this place, with her androgynous features, slacks, and bare feet, now looked more matronly than she could have ever imagined.

Alice had always been awkward with babies. She had held a few uncomfortably over the years, reciting the necessary compliments and pretending to fawn along with the others. At baby showers, she oohed and awed over tiny outfits and made small talk about strollers and diaper pails. But truthfully, she couldn't understand all the fuss. She would rather have a dog or a horse any day than a baby that spit up and pooped and screamed. She'd never even found them cute—they were fat and bald and they all looked pretty much the same to her. She felt in those moments that there was something missing inside her.

She wondered whether her lack of maternal instinct was linked to the cold practicality of her mother. But then, beneath it all, Mabel had always been soft and kind. At the end of the day, when no one was looking and she removed her jewelry and rubbed lotion on her hands, Mabel always had time to recite nursery rhymes and count sheep. And as a child, Alice had always known she could come home to her mother's plump arms. If she was sick, she could envelop herself in Mabel's chest and heave and cry until she drifted off to sleep on a cloud of perfume. In her mother's arms, she could block out all the sounds except for her gentle voice saying "hush," like the wind in her ears. No, she couldn't blame her mother for her failure to want a baby. It was her that was broken.

Watching Diz, Alice caught a whiff of a nearby woman's sandalwood perfume mingling with the cigarette smoke, and she was overcome by a sudden wave of nausea. She put down her glass, steadying it on the coffee table. Her mouth was dry and her tongue felt like lead in her mouth. She contemplated where the nearest restroom was in case she had to run. "Excuse me," she said, avoiding Diz's square gaze. "Have to powder my nose."

Alice made a beeline for the restroom, but halfway there she paused, trying to slow her breathing. Her vision centered and focused on something on the kitchen table—a newspaper article, a black-and-white photograph, a familiar face. It was the famously unfinished painting of Roosevelt. She stared at the deceased president's likeness until the nausea subsided.

She straightened, but kept her eyes locked on the page; something lurched inside her. She realized she was terrified. Not only of what Roosevelt's death signified, not only for the project and its implications, but for the frailty of men everywhere. First Warren's body had disappeared, lost somewhere in the Belgian forest, and now the president had died quietly in the middle of sitting for that portrait. In the painting, the details of his suit would never be fully sketched in, and his background was blank, but his eyes had a look that could only be described as surrender. Over the last few months, Alice had read nervously about the countless kamikazes piloting toward their deaths with their eyes wide open. They had been instructed never to close their eyes for fear of missing their targets. Their planes erupted into plumes of smoke—flying coffins. It was all so grand.

But according to the radio reports, Roosevelt had simply murmured, "I have a terrific pain in the back of my head," then he had slumped forward in his chair. That was it. That was this great man's flying coffin.

With turmoil in the headlines, work in the labs hit a stalemate. But the recruits still had to report to drill, so Alice hadn't had a chance to see Caleb—to see how he felt about all of it or finish their conversation. All the shoppers in the commissary that week seemed to be sleepwalking, meandering aimlessly while they listened to the radio on the overhead speaker. "He only had two private meetings with the president in his entire time serving as vice president," worried a political pundit while residents picked at the dairy aisle.

Time and again, the infamous recording of Truman's voice reacting to the president's death crackled across the airwaves, interrupting the shoppers, impossible to ignore. His voice was defiant, belying the content of his words: "Boys, if you ever pray, pray for me now. I don't know if you fellas ever had a load of hay fall on you, but when they told me what happened yesterday, I felt like the moon, the stars, and all the planets had fallen on me."

Stars didn't fall, of course. Alice knew it was just something people said. Shooting stars were just tiny specks of dust plunging at terrific speeds into the upper atmosphere. Still, she had always admired meteors. She and her father had spent hours watching them. "Like fireflies," Ishmael would say, watching the sky. "Nothing is permanent."

While she walked the fruit aisle, she couldn't shake the horror of impermanence. On the display, cherries winked at her beneath the light fixtures, red and ripe as rubies. In a week's time, they would be withered, caked with mold. Death was everywhere.

When she had first heard the rumor about Oppie soaking an apple in noxious chemicals to kill his high school tutor, she'd been taken aback. It was the first time she'd thought of him as dangerous. But now, scanning the produce, she thought how funny it was that Oppie had gone to that trouble when that apple could have killed on its own. Apple seeds could be brewed into a deadly elixir. She plucked a red delicious apple from the pyramid and inspected it. It had a bruise that looked like it belonged on a human body.

Her house stunk of rotten fruit. The putrid scent lingered in her nostrils and no matter how many times she washed her hands, there were traces of it on her fingertips. She cleaned out her whole kitchen, disgusted at the sharp smells of swiss cheese and coffee grounds.

She wondered if maybe it was some bizarre form of mourning for the loss of the nation's fearless leader. Without his fireside chats and calls to action, she couldn't picture the increasingly panicked country ending the war—all those soldiers returning to their spouses in gleaming uniforms and crew cuts, and the whole navy shipping home on boats, carriers, and submarines. She knew her contract would be up in August, but without Roosevelt, she had lost hope. She tried to repress a rising certainty that she was trapped and would never leave this place.

19

April 1945
Alice

Alice held her head in her hands and hung heavily over the toilet. She wiped her lip with the back of her hand and forced herself to take a few swallows of water and a bite of a saltine. She swished it around in her mouth, feeling the doughy texture congeal on her tongue. It took a lot of effort to swallow.

Everything considered, it took her longer than it should have to connect the dots. She had missed her period a few times, but she didn't keep track since she'd always had an irregular cycle, and with the extreme weather and the stress of her work, pregnancy wasn't something that was on her radar. The few times they had had sex, she and Warren had relied on a diaphragm. She had just lain there like a log while Warren hovered over her and stifled his moans with his fist. But Caleb was different. She had held onto him like he was the only thing tethering her to reality. She hadn't taken any precautions—truthfully, she hadn't been thinking.

She studied her belly in the full-length mirror. She couldn't be, could she? Her body didn't *feel* any different. She traced the contour of her abdomen. Her middle was as flat as the craters of the moon, as level as the mesa on which she was marooned. She pictured the cells dividing and multiplying beneath her navel. A tadpole. A guppy. A swamp swimming with life beneath the star-speckled sky of her fallopian tubes.

She made her way to the barracks hospital. A chime dinged announcing her entry, and a gargantuan Irish wolfhound nudged her with a large, wet nose, nearly knocking her over.

He was the size of a small horse. "Don't worry, he's very gentle. His name's Timoshenko." The redheaded nurse wearing a nametag that read

"Petey" grinned. "He's named for the father of mechanical engineering." Her smile faded when she saw the look on Alice's face.

"Congratulations," said a pale, blond doctor on her return visit the next day. His nose and cheeks were sunburnt. He seemed nervous, and picked his words cautiously: "Unfortunately, our medications are rationed. We can't prescribe you anything for pregnancy-related nausea."

He told her she was dehydrated, and that she needed to be careful to drink more water, especially with the extreme weather. "Pregnant women in wartime have been known to experience vivid dreams," he warned. "But don't let that stop you from sleeping. You need to rest."

She had stopped listening. She heard him droning on, but she couldn't focus. If she had been approximately four weeks pregnant at her first missed period, and it had been ten weeks since then, that put her at fourteen weeks, her second trimester. Her baby was approximately the size of a lemon. How come she wasn't showing more? Why hadn't the nausea subsided?

"Everyone carries differently," the doctor assured her.

A skeleton watched her from a medical poster, and she wondered what she looked like from its perspective. She observed it briefly from an anterior view, its clavicle and sternum, and its lumbar vertebrae all clearly labeled. Truman's voice was scratching through his prewritten inaugural address on the radio in the waiting room, seeping into their periphery through the crack beneath the door. The sound was muted and she could just barely make out the words: "heavy heart," "mortal remains," and "tremendous void." She sat on the crinkly brown paper and tried to dial down the bitter stench of antiseptic and illness while his voice carried through the wall, growing louder with the crescendo of his excitement: "Today, the entire world is looking to America . . ."

That weekend, Alice inspected her belly in the mirror. Her abdomen was becoming more swollen and hard to the touch. Occasional flutters beneath her navel made her stiffen and move gingerly through her household tasks. She knew it was likely just indigestion since it was too early to feel the baby. But she still found herself bending over cautiously to refill Pavlov's kibble, squatting from her hips rather than folding in the middle. Everything took longer and required more energy than before.

Thankfully, for the time being, her nausea had subsided and her appetite had come back full force—she was insatiably hungry. She wanted pancakes and syrup, buttery and flaky, and anything pickled—olives or peppers, soaking in brine.

Alice was still in her bathrobe, her wet hair swept back in a braid, when someone knocked. Pavlov charged at the entry, barking and snarling, but instantly quieted, wagging his tail. He pawed at the handle and nudged it with his nose. That's how she knew Caleb was on the other side of the door. She swallowed the lump in her throat and unlocked the bolt.

He was standing in the rain, looking sheepish. Raindrops dribbled down his glasses, which kept fogging up from his breath. She waited for him to say something. They stood there for what seemed an incredibly long time, the rain pattering on the boxy tin roofs of the McKee houses and plinking on parked cars.

Finally, she couldn't take it anymore. "I suppose I'd better invite you in before you catch a cold," she said.

Caleb shook his head solemnly. "No, ma'am. I just came to get something off my chest." He sighed and finally looked straight at her. Two pools of reflected light from his glasses bounced around in her entryway. "My mother's illiterate," he said, dropping his eyes again. "I remember watching her as a kid . . . the way she thumbed through the mail, holding letters up to the light trying to decrypt codes, shaking boxes, wondering what mysteries lay inside." He inhaled sharply, like it pained him. "You, on the other hand, are the kind of woman who opens the mail." He searched her eyes as though what he had said made perfect sense. "I guess that got me intimidated," he finally pressed on, "thinkin' you'd never want me."

Alice squeezed her eyes shut, pressing them with her forefinger and thumb until shapes of color splashed.

"I'm not askin' for forgiveness," he said, sensing her turning mood and speaking quickly. "I'm not askin' you to go steady or tell your mother. All I'm askin' is . . . join me in the common room for a game of bridge. Just bein' around you makes all this easier."

She opened her eyes and leveled him with her gaze. He seemed to shrink while he waited for her response, water droplets running down his glasses and off his nose. At a loss for words, she shook her head.

"You hate me that much?" he asked in alarm.

Frustration rose in her chest and her voice caught in her throat. "I don't hate you, Caleb."

"Then what is it? Are you upset about the president?"

You idiot, she thought. He was studying her, his light eyes filled with concern. He put his hand on her forearm, and she could feel his pulse throbbing. She knew she'd have to tell him at some point. But what would the news of the pregnancy do to him?

"All right," she said, pawing through the coat closet for her umbrella. "One hand."

Beside Alice in the common room, Caleb barely looked at his cards. He seemed to be in a daze, folding down pairs morosely, watching the deck get swept away and dealt back, expressionless. Time seemed to be passing without his consent.

She ached to tell him everything. The world seemed to be collapsing around them and so many unknowns lay in Truman's hands. Lacking his predecessor's charisma and public speaking skills, there were widespread fears about the end of the war and Truman's response to communism. She was troubled by all of it, but mostly, she longed to tell Caleb that she was pregnant with his child. Whether they made it out of there or not, their futures were aligned. But there were too many people listening. There were their bridge partners—they were playing against Diz and Al—and a circle of SEDs perched near the radio. None of them were really listening to the news, but after the death of a president, people get desperate for information. Everyone wanted the radio on all day just in case something new came up.

"You know what they mean by 'racial hygiene,'" said an SED, talking over the anchor on the evening news who was reporting on the war in Europe. Everyone turned to look at him. He paused, reveling in the attention. "Sterilization."

"That's the least of it," said another in the circle, shooing the former's claim away like it was a fly. "They've been experimenting with infecting children with tuberculosis." Alice shot a nervous look at Caleb. At least in public, she wanted desperately to avoid the topic of children. She knew all about it, of course: the wounds cut into prisoners then purposefully infected with dirt, bacteria, and glass. She had even heard of twins subjected to surgeries without anesthesia.

"The worst is if you're already pregnant," said Diz, rubbing her belly. Her mind seemed miles away.

Hot tears suddenly flooded Alice's eyes. It was not like her to be sentimental. She tried to breathe and hold herself together.

Diz didn't smile to soften her words. "What they do to Jews who are carrying future Jews, you wouldn't believe it if I told you."

"Try me," said Caleb. He was studying Alice curiously, seeming to have registered the emotion in her face. She lifted her chin and willed herself into composure.

Al shifted uncomfortably in his seat. "Honey," he said, "the stress isn't good for the baby, remember?"

"They're artificially inseminated with animal sperm," said Diz, raising her voice and defying her husband. "In tryin' to produce more Aryans, they're experimenting on mothers like rats."

The next morning, Alice rose early to take Pavlov for a walk and clear her mind. At the edge of the property, a small crowd had gathered to wave someone off at the gate. Pavlov started barking at the commotion. She yanked the leash and watched a Crown Coupe roll through the checkpoint, but she couldn't make out who it was. The windows were so clean she could see the desert glide by in their reflection. "What's all the fuss?"

Bonnie crossed herself. "Kitty's finally leavin' him." No one was surprised that Oppenheimer's marriage was falling apart. Things had gotten visibly worse since the birth of their baby, and lately, they'd been getting into drunk fights in front of party guests. Kitty had always drunk heavily, but she drank more steadily now, a constant stream of vodka lubricating her gestures and loosening her tongue. She no longer drank for the merriment of gossiping with the wives. She had begun accusing them one after another of sleeping with her husband, and now, there was no one left to drink with her.

"But," said Alice in disbelief, "Groves won't let anyone leave."

"Tell that to Kitty," said Bonnie, giving a princess wave to the taillights as the coupe descended out of view. Alice tried to repress the flickering anger in her chest. She had missed Warren's funeral, but Kitty, the German princess, could throw a tantrum and leave on a whim.

"Even Groves cowers when she comes around. She just packed up her things, kissed the children goodbye, and left Oppenheimer like a dog."

Alice hated herself for it, but she was envious. She could almost feel the gravel rumbling Kitty's steering wheel on her descent down the pockmarked road. She imagined the wails of her baby growing fainter as she sped away, the whole army town shrinking in her rearview.

Alice did her best to temper the fear growing by leaps and bounds inside of her. In her wildest dreams, she never would have imagined she'd be pregnant with such variables—a dead fiancé and a shameful affair. She was trapped inside a math equation all women understood: a baby without a husband added up to shame and disgrace. Not that she cared about that sort of thing, or anyhow, she tried not to. But she'd never imagined she'd be facing that undesirable sum, locked away in a secret world while explosions knocked her books from the shelves. Even though she knew it was only routine testing of dynamite, she couldn't quell her pounding heart. Perhaps, she worried, she and Kitty were more alike than they were different.

She didn't mean to end up on Diz's doorstep that weekend. Her feet just took her there. It was nearly ten o'clock, too late to call. But she had made it this far. Diz opened the door on the first knock. She peeked around the doorframe at first, then swung it wide with a pleasant smile, revealing a belly that seemed to have ballooned overnight. Alice tried not to stare. Diz wore only a battered, pink bathrobe, and it hung short on her due to the expanse of fabric required to stretch over her middle. Maternity clothes were limited due to the ration on fabrics and textiles. Alice glanced down self-consciously at Diz's bare legs and slippers. Her ankles were so swollen, the joints didn't seem to exist. Her legs just went straight from calves to toes.

"Al's due home any minute," she said. "You know how it is." She meant at the T. "We're lucky if we ever eat together. Won't you come in?"

Alice had it all mapped out, what she would say. She would only reveal what Diz needed to know. But when Alice stepped into the house, she froze.

Diz waddled across the room and lowered herself into the living room chair. She put her feet up on the ottoman and wiggled her swollen toes, then pressed her glasses up the bridge of her nose and blinked at Alice with curious eyes.

Following her cue, Alice perched on the couch and crossed her legs gingerly. She felt tears forming in her eyes and tried to hold them in. "When are you due?" she asked.

"I've got some time." Diz winked. Alice must have looked horrified because she said, "It's really not as uncomfortable as it looks. Worst thing is trying to sleep. Can I get ya anything to drink?" she offered, but it was clear she would not be getting up to retrieve it.

Alice took the hint. "Oh, it should be me waiting on you!" she exclaimed, hopping up to examine the bar.

Diz rubbed her belly. "Want to feel him kick?" She groaned and closed her eyes, holding her palm on her lower abdomen.

Alice wanted nothing less in the world, but there was no way around it. Like she was walking the plank, she inched her way over to Diz, squatted down to her level, and placed a cold, clammy hand on her warm belly. She caught a glimpse of her frightened face reflected in Diz's glasses, and felt the nausea inching back.

"Stinker knows we're waiting for him." Diz smiled. "Slippery little guy. He'll move any moment now."

Alice waited.

"There, did ya feel that? That was a big one."

She hadn't felt anything. "Yes, wow," she lied.

Just then Al bumbled through the front door. Both women blinked at him like deer in the headlights. It was bizarre, thought Alice, that they had assumed a guilty manner as though they had been caught at something shameful in this moment of female comradery. Al, however, seemed entirely unfazed to find a strange woman in his home at that late hour. He took stock of Alice's hand on Diz's belly but didn't break his pace on his route to the bar. With his back turned midpour, he offered: "He's a night owl, this one." He meant their unborn child. "Like his father." It did not strike Alice as odd that they both assumed it was a boy. That was just the way. Al turned back toward them and held his whiskey up to inspect the winking brown liquid in the light.

He passed Diz a glass of the brown liquid on the rocks and offered another to Alice. Diz accepted the drink and waved him away. Alice welcomed the beverage. She'd been prescribed champagne for her lingering morning sickness, so she figured this might help. She swirled the whiskey in her glass, staring down at the constellation of clicking ice cubes.

"We'll have to move," said Diz, looking around their little home at the Hopi pottery on the mantel and a vase of wildflowers. "We'll qualify for a bigger house, being a family of three."

Suddenly shining with sweat, she started fanning herself with a book on the coffee table. "These hot flashes," she said. "In this cold weather. You'd think I was an old maid!"

"Don't listen to a word she says," said Al. "Pregnancy makes her glow. She looks positively radiant."

"Interesting choice of words," quipped Diz.

Alice felt her heart flutter at the mention of the word that was just a hop, skip, and a jump away from the forbidden word "radium." She hoped no one had heard. She studied her fingernails. Bonnie was right—the walls in this place were waiflike. You could hear people having conversations two houses over.

The labs were no better. Only the other day, after a team meeting, she'd asked Bethe if she could transfer out of the darkroom and entirely away from Project Rufus. She would still calculate and study simultaneous sparks but perform her work in the theoretics lab. She'd made a case about Slotin's leadership style—her inability to focus in such a relaxed work environment. But truthfully, she'd been worried about the effects of the plutonium on the baby. Immediately after, she'd caught Harry's eye on her way out the door and worried he'd overheard, that he could see through her cover story. There were no secrets in this place.

Alice looked from Diz to Al and back again. She had come here because she longed to tell someone. These were kind people—they had nothing to gain or lose from her condition. They were trustworthy. Keeping it to herself was eating her up inside. But she had never said the words out loud.

"Have you ever thought," Alice asked finally, "in all your work with the Cockcroft-Walton accelerator, about the impact on the baby?"

Suddenly, there was someone home behind Diz's eyes.

"I don't mean to offend, truly. It's just that all this time, we've been building this gadget without knowing what it is or does. At some point, we have to ask, don't we?"

She and Al exchanged a look.

Diz's expression stiffened. "You came to my house to ask me that? At this time of night, when I'm in my robe and slippers?"

Al strode across the room and placed a hand on his wife's shoulder. "We know what we're building," he said pointedly. "And if you don't know by now, you'll know soon enough."

Alice nearly choked on an ice cube. She stared at her drink, feeling all the hairs on her forearms prickle.

"Of course we worry about the baby," Al breezed over her shock, turning his back and pouring himself another whiskey. "How could we not? Every day, we worry about the impact of oralloy on the fetus. If we fail, we'll all die. If we manage to build a bloody chain reaction, we'll all die. Not to mention what kind of life he'll live if he's ever cursed enough to be born."

"Oralloy?" Alice asked, unfamiliar with the code word.

"It changes everything, being pregnant at the end of the world," Diz said stiffly, staring into space.

"Did you say, 'chain reaction'?" Alice's nausea came flooding back. She'd been so afraid of the possibility of an atomic bomb that she'd been lying to herself, denying the evidence when it was right in front of her. Her mind raced through every measurable moment, every overheard conversation, every SED griping about the dangerous work of the explosives group, her endless hours diagramming hills and valleys and mapping every detonation on an axis. She'd filled her days committing to memory every detail of sparks: what caused them, what made them blaze brighter, and why they died. They were working on ignition, she realized. Then there was their work in Project Rufus, the numbers recorded as piecemeal work, bleeding one experiment into the next: it was a simulation. They were tampering with criticality.

On some level, she had already known. But it took Al saying it out loud for her mind to admit it, for her thoughts to rush back to Fermi's famed atomic pile under Stagg Field on a cold December day in Chicago in 1942. Fermi had built the world's first artificial nuclear reactor and set off the first manmade nuclear chain reaction, an event that, consequently, set off a chain of events leading to this very moment. Fermi had proved beyond the shadow of a doubt that the atomic bomb was a reality. She had noticed the short Italian Nobel laureate running around the hill, but she had never allowed herself to connect the dots. At the time, Fermi's explosion had been too weak to light a single lightbulb, but it was an explosion that had divided time into before and after. Something had awakened in that pile, and for four and a half horrifying minutes, it had stretched its legs. She realized with undeniable clairvoyance that the plutonium she had helped manipulate and mold into spheres might lead directly to the end of the world.

And suddenly she could think only of Caleb, wheezing in the smoke, his magnified eyes behind his specs no longer blue but gray and clouded, murky as the San Francisco fog. She couldn't save him any more than she could save herself, but she had to do something.

"Do the SEDs know?" She tried to make the question as vague as possible. "I'd imagine they're the ones closest to the dangerous materials."

"Not likely," said Al. He sounded a little guilty, like he had thought on this concern many times before.

Diz jolted up straight and grabbed her belly, reacting to the baby kicking. "Are you asking after Private Blum?" She huffed the words out through clenched teeth.

"Is it that obvious?" Alice had tried so meticulously to conceal every intimacy, but they did pair up for cards in the common room, only recently with Diz and Al themselves. Not to mention they'd been seen lingering on hikes and arguing in shady corners.

"Not so much. It's a small town. And I ain't so mobile anymore. Not much else to do besides watch."

"Is that the private that's been palling around with Dr. Feynman?" Al asked, taking a swig from his glass and swirling the brown liquid absently.

"That's the one," Alice admitted, her head in her hands. Now that the shock was wearing off, the edge of nausea was returning.

"He knows." Al said it in a hardened voice, making no effort to soften the blow.

Alice snapped her head up to stare at him. "Are you certain?" It was impossible. Not with the way he'd spoken of wanting to spend his life with her. He couldn't possibly know the world might end at any minute and look at her the way he did.

"He was in the red-card security meeting last month. He knows and then some."

She chewed on that for a minute, trying to plot out their interactions over the elapsed days on x and y axes, charting the opportunities he'd had to fill her in, the averted looks, the weak changes of subject, his quiet posture over bridge. Her hands and brow went clammy again. She didn't want to let her heart get sliced to fractions right there in front of Diz.

"Answer me this," said Diz, studying her with a morbid look. "Do you have any idea what the weapons of World War III will be like?"

"No," said Alice bleakly. "What?"

Diz shrugged. "I don't know. But I can tell you about the weapons of World War IV."

"What will those weapons be?"

She tossed back her glass and gestured for a refill. "Clubs," she said dryly. She stared hard at Alice.

"That's why her middle name is Riddle." Al laughed. "Elizabeth Riddle Graves."

Diz did not flinch. "If I could," she said, "I would hold this baby in forever."

T-Minus 10

May 1949
Haruki: A Story Told Backward

After his world had ended, math was the only thing that still made sense to Haruki. He could pinpoint the velocity and arrival times of two trains heading west from two different stations, traveling at an average rate of forty miles per hour and thirty-five miles per hour, respectively, for thirty minutes. Instead of trains, it could be cars or ships or planes. The variables didn't matter, so long as they were coordinates along an axis, vectors on a graph. The same basic principles could be applied to falling bombs, burn victims, atomic cataracts, and the minutes remaining to midnight. When all else failed, there were answers to be found in numbers.

Even after four years, Haruki still walked with a limp. His doctors assured him it would improve if he kept up with his stretches. But lying on his back, bending his knee was excruciating. He had a low white cell count, anemia, and whenever he got a papercut or a nosebleed, he bled for hours. Inner mouth lesions made it painful to chew, and he struggled to keep on weight.

By the end of the semester, it took all his energy to get through the lesson plan in applied mathematics. He felt particularly weak after class. When he stood up too quickly after dismissing the students at the women's college where he worked part-time, the room began to spin. He held the wall to support himself and inched toward the second-floor teacher's lounge.

Outside, the sunset had tinted the hallway amber. The sun felt so close, it seemed to be setting inside the building. He stepped into the box of cast sunlight on the linoleum floor and squinted through the blinding brightness. That was when he saw her for the first time.

Shinju was short and petite, but when she approached him, lit up by the drama of the sunset, the light exalted her clothes and exaggerated her height.

She wore a belted dress and a sun hat that cast a mysterious shadow across her face, like an eclipse. Seeing her, his mind illuminated with numbers. She had wavelengths in her hair and variables in her eyes.

She approached him, and he plummeted to absolute zero. The world went to fractions. Before he even knew her name, he was hopelessly in love.

20

April 1945
Alice

When Alice rapped on the barracks door, it was still dark enough to see the moon. Porch lights were switched on in a few of the homes up and down the drive, and all the windows were dark. The SED who came to the door grumbled, rubbing sleep from his eyes. He called for Caleb and slouched back to his cot.

Caleb emerged a moment later, fumbling through his pocket for his glasses. His muscular arms were on display in his undershirt, and Alice found his path of seven freckles peeking through the collar, a constellation to orient her in an unknown hemisphere.

"Coffee?" he offered, gesturing at the pot in the makeshift kitchen area. A slow trickle was dribbling into the pitcher.

She nodded.

He poured her a mug and they stepped outside together into the chilly morning air. Pavlov had been waiting on the porch behind her and rushed to greet him. He knelt to pet the dog before addressing her. "What's got you up before the birds?"

"Caleb," she said, searching for words, "does it ever bother you not knowing what we're building?"

He eased himself down into one of the deck chairs. His eyes were elsewhere. She paced the railing and peeked at him blowing on his coffee and warming his fingers on the mug. He was staring at something on the tree line. She tried to follow his gaze, to see what was calling him, but there was nothing there.

"No," he said finally. "I figure whatever it is we're making, it'll happen the same way with or without me. The way I see it, I'm just a cog in a machine." He rocked his head back and looked up at the rolling clouds. She watched his Adam's apple slide up and down as he took a sip of coffee. He seemed so untroubled lying to her. It almost seemed to calm him to do it—how effortless it was for him to sit there and pretend he didn't know they were tampering with atomic structures and explosions that might ignite the atmosphere. He felt no need to tell her they were in grave danger, that they were both the good guys and the bad guys.

"So I suppose," she said, changing the subject and hating herself for not being able to just come out and say any of the things she had come there for, "justice has been served in Italy."

She meant Mussolini. It was supposed to be good news—a turning point in the war. The corpses of the dictator and his mistress, Clara Petacci, had been mutilated by an angry mob.

He nodded. "They say he was dressed to die," he said dryly.

"I feel sorry for his beautiful mistress," she said, gauging his response. "Her only crime was falling in love."

His face reddened, but he plowed on, avoiding the dangerous words gathering like storm clouds between them. "You know one woman shot his corpse five times with a pistol?"

"It's horrifying," said Alice, "what people become." But Caleb didn't look horrified. Instead, he looked eager, like the potential for violence was brimming, filling him up. Maybe she didn't know him at all. Maybe he was just fine with contributing to this work, keeping it from her, letting her get so close to the end of the world that she might get blown through to the next one.

Across the horizon, the sun was beginning to rise over the desert, the shadows stretching their legs. The lineup of trees looked like a militia of men in the trenches in Ardennes, aiming their crosshairs at her.

She thought again of Mussolini, and his mistress. On the front page, army photographers had them posed like dolls. One of the dictator's eyes was missing. The other was pried open and glossy, still in a dream. Driven by morbid curiosity, Alice hadn't been able to look away. In the photo, the fascists' heads had rested softly against each other, like sleeping children.

"Caleb," Alice said finally, staring hard at the horizon, unable to bear the things in his look. "I'm pregnant."

Caleb froze. He didn't seem to be breathing. He spilled his coffee, the mug rattling as he set it on the deck at their feet. "Are you certain?"

Alice nodded vigorously. Tears formed in Caleb's eyes. He took off his glasses and wiped them away briskly.

Without his glasses Caleb was helpless, embryonic. He eased himself up from the chair, feeling for the world with his hands like a blind man. That was the intimate world in which he slept and dreamed, and it was the dimensionless world in which he made love.

"You don't have to do anything," she said stiffly to his turned back. "It's my cross to bear."

He was staring out at the pond, although she was certain he couldn't see it. She wondered what it looked like in his foggy vision—a mirror of shimmering, rolling currents.

"When are you due?" he huffed without looking at her.

"September," she said gently. "After contracts are up."

"September," he repeated, like he'd never heard the word before. "September." He turned back to her. Wordlessly, he pulled her to him.

Caleb

He should have been horrified by the scandal. Falling pregnant out of wedlock could destroy her family back in San Francisco. It could annihilate her career. There was so much to worry about when it came to the world beyond the two of them—three of them, he corrected. But he couldn't find it in himself to regret any of it. He was thrilled.

He started plotting out how he would propose, the things he would say. He fantasized about her response, her teary embrace. He envisioned Sunday walks and summer camps, play structures and zoos. He could never afford the ring she deserved. He'd have to think on that part.

It was hard to focus on anything else—he had to see her again. He showed up at her door with ginger candies and herbal tea.

"They help with morning sickness," he said, brandishing the gift basket, "and you need to eat double the calories—broccoli, sweet potatoes, whole grains."

She thanked him weakly but over and over she refused his help, insisting she just needed to rest.

His thoughts shifted and he started worrying long and hard about what was coming next, and how he could protect her. Ever since Saul's accident, Caleb had been wary of government secrets and mislabeled packages. He was becoming disillusioned with the need-to-know basis by which they worked.

Dick had allowed him to know so much more than he had been meant to, and it made him wonder what else was being kept from him now as things unfolded. He was tired of not asking questions. With Alice pregnant, too much was at stake.

In the barracks, everyone was still buzzing about Paul Tibbets's arrival. Only the other day, Tibbets had ridden the bus up the bumpy roads with the cloud of Hopituh cleaning ladies who infiltrated the secret city daily. The cleaning ladies had become a routine sight on the hill with their ornate cumulus-puff hairdos and their turquoise jewelry with whole skylines trapped inside. Caleb had paused on his morning walk to watch the women file off the bus and await the colonel. A small crowd had gathered. Tibbets had stood out like a sore thumb in his pristine uniform. Everyone knew that his presence signified that something was about to happen, but they weren't sure what. Even Oppie, with his puff of irreverent hair, had greeted him nervously.

While everyone gawked at the colonel, Caleb studied the cleaning ladies. Although the town was kept top-secret from the Caucasian population of Santa Fe, the Indians and Spanish Americans were bused daily to the project. The scientists needed them to stoke their coal and clean their houses. These Hopi women armed with mops and brooms were considered too unimportant to be a security threat. But Caleb felt rattled by their presence that afternoon. They reminded him of his illiterate mother. He had seen that same expression many times before on his mother's face when she desperately pretended to understand something she didn't. In their proximity, he caught a whiff of bleach and vinegar and pinpointed his mother's most trusted cleaning agents. He couldn't help thinking of her as he watched the women descend from the bus, bouncing down the steps and lining up to await their assignments. He felt a deep sorrow for these women who were by far the most invisible of all the invisible people in that town.

On Friday, Oppenheimer called a community meeting by the water tower. The sun beat down relentlessly, reflecting on the melting snow, making the landscape so bright it was hard to see. Caleb searched everywhere for Alice. He scanned the backs of people's heads for a woman in trousers with jet-black hair. She was nowhere to be seen. Instead, he found Dick in the crowd.

"What's all this about?" he asked. He shielded his face with his hand and squinted up into the brightness.

Dick looked about to be sick. "Don't ask questions you don't want the answer to," he said.

Harry was making his way through the crowd and bee-lined for Caleb. "Howdy," he said. "What you figure all the fuss is for?" He looked right at Dick. Caleb figured Harry was sizing the celebrity scientist up, wondering whether he would recognize him from the red-card meeting. Harry waited expectantly for Dick to address him, for some preliminary salutation, but Dick only stared somberly at Oppenheimer, who had approached the make-shift podium in his cowboy jeans and dirt-caked boots, looking waiflike, like he might blow away in the wind.

"Ever since Kitty left, he's had one foot out the door," said Harry conspiratorially. It hadn't occurred to Caleb that Oppie might leave. He knew that the children were being cared for by a friend on the mesa since he couldn't do it himself. He hadn't thought too much of it.

"At least in public, he's made a big display of falling in love with her all over again," said Harry, still eyeing Dick, who had gone uncharacteristically quiet. It was true, Caleb thought. He had seen the director meandering the mesa, picking bouquets of freshly bloomed wildflowers for Kitty on his isolated hikes: lupine and Indian paintbrush, sundrops and marigold. He had arranged them for her in vases and placed them in the windows of his home, beckoning her back. But Caleb had his suspicions that the director was worried about something more severe than his marital status. Since Tibbets had arrived, he hadn't seemed focused on what was being said in meetings; he was always staring off.

Just then, on the platform, Tibbets stood, in perfectly pressed attire, and saluted Oppenheimer. He held eerily still, like a statue. A quiet swept the audience.

"Colonel Paul Tibbets has got more admirers than you can shake a stick at," whispered Harry. Dick shot him an irritated look, but Harry, who had finally lost interest in Dick, didn't pick up on the subtlety. "He escorted Eisenhower to the Gibraltar Trench and all."

"Lay off," Dick hissed, shushing them. "This is it."

The crowd watched Oppenheimer contemplate the sky. He adjusted the microphone to his height, and the last whispers extinguished. Overhead, three turkey vultures circled, their squawks echoing.

"We have been ordered to run a test," Oppenheimer began, "of the world's first nuclear explosion." It was the first time the word "nuclear" had been uttered aloud. A collective gasp escaped the audience. Guards on the periphery lifted and poised their weapons, training them on the crowd. Oppie took off his hat in what resembled an act of respect and mourning. A patch of his night-black hair stood straight up with static electricity. "On the plains of the Alamogordo Bombing Range, in the Jornada del Muerto desert."

Caleb muttered, "Dead Man's Journey," translating the prophecy. Dick met his eyes.

"Holy smokes," Harry called out, clutching his chest.

Oppenheimer ordered, "After this announcement, we won't speak in these terms again. From here on out, the official code name for the test will be 'the baby.'"

"Weird name for it, if you ask me," murmured Harry, scratching his chin. Caleb felt like he must have dreamed the name. He searched helplessly for Alice in the crowd.

"The baby is due on July sixteenth," Oppie continued. No one said anything. In the company of so many scientific minds where numbers determined the order of things, the fact of a numerical date made the dream undeniably real for the army of physicists. A countdown had started. They had two months left to solve an equation and save the world. Caleb glanced at Dick. His young face had twisted into a pink knot. He was grinding away at something with his jaw.

"I have elected to name the baby 'Trinity,'" Oppenheimer continued. "I chose this name, not solely for its religious symbolism, but in commemoration of John Donne's poetry."

Caleb remembered Alice reciting Donne once on a hike. It had been the first snow of the season, and the fresh powder and the quiet had made her seem even more beautiful, like she belonged there among the snowcapped trees, a part of the frozen ecosystem. Her cheeks had flushed when she had said something about her father making her memorize the verse. He recalled it now aloud: "Batter my heart, three-personed God."

He realized Harry was staring at him. "He thinks who he is," Harry muttered. "He's talking about Jean Tatlock, ya know, with that reference. Everyone knows her daddy was an English professor. She was as much a highbrow as a communist." The town hadn't forgotten the drama of his suicidal love affair, and it seemed Oppie hadn't either. This was a man who loved his mistresses like his own family.

"I didn't think he'd go through with it," said Dick. He rushed off like he had somewhere to be. He squeezed between bystanders, and the hole closed up behind him. Caleb chased after him, but he was lost to the crowd.

Caleb scanned the audience, parsing reactions, and still searching for Alice. A whole sea of people had just learned what they were building, and emotions were flying high. So long as Oppenheimer kept talking, he could keep riotous protesting and infighting at bay. Alice, on the other hand, was smart enough to know what the research meant and what they were up against, and that was almost worse than the SEDs who were just now making guesses based on movies and superstition. He saw the back of Saul's head a few rows ahead, pacing back and forth. He had finally had his bandage removed and replaced with metal splints, and the concealed skin had gone gray and lifeless. It didn't seem to be bouncing back. The lumps of his deformed hand and the dark stitches against the pale flesh reminded Caleb of Frankenstein's monster. He could smell the rancid odor of decay wafting back to him on the wind. Or maybe he was just imagining it.

"Saul," he said in a forced whisper, shaking him, keeping his eyes locked on Oppenheimer. "Have you seen Alice?"

"I knew it," Saul said, his eyes glazed over. "I knew it was nothing good we were doin' here. But I never imagined in my wildest dreams. We're murderers."

On the podium, Oppenheimer elaborated on the plans for the "celebration." What he described sounded eerily similar to the Fourth of July. He would host a barbecue at a nearby base camp, and all the scientists would watch the bomb from a safe viewing distance. While he cataloged the holiday, Caleb knew that all the logical minds around him were fully aware the world might end on July 16, 1945. "It's time to tell your wives," Oppenheimer said, "and kiss your children."

Finally, crowds parted and there she was, standing at the foot of the water tower. She was staring up at the empty podium while everyone around her argued. Some of the men were shoving each other, pointing fingers. Others were celebrating.

"Alice," Caleb said, reaching protectively for her belly, "let's get you out of here." He escorted her away and watched her closely while around them, the mesa went up in a blur of activity and dust.

"You knew," she said flatly.

"Knew what?"

"You knew," she repeated. "And you let me go on like this."

"Alice," he began, but she held up a slender finger to silence him.

"What world will be left if our child is cursed enough to be born?"

He recoiled. He'd had the same fears racing around in the back of his mind while he read up on pregnancy and parenting. But for her sake, he had to try to be hopeful. "Maybe a world without Hitler. A democracy. A world order."

"That's a lot to ask of men who are busy playing God."

"It is," he agreed. "But what other choice do we have?" He took her hand amid the chaos. She stared at his fingers on hers, expressionless for a beat. They were in the middle of the turmoil, but they were still in public. She flinched and pulled her hand away.

"If we live through this, what will you do?" she asked finally.

"I'll finish my degree, marry you, and give you the life you deserve," he said without hesitation. It was only after he said it that he regretted it. He hadn't meant to lie. But there was no way he could afford it. What life could he truly offer her?

She nodded and began to sob quietly beside him. He'd never wanted to believe his own words more.

In the lab that week, the scientists conferred rapidly about outcomes. The explosive impact of energy might start a chain reaction leading to other unknown explosions. The atmosphere itself could catch fire.

The physicists organized an informal betting pool over the size of the pre-ordained explosion. They congregated in the hallways of the tech area, leaning or squatting against the walls, taking frequent breaks from their research to argue over the future in frantic whispers. The official scientific prediction was twenty thousand tons of TNT. But this was not a popular suggestion among the scientists, who waged bets that ran from zero to forty-five thousand tons.

Things reached a climax at a movie night in Fuller Hall. The scientists and their wives reclined on haybales while *Masie Goes to Reno* lit their faces in shifting flashes of light. But no one was watching the film. Caleb was seated cross-legged between Alice and Dick on the floor. The smell of Alice's perfume mingled with the buttered popcorn and the metallic tang of sweat in the room.

Caleb and Alice had been inseparable since Oppie's announcement. There was a book of baby names in the common room, and they had thumbed through it together. At meal times they talked about San Francisco neighborhoods with good schools. All the while, Alice had a clipped look on her face, like she was holding her breath. Aside from during the immediate aftermath of Oppie's announcement, they hadn't dared discussed the bomb, or the fact that Caleb had lied to her. It was as though the topic was too fragile, too threatening to the future they had dreamed up, to utter aloud. They also hadn't touched, even behind closed doors. Any time his skin grazed hers, she shuddered and moved away. Caleb was determined to be patient. There was nothing to do but wait for her to be ready to let him back in and hope they lived long enough to meet their baby.

Now, seated on the floor, Caleb was uncomfortable, and he kept shifting his weight around. His legs kept going numb. Whenever he leaned near her, Alice leaned almost imperceptibly away. Neither Dick nor Alice had said anything since the film had begun.

The brilliant and speculative scientist Isidor Rabi interrupted the film. He stood up in the middle of the projection, casting a man-shaped hole into the picture, and wagered his prediction loud enough for everyone to hear, "Eighteen thousand tons." Everyone turned to look. He stared back at the crowd. It had never been done before, this sort of acknowledgment of what was being built, in front of the wives. Rabi was challenging them to break protocol. And why not—they were as good as dead anyhow. The glow of the film lit his glasses, concealing his eyes. His claim hung over their heads momentarily while the film rattled on.

Then, Hans Bethe stood up too. "Eight thousand tons," he guessed. He had dark circles under his eyes that Caleb hadn't noticed before. Behind Bethe, the men on his theoretical team exchanged nervous looks, grinding their jaws like cows chewing cud, and their balding scalps shone in the projected light. Nearby, Fred tilted his head back and took a long, sinister pull of his drink, staring hard at Alice. He hadn't tried to approach her since that night of the party at Oppenheimer's house, but he was always staring at her. Caleb saw her stiffen.

Kistiakowsky spoke with clout. He headed the entire explosives testing group and worked intimately with the trigger device, so his hypothesis was not to be easily dismissed. He projected across the crowd: "I predict a figure closer to fourteen hundred." After that, the betting took a sudden turn.

"I bet it will ignite the atmosphere," ventured a young scientist in the back of the room, his voice heavy with emotion. That started everyone grumbling. Somebody paused the film, and Ann Sothern stood frozen on the screen in her evening dress, with three wiggling lines trisecting the frame.

"I think it will destroy all of New Mexico," asserted a vapid response in the front.

"He don't know from nothin'," said Dick beside him. "Push comes to shove, it'll destroy all the world." His affect was cold. Arline had been doing worse lately. Caleb thought of placing his hand on Dick's shoulder but hesitated.

Afterward, nervous energy hung in the air while the movie concluded. Dick picked at his fingernails and Alice stared straight ahead, ignoring Caleb's concerned glances. When the credits rolled, nobody said a word. Everyone seemed afraid to make the first move after what had transpired. The lights came up, and after some hesitation, the room slowly came back to life. "Well, better get back to the grind," said Dick finally, hopping to his feet.

"You're headed back to the T? Now?" Caleb asked.

Dick shrugged. His eyes were bloodshot.

Caleb walked Alice home in silence. She was halfway through her door, and he had already trotted back down the steps when she turned back.

"What's your wager?" she asked. "I gotta know."

He paused with his back turned and gazed up at the winking stars. According to Alice's meticulous research, the stars weren't actually there anymore. To look at the night sky was to look at the past. Yesterday was sparkling overhead. He took his time picking his words. "Oh, you know," he said, dodging the question. "I've no money to wager."

Dick strode frantically back and forth in the lab, scribbling diagrams on the chalkboard and talking electron volts with renewed tenacity.

"Dick," Caleb asked, feeling it out. "When's the last time you had a bite to eat?"

"Who has time to eat?" Dick rubbed his eyes. "Every day that passes is one day less to get it right."

"If you go belly-up before Judgment Day, that's one less genius to keep us alive."

"I can't eat a bite," Dick said, staring at the chalk in his hand like he didn't recognize it. His face changed, his gaze settling on Caleb. "You work on Project Rufus," he said, his golden eyes flickering. "Tell me everything you know."

"I'll tell you over dinner."

A little while later, in the mess hall, Dick threw his head back and belly laughed at Caleb's description.

"Fat-heads," he said. His eyes were tearing. He snorted and launched back into another round of hysterics. Caleb pushed the potato salad around on his plate. Nothing about this was funny.

Finally, Dick stopped laughing and wiped his eyes with his napkin. His cheeks had flushed and his face glimmered with excitement. He seemed younger than he had in all the months Arline had been sick, animated by this proximity to danger. "What you're describing is suicide," Dick said. "If it's really a plutonium core surrounded by tungsten carbide." His grin vanished. "Otto Frisch might as well be tickling the tail of a dragon."

Behind him, outside the window, the snow was falling in thick, puffy flakes. Caleb's mind drifted through the weather into that dimly lit room where the Rufus core was watching him from across the canyon.

"Can I see it?" Dick asked, pushing his tray to the center of the table and leaning forward. He had barely touched his food, and the oatmeal on his plate had congealed.

"Whole place is closed off," he said. "Besides, why on earth would you want to do that?"

"I've seen just about every other way there is to die," said Dick. "This one might just be the ticket." Caleb feared, as he had many times in the recent weeks, that Dick had a death wish.

Dick cupped his palm and tried to light a cigarette. But the match kept going out. It was then that Caleb realized Dick's hands were trembling.

First thing Monday morning, Caleb demanded answers. "Tell me, Harry— what exactly do you *do* in here?" All this time, he hadn't had the courage to ask about Project Rufus outright. He was only in there part-time, and all the work was dangerous. But if Dick was right, this project meant death. Panic was rising in him, but first he had to be sure.

The two faded into a quiet corner while Frisch debated something with Slotin in his heavy Austrian accent. "I mean, what's it *for*?" He nodded at the orb. "It's functional, right?"

"You betcha," said Harry, grinning ear to ear. He had gotten something stuck in his teeth at breakfast, and Caleb stared at it, trying to figure whether it was spinach or broccoli. "It's the heart of a boat," he said, using the code word for "bomb," even though now everything was out in the open. Caleb had figured that much, standing around taking notes, but he hadn't allowed himself to consider the implications. Even after the red-card meeting, when he made the leap to fissile energy, he hadn't revisited the issue of the core. Next to them, the orb was so bright to look at, it gave off the impression it was floating over the dull metals making up the platform on which it rested. When he finally looked away, the imprint of its rotund shape remained stamped in a white gaping hole in his vision. Everywhere he looked, he saw plutonium.

"It's a simulation," Harry explained. "With a thicker material, we can reflect the neutrons coming out of the core back on itself like a mirror," he said. Using the designated code words, he described the risky procedure of assembling an explosion of Uranium-235, leaving a large hole, so that when the missing core of uranium hydride was dropped into the waiting chasm, it would cause the material to go supercritical, but only for a fraction of a second. Caleb clenched. Dick had been right about everything. "Just think what we can learn"—Harry winced—"as long as we don't get roasted."

"So that's why all the security?" He nodded at the guards with slow understanding.

"Can't be too careful," he said. "It's too close to the action for most. Don't tell me you're goin' to transfer too?"

"Sorry?"

"Your honey, Dr. Katz, put in for a transfer to a different project last week."

"I didn't realize," he said, wondering if it was because of the pregnancy. Why wouldn't she have told him? It made him wonder what else she was hiding behind her pinched expression. He wasn't even sure they were really together these days. She could hardly look at him. He spent so much time daydreaming about their future, about pushing a stroller along the Embarcadero in the fog while the streetlights shifted red to green. But he was plagued by her icy silence across the dinner table. He wanted nothing more than to marry her, but he couldn't shake the nagging thought that she'd never actually said yes. What if they survived the bomb, and the war ended, and then she didn't want him after all? It would be better to die, for the atmosphere to catch fire. He realized Harry was staring at him, scratching his head. He had to say something, and quick. "I don't think SEDs get a choice. I'll probably be here long after you," he grunted.

"Good," Harry barked. "Besides, you're more likely to get killed crossin' the street in Santa Fe."

"Sure."

"But you never know. That's why the strict list of operating rules, you know, since the smallest mistake means suicide."

Caleb's panic must have shown on his face because Harry placed a concerned hand on his shoulder. His palm was soft and plump as a knish. "That's why we don't work alone," he said. "And we keep the engines in our cars running and the doors open so if we need to escape, we can run."

T-Minus 9

January 1946
Haruki: A Story Told Backward

On New Year's Day, in his Imperial Rescript, the emperor issued his official statement: "The ties between Us and Our people have always stood upon mutual trust and affection . . . They are not predicated on the false conception that the Emperor is divine, and that the Japanese people are superior to other races and fated to rule the world." Around the world, debate spiraled about the exact meaning of Hirohito's archaic Japanese. He never explicitly denied his divinity, although the West hailed the statement as a "Humanity Declaration."

Haruki read the rescript over and over, trying to make sense of the use of the word "akitsumikami" rather than the more common word, "arahitogami," meaning *living god*. He seemed to have avoided that word on purpose. The emperor never directly denied his tie to the gods.

That afternoon, as he underwent excruciating pain clutching the parallel bars for balance while his physical therapist moved his legs to simulate walking, he wondered what the rescript meant for the kamikaze. If there was a chance that the emperor wasn't divine, and if the Japanese people weren't a superior race, what did that make of all the deaths on the battlefield? If the messianic soldiers would never be rewarded in the afterlife, were their bodies just decomposing at the bottom of the ocean? Were they rolling in the waves, being fed on by fish and sea birds?

His therapist instructed him to lift one leg and then the other for balance, and he tried not to think about the algae taking root on the remains of the dead warriors, the anemones and starfish swallowing their features and nesting in their cavities until their bones became a coral reef, coded in a network of polyps. He tried not to think of the Yasukuni Shrine forever awaiting their arrival, cavernous and empty.

186

"Don't be so hard on yourself," his therapist said when he winced. "It takes time to reeducate your muscles. Before you know it, it will be muscle memory."

"I can't do it," he gasped, collapsing on the bars. The pain of the last six months was cumulative.

"It's not *you*. It's your vestibular system," she said, implicating his eyes, muscles, and inner ear's ability to send signals to the brain.

Feeling the cold steel bars against his skin, he wondered why he was still alive. At home, beneath black clouds, human remains were attracting flies. There was no headstone he could visit to mourn his family. No flowers would ever grow from the place they had died. Two words filled his mind and he held them in like he was holding his breath. In Japanese, implying both honor and self-determination, there were two words for *suicide*.

21

May 1945
Alice

"Alice, come quick!" Bonnie rapped on her door. It was a little before eight in the morning, and Alice was still in her nightgown. By the time she had made herself decent, unbolted the lock, and pried loose the screen, she could just make out the tail of Bonnie's robe flapping behind her. She trailed her to the common room, which was packed with huddled residents. Everyone stared at the television. Judith had gotten there early and had claimed one of the few upholstered chairs. She was dabbing her eyes with a handkerchief and smiling through tears while Milo scribbled in a coloring book at her feet.

"What's happened?" Alice asked, sidling up to Bonnie, who seemed to only realize in the presence of the crowded room that she was undressed. She pulled her robe closed around her frilly nightgown.

"Part two," said Bonnie soberly. "Or if you'd rather, a parallel universe."

Alice noticed Caleb in the back of the room in his civilian clothes, alongside Dick, who was unshaven, and Harry, who was puffing on a cigar. Harry's clothes looked rumpled, like he'd slept in them, and Dick's hair had grown long enough that he needed to tie it back. Caleb glanced up when she entered and gave her a weak smile. She felt his eyes on her while the coffee maker whirred and dribbled into the pot. A precarious stack of board games teetered on the table, ignored by the onlookers. Bonnie's husband, Vic, got up to adjust the rabbit ear antenna and the screen buzzed through the static, homing in on a military voice speaking in crescendos. She leaned in.

"Again, we are confirming the death of Adolf Hitler. Though the details remain unclear at this hour, Hamburg Radio is reporting that Adolf Hitler is dead."

Everyone started talking at once.

"There were mass suicides in Berlin this morning when the news broke," said Judith, pulling Milo close with his fistfuls of crayons. "Parents shot their children before shooting themselves."

"Mommy, you're squeezing me," Milo protested.

"I'm sorry, honey," Judith said, but she didn't loosen her grip.

"*Promise me you'll shoot yourself*," said Bonnie beside her. "That was the battle call—in German, of course." Alice hadn't looked at her very closely in all the adrenaline, and only now she noticed that Bonnie's blonde hair was still twisted in purple curlers and her eyes looked tired without makeup.

The more they learned, the more questions they had. Rumors abounded—some sources claimed that Hitler was killed by an exploding shell as he walked down the steps of his Berlin chancellery. Others reported that after arguing over the continuation of the war, his own Nazi leaders had placed a bomb in his underground fortress and blown him to pieces.

The predominant theory was that Hitler, knowing they were defeated, had taken his own life via cyanide. He and Eva had retreated to their private room where they bit into the glass capsules, side by side, like Romeo and Juliet. Just in case, Hitler also shot himself in the head. He was rumored to have died fully upright on the couch, his pistol laying on the floor, having fallen from his hand.

"However he went, it's cause for celebration," said Harry, puffing out plumes from his cigar in the back of the room.

"Hear, hear!" cheered several others, toasting and clinking coffee mugs.

"How do we know the bastard's really dead?" asked one of the SEDs, citing reports about body doubles. "Nobody's been able to produce a corpse. It could be a bunch of hoopla."

A momentary silence descended over the celebrations, and then everyone started shouting over each other.

"Don't be a fat-head. Hitler's deader than a doorknob."

"If they poured gasoline over the body, there'd be nothing to find. What more do you want?"

"You saw it with your own eyes—his jarring walk and the tremor in his left hand. He was already good as dead."

"He was just a junkie—hopped up on Pervitin and cocaine."

Suddenly, as though he was some sort of desert messiah having already lost his hand to the war, Saul stood up in the heart of the room. He stood with such urgency that he seemed to be levitating, his feet barely touching the ground. Alice tried not to stare at his splinted, unbandaged limb. She'd heard the rumors that he'd lost all feeling in the stump, that only last week he'd slammed it in a car door without noticing. Now, his somber presence and his mangled body demanded attention. Finally, the frantic arguments quieted and everyone turned to him.

"You know," he said, "I only came here because Hitler called quantum physics Jewish science—to Einstein, no less. But if Hitler was our reason for building the gadget," he said, finding the words slowly, "who's the target now?"

Alice glanced over at Caleb and found his eyes glued on her. It made her pulse race. In all the hours they'd spent together, she had been trying to forgive him for lying. She wanted to have hope for their future together, but her body tensed up when he was close to her. Could she trust him? Was it possible to be so furious with someone and love them at the same time? That was his baby growing inside her. He'd said he would propose. He hadn't done it yet, but given the chance, would he?

The broken look on his face at Saul's words would be permanently imprinted in her mind, she thought. Beside him, Harry stubbed out his cigar, his expression gone grim. Dick Feynman stood up and stormed out of the room like something had bit him. Caleb chased after him.

The frantic conspiracy theories and debates about Hitler's death ramped up as additional narratives hit the news. A rumor attributed to Heinrich Himmler had it that Hitler had died of a cerebral hemorrhage on April 24. A United Press war correspondent liberated after eight months in captivity claimed Hitler had been dead for over a year. Soviet soldiers reported digging deep into the rubble of the Reich chancellery in search of a corpse that seemed to have vanished into thin air. There were frantic rumors that Hitler was on his way to Japan in a U-boat. Nervous energy filled the labs amid the unknowns as the test date loomed closer. The desert warmed and bloomed, but with every cactus flower that opened, Alice heard the clock ticking.

Worse still, she was starting to show. Her baby bump had grown from the size of an heirloom tomato to the size of a sweet potato. She could conceal it under high-waisted dresses and baggy jackets, but as the weather heated up, it would be harder to hide.

She looked down at her weather-beaten fingernails. She had changed so much in the desert. No longer the singular self she had once been, she was a homogenous mixture, like sugar water or steel. The old parts of her identity couldn't simply be teased out. She could never go back to the way things were. It suffocated her thinking about it. She was utterly, helplessly, in love with Caleb. She wanted to live her life with him. He'd been dishonest, she knew, but then, he'd only meant to protect her. Learning to communicate took time, and he'd come from a world where people didn't talk about things, where intimacy itself was aberrant. It was his heart she wanted.

She bolted upright in bed. This was her whole life's happiness at stake. Coming to this decision, she was suddenly overcome with a need to tell Caleb immediately, to find him right then and there. She cinched a trench coat around her nightgown and raced to the barracks. She rapped on the door, her heart fluttering.

Her chest sank when Saul answered, chewing on a cigarette. He looked at her bemused, the trace of a knowing smile on his face. She wondered fleetingly what Caleb had told him about her. "Caleb's in the computing room," he said, nodding across the mesa in the direction of the lab. "He hides out there with Dick when he gets fired up."

Alice hadn't seen Saul's stumped arm up close before. It was discolored and marred by stitches, and he was using the suction from the folds of the appendage like a hand to prop open the door. He caught her looking and she averted her eyes.

"It ain't so bad." He grinned. "I can't lace up my boots, but the army don't make me make my bed anymore."

"Oh, I didn't mean to stare."

"It's quite all right," he said, placing his intact left hand on her shoulder to assure her. They locked eyes for a moment, and she quickly broke the gaze. "You know," he said, as she turned to leave, "Caleb's a good guy. And he loves you. But in my book, a girl like you deserves to know."

"Know what?" She turned back and faced him head on.

He flinched and scratched his head. Then he stepped out into the blooming light. He stretched, taking his time. "Lord forgive me," he said, staring up at the sky, puffing out clouds on his cigarette. "Caleb will never finish his degree." He drew a shape in the dust with his toe and stared at it. "Look, I love him like a brother, but you spend your life doing things with two hands and then you lose one and it gives a little perspective. You deserve to know what you're getting into, even if you might not live to see it through."

Whatever it was, she didn't really want to know. But she had a sinking feeling, and realized there was no turning back. She braced. "What on earth do you mean?"

"I mean, there's no money left. He can't afford to go back to school. He'll never get out of the Fillmore. Odds are, he'll never ask you to marry him because he's too ashamed and can't afford another mouth to feed. And if, God forbid, you do marry him, it'll be you stuck there with him too. You can kiss being a professor goodbye."

Alice sank down into one of the folding chairs. The lapels of her trench coat flapped in the breeze, revealing the folds of her lacy nightgown. She crossed her legs, the frills of the slinky fabric visible, spread across her knees like flower petals. She was indecent. She didn't care. She thought of the conferences, the publications, the lecture series she'd pictured for her future. She thought of Abigail rinsing her microscope with distilled water. In his own way, she realized, Caleb had been trying to warn her. She felt Saul staring at her hungrily. She didn't have the strength to stand, to pull her hair into twists, to button up. She was exhausted. On some level, she had known Caleb was lying about finishing his degree. He had already lied about everything else.

She thought of her mother's furs, her father's discarded oxfords by the fireplace. Her life was composed of silver polish, leather totes, and brick facades. While Caleb had been counting up spare change for the dirty city buses, Alice had been driven around in her family's Coupe de Ville. She and Caleb hadn't frequented the same intersections. They never would have met if not for the horror they were building in the lab.

Alice burst into the computing room, startling Caleb, Dick, and Harry, all three of whom were bent over a row of enormous PCAM machines. Dick was chewing on a toothpick and grinned at her, his eyes flashing with mischief. He elbowed Caleb. "Now you've done it, Ace."

Alice ignored him. "Tell me the truth for once," she ordered Caleb.

"That's my cue to leave," said Harry. As he turned, he tripped over an extension cord and collided with a control panel that was swung wide open, tangling with the exposed wires. The scroll of paper that was being fed through the machine, churning out stilted lines of calculations, jammed and an error code flashed. He straightened, brushed himself off, and having stubbed his toe, limped out of the room.

Dick trotted after him. "Hoo boy, wait up!" He turned back to address Caleb and gave a helpless shrug. "I wasn't sure I was so fond of the kid," he said, meaning Harry, "but one thing's for sure—he knows how to make a grand exit!"

But Caleb only had eyes for Alice. Dick saw that his friend's mind was elsewhere. "As for you, Ace, Godspeed!" Dick saluted and darted into the hall.

Alice marched up to Caleb, jabbing him in the chest. "Be straight with me. What are your plans when you leave here?"

"Alice," Caleb said, his face wan and serious. "I meant every word I said. I just need a little time." He scratched his head. "You're accustomed to a certain . . . lifestyle. And I want to provide that. For you and the baby. Not a penny less."

Alice's palm found her belly. "We don't have time. This baby is coming whether you're cash poor or not."

His face dropped.

Even when she was so mad at him, she pitied him. *Stay angry*, she urged herself. Despite everything, she softened. "Caleb," she sighed. "I can take care of myself. I always have. And my family . . . they'll be furious, especially my mother, but they will help. I just want to know you'll be a part of this baby's life."

Behind Caleb's specs, his light eyes were unreadable.

"And," she continued, her voice shaking, "I need to know that you'll go back to school. That's no small thing to me."

He stiffened. His hand, which was still glued to the PCAM machine, went rigid like a claw.

"Someday," he said. "I truly want to. Honest. But at the moment, that's a luxury a guy like me can't afford."

She stepped closer to him. "A guy like you?"

His eyes were suddenly glued to the tile pattern on the floor.

His voice dropped to a whisper. "Oppenheimer grew up on Riverside Drive. They have Picassos, Vuillards, and Van Goghs hanging in their living room. Meanwhile, my mother sold a tooth to pay for my tuition. I'm hiding in plain sight."

Alice was suddenly aware of how close they were standing. Their boots were almost touching. If she wanted to, she could reach out and place her palm on his cheek. But instead, she placed both hands rigidly on her hips and stared at him fiercely.

"If this gonna work," she said, "you're gonna have to let me in. I'm raisin' this baby with you. And you need to stop trying to be perfect and just be."

"You weren't meant to end up with me," he said, turning away. "I'm supposed to be a page in your diary, then you live happily ever after with a doctor or a lawyer."

"Yeah, well, Warren's dead." She felt a sudden rush of emotion, like she had forgotten it until just that moment. Her mind flashed to Abigail—the time she had chopped her hair into a bob back in high school and the math equations she had solved in lipstick on the bathroom mirror in the middle of the night. "I don't have a past to speak of. If we survive this," she turned to leave, refusing to let herself look at him and see what was written on his face, "I'd like you to be my future."

22

June–July 1945
Caleb

Like someone had flipped a switch, the weather had turned blazing hot. In the middle of the melting landscape, the test preparations began. In the Jornada del Muerto desert, army trucks containing hundreds of mattresses encircled the designated tower. Nervous about the danger of any sort of turbulence after the gadget had been hoisted the first fifteen feet up the firing tower, residents had gathered piles and piles of laundry and placed it under the contraption to cushion a potential fall. Great piles of linens loomed toward heaven, in patterns of stripes, solid cottons, and army-issued sheets stamped with the words "US Military."

Scientists craned their necks watching GIs wind the gadget one hundred feet into the air, and haphazardly piled more and more bedding beneath it, just in case. In addition, they'd decided to utilize a 25-foot, 214-ton steel vessel to encase the bomb, which they lovingly christened "Jumbo." After transporting it across railroads and on custom-built sixty-four wheel flatbeds all the way out to the test site, the men began to have doubts.

"What if it sends jagged pieces of metal hurtling across New Mexico?" asked Saul, staring up at the contraption. He wore his mangled stump inside his shirt, curled into the cavity of his chest, so his empty sleeve hung limp. "Or worse, what if the steel impacts our calculations?"

Caleb stared at the device teetering in the air for a very long time. He hadn't been sure of anything as the work ramped up. Since their confrontation, Alice had been avoiding him. It was his move. He had no desire to be a hero, risking it all. He didn't want to die before seeing her again. He was trying his best to hide his heartbreak from Saul, but he couldn't help moping. "I still don't understand why we're goin' through with this with Hitler dead and gone."

Saul shrugged. "It bothered me at first. But then I realized. You don't just kill someone like Hitler. It's like a disease. You gotta stamp it out."

"How do you mean?"

"I mean, Hitler never killed anybody."

"Come again?"

"Think about it. Hitler never got his hands dirty." Saul seemed aggravated, but it might have just been the heat. There was no shade in the desert, and they were sweating through their shirts. "All those people shoveling bodies into ovens were following the laws of their country. This"—Saul nodded at the steel casing, swaying overhead—"is the only hand we've got left to play." He averted his eyes, seeming embarrassed by his use of the word "hand." Or maybe it was something else. He had an almost guilty look, like everything was his fault.

When it was time to set up camp, Caleb struggled to pull himself away from the construction site. He turned his back on Jumbo, but he could feel the contraption rocking from its wires, swinging behind him like a hung man.

The test site was a good distance from the population in Santa Fe, so they figured it should afford the scientists the opportunity to measure the fall-out without any immediate dangers to the inhabitants. It was a practice bombing and air gunnery range, so in theory, a large explosion shouldn't turn any heads. That logic, of course, did not take into account the Hispano and Mescalero Apache tribal families who lived just downwind. And then there was the concern that the scientists themselves might not survive the initial blast.

Caleb couldn't help marveling at the irony. He hadn't spoken to Asher since their strange phone call, but he committed every detail to memory of the B-29 and B-17 planes that soared overhead every morning, eager to tell him about their tails of smoke and the force with which they cut through the sky in military formation. Asher would know the weight and draft of each model. He would know what it felt like to steer straight up into the firmament. In his own way, Caleb had found wings. But unlike his brother's bird's-eye view of the ocean jostling and glistening like shattered glass, his cockpit was sealed with government secrets.

By mid-July, the heat flared. Dead flowers hung their heads. The temperature hovered above 100 degrees Fahrenheit. There were almost five hundred men stationed at base camp, broiling in the summer heat. They stripped down to shorts and removed their shirts, revealing pale flesh.

The day before the test, Groves and Oppenheimer made their way to their designated positions. They were not to be in the same place at the same time so that if something catastrophic happened, one of them would still be there to provide order. Groves stayed near the bunkers at base camp and made plans, if necessary, to evacuate nearby towns and institute martial law. By contrast, Oppenheimer wanted to witness the explosion with his own eyes.

Dutifully, Caleb joined the ranks of the scientists on their final pilgrimage to base camp. It felt like a death march. The army of misfits reported to "safe" viewing grounds. Each of them had prepared in their own small ways. They mapped out escape routes from the test site. When they drifted off to sleep at night, they recited their evacuation plans through the desert—their Los Alamos lullabies. Some wrote in journals or sent letters. Others kissed their children. Most stayed awake all night.

When they stood at attention and underwent inspections, one young SED, his lips gone white from severe dehydration, collapsed. His knees buckled and he fell hard, hitting his head. The noise startled Caleb, who broke from his salute. Everyone swarmed the young man, fanning him and pouring water down his parched lips. They were excused early, and most took cover from the sun in their tents.

When Caleb retreated to his shared tent, Pavlov trotted to greet him, and he found Alice waiting for him on his bedroll. He'd been longing for her to turn up for so long, it took Caleb a moment to register that she was there. But he couldn't turn off the countdown in his head. With only eight hours between them and the scheduled test, every minute was accounted for.

They were enclosed, zipped into the cocoon of the tent, but other recruits were reclining on bedrolls nearby, playing cards and thumbing through magazines. Alice whispered, eyeing the men around them: "I've found a bed and breakfast far enough away that I should be out of harm's way . . ." She hesitated. "If things go south."

"There's somethin' I've been meaning to say to you," he began.

"I've been waiting for you to say it," she said stiffly. "You're hiding out here, avoiding me."

"Alice," he whimpered, reaching for her.

She shrugged him off. "I know, Caleb. You can't marry me because you're already married to the Fillmore."

She'd said what he feared most in the world. He stared down at his hands, unsure where to put them or how to stand. He was erased in every way a man can be erased.

"We can't talk here," he said when Two Face looked up at Alice with interest from his magazine. "Let's walk."

A gust of wind rattled the armature of the tent. They unzipped it and scanned the desert horizon that was spread as far as they could see. The sun had gone down, but they couldn't see the stars. The heat had not yet subsided in the darkness. Overhead, thunder cracked, and a flash of lightning broke the sky in half. For an instant, it lit the whole camp, then the rain started with such force that they ducked. The downpour felt biblical. Caleb couldn't shake a nervous feeling that nature was warning them away.

He held a newspaper over his head and trotted beside Alice, who was following Pavlov's lead through the sideways sheets of rainwater. Pregnancy had exaggerated her bust, and he stole a look at the way her blouse clung to her chest. Raindrops dripped down her nose and weighed down her eyelashes. He would have liked to think she was crying, but he knew she was far too practical for any such display of sentimentality.

They walked wordlessly, soaked to the bone, taking shelter finally under a canopy. The rainwater plinked out musical scales on the metal frame and the nylon roof. Unbothered by the downpour, Pavlov splashed through puddles and pointed his quivering nose up into the weather.

"Right," Alice said. "I'm all ears."

"Please be patient with me," he begged. "I am trying. I can't just turn my back on my past."

"No one is asking you to," Alice spewed. "If I've learned anything from starlight, it's that it is possible to have both a past and a future simultaneously."

Caleb ran a hand through his curls. "You picked an awful weird time to talk about the future," he said, scanning the peaks of the tents through the mist and the downpour.

She sighed and threw up her hands. "You can't say I didn't try." Then she stormed off toward her car. He chased her out into the weather and grabbed her arm, the same way he had that first night by Ashley Pond, dropping his newspaper into the puddle at their feet where it warped, the fibers separating.

She stared at him, the mask of her composure wilting, melted by the buckets of rain. "You could just ask me. I don't understand what's stopping you," she said weakly. "Tomorrow might as well be seventy years away. But I would say yes."

He stared at her shape through the rainwater. His glasses were so fogged up he could barely see her. He played dumb: "Ask you what?"

She looked like she'd had the wind knocked out of her—her mouth fell open, but no words came out for a beat. "If you ask me to marry you," she said finally, "I'll stay the night here with you. If the world ends, at least we'll be together for it."

It was everything he'd ever wanted. But he worried over the sacrifice she would be making, the world she'd be giving up, the limitations of what he had to offer. He had never been enough for anyone; how could he be enough for this woman who owned every room she entered?

Dejected, she averted her eyes. The rain was pelting her sideways, flipping her hair around. She didn't make a move to fix it.

In the distance, men were shouting. Some dynamite had gone off, and they were fleeing and shouting, terrified of potentially triggering additional fuses in proximity to the gadget. Caleb realized with a sudden urgency that he had to get Alice out of there.

"Alice," he tried to reason, "you can't stay the night."

"I'm so tired of being told what I can't do." She was shaking. She'd catch a cold. The lightning was flashing, lighting her up like flashbulbs.

"You have to get out of here. Things are escalating."

"I spent my career imagining what it would be like, hearing the stars. This will be the sound of a thousand stars right here on earth. I have every reason to stay."

Her expression turned. She was determined. But he couldn't let her spend the night here and be incinerated in the explosion, or else wake up so close to radioactive fallout, breathing in toxic air. Who knew if any of them would live? And what might it do to the baby? The longer he waited, the more he put her in danger. But still, she stood there, waiting for him to love her. He knew she'd never get in her car and leave unless he broke her heart. Even though every fiber of his being wanted desperately to make her stay, to hear the sound of a thousand stars alongside her.

He knew what he had to say, but uttering it out loud would hurt him as much as it hurt her. "Alice," he said, with careful eyes, "you don't love me. You never did. We both know you were just trying to sleep your way into the boys' club. You want your name recorded in the history books, but even that won't bring your sister back."

She made a single sound, a hollow suck of air. She stooped into the car and called for Pavlov, who bounded after her. When she disappeared behind the closed door, he felt the invisible threads that bound them together sever and snap. It was a chemical breakdown—a single chemical entity simplified into fragments.

After she drove away, he stared at the glowing red taillights of her Dodge until they disappeared.

As the storm raged on, it got harder to believe tomorrow would come at all. They were scheduled to detonate at 5:00 AM, but at 2:30 AM, thirty-mile-per hour winds swept the world sideways. The desert flooded, and they had to take cover from blowing sand. The rainflies of the tents flapped in the wind. The atmosphere kept catching fire—lightning illuminated the horizon like striking matches.

There was no point in trying to sleep. Caleb was certain that nobody was sleeping, but there they all were, an army of scientists lying in the dark, pretending. Twice, he had the sensation of something crawling on him and swept phantom scorpions from his bedroll in a panic. Around 3:00 AM, he gave up the ruse and got up to walk the camp, holding onto his hat in the sideways rain.

He saw Dick squinting straight up into the storm like a kid, getting drenched. He trotted up to him. From far away, it had seemed like a playful gesture, but up close, Dick had a desperate look in his eyes.

"What's good?" Caleb failed at sounding casual.

They walked silently side by side through the weather, their undershirts and cowboy jeans clinging to their bodies. They approached a small gathering of men finding temporary shelter under a canvas awning. A small waterfall poured from the eaves. Caleb recognized Louis Slotin's and Otto Frisch's faces in the flashes of lighting.

"Hallo," called Frisch in his heavy accent, greeting them without a trace of welcome in his tone. Harry was behind them, swatting at mosquitoes.

"We need to delay," Slotin said, ignoring the newcomers. "He's tryin' to toe the line, but he'll get us all killed." He meant Oppenheimer. He was dead set on running the test. They watched the dark horizon flashing with heat lightning then vanishing again on an endless cycle.

"Ja," said Frisch. His eyebrows pinched together.

"God knows what could happen," agreed Caleb.

"You said it, Ace," said Dick. "The weather could propel the gadget to Timbuktu."

Harry successfully clapped a bug and swatted it from his hands. "Has anyone heard from Oppenheimer?" he asked.

"He's been pacing in the military mess tent since midnight," said Caleb, nodding in the direction of the large tent that housed a buffet of mostly dry, salted, prepackaged foods.

The group made their way through the pelting rain, bowing their heads into the wind. Inside, they shook out their boots. A small gathering of men was pretending to pick at the food, but all eyes were on Oppenheimer. Caleb studied the director from between the stale bagels and the individually wrapped muffins.

Oppie was staring out the unzipped tent flap at the test site being racked by horizontal wind. The raindrops reflected on his cheeks, giving his skin a spectral look, like he wasn't all there. He stirred his instant coffee mechanically. "Perhaps God has his thumb on the scale," he said finally to the audience of waiting men.

"Sir?" asked Slotin, who stood closest to him, placing his cowboy hat over his heart.

Oppie took a slow gulp of his coffee then looked down at the dark liquid, rotating his mug with his wrist like it was a fine wine. He turned to face the onlookers. His hair had been slicked back, and Caleb could make out the squiggly toothed path left behind by the comb, but enough time had passed that the curls were beginning to break free and stand tall again. In the lantern light, his furry eyebrows cast heavy shadows, beneath which his eyes glittered. "So death doth touch the resurrection," he mumbled.

Caleb recognized the line from John Donne. He feared suddenly that this man who was the brains behind the whole operation had mistaken poetry for prayer.

Oppenheimer was a broken man, Caleb thought. It should be easy enough for this crowd of scientific minds to convince him to hold off. He still had time to drive across the desert, go after Alice, explain it all. These men could draw out the equations, they could hypothesize, and they could persuade him with reason and logic. Oppenheimer was already defeated, standing there, watching the desert flood through a canvas flap. But no one dared.

Caleb had never stood so close to Oppenheimer before, at least not without others pressing their way in front of him, even back in graduate school. He had always seemed larger than life, more myth than man. That's why he was surprised by how frail he seemed.

Caleb should hate him. This man was solely responsible for the turns his life had taken. It was Oppie who had drawn him across the Bay Bridge to Berkeley, away from his mother, leaving her alone to scrub wealthy people's houses. It was Oppie's science that had seduced him away from his father and sealed the coffin on his Jewish faith. It was men like this, men who flew too close to the sun and stole from the gods that had inspired Asher to take flight. And then, there was the morality. Oppenheimer had no remorse for the women he slept with. He'd left a trail of broken hearts all over New Mexico. If not for this man, Caleb never would have dared to so much as touch Alice's hand. And now she was unwed and with child.

Oppie began to pace, breaking the spell that had settled over the room. The wavering lantern light magnified his shadow into a monster on the wall behind him. He paused and turned to the audience of men before him with a pained expression. Instead of hating him, Caleb was overcome with pity.

He had the face of someone already dead.

T-Minus 8

September 1945
Haruki: A Story Told Backward

Haruki had been slipping in and out of consciousness for about a month. It was difficult to tell what was real. Behind his eyes, he wandered through the barren wasteland of ground zero. Even though he was breathing through a tube in a sterile hospital room, phantom smoke filled his lungs. A woman called for help in the distance. Her screams sounded like the beeping ventilator and heart monitor at his bedside, getting louder as he approached. When he reached out to help her, her skin peeled off in his hands.

Each time Haruki startled awake, he was stunned to learn that the war was over. He insisted on hearing it for himself, so, every time, the nurses would switch on the radio for him. Since he was meant to be godlike, most Japanese people had never heard Hirohito speak before. In fact, his surrender speech was the first time that most Japanese citizens had ever heard the voice of any emperor. Haruki was startled to hear Hirohito's voice cycling through an endless soundbite on the radio.

"Should we continue to fight, not only would it result in an ultimate collapse and obliteration of the Japanese nation, but also it would lead to the total extinction of human civilization." Hirohito spoke in formal Japanese. Rather than broadcasting directly, his speech was replayed from a phonograph recording with poor sound quality and characters missing. Consequently, his famous words went misunderstood by the vast majority of Japanese families, who were confused by both the accent and the poor audio. Since he made no direct reference to surrender, instead accepting the "joint declaration" of the United States, United Kingdom, China, and the Soviet Union, Japanese civilians were unsure whether or not they had surrendered. Haruki strained to hear, his dismembered ear aching and throbbing, a phantom limb. All he could think was that he had to find his family.

At the heart of the blast, the factory where his father worked, the building responsible for the torpedoes that had decimated Pearl Harbor, was incinerated. The Americans had targeted it on purpose. His mother was assumed dead, too, since her garment factory had been in an adjacent strip mall.

"Please," he begged his doctors while they treated his bedsores. "What has become of the schools?"

"According to recent reports," said a nurse gently, clearly weary from treating the dying in an overfilled, understaffed hospital, "seventy-eight schools were damaged."

"What has become of Honkawa Elementary School?"

Her face softened. She seemed to hesitate. "That was the campus closest to the bombing. The latest death toll was around four hundred students."

"Junko," he mourned, forgetting the nurse beside him.

When his sister was born, a surprise baby for his parents when Haruki was twelve, his parents had let him name her. When he first met her in the hospital, he had looked into her tiny face and chosen the name that meant *innocent child*. Since both of their parents worked long hours, their father at the torpedo manufacturing plant, and their mother sewing uniforms for the Imperial Army, she was always his responsibility. She was more like a daughter than a sister.

"Yes," the nurse said now, agreeing with the sentiment implied by Junko's name: *innocent children*.

"I have to go to her."

She gave him a pitying look. He wondered fleetingly how many families she had seen separated, searching for each other in the rubble. She patted his arm and he braced against the pain.

"You can't visit the site," she said. "It's radioactive." She turned away from him. "Besides, there's nobody left."

23

July 1945
Alice

She gripped the steering wheel with both hands. The rain was coming down so hard, she had to brace against it. The slippery road and jolting rocks beneath her tires kept taking control of the vehicle. There was no guardrail. She could easily spin out and end up in a ditch or nose-dive right off the side of the cliff. So what if she did, she thought bleakly, picturing the look on Caleb's face as she'd gotten into her car and driven away. There was no one to help her now, and no one to notice she had gone missing. Maybe it was better that way. She pressed the gas pedal to the floor, accelerating the force of gravity that propelled her down the hill, away from the secrets, back into the blissful ignorance of society.

Alice was the sort of driver who always sat up straight and held the wheel at ten and two. She never ate in her vehicle, and she wiped smudges from her mirrors, always double-checking their placement before she drove anywhere. She was careful about things. Now, she splashed through puddles that shined in the light on the road before her like silver coins. She ran her wipers, but they only rubbed the grime in. She leaned forward, squinting to see through the sheets of rainwater. What on earth was she doing here? She stared at her haggard, dirt-caked nails on the wheel. She didn't recognize her weather-beaten hands.

Back home, in civilized society, nothing would have changed. She could picture the sun sinking behind the bay, and the neon lights of San Francisco flickering awake beyond the Golden Gate Bridge. She missed the way the heat steamed up from the sewers on the Embarcadero, and the throngs of tourists dragging their screaming children, arguing in different languages on the piers.

She couldn't shake Caleb's parting words.

You don't love me. You never did. We both know you were just trying to sleep your way into the boys' club. You want your name recorded in the history books, but even that won't bring your sister back.

It was the most hurtful thing anyone had ever said to her. And yet, she couldn't help picturing a life with Caleb beneath the fog that hung like a low ceiling over San Francisco. She imagined herself in a wedding dress and Caleb beside her, standing straight as a rod in his suit. They would be like children playing dress-up, and beside them, their own small child.

But by tomorrow, all of San Francisco might be leveled into the ocean. Outside the car, the rain roared, nature rearing its head. She swerved abruptly to avoid a broken bottle. Her tires skidded, and for a moment, she felt weightless.

At the bed and breakfast, she bolt-locked her door. A lock couldn't keep out what was coming, but it made her feel a little bit better. She pulled off her wet clothes and towel dried her hair. Then she gingerly constructed a maze of crisscrossing wires for a makeshift Geiger counter. She tuned the dial on the shortwave radio, searching for Sam Allison's voice.

She had always liked Sam. He was a prominent figure—the head of the metallurgical lab at the University of Chicago. He was a no-nonsense kind of guy, and he had a severe look. Each day in the lab couldn't possibly all be watershed moments, but Sam insisted otherwise. He saw interconnected tributaries between every peer-reviewed study. He'd worked with Szilard and Fermi and had an impressive résumé and a complex understanding of the moving parts of the gadget. Alice had run into him only last week in Fuller Lodge and he'd said something about needing his watch fixed. "I've left messages and I've sent mail. What more can I do?" He'd described his black-faced A-11 wristwatch with complete hacking second-hand abilities, meant to be synced to precision with other military watches. "They don't realize," Sam had said, "that this watch might save the world."

Alice hadn't understood much of anything that he said that day. But later, it all became clear when she learned he'd been selected as the countdown man.

It wasn't until 5:30 AM that she heard Sam's voice on her radio. By then, her hair had dried, and the storm had softened to a patter on the roof. Through the window, the clouds had cleared enough that she could see the stars. She cranked the volume.

"T-minus thirty. T-minus twenty-nine."

She tried to focus on the landscape outside, but in those final seconds, she wondered about the lives of the residents that might be caught in the cross-fire of this test run. There were innocent families and children all over New Mexico who might be about to be swallowed up. As furious and hurt as she was, she worried for Caleb. If things failed, there would be nothing left of him, not even a body to bury. He would just vanish into the heart of the blast.

She thought about the fetus, rustling inside her. What kind of world would her child inherit? Then, for the first time, she began to wonder what would happen if the test worked. What came next? She had been chasing answers for so long, she'd forgotten to consider the ethics. Caleb was right. If all went to plan, her name would be remembered in the history of science—not just as a woman scientist, but as one of the mothers of the atomic bomb.

"Water is attracted to water," she mumbled, watching the lingering raindrops collect on the window. "Water is attracted to other substances."

In the final seconds of the countdown, she lost reception. Sam Allison's voice buzzed with static then was swallowed up into white noise. She tuned the dial but found nothing out there in the radio waves. *This was it*, she thought. *The beginning of the end*. She held onto the windowsill and braced, waiting for the atmosphere to ignite. She wondered, given the opportunity to say last words, if she would have anything to say.

She stared into the distance, pressing her forehead against the glass for a better look. Was that the sun rising out there on the horizon, or something else?

24

July 1945
Caleb

At 5:30 AM, five men threw the safety switches and sprinted for their Jeeps. One by one, everyone at base camp shielded their eyes with wellness glasses, except for Dick.

"Dick," Caleb nudged him, "you'll go blind." Dick continued to stare hard at the horizon, and Caleb realized that was the point. His friend was heartbroken. Arline had weeks left at best. To him, the world was ending whether the test worked or not. No wonder he had thrown himself so relentlessly into this work that would precipitate Armageddon. It was suicide.

They all lay facedown in the sand, turned 180 degrees away from the blast for safety. It looked like a war zone. Suddenly, an otherworldly white light filled the sky from corner to corner. It pulsed. The dark of night transformed into the light of morning. The light was so blinding that Caleb was certain they had miscalculated and blown up the world. Then came a sudden blast—so intense they all covered their heads with their hands. Even through his dark glasses, Caleb had never seen anything so bright. It took nearly forty seconds before the detonation hit him like a strong gust of wind.

A mass of flames rose in the distance. Even from ten miles away, he could feel the heat on the exposed parts of his skin. There were flashes contained inside the massive fireball of heat and ignition. The fire pooled into a pillar of smoke with a horrific mushroom shape, casting an evil shadow over the morning. A full minute and a half later, an enormous bang ricocheted off the mountains: the world's first manmade thunder.

Caleb stared at the dust cloud shimmering outward in concentric rings like rippling water. The shape reminded him of the body's circulatory system, bicycle tires in the mud, tree rings in the woods, the weeping rings inside an onion, and the yolk sack in Alice's womb. He struggled to see his own hands and feet in the ash it kicked up. But it was like he had no body—he'd become the dark cloud.

For many hours after, Caleb saw a purple-splotch afterimage.

For days, he saw that purple splotch every time he closed his eyes.

And for many months, before he fell asleep at night, he heard Oppenheimer mumbling in Sanskrit as those final seconds ticked down: "The good deeds a man has done before defend him."

T-Minus 7

August 1945
Haruki: A Story Told Backward

Having been nearly burned alive themselves, mothers gathered their bleeding children on Miyuki Bridge.

"Have you heard about Honkawa Elementary School?" Haruki asked one of the mothers.

She clutched her baby to her chest, seeming afraid of him. He didn't blame her—he had inhaled so much toxic smoke that he didn't recognize his own voice.

"Do you know if any of the schools are still standing?" he tried asking a man with cloudy eyes. He didn't seem to register his presence, just stared past him. He repeated himself. "My sister, she's only seven . . ."

He had to find Junko. After hours of lying on the ground going nose-blind to the burning corpses as the screams in his ears grew fainter, the thought of his sister was the only thing keeping him alive. Only after asking a third time did Haruki realize that the man had a shard of glass jutting out of his neck.

It got harder to hold up his head. His vision dimmed. When he closed his eyes, he was transported back home. In his vision, Junko was only a toddler, staggering around the kitchen, pulling herself up to stand on the kotatsu and holding onto him for balance. Her hair was barely long enough to put up; two choppy pigtails stuck out of her head like horns. The thousands of people wailing around him morphed into her single cry waking from a nightmare in her crib.

Suddenly, a voice that seemed very near to him yelled, "Young man over there, hurry up and get on!" Haruki opened his eyes and found himself still on the bridge under a roving black sky. Some military men had arrived on a truck and were pointing at him. He was overwhelmed with emotion as they helped him board the vehicle. He asked the man for his name. He knew enough to understand that by letting him on this truck, the man had just saved his life.

"My name doesn't matter. Get well soon and kill as many enemies as you can," said the soldier, handing Haruki the shirt from his own back. But he was also shouting and fending off the desperate women and children who were clawing at the truck. "Only young men get on board!" he shouted.

One woman tried to throw her infant into the bed of the truck. The baby was swaddled in a blood-splattered blanket. He couldn't tell whether the blood was from the baby or its mother. The man shoved it off the bed of the truck and it must have landed hard because it wailed. It was the same sound Junko had made when she was afraid of the dark.

Haruki watched the burned women and children shrink into the distance. They stumbled after the truck, their missing limbs and gaping wounds visible as they sped away. The baby had left a tiny handprint of blood smeared on the tailgate. Haruki stared at it. They had been left to die because they were no use in fighting the war.

Bushido is a way of dying, he thought.

For many years, late at night, he would hear that baby crying.

25

July 1945
Caleb

In the brightness, Caleb scanned the crowd of whooping and hollering scientists. The bomb had transformed night into day. Everywhere he looked, men were hugging, embracing, and running their hands through their hair. He glanced over at the theoretical team. Bethe's eyes were sparkling with tears. Beside him, Fred was strutting around, whistling what sounded like bird calls with two fingers in his mouth.

Caleb pinpointed Oppenheimer in the crowd, standing quietly amid the commotion. His face had relaxed from sheer relief. Beside him, Enrico Fermi was running around tossing torn bits of paper into the air to measure the displacement. In the excitement, his companions forgot to call Fermi by his code name, Farmer, as they clapped him on the back and congratulated him.

Beside Caleb, Dick was seeing spots, but he hadn't gone blind. His eyes looked marbled, like they belonged in a much older face. He was a little off balance at first, like a sailor with sea legs. But he seemed to have been rejuvenated. He was particularly taken by the distance the heat and ignition had traveled. He marveled, working up an estimate. Then he pointed a thumb over his shoulder at the explosives crew. "These duh-ta-duhs are callin' them lethal coat tails." Caleb followed Dick's accusatory thumb toward a group of SEDs who were making felicitous toasts and passing around a flask. Looking at them, Caleb couldn't repress the looming fear that in the excitement of the success, all the young people had forgotten what the gadget was for.

He did not take part in the celebrations. He had to find Alice. He could picture her clearly, straining for a better look at the end of the world with one palm pressed flat against the windowsill and the other on her belly.

Caleb was overcome with guilt. He wanted nothing more than to marry her and run far away from this place, to shed who he was and become what she saw in him. But wherever they went, the specter of the bomb would follow.

He made the trek back to base camp at a clipped pace. His sweat fogged up his specs. He realized with new clarity that he would be in large part responsible for whatever happened once the bomb was in the hands of the military. Whatever that was, it had to happen, he rationalized, to end the war. But still. His work had been meant only to save his house and his family. At least when he'd first come to the desert, he was not a murderer. What was he now? He wondered if a prayer existed for this moment. For the first time he could remember, he longed for his father's steadfast company. Only now, when it was too late, he understood him.

Back on the hill, fireworks erupted overhead, and people feverishly described the mushroom cloud to neighbors. The barracks exploded with celebration. People were dancing in the streets. Others were arguing with wild hand gestures. An SED who had celebrated too hard was vomiting in the bushes. Someone set off a firecracker by Ashley Pond and it made Caleb jump. The tail of the explosion snickered and burned off like a snake in the middle of the road.

He was trying to figure out a way to locate Alice in all the commotion when someone clapped him on the back. He jumped, recognizing the blunt shape and the coarseness of mangled skin through his shirt.

"I got decked out just for you, sweetheart." Saul laughed heartily like a schoolboy.

Caleb spun around to find Saul standing by his bunk, stark naked. Given that it was still so early in the morning, it took him a moment to realize his friend was drunk. Saul sloppily dropped a sack at his feet that clunked with the force of a bowling ball and began unwinding his bandage and removing his splints. "Might as well go au naturel," he said. The stumped nubs of his deformed hand and his coiled remaining fingers were appalling, yet Caleb couldn't look away. He desperately wanted to see what was concealed beneath the splint. He realized that several of the other SEDs were naked as well, dragging similar heavy backpacks as though they were filled with bricks.

"We've been on a treasure hunt." Saul winked. "It's harder than it looks with one paw."

"Where on earth are your clothes?" asked Caleb.

"Green-gold," Saul said dreamily.

"What?"

By way of response, Saul fished a mystery item from his sack. It was the size of a pebble, but it wasn't a pebble. He held the strange green gem to the light, inspecting it. It looked like sea glass, but when he moved it, the colors shifted like gasoline on pavement.

"What is it?" Caleb asked, reaching for it, mesmerized. The stone seemed to have its own light trapped inside.

Saul shooed his hand away playfully and turned mischievous eyes on Caleb. "The sand and the explosion fused into a strange new element," he said. "No one has seen the likes of it before."

"Is it safe?" Caleb worried, but Saul interrupted him.

"We named it Trinitite," he cut in proudly. Of course, Caleb thought, they had named it after Trinity. Saul squinted at the stone. His nose was peeling from sunburn, and he had a tan line from his sunglasses, which he had also removed when he undressed. The white, naked appendages of his body looked soft and tender. Caleb tried not to stare at Saul's mutilated stump of a hand. He thought he would be sick from the stink. A putrid, rancid odor wafted from the sutures. It had to be infected.

Saul gestured for Caleb to take the stone.

"Is it radioactive?" Caleb asked, stepping back and holding his hands up defensively.

Saul let out a defiant laugh as though he wouldn't care if it was. "We asked ourselves that same question," he said, "when we collected it off the desert floor."

"Is it?"

"If it is, it's too late." He tossed the hair from his eyes with a youthful headshake. "After we realized it might be, we tore off our infected clothes in a frenzy. I'm not so superstitious," he boasted, gesturing at the other naked SEDs, "but I'm not taking any chances." He grinned with pride. "Picture it," he said. "An army of men walking the desert in their birthday suits."

"You're drunk," Caleb said.

"Here," said Saul, teetering on legs that would not bend. He tossed him the stone with his good hand. He wasn't much for aim with his left arm, so it fell short. Caleb flinched and leaped back. "Jesus," Saul exclaimed. "It's not gonna bite ya."

✦✧

Alice

The redheaded nurse, Petey, looked up with a serene smile when the door chimed signaling her entry. Timoshenko, the large Irish wolfhound who still presided over the barracks hospital, was unaware that the world had changed a few hours before and sleepily wagged his tail against the floor.

"We've been booked solid all morning," Petey said. "People are falling apart. What brings you in, dear?"

"I'm having sharp pains in my abdomen," Alice said. At the bed and breakfast, she'd managed to sleep for maybe an hour, then jumped up thinking of Caleb waking up on the other side of that second sun. She'd raced to the barracks first thing when she got back to town, but he'd been nowhere to be found. She was still hearing his words over and over. She rubbed her temples. "And my head."

"Take a seat," said Petey gently. She gestured toward two folding chairs beneath an inspirational poster with a bald eagle that read, *Victory: Now you can invest in it!*

Alice was settling into *Ladies' Home Journal*, about to flip the page from an article on innovative ways to can fruit, when Saul staggered in.

He was tomato red with sunburn and his shirt was damp. His temples glistened with sweat. "Just lookin' for your run-of-the mill pain reliever," he said.

"You'll have to see the doctor," Petey instructed, offering him a clipboard. Her eyes lingered on his deformed right hand. It was a cesspool for infection and unlikely to heal properly without the splints. Even Alice knew that.

He nodded weakly in Alice's direction, embarrassment registering on his face when he recognized her. Still, despite the other empty chairs, he stumbled over and sat right next to her.

"I sincerely hope you two lovebirds worked things out," he said.

She tried not to show anything on her face. "Thank you," she said, "for what you told me."

He nodded with importance and cocked his head back. He stunk of booze. Alice crossed her legs away from him and shifted her weight subtly, careful not to offend. Saul struggled to uncap the pen one-handed. She was about to offer to help when he finally used his teeth, and still chewing the cap, began to scribble.

"What a bender," he said. "Nausea, headache, shakes, you name it," he said, checking off boxes.

"How awful," said Alice, feigning empathy. She wondered whether he had noticed the size of her belly in his stupor. Perhaps Caleb had already told him.

"It's nothing," he scoffed. "I've had worse." He indicated his stumped arm and winked at her. He was struggling to hold the pen steady between weak fingers.

"Alice," Petey called.

She glanced back at him one last time before passing through the swinging door. "Feel better," she said fleetingly. She didn't mean it. She didn't care if he drank himself into oblivion. She just hoped he didn't understand what he had seen or why she was there. There were no secrets in those tightly knit barracks. She knew she couldn't hide it much longer, but every day helped.

Petey listened to her breathing, looked down her throat, palpated her abdomen, and measured from her pubic bone to the top of her uterus. She seemed empathetic, but she firmly declined her request for medication. "Since this morning's events, I've had such demands for headache and nausea pills, anxiety, you name it. All our supplies have already been dispensed. We're waiting on the next shipment."

Alice did not feel reassured that others shared her symptoms. People were picking fights over rotten milk and provisioned tires. What had begun as a celebration of man's triumph over nature had devolved quickly as people worried about what was coming. She couldn't shake the feeling that they were living on borrowed time. Los Alamos was a secret about to get out.

T-Minus 6

August 1945
Haruki: A Story Told Backward

It seemed the sun had fallen from the sky. Everything was dark. Haruki could smell the stench of burning bodies wafting from the parking lot that was being used as a crematorium. He overheard some women saying that a temporary clinic had been set up at Miyuki Bridge. He couldn't move his legs, but he dragged himself with his arms. Fire crackled on his clothes and a tail of smoke trailed him through the rubble. But when he arrived, there was no clinic. There were only police officers pouring cooking oil onto the skin of children to ease the pain of the burns. He stared at the burned children. It was hard to see the details of their faces under the flayed skin and boils. Their hair and clothes had been burned off. He scanned their gory features, praying that none resembled Junko.

"Please," he said. "I have to get my sister." But the words came out garbled, sounding more animal than human.

One of the police officers looked at him with concern. He took his pulse then lost interest. He focused instead on a woman having a seizure, dying on the ground.

This is it, he thought. *I will die here.* He thought of the letters the kamikaze wrote their families on the eve of their final service, the attack from which they would never return. They ascended into the sky with fresh cut flowers to drop from heaven, and special-issued pistols to end their lives in the event of their capture. Preparing to die, they wore senninbari, belts of a thousand stitches, sewn lovingly by their mothers. He pictured his mother's silky hair, his father's fixed stare. He thought of Junko, running with joy to meet the other children. "I'll meet you at the Yasukuni Shrine," he whispered.

He found a small rock and etched his epitaph into the bridge: "Here is where Haruki Sato found his end."

26

July 1945
Caleb

Caleb had been camped out on Alice's doorstep for over an hour when she finally made her way up the drive. "Alice! I've been looking everywhere for you!" He jumped to his feet. "Are you OK? Are you hurt?"

She blanched. "I assume you'll understand if I don't invite you in."

He had known she wouldn't be thrilled to see him. But nothing could bring him down—there they were, both alive in the *after*. "Did you just make it back?"

"I've been back. Just came from the hospital."

He rushed down the steps to her. "Why? What's happened?" His hand found her belly.

"I didn't think you'd be too bothered."

"Alice." He removed his patrol cap. "I don't expect you to ever speak to me again. After what I pulled."

"It's nothing that hasn't been said before."

"Alice, you have to believe me, I was just sayin' what I had to." He paused, forcing out his next words. "I know I don't deserve another chance and I've royally mucked this up—but that's still our baby in there. I may not be a lot of things, but . . ." He thought of his father rising to his tiptoes during the Kiddushah to be closer to God and gathered himself. "I will be a good father."

"I know you will." She nodded.

He rushed on, encouraged. "I'm going to be a part of this baby's life, and if you'll have me, a part of yours. But we all have chapters already written for us. Some more than others. You seem convinced I can revise what's already in print."

"Look at me," she said. "My mother always said that the whole point of college was to get an MRS degree. If I hadn't broken away, I'd be locked in a tower, caked in makeup, with hair that remembers the shape of its bouffant at night, and a pheasant-tail feather hat that's forgotten it once knew how to fly."

Caleb felt his composure cracking. "I've been tryin' so hard to make you see. Don't you get it? It doesn't mean we can't be together, but you have your dreams and I have mine."

"I know your dreams," she interjected. "The question is do you?" She finally looked at him. She seemed to register for the first time that he was in uniform. "Why the getup?"

"Most of the recruits didn't even have time to sober up before we had to report to drill."

"Isn't the work done now? I mean, we did what we came for."

"Sergeant Moony said something about not celebrating prematurely. That the real work starts today."

"What are you meant to do?"

"We're loading flatbeds. No one's said anything directly, but we're no blockheads. It's all the puzzle pieces for another bomb."

Her eyes widened. "Already?"

He shrugged, helpless. "It's out of our hands now."

"Caleb," she said, "as soon as our contracts are up, we've got to get out of here." Then, without any further explanation, she closed and bolted the door.

"They sent me over from Rufus, said this was more pressing." With worried eyes, Harry shrugged off his lab coat. He draped it over a bush and rolled up his sleeves. "I don't think we can keep pretending we don't know what it's for," he said as they gingerly loaded a truck with U-235 target rings, bags of cordite powder, tungsten-carbide tamper cylinder sleeves, baro switches, tubing, and electrical plugs. Saul, unable to help with the lifting, was strutting around the recruits, barking instructions with a clipboard.

"I keep hearing more about the area outside the Trinity test site," Caleb said tightly. "Our first 'baby' is still making the rounds. We're not even waitin' to see the fallout."

Harry nodded stoically. "I don't know about you, but I can't pretend not to see the cattle with singed coats or the broken windows when I drive into town. Did you know ash got into cisterns and infected the water supply? Who knows what that will do to people."

"Come on now," said Saul, shouting over them. "No dilly-dallying. No, no, the oralloy rings go in the north bed. Those are headed directly to the

C-54 transport plane. The rest will go by train to Frisco, then hitch a ride on the USS *Indianapolis*."

"Who put you in charge of this rigamarole?" Harry rolled his eyes.

"I enlisted to take the plunge," Saul announced with pride. "All this junk is headed to the same place . . . Tinian Island. And I'm hitchin' a ride."

"You're headed to Tinian?" Caleb asked, startled. "I hadn't heard you were leavin'."

"Sure as shit and taxes, I am. Somebody's gotta assemble the parts and train the pilots. Besides, it's just for a few weeks."

"What about the . . . target?" Caleb asked, breaking into a whisper like the word pained him. "I thought you were just tryin' to stamp out Hitler."

"The way I figure, history's gonna happen whether I help out or not. This train has left the station." He indicated the flatbeds. "Besides, I'm more use up here these days"—he rapped his knuckles on his forehead, indicating his brain—"than for manpower. Next stop is the Northern Mariana Islands."

"They've been recruitin' us over there left and right. Is it true," asked Harry, his interest piqued, "that the island is shaped like a pistol?"

"That I don't know yet, partner. But I can tell you this much: it beats bein' stuck here in the sticks. There are beaches of golden sand as far as you can see. They say the island was once a large sugar cane farm, so even the air smells sweet as sugar."

"I think you misunderstood," Harry grunted. "It's the 'comfort women' the soldiers were callin' sweet as sugar, not the air. And we both know they're just young Korean girls, not pastries."

Caleb, who had resumed work, lifted a panel and recoiled. "What on earth?" The target case forging was graffitied with the words *Flatbush Avenue*. The letters were wobbly enough that they could have been written by a nondominant left hand. "Saul, was that you?"

"Honestly," Saul huffed. "It makes a guy wonder what you really think of me."

"Saul, this isn't just your run-of-the-mill graffiti."

"There's writing all over the casing," Saul replied, defensive. "Take a look."

Harry and Caleb started turning the steel panels over. Some bore love letters—initials inside lopsided hearts. One read, *Easter eggs for Hitler!* The last in the pile fronted, *A kiss for Hirohito!*

Saul came up beside them, admiring the scrawled text. "I can't say for sure I didn't write 'Flatbush,'" he dodged, "what with all the booze involved. But the boys are artists—they just wanted to sign their work."

Caleb shifted his gaze from Saul to the other men, astonished. Most of them were strutting around like heroes. "They really think they've saved the world," he muttered.

Harry said, "Well, the jury's out on whether or not we're the good guys."

Caleb turned over the last spring coil in the pile. The spiral reminded him of the Fibonacci sequence. Like the structure of DNA, a ringlet of Alice's hair, a pine cone, or a hurricane, a built-in numbering system was holding the world together. And he knew that what was about to happen could not be undone.

August 1945

Aside from Saul's empty cot, things continued as normal. Caleb went through the motions of drills and reporting to Rufus. Then one morning, he returned from an early morning walk with Alice and Pavlov to find pandemonium in the barracks. Caleb joined the ruckus, trying to make out what had just taken place.

Everyone was facing the radio with their backs to the windows. A recruit had strung up a glass crystal from the leg of his bunk and it wobbled from its chain, casting several shifting rainbows on the floorboards and the backsides of some of the SEDs. Caleb's mind wandered to the way the white light separated at varying angles corresponding to wavelengths. 400 nanometers for violet. 425 for indigo. 470 for blue.

He thought back to that first afternoon on horseback with Alice. After the storm had cleared, before the campfire, a rainbow had formed overhead while the horses trod the final leg of the pass. He had held onto his hat and recited the dispersion for her then like a love poem: "550 nanometers for green. 600 for yellow." She had laughed, saying something about missing the forest for the trees. "630 nanometers for orange," he had droned on, just wanting to say anything to keep the conversation going. "665 for red." Back then, he would have talked to her forever. They'd been through so much since, and it wasn't all roses, but the forever part remained true.

Across the room, one of the rainbows settled on a hunched back, and Caleb leaped out of his skin realizing it was Saul. When had he made it back? Had it really been two weeks? Saul was wearing an unbuttoned Hawaiian shirt and sandals, with an impressive suntan to boot. Apparently, the lackadaisical work culture of the island had agreed with him. His severed hand was folded into his chest protectively. He seemed to sense Caleb's gaze, and he craned his neck around, searching the room. His eyes were bright, the sort of eyes that flicker on a night vision camera on a mountain trail alone in the night. His gaze finally settled on Caleb, and he shuffled over.

"Did ya hear?" he said, wasting no time with pleasantries.

"Somebody had better tell me, and quick," said Caleb.

"It doesn't seem real," said Saul.

Someone in the front cranked the radio dial as the soundbite repeated: "Sixteen hours ago, an American airplane dropped one bomb on Hiroshima, an important Japanese army base . . . The force from which the sun draws its power has been loosed against those who brought war to the Far East." Truman's voice was deadpan, but the message was astounding: scientists had captured the sun.

Caleb gathered the details from scrambled conversations. Tibbets, who had piloted the plane, had painted the name *Enola Gay* proudly on the nose of his aircraft. He had named the plane for his mother, the radio explained, who had been named for the book *Enola; or, Her Fatal Mistake* by Mary Young Ridenbaugh. The title character, Enola, is doomed to isolation. Pundits on the radio even quoted the text:

> "In calling me by the strange name of 'Enola,' I wonder if my dear departed parents received a glimpse of the future life of their child in a camera, speaking to them of her life of loneliness," mused Enola, "for truly I am alone . . ."

In every way, it was a story without an ending. One broadcast bled into another. Correspondents debated the theater in the Pacific like it was a game of chess.

At precisely 7:15 AM, the *Enola Gay* deployed the gadget. After that, it was fifty-three seconds before anything happened.

"But what happened next?" Caleb asked.

"Nobody knows for certain," said Saul.

T-Minus 5

August 1945
Haruki: A Story Told Backward

Haruki did not know that that morning was the last of its kind. He took his last sip of tea. He dropped Junko at school, and he watched her run into the swarm of first graders for the last time, her backpack flapping loose behind her like wings. He walked his commute for the final time, crossing the churning rivers and making his way to the Hiroshima College of Technology campus, where he was a senior. For the last time, he made his way to class.

It was a humid day, and Haruki wiped the last beads of sweat from his brow.

A strange sensation made him look up, and he squinted at the shadow moving across the sky. A faint plane emerged through a tuft of fog, and Haruki watched as it released a small silver speck. It seemed to fall very slowly, whistling as it dropped.

In that moment, Haruki knew they were under attack. He threw his body to the ground and plugged his ears with his thumbs. Through closed eyes, he experienced a bright flash followed by a deafening boom that echoed over and over. The next thing he knew, he was airborne. The only thought in his head was Junko.

When Haruki woke up, he wondered how long he had been unconscious. What day was it? His first emotion was anger. "Damn you, Americans! How dare you do this! You'll regret it!" He had been raised under Japanese imperialism. This was the response he had been conditioned for. But when he looked down, he saw that his shirtsleeves and pantlegs had been incinerated. He pressed his hand over a throbbing wound on the side of his head. When he removed it, his palm was coated in blood.

Finally, he looked up. People were trying to walk but stumbling on broken bones. A man staggered past, his eye hanging from its socket, jiggling with each step. He noticed another with a chest wound so deep, he could see his lungs expand and contract with each breath.

Beside him, a woman's face was caked with ash. She was holding her abdomen together with her hands, trying to keep her intestines from protruding. People cried for him to help them. Some were trapped under the rubble. Others were drowning in the river. Corpses bobbed beside them in the water. Many of the drowning were children.

27

August 1945
Alice

There was mayhem all over the hill. Two men had shoved each other and were still arguing in front of the mess hall. Couples danced in front of the water tower, skirts twirling and saddle shoes kicking up dust.

Alice hadn't been able to stop thinking about the name of Tibbet's plane: *Enola Gay*. Had he intended for the newspapers and the headlines to measure their own reflections? When the plane was mirrored by the clear ocean water as he crossed the Pacific, the reflection would have read "Alone." Enola spelled backward was its own lost city.

Supposedly, Tibbets had named the ship for his mother. Alice held her belly; thinking about the climbing death count, she was terrified that her child would have to live in the world she had helped build. She tried to picture Tibbets's mother. Was she proud? How did she feel about what her son had accomplished in her name?

Outside, it was strange that the sky had not fallen. People were still celebrating late in the day beneath the low sun, casting long shadows. Groups congregated on porches. They sipped chilled drinks and popped off bottle rockets in the street. She stumbled through the celebrations, deaf to the excited voices and congratulatory remarks.

"Here we are at the end of the world!" called Bonnie from her porch, toasting with an iced tea. The drink fizzled and the ice cubes clinked.

"It took some moxie, but we made it to the other side!" Judith smiled beside her, fanning herself with what looked to be a Japanese fan. Alice wondered if she had given it a second thought, that she was fanning the heat with a relic of the culture she had helped to incinerate. Judith's puff sleeves billowed as she waved. Alice wanted to run. She sped up her pace to a jog as they called after her, and immediately her belly tightened, and she had to stop and hold herself together. She glanced back, wondering if they had noticed. But no—they were leaning toward each other, blissfully gossiping, and the pitcher of golden tea Bonnie clutched to her breast was illuminated by the sunset.

Outside the barracks, the SEDs were wandering around in their undershirts. Several were skipping stones on Ashley Pond while the sun was sinking twice, once in the sky and again in the reflection. The young men stared at the fiery horizon like they could make out the bomb in the distance.

Behind her, a few young men were talking at a clip with ecstatic eyes. She approached them numbly.

"A few of them knew what was comin'," the shorter one said conspiratorially, staring at the darkening trees on the far end of the pond like he could read something written in the spreading shadows. A few bats swooped low over the rippling water, then flapped up and seemed to vanish into the tree line. "What with Tibbets and the private committee discussions about bomb bay doors and target cities."

The taller one nodded. Alice had heard enough rumors to know what they meant. The military had needed a fully developed city to ascertain the destructive power of the bomb. They didn't want to bomb some place that had already been burned to a crisp. It was thought that by the end of May, the list of target cities had been shortened to Kyoto, Niigata, and Hiroshima.

"Have you seen Caleb?" she interrupted. "Private Blum?"

They hadn't noticed her, and they looked displeased, now, that she had been eavesdropping. The taller one hiked his thumb over his shoulder in the direction of Fuller Lodge. A lantern was glowing in the entrance, casting a flickering light.

When she approached, even though the voices inside were muffled through the closed door, she could tell they were in the midst of a furious debate.

Caleb

In the barracks, recruits were disputing everything from displacement to the aerodynamics of the escape route. Some were seated backward on chairs, others paced nervously and talked over each other in elevated voices. "The *Enola Gay* couldn't be right over the top when she blew, or no one would have ever known it had been there," Saul was saying to a group who usually only hung around for cards. He'd been talking around the clock about the work he did to train the pilots, filled with importance. Caleb studied him, wondering what had happened to his buddy who only a short while back, had been an avowed communist, marching for peace. "They would have been incinerated." Now, he had the room's rapt attention. "They had to swing a hundred and fifty-nine degrees, tangent to the explosion. That would get them the greatest distance in the shortest length of time," he continued.

Caleb couldn't stomach any further discussion. All he could think about was the strange black rain that they'd been told had fallen over ground zero. It felt biblical.

By contrast to the barracks, the common room was very quiet, almost funeral. A handful of men sat listening to the broadcast of Tibbets's interview upon his return. Caleb was thankful to see Dick seated closest to the radio. Through the speaker, Tibbets's voice was stifled, like he was afraid of his own words. No one moved as he recounted his experience. The moon had been a spotlight on the dark ocean, Tibbets recalled. The waves had scattered into a wake beneath the fan of the plane and the crew's chatter had dispersed into periods of reflective quiet. "It seemed everyone was dreaming," Tibbets said.

Just then, Harry flung open the door and stomped into the room, disrupting the spell of the broadcast. Everyone stared at him. Harry had spent more time in the common room lately, listening to the news, seeming to withdraw from the scientists who were racing forward with new research—larger explosions, the use of hydrogen. "No need to flip your wig," he said, dismissing their glares with a wave of his sausage fingers. His eyes settled on Caleb and Dick, and he flashed his sharp canines, breaking into a grin. "How's it hanging?" He plopped down beside them, smelling of coffee and sweat.

Tibbets was describing leveling out the plane despite the looming column of smoke. Explosive bursts had twisted through the sky, blinding the crew. "It seemed God had taken ahold of the plane and was shaking it," he said.

Caleb immediately thought of Asher. This was the realization of their childhood dreams. Tibbets had flown the barrier between this world and the next.

The broadcast continued: "The city was hidden by that awful cloud . . . boiling up, mushrooming, terrible and incredibly tall. No one spoke for a moment; then everyone was talking." Tibbets described an overwhelming taste of lead in his mouth as they sped away, putting as many miles between them and ground zero as possible. In closing, he repeated the words of his copilot, Robert Lewis. While watching the plumes of smoke, Lewis had asked him: "My God, what have we done?" When Tibbets fell silent recalling the exchange, so did everyone in the room.

After a minute, Harry seemed unable to stand the quiet. "You know the bombardier, Tom Ferebee, spent the getaway flight worrying the radioactivity would make him sterile." He nudged Caleb.

The broadcast picked up again with its twenty-four-hour coverage of the destruction. "At almost the exact center of the blast, the Mitsubishi factory that had constructed the torpedoes responsible for Pearl Harbor disintegrated," a stoic pundit explained. Several in the room cheered, celebrating with congratulatory handshakes. The news reviewed all the things they could count: at 8:15 AM, the bomb had been dropped from thirty-one thousand feet. It exploded fifteen hundred feet above the city and destroyed approximately five square miles. The scientists had already committed the numbers to heart. They all started talking at once.

"It must be horrific on the ground over there," said Harry softly. He caught Caleb's eye and hardened, seeming desperate to conceal his vulnerability. "God willing, it's over now and we can forget all this nonsense and go home."

"Roll up your flaps," said Dick. "No one is going anywhere."

"If that's true, I'm liable to go AWOL," said Harry, setting his jaw.

A harrowed look crossed Dick's face. "It ain't even begun," he said.

Fuller Lodge was full of people bickering. At first, Caleb tried to piece together the crisscrossing conversations, but soon, he stopped listening. He pulled off his glasses and pressed his thumb and forefinger into his weary eyes. He tried to count 33,000 names. If he thought of everyone he had ever known, he could get to a hundred, maybe two. And that didn't account for the 13,950 wounded. He tapped the toe of his boot on the floor, animated with nervous energy. Alice had taught him Morse code, and he thumped through the alphabet mindlessly: short-long/long-short-short-short/short-short-short.

Then, like he had summoned her, Alice appeared in the doorway. Without his specs, his vision was blurred and he saw only her silhouette at first, lingering and hesitant. The lantern shifted in the wind from the open door, making the shadows on the wall behind her rove like a turning carousel, distorting her face. He put on his specs and sighed with relief. What had looked like blood was only lipstick. Her eyes did look swollen, but that was likely because she had been crying.

It took all his courage not to run to her. Out of respect for Warren, she still wanted to downplay the public displays although it was clear that they were together. Without a word, she sat beside him. His heart was beating so loud, he could feel his pulse in his hands. He reached for her—and there, in a fresh new world, she held his hand in front of everyone. He squeezed her fingers, and she squeezed back.

More and more people came pouring in. All the belt buckles gleamed in rows. While they waited for Oppenheimer to take the podium, a laminated photograph made its way around the room. When it reached Caleb, he paused, trying to make out the grainy figures.

"Miyuki Bridge." Alice nodded. "It came our way first." She meant the PhDs. "It's one of the only surviving images," she explained. "Taken approximately three hours after the bomb." Caleb held the picture up close, then at an arm's length from his face, trying for a better look. In the pixelated image, beyond the remaining bridge structure, the world was a wasteland. There was a central cluster of entangled bodies. Off to the side, police officers were tending to children's burns. It was hard to distinguish exactly where one figure stopped and the next started. It reminded Caleb of a classical painting, something by Giotto, with torsos and thighs overlaid and foreshortened toward the viewer, and all the gazes and limbs pointing toward a distant focal point, an absent messiah.

Because the hair had been burned from the survivors' bodies, it was difficult to tell the men from the women, or whether he was looking at people's fronts or backs. He stared at the only distinct figure, captured in focus just at the crest of the pyramid of human bodies. His hair and clothes had been incinerated, and he was scathed by burns, his layers of skin removed in peaks and valleys like a topographical map. He had turned his face to gaze directly at the destruction, beneath a sky of churning smoke. His ear had been severed and looking at the spiral-shaped cavity of his bony labyrinth made Caleb dizzy; it was a swirling galaxy, a wormhole to another world.

The room hushed. Oppenheimer stood up somberly and leaned against the lectern, as though he needed it to prop him up.

Oppenheimer had always been a hero among men, but now he was a god. They all saw themselves in his porkpie hat, a synecdoche for the community of cowboys. Everyone celebrated him as the leader of the new world. Caleb was beginning to have his doubts.

Now that Oppie was a hero, even Kitty had returned to him. The two had picked up where they left off. The children had been returned, and when asked, Kitty claimed that she had been refreshed by her vacation. But from her glazed expression, it was obvious to everyone that she was barely subsisting through a drunken stupor. She was constantly smashing into things and banging herself up after drinking her dinner. Now, she was beaming triumphantly in the front row beneath an oversized sun hat. She had angled the large brim to conceal a bulging bruise on her left eye that was rumored to be from a run-in with the kitchen cabinet. She had always been accident prone due to her drinking, but now the swollen bracelet of plum-colored bruises around her wrists and her bony, cut-up knees told a more formidable story about the turn her drinking had taken.

Alice followed his gaze and acknowledged her, sitting stiffly in the front. "Nice for Oppie that she's back," she said. That their marriage had survived the blast despite its pitfalls seemed a sort of triumph to the residents who admired them. Perhaps it was even inspirational to Alice, Caleb wondered. But of their own feverish debate about whether to marry if they survived the test bomb, Alice said nothing.

When Oppenheimer finally spoke, his voice shook. He quoted from the *Bhagavad Gita*, the holy book of Hindu: "If the radiance of a thousand suns / were to burst at once into the sky, / That would be like the splendor of the Mighty One— / I am become Death, the Destroyer of Worlds." His eyes were as blue and cold as the sky.

He confirmed that, in a visual display described as far greater than the Trinity test, an orange fireball filled with internal lightning had ballooned over Hiroshima. He hesitated, then confirmed the facts. "The nuclear fission weapon named 'Little Boy' was deployed successfully." He didn't bother explaining the gadget's adjusted code name, but Caleb had heard some higher-ups in the military had worried that his proposed moniker, "Thin Man," too nearly resembled Oppenheimer himself. Neither did he describe the charred sides of the telephone poles that had faced the blast, beside the obliterated rubble of houses. He did not describe the two miles of earth scorched to red. There was much he left unsaid.

Caleb tried to listen to Oppenheimer, but in the bright lights, his glasses were giving him a headache. He kept taking them off to rest his eyes, and every time he did, the details of the room smeared into foggy nightmares at the edges of his vision. A few rows in front of him, just far enough away to have blurry features, a man looked just fine from behind, but when he turned his head, half of his face was burned and his ear had been severed. The dismembered ear lay in the aisle beside him like a dried peach slice. Caleb stared into the spiraling universe of the cavity in the man's head, realizing he was peering into the mind of the man from the photograph. His facial muscle tissues and ligaments hung loose like spaghetti. The mutilated ear kept seizing on the floor, like a halved insect. Caleb recoiled in horror and decided the migraine was safer. He put his glasses back on and immediately, the edges of the room aligned and straightened. The man in question was wearing black headphones. The phantom ear was only a stain in the carpet.

"If atomic bombs are to be added as new weapons to the arsenals of the warring world," Oppenheimer was saying with morose eyes, "then the time will come when mankind will curse the names of Los Alamos and Hiroshima."

Afterward, the community milled around for a while in the packed room, under the watch of two mounted deer heads with glinting eyes. They took their time before they filed out the doors. Outside, night had fallen. Stars were in the same places. It still seemed like the same world. It was hard to wrap their minds around the ways everything had changed. No one was in a rush to go home and be alone.

"Maybe we can say something for the people who died," Caleb said. "I mean the families with children." He paused and looked away from Alice before he dared to say, "Mothers with babies." He didn't mean that they should recite the Mourner's Kaddish precisely, but he couldn't stomach the way everyone was celebrating a mass killing. He was terrified of what horrors he would see later when he took off his glasses to sleep. Words were better than no words. Light was better than darkness. "We could light a candle," he suggested, recalling the Yahrzeit candle his mother had burned in his grandmother's memory from sundown to sunrise in the kitchen sink. He was frustrated with himself, but in times of distress, despite it all, Judaism was all he knew.

"Any one of us could go next," Alice said, a sort of nonanswer. "Our bomb is now part of the world." Her eyes bored through him. Usually, they were flecked with streaks of waving color like a miniature aurora borealis, but now they had gone flat. Still, standing near her made him feel alive.

"Listen," he said, smoothing her hair proudly in front of everyone in the room. "They say there's more to death than burial." He kissed her brow.

She looked up at him with fragile eyes. "They won't be able to bury them if they can't find the bodies," she said.

"In Mexican tradition, there are three deaths," he said, finding some comfort in soothing her. It was easier than being terrified himself.

"One's enough for me," Alice bristled.

"The first is when your heart stops. The second is when you are lowered into the ground."

"Stop," she said, turning away. But still, she held his hand.

"The third," Caleb continued, scanning the room for the back of Oppenheimer's head in the crowd, "is when there is no one left alive to remember you."

T-Minus 4

August 1945
Haruki: A Story Told Backward

The cashier's pink fingernails flashed as she rang him up. They made everything she touched seem more interesting and more beautiful. Her stick-straight ponytail hung past her hips and bobbed. She smiled at Haruki's overloaded tray. "Would you like a second breakfast?" She explained the discount, a promotional deal for students. She had to speak loudly over the bustling energy of the morning rush in the Shima no Kaori cafeteria.

He would have loved a second breakfast. He had spent so many years foregoing meals to provide food for Junko that he was perpetually hungry. Food was sparse due to the war, and his parents were hardly ever home, working themselves to the bone. But he was embarrassed. He didn't want her to think he was greedy. He refused and ate quickly. After he bused his tray, he was still starving. He glanced back at the cashier, too ashamed to go back for seconds. How would it look? It was a quarter to eight, according to the overhead clock. He had to get Junko to school. He decided he would grab something after class. He pressed through the rotating doors out into the brightness.

Outside, it was humid even though it was still early morning. There was no breeze. After a few moments, he was sweating through his shirt.

Thirty minutes later, the cafeteria was gone.

28

August 1945
Alice

A lice lined up at the post exchange to learn what she could of the bomb from the local papers. The nearsighted *Santa Fe New Mexican* became the talk of the town. Its headline had been rushed overnight, and consequently launched into the atomic era with a typographical error: "Now They Can Be Told Aloud, Those Stoories of 'the Hill.'" There weren't enough papers for all the inhabitants, so they passed them around the mesa, and the papers wore thinner and more translucent each time they were exchanged.

One lead article cited President Truman as accounting for six thousand persons working at Site Y. "We have spent," the president explained, "two billion dollars on the greatest scientific gamble in history—and won!" Elsewhere, a headline boasted, "THE BOMB THAT CHANGED THE WORLD." From yet another article, residents learned that they had twenty-seven technical buildings and 620 family units—and that two-thirds of them were civilian families. They read facts about their secret existence that they hadn't known before, published for all the world to see. After so much isolation, their Never-Never Land was catapulted into the limelight. They were written into history as heroes.

Around the country, cities were celebrating them. Las Vegas had rebranded itself as Atomic City, she read. On subsequent pages, she skimmed recipes for atomic cocktails, each stronger than the last. She lingered over a spread of atomic beauty queens. Vegas had crowned a "Miss Atomic Blast," declaring she was "radiating loveliness instead of deadly atomic particles." Her atomic-style hairdo required a roll of toilet paper and two cans of hairspray to hold it upright, but in a still photograph, it looked the essence of glamour. Alice was disgusted, but she couldn't quite bring herself to look away from the airbrushed smiles.

Pavlov was thrilled that Caleb was sleeping over these days, sniffing after crumbs he dropped in the kitchen and shadowing his movements around the living room. Now, Caleb seemed hesitant to go to bed. He lit a candle in Alice's sink and sat up most of the night, watching the flame burn down with Pavlov curled up at his feet. Alice tossed and turned, staring into the flickering darkness.

Early the next morning, she made as much racket as she could putting away dishes and clinking pots and pans, but she couldn't bring herself to shake Caleb awake. Even if he had nothing to say, his communal silence would prevent her from being alone with her thoughts. She doubled her efforts, switching on the radio and flinging open the drapes. Outside, birds chattered in the trees, hopping branches, unaware that the world was at war. Finally, Caleb startled awake. He clutched the bedframe like he was seeing things.

With nervous hands, Alice burned the eggs to a crisp and spilled coffee grounds through the filter. Caleb quietly stared down at the floaters in his mug.

"My father always says it's the favorite drink of the civilized world," she said. "Anyhow, it sure beats the mud they serve in the mess hall."

"I've been meaning to ask you," he started to say. "Seein' as our contract's almost up, we could just pack up and drive away—" But before he could finish, they both turned to look at the radio.

"Major Sweeney targeted the city of Kokura in his plane *Bockscar*," announced the broadcaster. "Due to a major firebombing raid on the nearby city of Yawata, the city was masked in black smoke."

The crew had grown uneasy since they were attracting unwanted attention from Japanese fighter jets. When a hole opened up in a cloud, Sweeney made a rushed decision. The radio did not mince words: Nagasaki was in the wrong place at the wrong time.

"One wasn't enough?" Caleb said. His voice cracked and his hand shook as he adjusted the volume dial. "All this time, I've been trying to get behind what we've done. How do you justify this?"

"Fat Man was unleashed two miles away from its target," commentators elaborated. They described the fireball that billowed up to twenty thousand feet, proving much more powerful than Little Boy. A column of smoke had vortexed through the sky and swallowed the plane. The crew had been warned not to fly through the atomic cloud because of unknowable dangers. Sweeney had reflexively throttled *Bockscar* into a steep dive. It had been hard to tell whether they were escaping the cloud, or whether the cloud was gaining on them. "Immediately thereafter, the plane lost all communication."

They waited. Occasionally, the broadcast checked back in with the crew, playing the static of the transmission on the air. "Still no word from our pilots," they said as they counted down the minutes. Alice watched Caleb run his fingers through his hair. He dumped out his coffee and poured himself a stiff drink, but he just stared at it. She remembered Warren doing the same thing the night before he left for boot camp. His bourbon on the rocks had melted a ring into her coffee table. She had stared at that ring every morning, unable to scrub it away. This was her curse, she thought. This exact moment.

They chewed breakfast in silence. Outside, it was perfectly sunny and eerily quiet. It couldn't have been more different from the celebrations and fireworks after the Trinity test. Everyone was hiding behind shut doors. The scientists had lost control. But they had built this world, whatever it was.

It wasn't until Sweeney's copilot, Fred J. Olivi, recalled the experience on the evening news that the waiting world was able to fill in the holes in the story. While they listened, Alice's heart raced. She knew enough to explain the phenomenon—being pregnant, and large as a watermelon now, she had an increase in blood volume that required her to pump anywhere from ten to fifteen extra beats per minute. She had read somewhere that pregnant women's hearts actually grow. But the scientific understanding didn't quell the pounding in her ears. Beside her, Caleb jiggled his legs listening to Olivi's description: "Suddenly, the light of a thousand suns illuminated the cockpit."

Even though she had no work left to do, that night Alice went to the lab. A cohort of theoretical scientists were dedicated to improving upon the bomb, building something even bigger and even more lethal, and they gathered frequently in the T, arguing in frantic voices. But as a woman, she was excluded from the new research, which, for once, she was thankful for. Even they would be absent this evening, camped by their radios, tuning the dials.

A summer storm swept in, and she huddled under her raincoat for cover as she jogged down the path to the barbed wire perimeter. She had thought getting wet would feel better than sitting at home in the stifling heat of the kitchen, afraid to turn off the lights. She had left in a hurry, not accounting for the explosive thundercracks. With each lightning strike, Warren's lifeless face flashed in her mind. She fled.

Inside, she was thankful for the familiar scents of chlorine and vinegar. An odor like that of burning hair wafted from the Bunsen burners, calming her. This building gave her something to do—someone to be.

In light of the news, the lab that was usually buzzing with energy had been abandoned. It felt cavernous and dystopian walking the halls; most of the lights were off and her footsteps echoed. The spaces felt bigger in the dark. She settled into the familiarity of her desk, reviewing research findings with a highlighter and occasionally keeling over in sobs. Time and again, she wiped the makeup from her eyes and returned to her work, only for her mind to wander from a passage on electromagnetism to the flashing skies over Nagasaki, or from findings in thermodynamics to what would become of the radioactive ecosystem and parched soil. She felt the baby kick, and her belly seized up. She was overcome by images of dead children, incinerated on their swing sets or scorched in their sandboxes.

She chased the thoughts from her mind. Her back began to ache from bending low over the page. A few times, she got up and rolled out her neck. Finally, she stood up to stretch and checked the clock. It was nearly two in the morning. The rational thing to do would be to go home and sleep. But the baby had been most active when she lay down, and sleep hadn't come easily lately. These days, there was no concealing her belly. Her secret was out—and to her surprise, even the wives had been supportive, thrilled at the prospect of another baby in town. But it was impossible to get comfortable in a chair, or on a couch, or in her bed. Anyhow, she told herself that was why she wasn't sleeping.

She peeked out the door. There was not a soul in sight. An idea came to her, almost greedily, and she tiptoed to the end of the hall. She could sense the heat of the plutonium glowing on the other side of the wall before she even opened the door.

She startled when something moved in the room. The shape shuddered, seeming as surprised by her presence as she was by it. It took her a moment to see him in the dark—and likewise, it took him a moment to see her standing there in the light of the doorway. Sitting in the shadows, she got a glimpse of his profile in the brief glare of his cigarette. Oppenheimer himself inhaled a mouthful of smoke and exhaled slowly.

He sat dangerously near the samples with no protection, in a partially unbuttoned shirt, his bare chest exposed, cradling a fifth of vodka. Behind him, several of the samples were combusting, glowing red and churning. His eyes glowed with the reflection of the plutonium.

He seemed to have aged dramatically even though it had only been a few days since she had last seen him in Fuller Lodge. She recalled the pristine way he had folded his napkin back at the steak house in Berkeley, shrinking it down from a rectangle to a square and finally a smaller rectangle. When he laid his steak knife across his polished dinnerplate with the teeth of the blade facing in, it was always at a forty-five-degree angle. Even her mother would have approved of his impeccable manners. But before her now was a very different person than the thin man who had leaned on the podium and recited the *Bhagavad Gita*. This was Dr. Oppenheimer, the insomniac dreamer.

She recalled that very drunk night on the mesa when he had professed that he couldn't love. She wondered how lonely it must be inside his noisy head. He had taken an interest in her back then—possibly, she had supposed at the time, for being one of the few women on the theoretical team. Or maybe it was simply that the dimensions of her face were familiar to him from his seminars. Since then, he had moved on to chasing other women and other scientists' wives. But at the least, he always seemed to remember Alice. He always really listened to what she had to say. He had only ever been perfectly kind to her, and that was something, considering that he wasn't always kind. That's why it concerned her so completely that he looked at her now like he couldn't quite place her.

He offered her a sip. What was the harm, she thought, perching beside him on the floor. She took a gulp straight from the bottle, gasping sharply and squeezing her eyes shut to quench the burn as it slid down her throat and warmed her chest.

She left a lipstick imprint on the rim. Not taking any notice, he held the bottle up to salute the linoleum ceiling and flickering emergency lights like they were God watching over them. "I've always been fond of saying that no man should escape our universities without knowing how little he knows," he mumbled.

"Or woman," Alice added. She kept her eyes locked on him, but she could sense the plutonium glowing in her peripheral vision.

"Little did I know," he said.

After a long moment, she asked, "What happens now?"

"We're due for a forty-day flood."

"I mean, what happens"—she gestured around the room—"to all of this?"

He grunted. "We've dumped enough nuclear waste into the canyon for a hundred lifetimes. Let's give it back to the Indians." He flicked the glowing end of his cigarette on the floor by his feet and took another swig.

What he had come to build had been completed. Contracts were almost up. He was looking to step down, she realized. He was as desperate as she to put this chapter of his life behind him.

"Dr. Oppenheimer, without you, this hill will cease to exist. And just think what could happen to it in the wrong hands."

"I have blood on my hands." He dangled his palms. His thin fingers looked skeletal white in the darkness between them. "They're listening in on my phone calls. They pick through my garbage. Everyone knows." He pushed himself up to an unstable stance. "The craziest part is," he began, teetering on stiff legs in the pitch-black room, "in all my life, physics and desert country were my two great loves."

She noticed that he did not mention Kitty. Alice pictured his slender wife in her starched keyhole blouse and her bangs swept up into a pompadour, staring at nothing through French windows. Only that morning, Alice had seen the fresh burn on her forearm, rumored to be from an intoxicated incident with the stove. She noticed also that Oppie did not mention Jean Tatlock's grave, the offerings of flowers collecting rainwater in their petals. He did not mention his son, Peter, building a tower of Babylon out of blocks, or his daughter, Katherine, crying out in her crib for something she could not yet name.

"We won," he said, his face setting. "The sons of bitches asked us to bottle the sun and we did it. Any morning now, you'll wake up and the war will be over." He stood, and took a wobbly step toward her, but stumbled and fell hard on the floor. She jumped to help him but hesitated. He lay there quietly, cradling his head in his hands. He was so thin, she wondered whether if she touched him, her hand would pass right through.

She decided to leave him alone to mourn. On her way out, she turned back for one last look. What remained crumpled on the floor wasn't the messiah of science. He wasn't the father of the atomic bomb. He was just a shell of a man, watching a flesh and blood woman leave the room.

T-Minus 3

March 1944
Haruki: A Story Told Backward

"We're winning," said Junko. "Banzai!" She looked on in glee as Hirohito celebrated victory on their grainy television.

On the screen, the emperor waved his snow-white gloves at the crowd. In the static, his waving hands looked like snow flurries. Beside him, his prime minister, Hideki Tojo, who doubled as the general of the Imperial Army and leader of the Imperial Rule Assistance Association, wore a neatly trimmed mustache, his bald head shining in the light. On their balcony in the Chrysanthemum Palace, they were the perfect image of glory. Beneath them, a sea of fans waved red dots: Japanese flags. Seen from an aerial camera, the billowing fabrics looked like an unfurling creature with millions of eyes.

"Soon, we'll have more than we ever dreamed," Haruki promised Junko. But privately, he worried that their parents were working longer and longer hours. When their father made it home, he was too weary to rise from his chair. He stared at nothing, sipping sake. His mother's fingers were covered in blisters. She couldn't sew uniforms fast enough at the factory to keep up with the casualties in the Imperial Army. Despite the proclamations of victory, Hiroshima was suffering from food and medicine shortages. More and more, Haruki was skipping meals so Junko could eat. He'd gotten used to walking their commute instead of driving, but the lack of fuel had begun to wreak havoc across the country. For the first time, his college classmates had begun to question their divine emperor.

Tojo took his turn at the podium. He boasted that "there were so many volunteers for suicide missions that recruits were like a swarm of bees who die after they have stung."

But Haruki kept thinking about the stories that had begun to surface in town. People feared the newspapers were lying. Most of the kamikaze pilots were younger than him. Even if it was true that they were beaten so brutally that their faces were unrecognizable, it was still a death of honor, he thought. Even if they had to be forced into their planes, they died like heroes.

Still, some of the rumors were harder to justify. The official line was that the kamikaze were instructed to turn back if they couldn't identify a target, so as not to waste their lives lightly. But one pilot who returned nine times had recently been shot for his cowardice.

"It's our glory," Haruki insisted, staring hard at the screen, "to be Japanese."

"To restore past racial and spiritual purity," Junko agreed. Then she recited the Samurai Creed: "Bushido is a way of dying."

He turned to look at her. He shouldn't have been surprised to hear her repeat the propaganda. But she was only seven. What did she understand of what she was saying?

Even while he defended the glory of the kamikaze mission as he tucked her into bed, he knew that most pilots were only supplied enough gas to make a one-way trip.

29

September 1945
Caleb

Bright and early, while most of the recruits were still asleep, Sergeant Moony called Caleb to the office for a phone call.

"Is it true?" The intonation on the other end was so flat, he almost didn't recognize Asher's voice. A wave of relief rushed through him.

"Asher, are you home? Have you been discharged?"

"Is it true?" Asher repeated. His voice was more forceful now.

"Is what true?"

"Was that your bomb?"

Across his desk, Sergeant Moony was watching him. He had been scribbling something in a notebook, but he had stopped writing to meet Caleb's eyes. He pushed the notebook away and stared.

My bomb, Caleb thought. The words came from his brother, but the question was his own. He recited the excuse he often told himself: "I had to contribute to the war effort somehow. You were out there risking your life."

"You still don't get it, do you?" Asher's voice wasn't angry now, just defeated and small.

"Listen, the way it works out here, it woulda gone down the same way with or without me. I was just a face in the crowd." Caleb had repeated Saul's logic so many times, it was second nature. But he no longer believed his own words.

"You've never seen corpses floating in the water like logs. You don't have to witness the aftermath."

"Asher, all those people could have been dead American soldiers. It was us or them."

"I never thought you had it in you," Asher continued, refusing to weigh death against death. "The kid I knew was too goody two-shoes to shoot anyone. But as long as you didn't have to get your hands dirty . . . well. Look what you've done."

Caleb felt something crumpling inside him. He took a short, staggered breath. "Asher, don't say things you'll regret."

"On my worst day, I can only kill one person at a time."

Caleb bristled. He was racked with guilt, and the accusations made him furious and defensive. He had had no other choice but to come here, unlike Asher, who had abandoned his family and flown out of the hemisphere. Caleb was never trying to be a hero. He also wasn't a villain. He clenched. "I'm not proud of it."

"You're not?"

"I keep thinking about the other forty-three thousand and five hundred victims—the ones who were counted as being not seriously wounded. They keep dying mysteriously from slight burns and minor wounds. I'm afraid it's only just begun."

Asher sighed. "All those years when I was teaching you about the scientific method, lighting up lightbulbs with potato batteries, I never knew what you were capable of, what you had inside you. I wish I could take it all back."

Caleb tried to stay calm. His brother didn't sound well. "You don't mean that," he reasoned, but Asher had already hung up. He was only talking to himself.

An hour later, under the bright lights in the Project Rufus lab, morning didn't seem to exist. Around the plutonium core, it was always high noon. With the gadgets deployed, much of the work had come to a temporary halt on the hill. But at Project Rufus, there was a sudden mad rush to store up additional research, to record all the findings on official letterheads, and to push for new frontiers. They were on the verge of even larger explosions. It was unthinkable, so Caleb tried not to think.

While he put in extra hours alongside Harry, he tried not to worry about Asher. He looked around the room, past Harry, at Louis Slotin and the security team. These were the good guys. After the grotesque news about Nagasaki, he was less sure than he had been before, but he was still fairly certain.

Rough as he was around the edges, Harry had become one of his closest friends. In Harry's company, he had even begun to enjoy his time on the project. Harry wiped the sweat from his brow with the furry back of his hand, seeming self-conscious of his armpit stains. "Look at me, I'm sweating like a sinner in church," he said, elbowing Caleb with a laugh.

A few feet away, Slotin moved his slender fingers gingerly when he placed the uranium hydride, but he, too, was sweating. Finally, he unbuttoned his shirt and navigated the pile bare-chested.

"I'm in your corner," Caleb encouraged Harry, who was using just a screwdriver instead of the designated safety shims to keep the spheres separated. Slotin preferred the procedure be performed that way. "It's cleaner," he insisted. "Besides, it puts hair on your chest."

It was still cold outside, but under the bright lights of Project Rufus, and the blaring car headlights aimed through the propped door like spotlights, it was hard to breathe.

When Fermi stopped by that week for an impromptu safety check-in, he worried that no one was wearing their dosimetry badges to monitor radiation. "You'll be dead in a year," he said with a frown, "if you keep flouting safety protocols."

Slotin staggered back, holding his belly like Fermi had punched him in the gut. "That was below the belt," he said. Then he smiled and looked right over Fermi's short, balding head. "If we have to do it all by the book, I'm liable to throw in the towel."

Caleb was learning to let go of some of the rigid behaviors he'd grown up with under his father's meticulous watch, and he rather liked this relaxed approach to the work.

He and Harry worked side by side while the wind rattled the propped door against the cinderblock that supported it. They were building a stack of tungsten carbide bricks around the plutonium sphere to create a "neutron reflector." Harry gingerly lowered the mass plutonium required for criticality, testing the fit. He added another brick-shaped piece of metal around the plutonium, and then another, making it more unstable with each addition.

A single guard sat in the corner, charged with fire safety. He wasn't really looking, though. He kept nodding off, his head bobbing.

While they worked, Harry rattled on about conspiracy theories.

"They cut a man in two pieces vertically and pickled him in a six-foot glass jar," he was saying, staring hard at the mass. "A human preserve." He'd been glued to the news of Hirohito's top-secret Unit 731. There were rumors everywhere of biological warfare.

"Research for Operation Cherry Blossoms at Night." Caleb nodded, referencing Hirohito's abandoned plans to attack San Diego with bubonic-plague infected fleas.

"They'll cover it up, you know," Harry said. His combed hair had gone limp with sweat and was sagging into his face. His hands being occupied, he shook his bangs from his eyes.

"What?"

"In exchange for scientific data on frostbite and poison gas."

"Sure," Caleb agreed weakly. He was tired of discussing the horrors committed in the name of science. He wondered whether Asher regretted his whole childhood.

"The mother who shielded her daughter from the gas chamber with her body while physicians took notes on her spasms," Harry said, his hand rattling slightly, "will be wiped from history. A mom's a mom, you know?" His breath was labored. "It broke my heart into a million little pieces," he said, keeping his eyes locked on the sphere in front of him, "having to tell my mother I was leaving for the duration of the war without telling her where I was going."

"Not being able to tell them was the hardest part," Caleb agreed.

"Even now, they don't know where I've gone or what I'm working on," he said.

"Are you going to tell them?"

"Someday," he said.

"Same here," Caleb lied, knowing full well that after Asher's reaction, he would never tell his mother.

"I figure it's just about time for me to lick my wounds and head home, seein' as contracts are up," he said. It was the closest Harry had ever come to abandoning his tough guy persona. He must have lost his focus because his hand slipped just a fraction of an inch, but it was enough to get both their hearts racing.

"Eyes on the pile," Caleb instructed, his voice taking on urgency. As they approached criticality, he had the overwhelming sensation of a sour taste in his mouth. But it could have just been the placebo effect. He always got nervous with those final bricks.

Afterward, they broke for dinner, parting ways. Harry rested a chubby hand on Caleb's shoulder. "We'll be home again before we know it, brother."

Caleb cringed. He was homesick, of course. But he was homesick for a home that existed only in his memory, sweetened by the haze of nostalgia, improved by wishful thinking. He hadn't heard any news about the foreclosure, and even if the house was still theirs, he couldn't bring Alice to that ramshackle neighborhood. He also couldn't see his parents eating off her fine china. He could never go to the Fillmore with Alice on his arm and a baby in her lap, stepping over glass shards and getting cat-called by the loiterers. He refused to raise a child there, to subject his offspring to the traumas of his own childhood. He and Alice would build a home together, but it would have to be somewhere new. "Sure," he agreed. "Soon enough."

Harry nodded in the direction of the lab. "It might look like a hunk of junk, but it's a building with four walls and tomorrow inside."

Caleb nodded, but he hated that building. Wherever he went, whatever he did, he couldn't shake the tally in his head of the people who had died because of the science he had helped dream up. Every time he passed someone on the street, he wondered if the guilt showed on him. How many more would lose their lives because of his calculations? He had spent all his time in this secret city racing toward the future so eagerly, thrilled to have money to send home, and thankful to avoid the violence of the army. He'd felt so lucky to spend the war years admiring the natural world and dreaming about scientific realms of possibility, he hadn't ever stopped to question what world would be left waiting for him when he got out.

Caleb made his way to the mess hall. While he spooned around his mashed potatoes, he kept thinking about Harry's eyes when he had spoken of his mother. He had been manipulating the very material that made up the galaxy with his fat fingers, like a god. But like a little boy, all he wanted was his mother. Then, Caleb thought of his own mother, scrubbing the bathroom tiles till they gleamed in their corner store. "Pooh, pooh, pooh," she had said, spitting three times to ward off evil when he had first told her he was leaving for a top-secret project in a town without a name.

Suddenly a ruckus broke out in the dining area. People were shouting. Recognizing Frisch's harsh Austrian accent across the room, Caleb leaped to his feet, abandoning his tray.

"What's happened?" he asked.

Frisch had a pinched expression. "Slotin sent me to collect you."

"Why?"

"It's Harry," he said. "Hurry."

Caleb rushed to the barracks hospital. A chime signaled his entry and Timoshenko, caught off guard by his panicked movements, leaped to his feet and howled. Caleb backpedaled.

"Timmy! Down!" Petey chastised the Irish wolfhound from behind her partition, not even glancing from her clipboard. Timoshenko cowered and walked three indecisive circles before grunting and lowering himself to the floor. His beady eyes were buried beneath waves of silver fur, so Caleb couldn't be certain, but he seemed to drift back to sleep. He watched the great belly heave before regaining his composure and taking stock of the room.

Louis Slotin was sitting in the waiting room, staring through his round glasses at his steel-toe boots. Removed from the romance of the plutonium core humming in its cave, he looked frail. In that small secret layer, Slotin's movements were always purposeful, and he always seemed to know what to do with his hands. Here, he was reduced to just another man waiting out the clock.

Caleb eased himself down into the small folding chair beside his supervisor. The seat creaked under his weight.

He was so nervous, he couldn't sit still. He turned to Slotin. "Harry returned to his station? After we parted?"

"The guard was off duty. There was no one to prevent him from working alone," Slotin grumbled, never looking up from his feet. "He was drawn back like a man under a spell."

"He would have been wearing the monitor," Caleb said, meaning the precautionary instrument they all used, the one Fermi had been adamant about. He felt the need to defend his friend even if there was no justifiable explanation, even if it was a fool's errand. Harry should have known better.

"Those monitors are hairy at best, and you know it."

They fell into an uncomfortable silence. Timoshenko was dreaming now, yelping and shuddering, wriggling his enormous paws like he was chasing something. Caleb stared at the dog, running through it again. Slotin recounted it for him forward and backward. No matter how many ways he told it, the outcome remained the same. Harry had lain out four layers of bricks, then a fifth layer, no problem. When he was about to place a brick over the center, his monitor had illuminated. Startled, he had rushed to remove the brick, but it slipped from his fingers and fell directly on top of the plutonium core. He swept the brick away in one quick gesture, but it was too late to save himself. A blue flash lit the room and vanished just as quickly. If he had blinked, he would have missed it. But for that fraction of a second, the assembly had gone critical. That was all it took. He called for an ambulance and Slotin had been rushed to the scene as his supervisor and emergency contact.

"When I got there," Slotin was saying, "he was eerily calm, accounting for every detail. That ambulance ride was like a funeral procession. He knew what it meant."

"I shouldn't've left him," Caleb said. He shouldn't have left Saul, either, on the day he lost his hand. Slotin nodded. "It was a knockout punch."

Caleb noticed that his team leader did not disagree with his statement. He did not recuse him of his guilt.

"I coulda stopped it," Caleb said, realizing it fully only as he said it out loud.

Slotin didn't seem to hear him. "He's in there waitin' to die." Finally, he turned to look Caleb in the eye. "I don't know which is worse: dyin' or waitin'."

Inside, Harry looked away from him sheepishly. He seemed self-conscious about his hospital gown and shifted his weight in the bed, trying to conceal his naked backside without needing to move his hands, which had been rendered immobile. His already chubby fingers were swollen around the knuckles and he was unable to straighten them. He propped his opened hands on his thighs like dinner plates. The skin on his palms was rubbery and slick. Caleb tried not to look directly at the dark black spots on his fingertips, although he couldn't help feeling overwhelmed by curiosity. He didn't want to gape, but he desperately wanted to see.

"Fingertips are the first place to show changes," Frisch had said, back in those first few days. Caleb understood now. Frisch been referring to radiation poisoning.

Harry broke the silence. "I don't mean to pass the buck. I know what I done." He was staring out the window at the army-green buildings and the low blue sky.

Caleb stepped closer. "Harry," he began, but then he couldn't think what to say.

"I goofed," he said, "plain and simple."

"Did ya tell your parents?"

Harry turned to look at him. His lips had gone white. "Nobody tells 'em, you hear me?"

"Don't ya want them to come see you?" He didn't say what they were both thinking—that they would want to come say goodbye.

They sat there without speaking for a minute.

"It would kill my ma," Harry said eventually in a defeated voice, looking down at his hands, "to know what I been up to all this time. Suppose I got what I deserved." He turned back to the window. "I ain't alone in this, you know." The window shutters cast striped shadows across his profile, cutting his face to pieces.

Caleb remembered something he had heard about prisoners wearing striped uniforms so that even in fleeting moments when they weren't behind bars, they were still in a cage. Even if Harry could take it all back, even if he could go home tomorrow, he couldn't leave unscathed. "We'll all get what's comin' to us," he said.

Alice

Harry was asleep when she got there. He must have been given some heavy narcotics. She stood beside his hospital bed, uncertain whether to wake him. The room stunk of rot. His hand was swollen, resting on top of the covers, the size of a baseball mitt.

It was only a few minutes before a nurse flew into the room, flicked a needle, and rolled him on his side for an injection.

"Hiya," Alice said as Harry's pearly eyes focused on her, his pupils dilating and contracting.

He raised his eyebrows in surprise. "Hiya, stranger," he said weakly. "Didn't expect you'd turn up here."

"Ya, it's been a minute," Alice said, holding her swollen belly and searching for a place to sit. The only chair was pushed up right next to him.

"You got out of Rufus," he said. "You always were smarter than the rest of us."

"Oh, Harry," she said. She felt tears welling in her eyes and steadied herself. "This could just as easily have happened on my watch."

"Nah, you run a tight ship, Doc."

"Why in God's name were you trying to work alone?"

"I figured the sooner I got it done, the sooner I could go home." She could see from the way he refused to meet her eyes that this was a lie. He stared out the window, looking incredibly lonely.

"Is there anything I can do for you? Anything you need?"

He seemed to think this over for a long while. He was groggy and his head slumped forward. For a moment, she thought from the way his eyelids drooped that he was falling back asleep. Finally, he said, "Be good to Caleb. He's doin' his best by you."

She sighed and finally eased down into the chair at his bedside. She could see the enlarged pores on his nose, like the rind of an orange. Sweat was dribbling down his temple. "Oh, Harry," she said. "Here you are, and all you can think of is Caleb. Would it kill you to be selfish for once?"

He stared at her and his eyes were milky and flecked with points, like a galaxy. She could see herself reflected in them, twice over, her waft of curls, her chain necklace. "His parents are going to lose their house. While the rest of us pocket the dough, he's been sending his paychecks home all this time. He tells me stuff he won't tell the SEDs, you know. He's got a better heart than the rest of us, that's for sure."

She gasped. Alice knew by now that Caleb's home life was bleak, that he was ashamed of his past. But a foreclosure? "Their house?"

"Listen—" He reached for her and she shuddered. It terrified her. So little was known about radiation exposure. He yanked his hand back. "Most of these men are sexist as a door handle. They don't think a woman can understand the scientific complexities." He thumped the side of his head indicating intelligence. "I don't have to tell you that."

"You certainly don't."

"Caleb, he may have kept what he knew from you. Hell, he kept it from me. But he doesn't keep secrets for himself the way the rest of us do. He keeps them for other people—he holds the bad parts in so that other people don't have to. He didn't want you to know, not because you couldn't be trusted or you couldn't handle it. But because he wanted a better world for you. He was hell-bent on building you a better world."

Alice turned Harry's words over in her head as she exited through the waiting room where a small child was stacking blocks. Timoshenko perked an ear at the sound of her heeled oxfords. She considered Harry's wish. He was a man who'd spent more time in Caleb's company than anyone on the mesa, aside from Dick, Saul, and herself. She hadn't thought they spoke about anything of substance during their long work hours. Did he really know what was in Caleb's heart? But then, looking into his marble eyes had been like looking straight through into another dimension, into whatever world came after this one. He was seeing things with the clarity of a man about to die.

Caleb had lied to her because he loved her. Not because he thought she'd leave him for being poor, or because she was a woman who couldn't handle the reality of the gadget, but because he wished these horrible parts of the world and himself weren't true. He spent so much time daydreaming. It was this dreamy quality that had first drawn her to him. Since Trinity, they had gone through the motions of being back together, sharing a bed, eating meals, going for hikes. She'd even let him kiss her in public. And there was the way he put his hand on her belly and spoke to their child. It was the best part of her day. But she was holding him at arm's length. She had yet to forgive him. She was hiding out in this town, where a hierarchy of secrets governed them, shackling them to their stations, preventing them from just being two people.

She trotted down the hospital steps and broke into a run. They could pack up and leave tonight. Contracts were up. They were free to go. They'd make it work somehow. It was a new age out there. They could get married and start their lives together outside of the barbed wire periphery. The rest would sort itself out.

By the time she was at the barracks door, she was panting. She fanned herself with her hands and ran her fingers through her tousled hair. She summoned the courage to tell him she wanted to marry him. If they left now and drove as far and as fast as they could, they might just make it to San Francisco before nightfall.

But it was Saul who answered. "Alice Katz, in the flesh. Ain't that just the cat's meow?"

"Where's Caleb? I need to talk to him."

"Sorry, doll, he's gone with Dick to Albuquerque." He glanced over his shoulder and made his voice uncharacteristically gentle. "Poor man's wife is finally kickin' the bucket."

Caleb

Caleb watched the ceiling while a chorus of men snored in different octaves. On the nights he and Alice slept apart, he never slept a wink. If only she could be beside him, pressed against him between the covers.

He heard someone shouting outside. He felt blindly for his slippers at the foot of his bunk and slipped out. Dick was staggering by the pond, prying up small boulders, hoisting them over his head, and hurling them in. Minnows and tadpoles scattered in their wake. When he saw Caleb, he kept right on chucking rocks, but he clenched his jaw.

"Arline's dying," he said with his back turned. He flung a fistful of stones. "Any day now."

It was already getting colder after sundown. Caleb shivered in the thin material of his undershirt. He crossed his arms for warmth and stared at the rippling water, concentric circles expanding endlessly from the points where the stones had submerged. "It ain't the same thing," he said, "but my brother may as well be dead." It was the first he had said it out loud. "The man coming home from the Pacific is a shell of the one I knew."

"You never told me," said Dick, plopping down in the dirt beside him. They both stared into the jiggling water.

"Instead of enlisting alongside him, I traded up for all this." He gestured at the ramshackle houses.

"I made Arline come all this way," Dick said, "just to die alone in a sanatorium."

Caleb felt his Jewish star medallion, cold as ice against his chest. "There's something we say in temple," he began, but Dick interrupted him.

"Don't talk that hocus pocus at me," he said.

Caleb sized him up. It was common knowledge that the Jewish quota had kept Dick out of Columbia, that he had arrived at MIT not by choice but because even if he didn't consider himself Jewish, the world saw what it saw. So, Caleb pressed on and recited what he felt certain Dick needed to hear: "Love doesn't die, people do. So, when all that's left of me is love, give me away."

Dick wiped the snot from his nose with the back of his hand. "You know," he said, his eyes glistening, "I wanted to open 'em just to open 'em. But those safes were full of things I wish I hadn't learned." He looked at Caleb head on. His expression was deranged. "It's a paradox," he said. "The word *safe*."

Neither thought of sleeping after that. They buried themselves in work at the T, while they waited for the call from Arline's father. It was unbearably hot in the small computing center with just one tiny rotating fan. Dick stooped in the corner. He looked like he hadn't showered in days.

In the quiet, Caleb tried not to think of Harry in his hospital bed just across the pond.

When the phone finally rang, they both jumped, but for very different reasons.

"Dick here," he said.

"You'd better get down here right away, son." Caleb could hear the gruff voice through the line. Dick dropped the receiver, and it swung like a pendulum back and forth on its curled cord, just an inch above the floor. He could hear the sound waves of the echoing dial tone, higher pitched swinging toward him and then lower pitched swinging away. It was the Doppler effect, he thought, remembering Alice's description of Abigail's muted calls from the water, the way a siren sounds higher pitched and more powerful right before it reaches you.

Dick jolted and knocked over a stack of papers, and they snowed down around the room. He grabbed his hat from the rack and rushed down the hall without looking back. "Come with me," he shouted over his shoulder at Caleb.

Caleb gasped. "You sure?" The death of one's wife was not the sort of thing to which you brought just anyone. He couldn't just vanish into the wallpaper or fade away into the background if he was in the room with a dying woman. Also, if he was being honest, he was terrified. He'd never seen death up close. He couldn't stomach the idea of watching the light leave Arline's eyes. If he couldn't believe in religion, or any sort of afterlife, there was nothing spiritual to reassure him about dying. Death was just the end of a sentence. Like a telegram, stop.

"Listen," said Dick, turning back and looking him in the eye. "You seem like you ain't cut from the same cloth as all these blowhards. They don't even look at ya when they talk—too busy looking at their own reflections in your eyes. Everyone on this hill is so in love with themselves. It's Narcissus staring into the pond, for Christ's sake. I'm not looking for a drinking buddy. My wife is dying. You and your Jewish gobbledygook might be useful. She's about as religious as a water bug, but she deserves a proper send-off."

Later, while Dick knelt beside Arline's hospital bed, his face glistening with sweat, Caleb wondered what it had been like for Asher to watch his comrades die.

A water clock stood over Arline's bedside. Mechanically speaking, it was a dinosaur. "I spent countless hours trying to keep it running," Dick explained. It had kept malfunctioning no matter what he did. They watched the clock tick in silence. When the room finally darkened, Arline's clammy skin seemed to glow. By the time the sky was dappled with faint stars, dimmed by the city's light pollution, Arline's cold face lit the room.

Caleb came and went, retrieving coffees and snacks from the small vending machines. A metallic tang of antiseptic and stainless steel wafted into his nostrils each time he reentered the room, but he quickly went nose-blind to it. He was right beside Dick when a nurse pronounced her time of death at 9:21, reading from the little clock.

For some reason that no one could explain, Arline's clock froze at her time of death, 9:21. "Maybe the cogs caught when the nurse picked it up," Dick said in Caleb's direction, but he wasn't really speaking to him in particular. "Or the oscillator ceased to invoke perpetual motion." He seemed fixated on solving it. Of her death, Dick said nothing at all.

Caleb placed a hand on his shoulder. "If you'd like, we can recite the El Malei Rachamim." He suggested the prayer for the soul of the departed gently. It was the only thing he had to offer.

"I'm an atheist," Dick huffed. He seemed to have forgotten his request of only a few hours prior. He was a different man now than he had been that morning.

"Jewish is Jewish," Caleb urged.

"I prefer not to be classified as a Jew," Dick said, his face setting. He turned the clock over and over in his hands. "God was invented to explain mystery. God is always invented to explain those things that you do not understand."

Dick didn't say a word on the drive back up the hill. His movements were mechanical, his face vacant. It wasn't until they flashed their badges at the gate and waited for the blinking light to summon their entrance back into the secret city that he said, "You know, when I hugged her, right after she died, her hair still smelled exactly the same."

That night, Caleb never made it to bed. He scanned the laboratory, which was flooded by emergency lights in every direction. He bolted the door and emptied his pockets, sprinkling out a handful of pennies. They rolled along the counter, spinning like dreidels and drawing lopsided circles before they settled. He sorted them, selecting the ones that shone the most brilliantly. He was nervous. He knew that finely divided copper could react violently on contact with oxidizing agents, even in trace amounts on the lab equipment. It was an explosion hazard, and it was possible to produce poisonous gases in the fire.

Gingerly, he positioned the pennies in the mouth of a spoon and secured the end with a clamp. He investigated the blowtorch, filling it with lighter fluid and triple-checking the on/off valve to avoid accidentally igniting it. He had never used one before, but he needed something that would achieve a temperature above 1,984 degrees. When the fire made contact with the copper and the oxygen, it instantly changed color to bright green. He leaned away reflexively. The heat stung his eyes even behind his safety goggles. The ventilation was no good in there and he knew better. In melting down the combination of copper, zinc, and tin, he had released copper-oxide fumes. He was exposing himself to metal-fume fever, and he'd have to be wary of a headache, nausea, vomiting, diarrhea, or sore throat. He had read of cases where inhaling it burned a hole in the septum—the bone dividing the inner nose. His skin began to itch under his protective gloves.

He carefully poured the molten metal into a cylindrical tube. While he waited for it to cool, he recalled Alice's words: "I'm not interested in a wedding fit for a princess." She had explained that as far back as she could remember, her mother had threatened that no man would ever marry her in her lab coat. "What I need is a wedding fit for a physicist."

She might be from a different dimension, a world of fine china and French pastries. He looked down at the scuffs in his shoes and his frayed jeans. His shirt cuff was missing a button. He might nose-dive, roll cartwheels into the sea, and burst into plumes of smoke like the kamikaze on the evening news. But God help him if he wasn't already airborne.

With the hands of a surgeon, he cautiously rounded the edges and smoothed away rough patches. His drill sliced effortlessly into the soft heart of the metal. It had partially hardened, but it was still malleable, suspended in a purgatory between physical forms. He hammered the orb carefully, cautious not to move too quickly and tear it. It was strange that something that seemed so solid in one form could be transformed into a state so vulnerable and fragile. Finally, it began to resemble a ring. He sanded it down and buffed it with metal polish until it sparkled.

He began to feel light-headed. He knew that repeated exposure might cause a greenish discoloration of his skin, hair, and teeth. He was wary, but he did not plan on repeating the process. You only got married once, he thought. Besides, love was worth dying for.

He pocketed the ring. It was 4:00 AM, too late to show up at Alice's doorstep. He'd have to wait for morning. But, he thought restlessly, Harry would be awake. The lights never went out in that wing of the hospital.

It was impossible to prepare for what he saw on his return visit. He understood that his friend was dying by inches. But walking into that room, he still had hope. He believed that the war was over. The world would recover.

Even in its worst moments, he had always held onto a belief that they would make it through to the other side.

But inside that hospital room, Harry ceased to be Harry. The room stunk of excrement and rot. Caleb tried not to retch. Harry was emaciated. The skin that remained on his arms and chest was sloughing off in layers. He was a man-shaped hole. What had begun as black dots on his fingertips had multiplied, transforming his fingers to dark claws. His fingernails had gone blue. There were growths oozing from his knuckles like barnacles. Caleb stared at the gangrenous skin. The man was covered in scales and blisters like some kind of aquatic monster.

He left Harry at sunrise and went to Alice, the ring tucked away in his breast pocket—but in his mind, he was still trapped in that room. She let him in wordlessly and stumbled back to bed. He removed his glasses in the smudgy darkness. He nestled up close beside her, but without his specs, their army cot resembled Harry's hospital bed and the bedside lamp was an IV tube pumping fluids.

She drifted back to sleep instantly, and he tried not to wake her.

In the brightness of morning, he brushed his fingers through her silky hair, swept up. She met his hand in her dark curls. She gave the pin a tug and shook out her hair. The scent of lavender wafted as her jet-black hair cascaded over the pillow. Her eyes flashed and she looked at him like she was waiting for something.

Do it, he thought. *Marry me.* He could just say it. He couldn't bring himself to ask. Not after what he had just seen. Soon enough, he promised. Once this Harry ordeal was over.

Over breakfast, he told her about Arline. "It was like watching in slow motion," he explained. Alice poked at her food. "He just kept trying to fix that stupid clock." Neither one dared to take a bite. His coffee jiggled in the mug when he finally pushed it away.

"Sometimes when people don't know *why* something happens, they have to settle for how," Alice said. "Any girl would be lucky," she said, "to be loved like that."

Taking her words as invitation, he slid closer to her.

"I mean it," she said. "Some people live seventy years and never love like that." He studied her face. Was she trying to tell him something? "You were a good friend to go with him."

He had never met a woman like her before. He reached for her hand. Her skin was porcelain, unblemished and smooth. His skin awakened at the weight of her hand in his. He became suddenly hyperaware of the creases and folds in his palm, all the nerve endings on the tips of his fingers. They sat there quietly, their fingers grasping for each other across the unmapped border of the breakfast table.

Finally, Alice fumbled through her purse and snapped open a compact and began to powder her nose. All the shivering emotion blanched out of her face. The emotional glitter in her eyes dulled. She assumed a mask of composure behind that pressed powder. She smoothed the puffs of escaped frizz behind her ear with her fingers.

"Why don't we go see him together?" he said.

"Dick?" she asked.

"No, Harry."

When she went to get dressed, he dreamed of a world where he could spend his life growing old by her side. Seventy years from now, they would be sitting on a bench, watching the stars twinkle over the bay while hundreds of small windows flicked off their lights one by one across the San Francisco skyline.

Seeing Harry in the daylight, with the precision of his glasses, was a living nightmare. He and Alice went together to the hospital, and they witnessed in detail what hundreds of thousands had suffered in Hiroshima and Nagasaki. They could see the peach fuzz on his fingers, bright white against dead skin. They saw the flecks of vomit and blood on his hospital sheets, and the sweat stain he left behind, so similar to the shadows of Hiroshima—those horrific silhouettes of children flying through the air that had imprinted in the buildings in ash. They stared at the chafing bed sores on Harry's back when Petey rotated him or came in to clear his bedpan.

Caleb watched Alice's face cautiously. He knew that no matter where they traveled or how many miles they put between themselves and the mesa, some small part of them would always be trapped in that hospital room, prisoners in stripes.

The next day, Harry slipped into a coma. Caleb felt obligated to sit beside him, even though he realized Harry would never know. He was surprised to find that his friend's hands had gone from black to chalk white. It took him a moment to deduce that the color change was because his hands were already dead. His brain might still be alive, but his extremities had already extinguished. The only noises in the room were the harmonized whirring and whooshing machines and Harry's labored breathing. There was the heart monitor beeping on intervals and the endless ticking clock.

"He can hear ye," encouraged Petey, flicking the IV tubes for bubbles. "Talk to him. He's listening."

Caleb nodded, but he had nothing to say. He still had nothing to say the next day when the peaks on Harry's heart monitor flatlined and the doctor came in to pronounce him. Before they closed them, Harry's eyes stared at the ceiling, seeing nothing.

All this time, Caleb had been so afraid of proximity to death. He had made many choices to avoid being in the room with it. That's why it was strange that when they covered the remains in a white sheet, he felt nothing. He only thought that the hills and valleys of Harry's body parts beneath the sheet looked just like the snow-covered mountains.

That week, they threw together a piecemeal memorial at Fuller Lodge. It was a small affair by necessity since senior officials had hushed up the circumstances of Harry's death. Friends were permitted to celebrate his life but forbidden to discuss the details.

It felt disrespectful that it was such a beautiful September day. Sunlight flooded the room. Flies buzzed around the food. The wives made casseroles and pot roasts and put out doilies and linens. Alice made an eggplant dish that was as tasteless and jiggly as an undercooked egg. But it didn't matter. Nobody ate much. They just congregated around the food talking about how good it looked. Without any windows cracked, it got hot in there with so many bodies packed in close quarters. When they took their seats, the women fanned themselves with their programs and the men used their broad-brimmed hats. Row by row, they unbuttoned their collars and tugged loose their ties.

Caleb studied the photograph propped on the easel of young Harry with kinky curls and chubby cheeks. His skin glowed and his eyes glittered with youth. He couldn't stand looking at it. He took off his glasses and watched the image shiver into an unrecognizable blur.

He scanned the crowd. Sitting at the edge of his field of vision, on the cusp of a horizon line of his own ocular invention, he recognized the man from Miyuki Bridge. He was still in his shredded, bloodstained clothes, but he flipped through the program casually with his index finger, with the air of someone in church. His left sleeve had been burned to shreds, revealing flayed skin beneath, imprinted with the pinstripes of his incinerated shirt. Caleb crossed his legs and the man crossed his simultaneously. He wiped sweat from his brow and the man did the same, a perfect twinning. He stood up to leave, but before he could see if the man had done the same, Alice tugged his sleeve. He realized his abrupt gesture had interrupted the service. On the podium, one of the wives had been speaking and had paused to look at him. All the eyes in the room were trained on him. After that, he put his glasses back on and suffered silently through the look on young Harry's face in the photograph. When he checked again, there was no one seated in the corner. Of course there wasn't. He tried to focus, but he hardly heard a word of the service.

"Heaven needed an angel," the woman said from the podium, gesturing up at the ceiling. She wore a droopy derby hat weighed down by fake flowers. Her lip quivered, but she pressed on. "God called him back. Who are we to ask why?" Caleb longed to explain that while Harry had a heart of gold, he was no angel. These people didn't even know him. Beside him, Alice dabbed her tears with a tissue.

"I'll say a few words," volunteered Saul. The aisles were narrow enough that the tail of Saul's trench coat brushed Alice's knee when he passed by. He took off his hat and held it over his heart with his good hand. He searched the room. His eyes flickered over Alice with her curls swept up, her enormous pregnant belly concealed behind her black chiffon shawl. The gemstones in her teardrop earrings jiggled slightly, even though outwardly, she appeared to be sitting perfectly still. Saul's gaze landed on Caleb. He cleared his throat.

"We can take solace in knowing he has his hands back," he said. Despite themselves, everyone in the room looked at Saul's deformed hand. Even with the antibiotics he had been prescribed, he had developed nerve damage. He experienced abnormal sensations and involuntary spasms. Sometimes, in the middle of the night his hand was unbearably itchy, like he was being pricked by needles. At the mess hall the other day, he had failed to notice his hand was resting on a hot plate. Now, his forearm was shaking convulsively. "Wherever he is. If nothing else, there's that." Caleb shifted in his seat. He felt Saul's eyes settle on him again, but he also felt Harry's eyes in the picture burning through him.

Alice seemed uneasy. She squeezed his hand. He wondered whether she was trying to comfort him, or whether she wanted the reassurance for herself. Her teardrop earrings clacked, giving her away.

Dick had snuck in late. He was in his lab coat, underdressed and antsy. He ran his hands through his chestnut hair, attempting to coax the waves into a last-minute side part. He caught Caleb's eye and nodded.

Then Caleb spotted Oppenheimer sitting morosely near the aisle, his porkpie hat over his heart. He could see the blues of his eyes floating from across the room. He was larger than life these days, his porkpie hat gracing the covers of periodicals. Just last week, *Scientific Monthly* had proclaimed, "Modern Prometheans have raided Mount Olympus and have brought back for man the very thunderbolts of Zeus." *If anyone was to blame, it was Oppenheimer*, Caleb thought. This should have been his funeral. That was meant to be him laid out in the casket in Wranglers and boots with wild hair and a still, unflinching Adam's apple.

Just as quickly as he had the thought, he was ashamed of it. He couldn't blame Oppenheimer. They had all come here of their own volition, drawn to the secrets like mosquitoes to the light. *Besides*, he thought, when Saul finally ambled from the podium back into the ranks of the audience, *if anyone in this room is cursed, it's me.*

While they lingered around the buffet talking about the weather and the war, Dick wrapped his arm around Caleb and pulled him aside. He did not look well. His eyes were glossy and he stared past Caleb, tracking the movement of some distant figures across the room, but there was nothing there. "I told ya before, and I'll say it again. What you're doin' in that lab is suicide," he said, his voice strained. He plucked a grape from the display and popped it in his mouth. He scanned the room and grinned tightly as he made eye contact with the other mourners, but it was a Halloween mask of a smile. When he turned back to Caleb, his grin faded. "Look, Ace, you know me. I'm incurably curious. I would rather have questions that can't be answered than answers that can't be questioned."

"You've never been one for law and order," Caleb said.

"But with that humdrum, there'll be no one left."

30

September 1945
Alice

With contracts up, and decisions on the horizon, the reaction of the hill was divided into two camps: those who felt that something larger and even more powerful was within grasp if they forged onward, and those who had been spooked by Harry's death and decided that they had had enough of science being used for murder.

Since Caleb had told the SEDs over cigars and bourbon back when she first started to show, and the theoretical team's wives had taken to giving her baby gifts, Alice decided to finally tell her mother about her pregnancy. "Schrödinger's cat's outta the bag," she joked. "I'm pregnant." She hoped the joy of a grandchild might help ameliorate her mother's disapproval.

Although Mabel must have been horrified that her daughter had conceived outside of wedlock, to her credit, she had been polite. She had even been charming. Alice didn't trust it.

"Who is the father?" she asked with an expectant note in her voice. "Will there be a wedding?" Was she imagining things, or did her mother actually seem pleased by the prospect? Mabel had always wanted her to marry rich, distraught by the notion of her ending up with a poor scientist, but perhaps she wasn't all that surprised by this outcome. Sometimes, Alice marveled, her mother was wise beyond her years.

Alice braced herself. "His name is Caleb. We're not certain yet of the particulars, but we'll be looking for a house somewhere between Pacific Heights and the Fillmore."

"Good heavens," Mabel gasped. "The Fillmore?" But to her credit, she steered the conversation to nursery color palettes. "We'd better decide quickly between cloud white and sunlit coral; it sounds like this baby is well on its way."

"Any moment now," Alice groaned, feeling her abdomen twitch.

Alice was certain more was coming. Surely, Mabel would have a thing or two to say to her behind closed doors when next they were together, but at least over the phone, she had received the news with appropriate candor. She even seemed excited. Since then, she had begun stitching beaded throw pillows and hemming curtains for the nursery. She had purchased a bassinet and a swing. She had even prepared a basket of baby swaddles with giraffes and elephants printed on them in pastel hues that were all wrong for her usual midcentury modern design.

Alice took a seat beside Caleb in the back of Fuller Lodge. The weight of her pregnancy made her back ache in the rickety folding chair. The room was dimly lit aside from three bright spotlights that had been placed at the front by the makeshift stage, with a single extension cord taped down with duct tape, curling through the aisle like a snake. Beneath bright lights in the front of the room, Bethe's blond frock of hair looked snow white. Over his head, Oppenheimer's blue eyes smoldered.

She was surprised to spot Edward Teller, the moody Hungarian physicist, seated among the panelists at the front table. The joke lately had been that he was Oppie's mortal enemy. The two were old acquaintances who had disagreed about everything since back before the project had been founded, and their arguments had only escalated. From so far away, Teller's furry eyebrows looked like caterpillars.

Oppenheimer cleared his throat. The room quieted to the point that you could hear a pin drop. Finally, he spoke. "There are seven minutes to the end of the world."

Stunned listeners murmured, surprised by this Armageddon pronouncement. Several shifted in their seats, sending rustling noises around the room.

Someone in the middle of the crowd shouted, "Coward!"

"What better way to explain," Oppenheimer said, barreling onward, "than in the words of Leo Szilard on the eve of the Trinity test." He paused to collect himself and his eyes glittered. "'That night I knew the world was headed for sorrow.'" He scanned the air over the audience's heads, like he was reading a text that only he could see. "Together, with Einstein and a host of others, we have established the Bulletin of the Atomic Scientists. We aim to conceive of a doomsday clock, using our intimate knowledge of the innerworkings of the gadget to calculate how many minutes remain before midnight." He paused and glanced back at Bethe. Bethe nodded, urging him on, his broad forehead shining under the lights. He continued, "That is, how many minutes to the annihilation of the human race."

Alice and Caleb exchanged glances. "He had to do something," Caleb leaned close to whisper, "to rein it in."

Alice nodded. "We're dropping like flies," she said, meaning the empty lab. The T was a ghost town. Whether they were enticed by large university salaries, recruited back to depleted technical staffs, or morally opposed to the direction of Oppenheimer's leadership, there'd been a mass exodus from the hill.

Whispers and scuffling noises emanated from the audience as the room debated. Bethe unwound the string closure on a manila envelope and held up a document. "We have called this meeting to invite you to add your names to the list," Oppenheimer said, gesturing at the famous scientists in the front row and onstage.

Flanking him, Teller's features twitched on intervals as though in some past life he had been a ticking analog clock. He rapped twice on the table and stood up, rudely interrupting Oppie's monologue. "I've said it all along. What if we used hydrogen?" Teller allowed the question to linger for a moment, and then pressed on. "Nuclear fission is the pathway to the future," he continued. "Why stop now? We could build a super bomb, more powerful than any atomic weapon."

Alice felt her stomach lurch at the suggestion. She wondered whether it was her own tightening gut or the baby protesting. Oppenheimer scoffed at Teller's suggestion with a dismissive wave of his palm, twirling his cigarette smoke into elaborate spirals that expanded around the room. "It's not only improbable," he retorted. "It's immoral."

Alice glanced at Caleb, who had gone tense beside her. "We should have left when we had the chance," he said, keeping his eyes locked on Teller.

"You heard what the doctor said—that I could go into labor at any moment, and that there are long stretches of road on that drive with no medical care."

Teller sat back down, but behind his eyes a fuse had begun to tick. Alice looked around nervously. She could see the shifting expressions. There were rumbles around town that Oppenheimer had gone soft. Some of the scientists had begun calculating, talking hydrogen behind closed doors. Hydrogen would be expensive, but with the conservative bent of the government, and the looming fear of communism, it might just get greenlighted. This was the first it had been said in public.

Oppenheimer had a sunken look. "May the Lord preserve us from the enemy without and the Hungarians within," he groaned. He sat down. The

audience erupted in debate. Some were busy working through the mathematics and practicality of Teller's proposal, and others weighed the ethics.
No one took any notice when Oppenheimer stood and, like a cowboy, staggered outside into the sunset.

His meek exit was a stunning pivot from his role as fearless leader into
the unknown.

Later, in a statement that resounded even louder than the strike of any
doomsday clock, Oppenheimer refused to renew his contract and resigned
his post. Just like that, he packed up and left. His house on Bathtub Row
stood empty. There was no skeletal cowboy riding the trails in a porkpie
hat to guide them. The community panicked. Everyone was certain the lab
would be shut down.

"Not to worry," asserted Groves, his buttons gleaming. He introduced
Norris Bradbury as Oppenheimer's replacement the way you might swap out
a tire.

Norris Bradbury had a friendly grin, regularly shaved, and he dressed
up for work in the labs—or at least he was overdressed by the hill's relaxed
standards. He routinely wore a tucked in button-down, slacks, and a tie.
It was a culture shock to say the least. Most pronounced inevitable defeat
regardless of the direction he led: either they would be out of work by the
end of the year, or they would build Teller's hydrogen bomb and blow themselves to smithereens.

"Let's give him a month," Caleb suggested when Alice worried over the
bloodthirsty direction of the hill. "Get this baby out of you safely, and then
see what there is to see."

Caleb

That evening, he took Dick up on his invitation for a stiff drink.

"I've decided not to renew my contract," Dick said, forcing a grin. "Get
out while I still can."

Caleb had expected as much. After Oppenheimer left, all the greats
started fleeing like rats. Los Alamos was a sinking ship. Still, he was surprised how nervous the thought made him—life on the outside with Alice.

Despite all the hours they had passed together, Caleb had never been
inside Dick's house before. He tried not to stare. It was a mess of scattered

notes and discarded half-eaten plates of food. Abandoned and forgotten mugs were strewn around the room, and the coffee table was stained with hundreds of rings, like a fossil record of his movement. There was a musty smell to the place and Caleb wondered whether something was molding, or maybe it was just Dick's natural odor—he hadn't kept up with showering or shaving since Arline had passed. Caleb glanced at the window, considering whether to pry it open for fresh air.

Staring at the mess of science and philosophy books in heaps, he recalled his father's instructions to treat books as holy objects. Levi never dog-eared pages and was always careful to use a bookmark. He never ate while reading, and always read sitting up straight. Instead, Dick's books were beaten up, loved things. Several lay open on the couch and near the unmade bed, with double-underlined passages and exclamation points in the margins. It was like looking inside the mind of a genius.

"Pick your poison," instructed Dick. "I'm hankering for a Manhattan."

Caleb grimaced. "I don't know if I have the stomach for something that shares the name of this place."

"A wise man once told me to drink my sorrows."

When Dick left the room to stir up the cocktails, Caleb scanned the framed pictures of Arline around the room. It was hard to recognize the glowing woman in the photographs in the emaciated body he'd seen on her final day in the sanatorium. In the pictures, she was a dark-haired beauty with dimples. She wore her hair half-up in a glamorous pompadour with pin curls, or tied back with a playful bow. In every photo, Dick was grinning ear to ear, gazing at her like she was the sun and the stars. On the coffee table, they held hands in front of a Christmas tree. Bookending his collection of hardcovers on quantum mechanics, she sat on his lap and leaned into him with a flirtatious smirk. On the opposite wall, a collection of Arlines smiled in matching frames: riding a horse, posing in a bathing suit, wearing a floppy sun hat, and grinning on a pair of skis, looking like a kid.

He thumbed through the books on the shelf absently, embracing the opportunity to eavesdrop on Dick's private world. He noticed Proust's *In Search of Lost Time* fraternizing with the physics texts. It seemed at odds with everything else in the room, and everything he knew about Dick, so he pulled it out for a closer look. It was wedged tightly, and along with it, a folio spilled out on the floor. He scrambled to rearrange the scattered papers, but paused, recognizing Dick's loopy handwriting and the recurrence of Arline's name.

There were at least a hundred letters, he estimated, as he scooped them back into the folio. Every single one was addressed to his dead wife. He was startled reading the dates to find that they had all been written since she had died.

The first in the stack began, "D'Arline, I adore you, sweetheart," and ended, "You alone are left to me. You alone are real." On the back was scribbled something in nearly illegible cursive. He squinted to make it out: "PS Please excuse my not mailing this—but I don't know your new address."

When Dick reappeared with Manhattans in tow, Caleb nudged the portfolio closed. He pretended nothing had changed. But later, when Dick returned to his scribbled notes in the lab, racing the clock and refusing sleep, Caleb began to treat him more delicately, taking note of the weight he had lost and the things he mumbled seemingly to himself under his breath. Was he talking to her?

It did not escape Caleb's observation that Dick's letters had been written in the present tense. He remembered something he'd heard somewhere about how when someone dies, a version of the bereaved dies too. He'd had his suspicions before, but now there was no way around it. Dick had died that day in the sanatorium. This stranger sitting beside him in the lab was someone brand-new.

Alice

By the time her water broke, Caleb was already at the lab. Lately, he'd been back to working long hours at Project Rufus, filling in for Harry's absence. As her due date approached, and the beginning of their life together beyond the hill drew nearer, he seemed to grow distant. It was like Alice was looking at him through the far end of a telescope. At times, he seemed like a stranger in bed beside her. She knew he wasn't sleeping because she hadn't been sleeping either.

She was climbing the steps down from her front door, on her way to a theoretical team meeting. Something loosened inside her, and she felt a rush of release. She had to squat all the way down and squeeze her thighs together, afraid of soiling herself. She stayed that way, afraid to move, for several minutes. It was horrifying—her own body felt foreign. Whatever was happening, it had been put in motion without her willing it. She thought perhaps anxiety had triggered labor. Or maybe it was the shift in the weather. The wind had turned over trash cans and blew laundry from clotheslines. The sky went dark while she hobbled to the barracks hospital. She felt a sudden stabbing pain in her abdomen. It was hard to breathe.

Thunder shook the weaker leaves from the trees. Water shuddered in the puddles.

Alice found herself lying in the same hospital room she'd visited Diz in only a few months prior. In the end, she'd had a girl. "I've named her Marilyn," Diz had said then, while the sun set in the window, "Marilyn Edith." She had cooed at the newborn nestled into her chest. Alice had peered at the scrunched-up ruddy face and cone-shaped head and feigned admiration. She'd felt no motherly instinct kicking in, no desire to hold the baby.

"The whole thing makes you think about space," Diz had said. "How strange it is that between us and the sun there's only that—no atoms, no cells, just empty space. And that's not even as great a space as the distance from a nucleus to an electron. And yet this tiny body right here is composed of millions of atoms."

Alice had nodded. "If the nucleus was the size of a blueberry, that electron would be three blocks away, halfway to the checkpoint gate."

"Right," Diz said. "Left to my own devices, I sometimes get to thinking that there's an eternity of nothing inside us. There's no *there* there. Then Marilyn came along and made me believe we're really here."

Now, from that same hospital room window, the sky looked so low, it seemed she could reach out and touch it. It hadn't started pouring yet, but it was that moment before the storm, when the sky breathes in. Alice writhed through a contraction curled into a ball, losing herself and her sense of the world for thirty seconds: inhale, hold, exhale. *So this is what Diz meant by nothing,* she thought. *I'm disappearing.* She'd never been so simultaneously inside and outside her body. She longed for relief from the pain, to go numb, to be *nothing but space.* The feeling came and went with each contraction. She returned to herself and her thoughts about the world, then washed away again, like lapping waves. She thought fleetingly of Abigail, being pulled under. *She must have felt like this,* she thought, *before everything went dark.*

"Pretend you're blowing out a candle," instructed Dr. Hempelman, the statuesque, blond medical director. Alice hated him for his chiseled jawline and polished comments. He watched her with removed intrigue like she was a remote butterfly preserved on a pin. He recited medical jargon by the paragraph, but he wouldn't quite look at her. She had heard rumors that he was great at clerical work but passed out at the sight of blood.

In the reprieve between contractions, she was instructed to pace the halls. She staggered back and forth, marveling that walking had come easily to her only a short while ago. "I was told they contacted my baby's father," she begged a young nurse rolling an IV pole down the hall. Alice was ashamed that she didn't know what else to call Caleb. "Did you get a hold of him? Is he on his way? He should be here by now."

The nurse tried to comfort her. "I'm sure he'll be here any minute," she rationalized. "This town isn't that big." Alice nodded and willed herself to keep pacing. She was terrified of what was coming. The pain of a contraction crippled her again, this time in the middle of the hall. She buckled over. The nurse was at her shoulders, offering support, but she didn't try to get her to her feet. "There's a difference between pain and suffering," the nurse said when the contraction eased off and Alice could breathe again. "Pain is in your body—it's perfectly natural. Suffering is psychological—it's in your mind. When you panic and start to feel out of control, remember to breathe."

Alice resented being talked to like she was hysterical, like her pain was of her own making. The anger flaring through her made her feel stronger. "It's just the noxious stimulation of my sensory nerve endings," she said, boosting herself to her feet and walking on, leaving the nurse slack-jawed in dismay. But as soon as she was on her feet, she could hear her pulse in her ears. The clock was ticking down to her next contraction. She wasn't sure she could survive this without Caleb.

The rain had started. It tapped on the roof and drops slid down the window. "Water is attracted to water," she recited, trying to comfort herself with the familiarities of science. "Water is attracted to other substances." The sky blackened until it felt like the middle of the night. The noise escalated to a deafening roar.

She had to keep moving. She strode into the waiting room and walked endless circles. A flash of lightning lit the room, and seeming to step right out of the electric current, Caleb finally rushed through the door. He was soaked through, water beads dripping from his nose. All the things she had ever longed for him to say were evident in his look. She ran to him and flung her arms around him. She sobbed quietly into his chest.

In their private room, she got on all fours, then squatted on a medicine ball. The nurse instructed Caleb to perform a hip squeeze to alleviate some of the pain of the contractions. When she was in the throes of the next one, he applied pressure to her lower back, but his touch made her reverberate with pain. It felt like echoes of the contraction, shooting all through her limbs and extremities. Then, restored to herself again for a moment, she decided to bear down. She sucked on ice chips and tried to open her hips. She realized that through it all, Timoshenko had been barking at the storm. "Quiet!" Dr. Hempelman ordered. The dog cowered, then curled up beside her hospital bed, fitting his large body into a very small space. Alice wondered for a moment whether the terrified, enormous dog was an apparition of her labor pains.

Another thundercrack flung the obstetrician, Dr. Stout, into the room. He burst through the door sopping wet and leaped into action, shooing away Timoshenko and flipping through a cabinet of the hospital's rationed medical supplies. "We are terribly limited," he apologized. "There are only two of us on call tonight and a hospital full of inpatients." He looked at Alice convulsing and then studied Caleb wringing his hands. "First-time parents?" He smiled weakly.

In the fleeting minutes between contractions, Alice felt Caleb's eyes on her from across the room. She knew he was agitated for her. He didn't seem to know what to do or where to stand. It comforted her just knowing he was there. The rain was roaring louder on the roof now. Alice counted the seconds between the flash of lightning and the thunder, then divided by five to calculate their distance from the storm. It was 2.4 miles away, she determined.

"All right," Dr. Stout said, polishing a surgical instrument on the dressing tray. "It's showtime."

Caleb seemed reluctant to leave when he and Timoshenko were expelled for sanitary reasons. "Please," Alice begged. "I need him to come back."

Nobody listened to her. Her pleas were just the nonsensical wails of an animal in pain. She had no more tears to cry, so she closed her eyes and tried once again to *be nothing*. The storm carried her oceans away. The wind became bombs whistling overhead. She saw Warren ducking for cover while the earth exploded into a cloud of dirt around him. Her exhales were the powerful fans of army helicopters blowing the treetops outside her window. Dotting the horizon, she saw children in small backpacks on their way to school, and mothers pushing baby strollers, and when lightning flashed, they were swallowed by a sudden explosion of brightness that took over the sky.

Finally, she heard a cry that wasn't hers and she began to sob. The doctors had their backs turned while they pumped the baby with air. "Congratulations, it's a boy," said a voice that seemed miles away.

"He needs to be incubated," someone said urgently. She could only make out the blue hospital scrubs floating around the room. Dr. Stout seated himself beside her, reading off a clipboard and explaining flatly that the baby's temperature wasn't regulating. He said something about jaundice and vital signs. "It's unusual," the doctor said, chewing on his pencil like he was working a math equation, "since he's only a few weeks early."

"Can I hold him?" Alice asked.

"Soon," the doctor said.

"Where is Caleb?" She needed him there to help her make sense of it all. During the height of the pain, it had never once occurred to her that she might not be able to hold the baby when it was over. At least there had been that happy ending waiting for her on the other side. Now, she was shattered. She was nothing and she had nothing.

"They're briefing him in the waiting room. He'll be in momentarily."

The doctor had barely gotten the words out when Caleb tore into the room and flung himself down at her bedside. "Are you OK?" he asked, combing his fingers through her hair. She interlaced her hand with his and nodded.

"As long as I don't move," she said.

She had no idea whether it was minutes or hours later when they helped her out of the hospital bed, and she finally looked down at the small wiggling creature through a protective glass cylinder. Beside her, Caleb gasped. He wiped his tears on his shirtsleeve. She had no tears left. She looked at the small body, wrapped in a swaddle, and wanted to feel whatever Caleb was feeling.

Alice had expected to be overwhelmed with love when she saw her baby, like Diz had said happened for her. But when she watched him cry, she felt nothing. That could have been any baby crying. She had heard that new babies had an intoxicating smell, but all she could detect in the room was the scent of metallic tang and sterile swabs. She worried that he would memorize test tubes and monitors instead of her face. She touched him through metallic sleeves and gloved fingers, like an astronaut running her padded fingers through the rocky shores of the moon.

He was so skinny, he looked more alien than human. A feeding tube was taped across his upper lip and through his nostril, squishing all the features of his face to mush. His tiny ribs rose and fell with each breath. His skin was so red and shiny, he seemed made of rubber. His eyes, when he opened his puffy lids, were too blue for his red face. She worried deeply and privately that there was something messianic about those eyes—a cowboy quality. The sort of blue that looks right through you.

Outside, the sky opened up. The rain that washed the hospital felt biblical, like it was raining holy water. The doctors assured her the baby would live, and that his birth certificate would be issued soon. Like so many censored letters home, and the stories of so many who had lived, loved, and died on the mesa, Alice's baby had been born in Postal Box 1663.

T-Minus 2

April 1938
Haruki: A Story Told Backward

Haruki removed his white headband featuring Japan's rising sun emblem as he made his way through the rotating doors of the hospital. He had been pulled out of secondary school to meet his new sister. He couldn't quite believe it was real.

A nurse rolled back a protective curtain, revealing his mother's frail body in a hospital bed. She was lying in the dark, so the nurse flipped on the light. His mother was curled on her side, sobbing quietly. "You have a visitor, Sato-san," the nurse said gently. His mother didn't respond. His father grunted a tired greeting from his perch by the foot of her bed. He was seated in a high-backed chair, resting his head on his hands.

"Ma?" Haruki knelt beside her and brushed back a sweaty lock of hair that had fallen in her eyes. "Are you all right?"

"She'll be fine," his father answered for her, massaging a headache in his temples. "It's just the nitrous wearing off."

"Ma?" he asked again, trying to reach her. She looked right past him into the distance, her eyes glossy. She emitted a slight whimper. Then he heard a cry that hadn't come from his mother, and he noticed the tiny creature bundled in her arms.

"May I?"

His mother didn't resist as he lifted the baby. His father leaped up. "Hold her this way," he instructed. "You have to support the head." Haruki cradled her in his arms, staring down into her pale eyes.

"Can she see me?" he asked. Her eyes were colorless, but she seemed to be watching him.

"Sure she can," said his father. "But she can only see an arm's reach."

Haruki took his rising sun headband out of his pocket and draped it around the swaddle blanket. She was surprisingly warm and dense. It was like a math equation they had worked at school that morning in algebra—solving for an unknown variable. It felt like she had always belonged with him; he was the constant and she was a variable he had been missing all this time. He decided he would hold her in his arms forever.

"Hi," he said. "Hi," he repeated, over and over. "Welcome to Hiroshima."

31

September 1945
Caleb

Caleb had forgotten his glasses in his mad rush to the hospital. He stared down through the glass partition at the limbs and open gaping mouth of the tiny creature. If he pressed his face against the glass, he could just make out the small chest puffing up with each labored breath, making a strained wheezing sound. A machine that reminded him of a fireplace bellows opened and closed on an endless, sleepy cycle. The small torso was covered in round, white stickers and tangled wires connected to various monitors. In Caleb's dimensionless gaze, it was difficult to tell where the wires stopped and the baby began. He was so thin, his ribs bumped through his skin.

In Japan, in the immediate aftermath, pregnant women suffered loss of hair, bleeding, and inner mouth lesions. They gave birth to stillborns. Some were born with malformed skulls, their brains exposed. Some babies were born without eyes or noses. Some were born without legs. Some were born with too many legs, and they were bulbous and malformed, like the limbs of an octopus, wiggling on the operation table. Some had gelatinous growths oozing from their necks, the size of a second infant, beating like a heart. Babies looked like mythological creatures instead of humans. A baby cyclops made the *New York Times*. The future was a generation of tortured souls.

"Let's name him Harry," Caleb said, avoiding Alice's look.

"I thought you'd want a Jewish name," she said. She hadn't exactly agreed, but it also wasn't a refusal.

Caleb counted the strained rise and fall of the infant's chest every few minutes to make sure he was breathing regularly. He longed to bend the baby's limbs, to make sure he wasn't stiff as a board. He couldn't be sure he would love him. But at least this was something to hold onto, he thought, watching the baby clench its tiny fist around his gloved thumb.

October 1945
Alice

At his follow-up appointment, Nurse Petey took Harry's head circumference and weight several times and scribbled on a chart with a stern look. She seemed unfazed when he screamed and turned red on the exam table. Alice scooped him up and held him close, but the infant clawed away.

"We're not seeing enough of a growth curve," she said. She asked a series of questions about breast feeding and milk transfer. Alice tried to answer, but she was so tired, she kept forgetting what had been asked. She hadn't slept more than two consecutive hours in the weeks since he'd been born; sometimes, when Harry slept with one arm curled under him, she worried he had been dismembered. Other times, when she nursed him in the dark, the shadows on his face made him look like there were no eyeballs in his sockets. Occasionally, when she drifted off to sleep, she shot up in the dark, convinced she heard thousands of children screaming. She would try to reason with herself, to make the most of the chance to rest, but by then the milk would be leaking through her blouse.

After Alice had to ask Petey to repeat herself for the third time, the nurse put down the clipboard and looked at Alice with pity. She began to fear they were going to take Harry away, that she was one of those mothers you hear about. She clutched her infant tightly and, possibly responding to her anxiety, he cried harder.

"Baby blues," Petey said, "is only temporary."

"Baby blues?" Alice repeated, angered by the patronizing alliterative phrase.

"It clears up," she promised. "And you get a baby after." She emphasized the word "baby" like it erased the need for her own shadow.

"Trust me," Petey said. She retrieved a packet of trail mix from a cupboard and placed it in Alice's palm. "You need to eat," she said. "For both of you."

"What if it doesn't?" Alice began, standing up to soothe Harry. "Clear up, I mean." She bounced him, and he settled.

"Oh, honey." Petey made her face look very kind. Alice wondered if she was a mother. "Did you know, mothers can feel their babies' hearts beating from across the room?"

Alice wasn't across the room. She was holding the infant in her arms, and still she couldn't feel anything. She wondered how she was measuring up.

"A mother's heart pumps faster when her baby cries," Petey elaborated. "Like magic."

Motherhood had never struck Alice as magical. She thought of Tibbets and the plane he had named for his mother. She imagined Enola herself, young and unaware, nursing the baby who would grow up to unleash the basic power of the universe. She peeked at the strange creature in her arms. She had memorized those wisps of baby fuzz while her own thick, black waves came out in clumps in her hairbrush. She had mapped the stork-bite rash on the back of his neck, just below his hair line. Now, she couldn't cut up a melon without worrying about collections of capillary blood vessels as she traced her hand across the porous rinds. Eventually, her red, puffy infant would grow accustomed to the world beyond the uterus, she thought, and become a man who made decisions and flew planes and went to war.

Motherhood sent her into a tailspin. When she couldn't take the noise in her head, she switched on the radio. A survivor by the name of Haruki Sato had woken recently after forty days in a coma and was telling his story. "There was so much smoke in the air that you could barely see one hundred meters ahead, but what I did see convinced me that I had entered a living hell on earth." His descriptions of horror were nothing new. The destruction had been so widespread that even the soil itself was singed, barren of vegetation. Scientists believed that no plants would ever sprout from the rubble again. That's why what she heard next flung her right out of her chair.

"Today, Hiroshima is dappled in red blooms," a voice explained pragmatically.

Alice jolted, nearly waking Harry, who was lazily suckling at her breast. His eyes opened for a beat, then drooped and closed, reminding her of a rocked baby doll. His lips were still clamped around her nipple, the visible crescent moon of her areola stretching like rubber into his puckered mouth. Every few minutes, he curled his lips into the demonic expressions of sleep reflexes.

Alice listened to the description of the deadly shrubs, staring down at her sleeping boy. "They release a pleasant perfume into the air, but they are still filled with nebulous cardiac glycosides, saponins, oleandrin, and other mysterious toxins," cataloged a dry voice entirely divorced from the devastation of its words. "Ingestion of any part of the beautiful flower could lead to serious illness or sudden death. Oleander is one of the most poisonous plants on the planet."

Alice stroked Harry's peach fuzz, and he emitted a dreamy hum. "I wonder if you will forgive me for what I've done," she said.

32

November 1945
Caleb

Every time Harry cried, Caleb leaped up in bed. He tried to soothe Harry, but the baby didn't want him. The instant he lifted him from the bassinet, Harry screamed like he was in pain, his whole body blushing red.

"He wants his mother," he would say sheepishly, handing him over to Alice. Harry would immediately latch and soothe, drifting back to sleep clamped to her breast. Alice spent hours sitting upright so as not to wake him. She shushed Caleb if he walked too noisily in the next room. She tried to sleep propped up on pillows, craning her neck. She shoved tissues into her bra to prevent her milk from leaking through her blouses, but eventually she stopped bothering to change out of clothes with spit-up and milk stains. She kept sleeves of crackers by her bedside table and snacked at crazy hours, filling up on prepackaged goods rather than preparing fresh meals. She rarely left the bedroom at all. Caleb worried about her, knowing her father's predisposition to depression and agoraphobia. It was in her genes to be sad.

He opened the sunshades to let the light in, but she would protest and hold her hand up to shield herself from the glare. He tried to give her breaks by watching Harry so she could nap. She would drift immediately into an unconscious sleep, face down in the pillow. Several times, it scared him that when he tried to shake her awake, she was unresponsive. He was certain that if he let her alone, she could sleep for a year.

After an endless rotation of rising moons and suns and no sense of the day of the week, she insisted he wake her before he left for Project Rufus so she could get on a schedule. He hated to do it. He tiptoed in after she had slept most of the morning with Harry in the crook of her arms. Something took hold of him when he stepped into the dark room, flooding it with light. It was musty in there—the scent of dried milk and spit-up. But it was also intoxicating: her bodily smell, mixed with the metallic odor of her sweat and vanilla lotion.

He fingered the ring in his pocket and knelt down beside her. He ran his fingers through her hair and up her arm until she blinked and her eyes cleared momentarily, slowly focusing on him. Her lips were a pouty heart and he found them with his mouth. *Marry me*, he thought. *Just say it. Marry me. One thousand times over.*

She reached for him, kissing him back, then smiled down at Harry, who wiggled and then settled. He gripped the engagement band in his pocket. *1,984 degrees*, he would say, placing it on her finger. *I fashioned it in a lab with a crucible and coins.*

"I think I love you," he began. His voice came out gravelly.

"You think?"

Her sleepy eyes flickered with the emotions of heavy dreams still present. The green band around her eyes seemed to shift in the light, like a drifting cloud.

He kissed her on the brow, and she emitted a dreamy hum; her eyes drifted closed and her lashes fluttered like moth wings.

"There's something I've been meaning to ask you," he said.

"Hmm?" she mumbled, her eyes sealed shut. Her hand went limp in his.

"Alice?" She had fallen back asleep. Whatever he said now, she wouldn't remember upon waking. She might as well be dreaming him there, beside her, clutching a lab-made ring.

It was Slotin's final day at Rufus. With his contract up, he officially resigned his post, determined to head back to academia. Since Harry had been the more senior research assistant of the two, Caleb had been consequently promoted to the position of Slotin's wingman, and now, with his resignation, Caleb was his replacement. He shadowed his every move and learned every trick of the trade. He flanked him and handed him tools diligently while he performed his daily task of placing two half spheres of beryllium around the core. He stood idly by while Slotin moved them closer and then drew away, monitoring the rate at which the neutrons multiplied. His heart raced every time they approached the edge of criticality. Harry's accident had made everyone nervous. The first few times, they buttoned up and wore their monitors, and did everything by the book. But day after day after day, Slotin performed the procedure impeccably. They gathered data and made their way home at night, slipping back into the routine. Still, they kept the door open and their engines running. They couldn't be too cautious.

After a matter of weeks, the group had begun once again to shun the safety devices used at cyclotron facilities. They relied only on a single neutron counter. So that morning, when Caleb left Alice dreaming in her cot and made his way to the lab with the wedding band in his shirt pocket, he probably should have seen it coming.

Slotin had already said his goodbyes but decided to perform one last test for good measure. Caleb stood close beside him when a flash of lightning lit the room, then a moment later, another. At first, they thought the plutonium had caused the flashes, not the weather. But as they all turned to look out the propped door and marvel at the dark sky, a sudden downpour burst from low clouds. Slotin pressed on, raising his voice to be heard over the roaring rain. He was using his favorite screwdriver to lower one hemisphere of beryllium onto the core when a gust of wind slammed the door and startled him. His hand slipped.

It happened in an instant. A glow enveloped the lab. In total, there were seven of them in the room, including the guard. Something clattered noisily on the floor. A blue light illuminated Slotin's face. The whole room flushed with a wave of heat. Even those some distance from the source felt the intensity. The Geiger counter ticked violently. Everyone was yelling. The security guard fled down the ramp and the rest dashed out into the wet weather behind him, diving into the fleet of idling cars puffing out fumes. The parking lot was locked in by a security clearance gate, and there was some commotion trying to get it open. The guard couldn't get a whistle out of his pocket to signal the alarm. In the chaos, Caleb's glasses were knocked from his face. He couldn't see anything clearly, just a three-dimensional blur and winking lights and colors.

Slotin had turned to block the others from the radiation, heroically taking the brunt of the exposure directly. Before fleeing, he used his left hand to scatter the material. Then he resolutely called for an ambulance. On the way to the hospital, he was already vomiting.

The men moved like a pack of animals. They burst through the hospital doors, sopping wet and disoriented. They limped and bumped blindly into each other, behaving precisely like the frozen rain particles colliding overhead to create electric charges and illuminate the sky. Caleb squinted at the room full of medical professionals trying to make sense of what had just taken place through the blur. None of the men had been wearing their dosimetry badges, so there was no way to assess their exposure.

In the hospital, Slotin complained of a sour taste in his mouth and a pro-longed burning sensation in his left hand, the one used to knock apart the spheres. "I suppose I just gotta roll with the punches," Slotin said, trying to sound tough, but his voice was strained. Back in the lair, a team was cleaning and taking measurements to file a report, trying to mark off who had stood where and how many rads each member had received. They had promised to retrieve his glasses by nightfall, but for the time being, his world was com-posed of squiggles.

In the hall, Nurse Petey placed a hand on his shoulder and escorted him to an intake room. "We need you to stay overnight for observation," she instructed. He waited there, thumbing the engagement ring in his pocket.

Finally, Dr. Hempelman knocked on the door. He strapped the cuff on Caleb's arm and puffed it tighter and tighter, watching his stopwatch to check Caleb's blood pressure. He never once looked Caleb in the eyes.

"Your vitals are normal," he said and seemed genuinely curious. This man seemed completely ignorant to the way Caleb's life had just changed. He felt certain Dr. Hempelman was the sort of man who saw charts, not people. "Although your blood pressure is a tad high." He scribbled on his clipboard and furrowed his brow. With his pronounced chin cleft, muscular stature, and blond Aryan waves, Caleb couldn't place him. Hempelman sounded like a Jewish name. He caught himself. It shouldn't matter. He told himself a doctor was a doctor.

"Let's take a gander at your hands," Dr. Hempelman instructed.

"What do I do?" Caleb asked, trying to comprehend the numbers and charts.

"Nothing." Dr. Hempelman grunted and flicked bubbles from a syringe. He arranged some shining medical tools on a tray and returned to his notes unceremoniously.

"Whaddaya mean?"

"I mean, God only knows what's in store for you seven."

Caleb looked out the window in the direction of Alice's house. Right now, she'd likely be rocking Harry to sleep, staring absently out her own window at the brewing storm. She wouldn't expect him home for hours yet.

"What do I tell my family?" Even though they were alone in the room, Caleb whispered it. He couldn't bear to keep secrets from Alice again. She had finally forgiven him for lying about everything he was. He had learned to be vulnerable with her, and she hadn't left him for it. But then, he was so worried for her well-being. He pictured her absent expression, the one she always wore when she heard her sister's name. It had been permanently etched on her face since Harry was born.

Maybe there was no reason to worry Alice unnecessarily. After all, Caleb wasn't visibly irradiated. The recruit directly to Slotin's right had had all the hair singed off the exposed side of his head. The doctors had determined that the radiation had gotten into the gold caps in his teeth and were in the process of fashioning him metallic dentures to protect him from his own bones. Caleb had left seemingly unscathed. And, as the doctor had said, his vitals were normal.

"We've just had a baby," he pleaded. "What can we do?"

Dr. Hempelman finally glanced at him over his clipboard. "Pray."

"Can you at least tell me how much time I have left?" Caleb was surprised his voice came out strangled. He tried to steady his breathing.

"It could be weeks or it could be years," he said. He fiddled with his stethoscope and listened to Caleb's chest. "Exhale," he instructed.

Caleb complied, but his breaths were shallow and labored.

"Listen," Dr. Hempelman said, hanging the stethoscope around his neck. "None of us knows how much time we got. You're no different. Your clock's just wound a little closer to midnight."

It was only when Caleb went down the hall for coffee the next morning, reunited with his glasses, that he turned his sharp vision on Louis Slotin. He could see the flecked freckles and black pores on his nose. His team leader looked worse than he had imagined. His hands had swelled overnight. His skin was blistered and gangrenous and his palms were shiny and red. He was losing control of his bodily functions. They had given him a catheter to preserve his dignity. He was struggling to control the muscles in his mouth, so he was drooling and his speech was slurred. The Rufus team lined up to donate blood, but it made no difference.

Alice

When Caleb didn't come home, she figured he had gone to the barracks for a chance to sleep through the night uninterrupted by the wails of the baby. So, she didn't think much of it at first when he turned up twenty-four hours later with a grim expression. He took a long time getting ready for bed, running the water. Then he held her tightly all night, refusing to let her roll over to her separate side of the mattress. She finally broke away, turning to sleep in the hemisphere of the room filled with spent bottles and nursing pads, nipple butters and a galaxy of spittle stains on burp cloths strewn across the floor. She heard him breathe sharply beside her, tossing around.

Eventually he got up and shuffled off to the living room. She meant to go after him, but her limbs were so heavy against the mattress. Harry was snoring softly in the bassinet beside her. The next thing she knew, it was morning and he was gone.

When it was announced that Team Rufus's work had been brought to an immediate halt that week with no explanation, Alice began to wonder what Caleb knew. She didn't trust his nervous answers. He was far too quick to offer her nursing pillow or to wash bottles in the sink.

Caleb

It only took nine days for Slotin to die. First his legs went black as the infection spread closer to his heart. He spent hours staring out the window at the clouds, tears sliding down his cheeks. Caleb wondered whether they were tears of sadness or just the involuntary leaking of his tear ducts.

Caleb observed Slotin's descent, visiting him frequently and all the while obsessing over his own parallel symptoms, weighing whether or not to worry Alice. He might be imagining it, but under the bright hospital lights, Caleb was convinced his fingers were turning sallow; they were pruned with wrinkles like he had spent too long in the bath. He was plagued by a burning sore throat, and his eyes stung and teared—like he was permanently chopping an onion. After a shower, his thick, curly hair came out too readily in his hairbrush. He opened his mouth and investigated his tongue in the mirror. His teeth looked gray and silver, like plutonium.

The last time Caleb saw Slotin, he was emaciated and pale, disappearing into the same hospital bed that had claimed Harry. Caleb lingered in the doorway, a hesitant shadow. Slotin noticed him and stiffened but didn't turn his head. "I suppose it was my Hail Mary," he said gruffly, staring at the weather. A fresh storm was gathering, sitting low over the desert.

When they rolled him away on a gurney, Caleb recalled one of his first days on Project Rufus. Slotin had explained his predisposition to science while he lowered the beryllium with a screwdriver. "As a child, while other kids played in puddles, I looked up at the storm clouds and wondered about their chemical makeup. I knew that clouds were just water droplets suspended in the sky," he had said. "All those Sundays in church, I felt sorry for the children who believed in heaven."

T-Minus 1

October 1937
Haruki: A Story Told Backward

Because the snow was falling in big, puffy flakes, Haruki altered his route from school to take the long way home. Behind him, the flat rooftops in the compound were already capped with snow. When he exited the perimeter gate, he looked back at the muted buildings. With its gated entry, he always thought that his school looked more like a prison. At each river crossing, he paused to look down at the frozen waves that churned like ice cream.

He crunched through the snow, passing by the shuttered windows of the Jesus Fellowship building. Nearby, a florist was closing up shop, pulling down the railing on her storefront. He strolled by a factory compiling televisions on assembly lines at costs meant to compete with the West.

As Haruki passed by the homeless man at the bus stop, he picked up his pace. It made him sad to see the man sleeping in the cold. He had bundles and blankets piled up in his cart, and he had covered them in newspapers hoping to keep them dry. Everywhere except for the rectangle of dry cement under the eaves of his bench, the streets were turning white, the grime and corruption of the city transformed into the top side of clouds.

At Hiroshima City Hall, he paused to admire the photo of Emperor Hirohito astride his white stallion, named Shirayuki, or White Snow. Holding the reins in pristine white gloves, Hirohito sat stiffly and did not smile. When the snow came down sideways, decreasing visibility, and forcing Haruki to squint, the horse's fur seemed to glow.

Around the bend, he was overwhelmed to see hundreds of photos of Hirohito dappling every business and billboard. Many depicted him astride Shirayuki. There was a whole series of equestrian portraits where he saluted or stared directly into the lens. Others pictured him standing at attention in his military uniform, or resting one white-gloved hand on his samurai sword. A taxi splashed through the slush, running its wipers, and honked in reverence at the emperor's likeness as it zoomed by. Haruki turned to the cityscape of photographs, an entire colony of Hirohitos, and bowed.

It occurred to him that he had never seen a photo of the emperor smiling or laughing, or where he looked shorter than those around him. His likeness was a constant presence in the city, his image cultivated to relay his divinity—he was, after all, a direct descendant of the sun goddess Amaterasu. He was a living link to the land of the gods. Standing in proximity to his likeness was the closest Haruki would ever be to heaven on earth.

33

November–December 1945
Alice

They attended Slotin's bleak memorial. It was a warm, breezy afternoon, but the temple pews were chilly. Slotin's parents sat in the front row. Since they were Orthodox Jews, the military had arranged for them to be flown in before sundown on Friday.

Slotin's father, Israel Slotin, showed up dressed in a wool waistcoat with a watch and chain dangling from his vest. He kept checking the time absently during the proceedings.

More than once, Alice caught Caleb staring at Israel, looking morose. Alice bounced Harry on her knee while women in hats used their programs to fan tears from their eyes for fear of smudging their makeup.

When it was Israel's turn to speak, Caleb stiffened. "I think it's no secret," Israel began, letting the word "secret" wash over the audience for an uncomfortable span of seconds ticking audibly on his pocket watch, "that my family was opposed to the autopsy." A shocked silence held the crowd captive. "It goes against our religious beliefs and traditions. But Louis was a scientist all his life. It would be wrong now, when it can do him no further harm, to prevent him from adding to knowledge."

Throughout the memorial, they referenced the tragedy, speaking of Slotin's bravery. General Groves, heavyset and gruff in demeanor, even looked a little starry-eyed when he called him a hero. Rumor had it that they had had a casket special-made in Santa Fe with a mandatory metal interliner seal. But the official cause of his death was tightly covered up.

Beside her, Caleb's jaw set. In her arms, Harry hummed and dreamed, ready to take on the world.

Caleb

Some days, Caleb didn't feel like he was dying. Other days, he was certain of it. The doctors had said it might take anywhere from hours to weeks for symptoms to begin. The morning after the funeral, he woke with a low-grade fever, sweating through his shirt. He felt weak and light-headed when he stood up too fast, and he couldn't shake a pounding headache. Trotting down the hall to tend to Harry when he cried, he suffered a sudden shortness of breath and keeled over, his heart pounding.

He started thinking he better tell Alice. But it was hard seeing her worn so thin and exhausted caring for Harry. She had no defenses left, no time to curl her hair or starch her clothes. She was the rawest form of herself, existing on a never-ending cycle of waking hours and washing bottles. It made her seem more vulnerable, and that plagued him. He could just take a lukewarm bath to stave off the fever, and be mindful not to overexert himself climbing the stairs to the front door. Now that Harry's weight had leveled off, when they finished out the month, they could leave Los Alamos for good. It wasn't too late. They could still marry and grow old together. Maybe he'd be just fine once they got away from this place.

It wasn't until Niels Bohr paid the Project Rufus survivors a visit that Caleb was forced to confront his diagnosis. Like Oppenheimer, Bohr had tried to distance himself from Los Alamos. He had railed against Teller's hydrogen bomb, but the idea had continued to gain traction under Norris Bradbury. Los Alamos residents had had a taste of fame, and they wanted more. Those who disagreed had packed up and left when their contracts ended, and Bohr had been one of the first to leave. Now Slotin's tragedy had summoned him back.

At sixty years old on this visit, he was the oldest scientist on the hill. He stumbled into the room of twentysomethings who had just been handed death sentences. They looked to him with desperate reverence.

Bohr repeated his warnings about the consequences of their work to any-one who would listen, and in these seven infected men, he found a primed audience. His work on the neutron initiator, a secret within a secret at the center of the device, was so classified that it was still referred to in proxy by various code names: urchin, grape nuts, nichodermus, and melon seed. It was not lost on Caleb that the man was a walking paradox. He railed against the continued production of nuclear weapons, but it was undeniable that his private innovation, with its small burst of neutrons, was essential to kickstarting the whole chain reaction. Still, he had passed his time in Los Alamos repeating his creed: "The problem is what is going to happen *afterward*." Caleb studied Bohr's long forehead and heavy, Neanderthal eyebrows. His pinched features gave him the impression of being perpetually surprised.

Bohr knew better, Caleb supposed, than to moralize at these men who had just stood witness to their own future deaths. But everyone in the room knew what he thought. He had long been vocal about his disgust over the messianic role Project Rufus had taken with that plutonium sphere, which would now go down in history as the "demon core."

"What do we do now?" Caleb asked him. "Besides wait around to see if we live or die?"

Around the room, the men awaited words that might guide them home.

"You know, I had a son who died," Bohr said, very quietly. Nobody had known this. He spoke so softly, Caleb thought possibly he had misheard.

Bohr sat down, seeming to buckle under the weight of the memory. "Christian and I," he began, struggling to stop his voice from shaking, "were sailing side by side." He paced to the window. The men waited in silence. Someone's shoes could be heard clicking down the hallway. Finally, Bohr turned back to face them. His eyes had glossed over, and his whole face had changed. "I circled until nightfall." In that moment, he didn't look like a giant of physics. He didn't resemble the daunting genius whose cryptic words were embossed in lecture halls in universities across the country with searing proclamations like, "A physicist is just an atom's way of looking at itself." He looked old.

He suddenly seemed to remember the purpose of his visit. His nostrils flared, and he straightened. "Prediction is very difficult. Especially if it's about the future."

"We can't live waiting to die." The man who had only been in that room as a security guard bristled. "That's dying twice."

Bohr nodded. "What I'm saying is this: stop telling God what to do with his dice."

Afterward, Caleb picked his way home in the dark. Even though they had been declassified, Groves still refused to allow streetlights. The stars spiraled overhead, and the moon seemed close enough to touch. He thought about Galileo, three hundred years ago, looking through a telescope and realizing the marks on the moon were depressions—craters, not mountains.

Oppenheimer himself would one day have a crater named after him on the moon. Caleb would not live to see it.

The desert was freezing over. The plunging weather was a constant reminder that they were nearing the end of the month on their renewed contract. Alice was packing boxes, wrapping utensils in newspaper. Something had come over her lately. She was desperate to get out of there. Maybe she sensed it—the death grip this desert had on them. She just started packing, even though they had no idea where they were going.

Worried by the trunks and luggage, Pavlov kept whimpering and curling up in the open suitcases. Caleb watched her carefully wrapping cookware, bent over the mixing bowl and salad tongs. He imagined saying it to her turned back: *I'm a dead man.*

He peeled back the window shade. Two large rays of light swept through the room. In the brightness, he noticed a field of subtle gray freckles on his fingertips.

They stood in front of the car as the sunrise flickered between the mountains. The Sangre de Cristos seemed vast enough to cover the globe, their shadows looming taller as the light inched higher in the sky. They were glowing pink with alpenglow. Caleb looked at the steep vanishing point down the road before them. With switchbacks and potholes and veering cliffs, it looked like something drawn by a madman.

Alice swung open the door for Pavlov to jump in the backseat and strapped Harry in. She turned back for one last look at the army-green town. "I have the strangest feeling," she said. She had braided her smoky black hair into pigtails and several curls had wisped out around the nape of her neck. She looked youthful that way, like the best years of her life were still ahead of her. "Like we'll drive away, but the road will just circle right back."

Caleb glanced down at his fingers. The spots were still there. They were small as needle pricks, almost microscopic, but they were unmistakable.

"It's like how all rivers lead to the ocean," he said, staring past her. "We might as well just stay put."

Her smile faded. "You're not coming," she said, studying his face with slow understanding. "You never were."

He bit his lip and shook his head. "Sure I am," he said. Harry shrieked in the car behind them and Pavlov started barking, but neither one broke eye contact to tend to the child. "I'll be right behind ya, on the next train."

This was it, he thought. If he was ever going to tell her, now was the time. She would understand. She was a scientist. She knew about Slotin. They had named their child after Harry, for God's sake. He could just tell her what he was up against. If he went with her, she would be forced to slowly watch him shrivel away, the infection inching closer and closer to his heart. First, his joints would swell. The flecks on his fingers would bleed together, inching up his wrists, turning his extremities black and gangrenous. He could already smell rot in his nostrils.

But then, he knew all too well that if he told her, she would never leave. She would insist on nursing him through it. He couldn't allow her to see him that way, shrinking into a hospital bed, watching the clouds.

He recalled his last conversation with Dick before, he too, had packed up and left this town. "Telling Arline she was dying changed everything," he had advised him gently, with a hand on his shoulder. "A countdown started as soon as I said the words, and from that point on she just had to live in reverse, because she knew how it ended before she knew the rest of it."

Beside him, Alice's green eyes looked fiery in the sunrise. "You know, I've often joked that without this place, I might cease to exist," he said, gesturing at the cliffs. "And now look at me—a man without a religion," he said. He thought of his flat in the Fillmore, and his father, fearful of solicitors on Shabbat, pulling the blinds. Even if the government had foreclosed on the house, even if he never stepped foot in that peeling seafoam-green kitchen again, he would always be trapped there, beneath a city of marching shoes.

She began to cry. "Then we'll stay," she said. "Harry and me. We'll make our lives here."

He took her by the shoulders, towering over her. "I'll be right behind ya," he said. "Just give me a few months to clean up the mess I made."

Her eyes widened, flashing greener. Verdigris. "You promise? You'll meet me in San Francisco?"

He nodded. "We'll take Harry on the carousel at Fisherman's Wharf."

"Why don't we all just delay and make the drive together?"

"Listen," he said. He peeled off his glasses. The sunset seemed to brighten as the details blurred. "This is no place for a child. Harry deserves better than the world he stands to inherit from me."

"He deserves his father," Alice said, her voice breaking.

He began to doubt himself. This was the love of his life. Maybe he should just go with her and try his luck against the clock. Maybe they'd get some time together, maybe years. Then he pictured her burying him on the mountain pass, not far from where they stood, touched by the very same sunrise. It strengthened his resolve.

He thought of the hibakusha, the survivors of the bombs who had lived to tell their stories and were campaigning against atomic weapons around the globe. They were trying to save the world. He hoped they would, that there would still be something left.

A flyaway curl had blown into Alice's mouth, and she was too distraught to whisk it away. He bent close to her and swept the renegade hair behind her ear. He wiped her tears with his hand and let his enormous palm linger against her cheek. His hand was large as a dinner plate against her small face. Perhaps it was already swollen.

Tell her, he thought. *Just say it. "I'm dying. It's not a matter of if, it's a matter of when."*

Instead he said, "Somebody has to stay back and keep saving the world."

He squinted into the cascade of cliffs behind her. Silhouetted in the sunrise, he saw a lone figure limping toward him, wheeling an oxygen tank. He was standing in a field of blowing flowers. He didn't need to see his face to know who it was.

34

December 1945
Alice

She knew he was lying. He wasn't saving the world. He was afraid of what was waiting for him down that winding road.

"A token of my love," he said and fished something out of his pocket. She caught her breath, thinking it might be the wedding ring she knew he'd been trying to give her. She'd been waiting and waiting for him to get up the courage. Instead, he placed a greenish gold rock in her palm. It was rough on one side and smooth on the other. It looked to be composed of quartz and feldspar, but it was tinted seafoam green—fused with desert sand and something else she couldn't pinpoint, something strangely familiar. He pressed her fingers closed around the stone. It was warm to the touch. "A placeholder," he said, "until we're together again."

"Is this what I think it is?"

"In the army, we call it Trinitite. Jury's out," he said, "on whether it grants wishes or carries a curse."

"Is it radioactive?" She opened her fist and examined it in the light. It went teal, shifting colors before her eyes.

"Only a touch more than kryptonite." He winced. "Just don't swallow it."

It shimmered brilliantly in the sunrise, and Alice realized she didn't want it. It was a part of this place and part of what they had done. She tried to give it back, but he held his arms up like she had pointed a gun at him.

"Whoa, whoa," he said. "That stone has your name on it. Besides, if I want, I can hitchhike over to Albuquerque where they're selling fakes." He smiled, but it made him look sad. "They're just painting rocks Coke-bottle green, you know. People believe anything you tell 'em."

"Why would anyone want that?"

"Jewelry. They call it green-gold," he said, squinting into the distance like someone far away had called his name. She turned to see what he was looking at, but there was no one there. He stared into the expanse for a long time before he finally said, "They say it makes a beautiful woman a thousand times more beautiful." Alice imagined young girls across New Mexico, dazzling with fallout strewn about their necks and implosions dangling from their earlobes. "That you can hear the future if you hold it to your ear." He touched his ear then, and left his hand there, tracing the inner corkscrew, the perimeter fence guarding his thoughts.

The sun was up now. He looked like an aged man in that unforgiving light.

"The fury of a thousand suns locked inside a bead," she said. "Of course they would sell it."

The trinitite flashed in her hand.

"That pebble is a story you can never tell," he said, a note of warning coming into his voice.

She nodded and pocketed the stone. "Secrets are secrets," she said. He pulled her to him and kissed her. Pressed against him, she could feel his heart beating. His palm slid down to her waist, drawing her closer. When she broke away, he seemed reluctant to let go of the material of her blouse, to let her slip through his fingers.

She turned to her car, unable to bear the look on his face. Inside the sealed-off capsule of the vehicle, she turned over the engine. Realizing Caleb wasn't coming, Pavlov started whining in the backseat. Caleb stepped back from the car and gave a shallow wave. His glasses glinted in the sunrise.

"I'll be right behind you," he called, cupping his mouth to shout, but his voice splintered like he had had the air knocked out of him.

She rolled down her window. "You know, tailing someone is a crime in California," she said. She watched his expression splinter. If she didn't pull away now, she would never leave.

On the drive down, Alice's vision was streaked with tears. She watched Caleb's hulking body shrink into the distance in her rearview mirror as she sped away. Just before she turned a corner and he went out of view, he knelt and buried something that flashed gold in the sand. The ring. It was lost to the desert now.

She had planned to tell him before she left that she knew he was dying. She'd been trying to ever since she had gone to pack up her office and Fred had approached her, unapologetic with his greasy comb-over, twirling his janitor's ring of keys and sweating through his undershirt. He had loosened his bolo tie and said he wanted to meet the baby, but he didn't even look at Harry. He just started saying with a superior gleam in his eye what a shame it was that there had been seven other men in that room with Slotin.

It had only confirmed what she had already suspected from the gossip around the funeral, what she already knew in her bones to be true. She hated that of all people, it had come from Fred. She had felt him watching her, waiting for her to break.

After that, she had watched Caleb lie to her every day. She loved him for trying to save her from it. She loved him more and more with each mile she put between them.

She drove faster, until the mountains stretched into streaks of color in the windshield. She noticed a patch of red flowers by the side of the road. *It couldn't be oleander*, she thought. The toxic flower was an invasive species. But then she thought of the radioactive waste they'd been dumping for years—so much that the locals were calling it Acid Canyon. And she thought of the poisonous blooms opening across Hiroshima like bloodstains.

She glanced in the rearview mirror at her sleeping "little boy." He was clasping a toy warplane in his chubby hand, his head jostling over the bumps. She wondered how many children like him had been murdered in their sleep in Japan. Caleb was haunted by them. He was trying to avoid the ending he had written for himself, living backward.

Alice decided that Harry deserved a story that started at the beginning.

She thought about gravity. Einstein had proved that time is relative. The gravitational field is a curving of space and time. Clocks tick faster at higher altitudes, although the shift is so subtle that humans don't notice it much.

Caleb's wristwatch would already be ticking a little faster than the clock on her dashboard. The farther down the mountain pass she traveled, the faster his watch would tick. But to him, it was her clock that would be ticking slower and slower.

The difference was relative. Between them was a glitch in time and space.

Epilogue

August 1996
Alice: A Story Told Backward

While Harry went to pull around the car, Alice took in every detail of the Hiroshima Peace Memorial Park, trying to commit it to memory. Her memory wasn't worth much these days—she often forgot to take her medicine and couldn't keep straight the day of the week. She had stuck Post-it notes on her kitchen appliances to remind her to switch them off, and Harry had installed stove knob covers to prevent her from cooking alone. Ironically, she remembered every vivid detail of her youth while the events of her present were murky, written in sand. If only she could trade—find it in herself to forget the photographs of the twisted ruins on the evening news, forget the plume of Oppenheimer's cigarette smoke coiling on the ceiling, forget Caleb squinting into the sunrise.

Now, she felt confused, as though she had been to the hypocenter before. She knew she hadn't, but something about the landscape felt familiar. Red oleander flowers were tangled around memorials, and fields of the red toxic blooms lit her periphery, glowing in the summer heat. They painted the corner of her vision blood red. She found a bench in front of the Children's Peace Monument to rest, fanning herself with her bonnet.

A Japanese man prostrated himself to place a white paper crane at the base of the monument, among a field of paper cranes of every color of the rainbow. At the monument's peak was a sculpture of a small girl hoisting a wire crane over her head. The man had dark hair streaked with silver, and his face was disfigured by scars. He dragged an oxygen tank awkwardly across the pavement.

"Did you know her?" she asked him, indicating the memorial.

He startled and swiveled toward her. She gasped, seeing that his left ear was deformed, that in its place was a cavity, a cross section of the inner ear. It looked like the whorl of a shell. Staring into that vortex, she heard the sound of the ocean, Abigail calling under the water.

"Not her in particular, no," he answered in accented English, averting his eyes. "Someone like her."

"I'm sorry," she said. She wanted to say more, to apologize for the things she had done, for the part of her past that haunted her. But she knew that would only help her, not him.

"Everyone who lives here knew someone like her," the man said.

She nodded, avoiding his look by studying the modular origami forms, a flock of acute angles. "Why a crane?"

"It's a symbol of peace."

She waited for more.

He sighed. "I promised I would keep telling her story, our stories, as long as I can breathe." He waved her closer.

She got near enough that she could see herself reflected in his dark eyes. "This statue represents a child survivor. She was only two years old at the time of the bombing. She believed that if she folded one thousand paper cranes, she would be cured of her leukemia . . . that her wish for peace would come true." He swept his hand across the field of paper cranes, implying the entire flock. "After she died, visitors kept making more." Alice watched the cranes wiggle a bit in the wind as though they were alive.

"There's easily a thousand," she marveled, adding up the rows.

"When the wind comes up, they scatter, flying all over the park like they remember something." He looked at her curiously then, his eyes glistening.

"Ma?" It was Harry, back with the car. He gave the man a concerned look. "Are you ready?"

Alice nodded and took Harry's arm, then turned back. "Just a minute," she instructed her son.

She walked haltingly back to the cenotaph, holding her flapping bonnet to her head. She retrieved the Trinitite, pausing to take one last look. It flashed in her hand, the color of pond moss, iridescent as a drifting soap bubble.

She pressed it into the man's palm, wrapping his fingers around it.

"What is it?" he asked, turning it over, running his thumb across the rough vesicles.

"Instead of a birthstone, they call it a deathstone," she said, making her way back up the gravel walkway to where Harry was waiting, the man and his oxygen tank keeping her slow pace alongside her. "Someone once told me that pebble was a story I could never tell. But here I am, and I think it's about time I told it."

Author's Note

October 4, 1944

I'll write al I can about Sh█la. Please understand
that if I don't answer your questions there's a reason. I
have been told that our mail, both incoming and outgoing,

will be censored. If my letters have █en less coherence

than usual please blame it on the rules and regulations

of ~~the Never-Neverland~~. *our future home*.

Chins up, carry on,

Love,

"I wonder if my children can forgive me for what I've done." My grandfather Leon Fisher muttered these words in his living room late one night when he thought no one was listening.

It is one of the great regrets of my life that I never asked my grandparents about their time in Los Alamos. They never spoke about the bomb, and we never brought it up. It was an unspoken rule, a guest at the dinner table, a commandment we abided by. Even after my grandmother's death, sixty-four years after they'd left that top-secret mesa, my grandfather still rigidly avoided the topic of Los Alamos. Instead, he took me on dates to their special places and described the way she had stirred her tea, initiating the tea leaf paradox—a whirlpool that broke the rules of the spiral centrifuge.

What I do know is this: my grandfather worked on the plutonium core of the "Fat Man" bomb, and my grandmother, Phyllis Fisher, taught elementary school to the scientists' children, focusing on Longfellow and long division, afraid to ask questions.

My zaide was from an Orthodox family. He turned his back on his upbringing to pursue science. His love for physics was only ever overshadowed by his love for my grandmother, who was entirely out of his league—a socialite from a wealthy Jewish family, an heiress of the famous San Francisco de Youngs. When she fell in love with him, my great-grandmother warned her away: "If you marry him, you'll never have a grand piano." It seemed the only way for them to be together was to disappear. Together, they vanished into the mysterious community under J. Robert Oppenheimer that would go down in history as the "Manhattan Project."

During their time at Los Alamos, my zaide never told my grandmother what he was working on behind the barbed wire in the laboratory known simply as Project Y. But when she was pregnant with their second child, my grandmother pieced it together. As a joke, while debating baby names in their flat-top house in McKeeville, she suggested the name "Uranium." When she uttered the forbidden word, my grandfather stormed out the door. "Uranium Fisher" had been too close to *uranium fission*.

Years later, my grandmother published a book of her government-censored letters home, entitled *Los Alamos Experience*, for which the above excerpt was revised and repurposed. My grandfather remained tight-lipped and never attested to feelings of guilt, yet he stood pensively by her side while she traveled to Japan to lecture about peace. The signs that he was grappling with his role in creating the bomb were there.

My grandparents lived in Tokyo for many years, and consequently, their house was strewn with Japanese relics. I always wondered whether their fixation on Japanese culture was directly connected to their feelings of remorse. The house felt haunted by the Oni masks of ogres that guarded their entryway.

In carefully preserved news clippings, my grandfather meticulously tracked the bomb's evolution. In articles documenting the test bombings in Bikini Atoll and Vegas, which dubbed itself "Atomic City," and in his transcript of Oppenheimer's security clearance hearing, he scribbled desperately in the margins. I pored over those notations, trying to make sense of his words.

Then, in the years that followed my grandmother's death, my grandfather stopped documenting. He lost track of time. He kept forgetting my grandmother was gone. He went looking for her in the middle of the night and wandered aimlessly around his block. He left music on for all hours of the day to fend off the silence. He claimed it was to deter burglars, but I knew better.

When he died and was buried beside her, I placed stones on his grave, a Jewish tradition. In that moment, I recalled the eerie green stone in his study that looked like it was from outer space. On the plane ride home, with a suitcase full of their Japanese keepsakes, I wrote down my questions. Later, I tracked down his still-living friends, who have since passed away, to ask them my questions and listen to their stories.

Over flickering Shabbat candles, Murray Peshkin, one of my grandfather's colleagues in the Experimental Physics Division, described seeing a fellow SED's (Special Engineer Detachment) hand blown off by dynamite. Ben Bederson, a self-proclaimed communist and associate who had worked beside my grandfather, spoke about bunking next to David Greenglass, who later turned in his own sister, Ethel Rosenberg, for espionage.

When I pressed for more, Bederson avoided the subject. "That was seventy years ago," he said. "It's amazing how memory fades."

I knew he was lying. Using a cigarette, he had famously burned a hole through his diary on August 6, 1945, the day the bomb was dropped on Hiroshima. "Secrets are secrets," he said, meeting my eyes. He let me hold the damaged book, and I stared at the hole in the words. This novel is my attempt to stitch it back together.

Historical Notes

This book is a work of fiction. The names of some individuals have been
changed to protect their privacy. Where public figures were concerned, I
conducted extensive research and then tried to fill in the blanks for the things
we couldn't know for certain—the private asides and candid moments. For
the sake of narrative design, a few historical inconsistencies occur in the text,
and I want to clarify them here to encourage further research and discussion.

Female Scientists

There were approximately 640 women who worked at Los Alamos, composing 11 percent of the workforce. About thirty women were included among technical and scientific staff. Some of the female scientists expressed frustration at being segregated from their male counterparts, treated as assistants rather than equals, while others were able to rise through the ranks.

In the novel, Alice's research is based loosely on the research of Elda Anderson, who worked with the cyclotron, focusing mainly on spectroscopy. She produced the lab's first sample of nearly pure Uranium-235. Likewise, Alice is also inspired by many of the other pioneering women in STEM from this time, including Mary Frankel, a junior scientist in the Computation Group who used numerical methods to solve physical equations, and Frances Dunne, who worked in the Explosives Assembly Group, and proved an asset on the assembly team for the Trinity test since her small hands were more dexterous and therefore more able to maneuver small machine parts.

Alice's drive for career success is inspired in part by the legacy of Jane Hamilton Hall, famously the first woman to receive equal pay with her male counterparts on the Project. Hall also went on to become the laboratory's first female director. Elizabeth "Diz" Riddle Graves, Alice's sole female scientist companion in the novel, was recruited to Los Alamos along with her scientist husband, Al Graves, and, at seven months pregnant, she watched the Trinity test from a safe viewing distance—a cabin forty miles away. Graves worked to select a neutron reflector to surround the core of the implosion device. She went on to become a group leader in the Experimental Physics Division, and she did in fact give birth to a baby girl named Marilyn while living in Los Alamos.

Others included Norma Gross, who worked in the chemistry and metallurgy division, which studied shockwave behavior that contributed to the design of the plutonium bomb, and Maria Goeppert Mayer, who worked with Edward Teller and continued her research on the structure of nuclear shells, earning the Nobel Prize in Physics in 1963.

Historically, many female scientists were relegated to the role of "computers," performing calculations by hand or with the aid of a mechanical calculator. These vastly overqualified women opted into this role due to limited opportunities for advancement in the field. Needless to say, barriers to success in STEM fields still exist today for women, so there is an urgent need for these stories to be celebrated and told. For further reading, please refer to the Atomic Heritage Foundation and their archive, "Voices of the

Manhattan Project." Other books chronicling female involvement in the making of the bomb include the intricately woven tales of TaraShea Nesbit's *The Wives of Los Alamos*, Jennet Conant's *109 East Palace*, and Denise Kiernan's *The Girls of Atomic City: The Untold Story of the Women Who Helped Win World War II*.

Sunao Tsuboi

Haruki Sato's character and biography are closely based on the interviews and testimonies provided by a survivor of the atomic bombing of Hiroshima, Sunao Tsuboi. Tsuboi, who was a student at the Hiroshima College of Technology (present day School of Technology of Hiroshima University) was approximately three-quarters of a mile from the epicenter in Fujimi-cho (present-day Naka Ward, Hiroshima) when he heard a loud bang and was blown ten meters in the air. He suffered burns covering most of his body, and the skin of his back was sheared off. He was photographed at Miyuki Bridge three hours after the bomb was dropped.

He slipped in and out of consciousness for over a month and was told on three occasions that he was terminal. Tsuboi went on to teach mathematics at a women's technical institute, where he fell in love with a student whose parents wouldn't let him marry her because of his radiation exposure. The two really did attempt suicide with sleeping pills.

After retiring in 1986, Tsuboi committed himself fully to the hibakusha movement, taking on the role of cochairman of the Nihon Hidankyo. At the Ministerial Meeting of the Non-Proliferation and Disarmament Initiative, he urged foreign ministers of twelve countries: "We must never again repeat this tragedy." In 2014, he was again elected as a cochair, accepting the position, stating that he was "determined to serve to the best of [his] ability, as long as [he] can breathe." Alarmed by the decreasing number of hibakusha who live to tell the story, he advocated for younger generations to take on the mission, famously speaking with Barack Obama when he made the pilgrimage as the first sitting US president to visit Hiroshima. Tsuboi died of an abnormal cardiac rhythm from anemia at the age of ninety-six.

For further reading about the hibakusha and their experiences, please see the "So Tell Me . . . About Hiroshima" project, which features messages from hibakusha; John Hersey's *Hiroshima, The Ministry of Foreign Affairs of Japan: Testimony of Hibakusha*; and the documentary film *Atomic Cover-Up* by Greg Mitchell.

Homesteaders and Downwinders

In the aftermath of the Oppenheimer movie, there is renewed interest bordering on fanaticism regarding the Trinity site and the Manhattan Project. Just this past October, following the film's release, nearly four thousand people flocked to visit ground zero on one of the two annual days the Trinity site is opened to public visitors. But in all the hubbub, the plight of the local Indigenous and Hispano communities often gets overlooked. The term Hispano is noteworthy because it specifies the descendants of Spanish descent who settled in the southwestern United States prior to annexation. I referred to the dislocation of these Indigenous and Hispano residents obliquely throughout the novel, from the inhabited land that was either purchased by the government for a nominal fee or condemned under the Second War Powers Act, to the colonial guilt of the scientists tramping through holy sites. The removal of the homesteaders, who likely couldn't understand the evacuation orders written in English, remains a point of contention in history. The need for advocacy regarding that forced evacuation continues today in a formal petition to the US government requesting reparations. Many of these same displaced people returned to the Project, working as babysitters, maids, construction workers, janitors, and technicians. In this capacity, sheer racism contributed to the blind oversight regarding security clearances for those who were hired to dust and mop around atomic secrets and exposed to toxic chemicals without their knowledge or consent.

Likewise, there were families living as close as twelve miles to the Trinity site and thousands within a fifty-mile radius. In the fallout, cisterns, the only water source for these predominantly Hispano and Indigenous communities, were contaminated with radioactive ash. Since there were no grocery stores in the vicinity, all of the meat, dairy, and produce consumed in these communities was raised and harvested internally. In the aftermath of Trinity, their stock was contaminated. In the novel, when the scientists refer to the radioactive burns singed in the sides of cattle, they can't yet know of the increase in the infant mortality rates in the months following the Trinity test, or of the plague of cancer and other diseases that impacted these populations in the years to come. But it is telling that still in 2024, with so much media focus on the subject, few are aware of this inequity. The Downwinders in New Mexico have never been included or compensated by the Radiation Exposure Compensation Act (RECA) although they were the first in the world to be exposed to atomic radiation. For more information, please refer to the Tularosa Basin Downwinders Consortium or visit trinitydownwinders.com.

Jewish American Princess (JAP)
The term, which is an offensive slur for American women of Jewish heritage, was not actually prevalent as a stereotype until after the conclusion of World War II. The concept of the indulged, privileged Jewish girl first appeared in print in Herman Wouk's *Marjorie Morningstar* (1955) and Philip Roth's *Goodbye, Columbus* (1959). The acronym did not appear until 1969, when it manifested in a *New York Magazine* op-ed. *The Official J.A.P. Handbook* hit bookshelves in 1982.

While the word directly resembles the anti-Japanese slur that was prevalent during WWII, JAP was used, as many ethnic slurs are, predominantly within the Jewish community as a means of policing other Jews, and as a way of condescending against Americanized nouveau riche. It critiqued the trend of immigrant minorities attempting to become white.

Though the acronym itself wouldn't have been used during the war, the fear of moneyed Jews most certainly prevailed in this era where Jews were believed quite literally to have horns under their hair, with stereotypes ranging from money lenders to global conspiracy plots. I felt it was important to include this term in the book despite its anachronism for its phonetic link to the Japanese slur of the time as well as its thematic connection to the self-loathing and anti-Semitism that was a fixture of the lives of the characters in the book, and figured into the many Jewish scientists' lives on the Project, where they worked diligently on a "gadget" meant to defeat Hitler.

Deaths of Harry Daghlian and Louis Slotin
Harry Daghlian died a painful death after radiation exposure on Project Rufus, while working in Otto Frisch's Criticality Group. The exposure took place on August 21, 1945, shortly after the bombings of Hiroshima and Nagasaki, while he was working to create a "neutron reflector" by building a stack of tungsten carbide bricks around a plutonium sphere. He went to dinner, then returned to work alone, violating safety protocols. When his monitoring equipment informed him of the risk of criticality, he rushed to pull the brick away, but accidentally dropped it directly over the core, exposing himself to what resulted in a lethal dose of radiation.

In this novel, I've conflated the timeline of Daghlian's death with that of Louis Slotin's, his team leader, who suffered a similar fate nearly a year later, on May 21, 1946. Slotin was demonstrating the procedure of "tickling the dragon's tail," bringing together two beryllium-coated half spheres around a plutonium core, using a screwdriver instead of the designated safety shims to keep the spheres separate. When a bright blue light flashed, Slotin heroically threw his body in front of the sphere, shielding the other seven men who were in the room, which I used as fodder for Caleb's diagnosis and uncertain fate. Ultimately, Slotin took on 1,000 rads of radiation, and died only nine days later.

In the narrative, I push Daghlian's death to September 1945, delaying it by a few weeks, and I move Slotin's death all the way up to November 1945 to tighten up the story arc and emphasize the danger of the work as the aftermath unfolds in Japan. Both deaths were a sobering reminder for Americans of the horrific realities of radiation exposure and poisoning in Hiroshima and Nagasaki.

Richard Feynman

In a novel that at its core functions as a feminist critique of women in STEM, I would be remiss not to address one of the major players in the narrative who also happens to be one of the most polarizing figures in science today. Richard Feynman was one of the most profound minds in twentieth-century physics: contributing to the atomic bomb, earning a Nobel Prize for his theory of quantum electrodynamics, and acquiring international renown for his nail-biting exposé of the *Challenger* space shuttle disaster. His reputation as an eccentric is underscored by multiple accounts and lore from Los Alamos about his being the prankster who opened safes, played the bongos, and snuck in and out of the top-secret community through a hole in a perimeter fence. By turn, his heartbreak over the premature death of Arline Greenbaum is also historically documented—he truly did write her letters long after she died. Like Daghlian's and Slotin's, the timeline of her death is similarly conflated in the novel for the sake of the narrative. Feynman continued to write her letters through 1946, although she died about a month shy of the Trinity test, on June 16, 1945, conjectured to be his rationale for choosing to stare right at the blast with no protective lenses.

Feynman was so celebrated for his genius that he was more myth than man by the time Ralph Leighton's *Tuva or Bust!* came out in 1991, celebrating their quest for the lost country—which was annexed into the USSR. Yet in the decades that followed, accounts of his predatory sexual behavior sparked debates about science and misogyny. In well-documented sources ranging from Lawrence Krauss's *Quantum Man* to James Gleick's *Genius*, his predacious treatment of women is appalling. The list of affronts abounds: holding meetings in strip clubs while a professor at Cal Tech, drawing naked portraits of his students, pretending to be an undergraduate to ask women out, and having affairs with married women. There's also the troubling fact that his second wife accused him of abuse. In the aftermath, the question stands—can we separate the science from the scientist?

Concerningly, his mythos lives on today in a cult of personality that defends his behavior—he was featured on posters as part of Apple's "Think Different" campaign, and most recently as an inspiration for the character of Sheldon on the syndicated television series *The Big Bang Theory*. Feynman attests to many of these misogynistic behaviors in his own accounts in his autobiographies. In *Surely You're Joking, Mr. Feynman!* and *What Do You Care What Other People Think?*, he manages to cast his predatory behavior as charming and unconventional, a luxury afforded him by a misogynistic culture. I could not simply gloss over his behavior after working on this novel, with the advancement of women in the sciences at its heart, in an era where feminist critiques of unchecked chauvinism are sorely needed.

Black Holes

I began researching by reading about J. Robert Oppenheimer in *American Prometheus* by Kai Bird and Martin J. Sherwin, and *The Making of the Atomic Bomb* by Richard Rhodes. I've also referenced Rhodes's *Dark Sun* and *Masters of Death*. For intricate details of Oppenheimer's trial, I turned to my grandfather's official transcript: *In the Matter of J. Robert Oppenheimer Transcript of Hearing before Personnel Security Board*. For daily life in Los Alamos, I referred to my grandmother's book, entitled *Los Alamos Experience*, by Phyllis K. Fisher. It is a collection of her censored letters home and offers a fascinating look into her secret world, but it keeps the reader at arm's length. I approached *The Sound of a Thousand Stars* as something like a sequel to her story, attempting to get closer to what was being withheld in those pages.

In the process, I stumbled across Oppenheimer's study, "On Continued Gravitational Contraction," which he copublished with his student H. Snyder. I was immediately fascinated by the legacy of the man who went down in history as the father of the atomic bomb but denied having discovered the black hole. Oppenheimer's article published by the American Physical Society—which was overshadowed by the Nazis' invasion of Poland on September 1, 1939—used Albert Einstein's theory of general relativity to propose how a star could collapse indefinitely. For years, the discovery lingered, but nobody paid it any attention until the astronomer John Wheeler coined the term "black hole" in 1968. Eighty years later, when the Event Horizon

Telescope Collaboration released the first-ever image of a black hole in 2019, Oppenheimer's research on neutron stars still stood the test of time.

Archives

Perhaps the most important work I did in writing this novel was to connect with and interview my grandparents' oldest still-living friends. In the time it took to write this book, both Ben Bederson and Murray Peshkin passed away. I collected their stories of working on the Project, along with my grandparents' original letters and documents, and donated them to the Los Alamos National Laboratory archives. With fewer hibakusha and fewer Project scientists still living to tell their stories, it's more important now than ever to preserve these histories for future generations.

For further reading on the Project, and the risks nuclear weapons pose around the world, please refer to the Los Alamos Historical Society and subscribe to the *Bulletin of the Atomic Scientists*.

Acknowledgments

There are numerous people I need to thank for their patience, time, and support that enabled me to bring this book into the world. First, and foremost, my husband, Michael Robbins—for talking through countless drafts and making do with never-ending dinner table conversations relegated to the 1940s. My prior agent, Wendy Sherman, who first believed in this book when it was just an exercise in free association on the flight home from my grandfather's funeral, and who continues to send me articles about Los Alamos to this day. To Catherine Cho at Paper Literary, who represented this book in its current form on the journey from draft to sale, and to her editorial director, Melissa Pimentel, for her brilliant vision. To Jess Verdi, my passionate and patient editor at Alcove, for her zealous attention to detail, her contagious energy, and her commitment to representation and stories that can change minds. Thank you to the mighty team at Alcove Press and Crooked Lane Books who helped make this novel everything and more than I had hoped.

To one of my brilliant early editors and champions, Denise Roy, for reminding me when I needed to hear it most that "books are for the living." To Gerald Brennan of Tortoise Books for supporting this vision and believing in my poetry. To my inimitable author's critique group, Crystal Rudds, Tim Chapman, and Lani Montreal, for reading numerous iterations of this story and devouring new drafts with fervor. To my dear friend, the author Julia Fine, who was central to my journey with this book and inspires me daily both as an artist and as a mother.

To Kathleen Rooney, I should list her name twice—for believing in an early draft when the manuscript was still straddling the line between nonfiction and fiction and soliciting it for *Make Literary Magazine*, and for selecting a variation of it, along with Abigail Beckel, as a semi-finalist for The Rose Metal Press Hybrid Genre Contest. Kathleen, thank you for being my dear friend, charming poetess, divine collaborator, and for your insight and guidance. To Jessica Anne at *Make* for her editorial insight and for nominating that early iteration of the story for a Pushcart Prize. Thank you to the Illinois Arts Council Agency for the Literary Award for prose that allowed me to devote more time to writing.

Thank you to Katy Jones-Gulsby, and the amazing team in Archives & Collections at the Los Alamos Historical Society, for helping me pinpoint my grandfather's exact address in Los Alamos, and for your assistance in decoding Ben Bederson's horrific cursive! Thank you for the tireless work you do to preserve these stories for future generations.

Thank you to Melanie Amano for sharing your family's experience with racism and Japanese internment. Thank you to my oldest and dearest childhood friend, Rumi Okazaki. It was a pleasure to reconnect after all these years and I can't overstate the value of your insights regarding the Japanese perspective. For sharing memories of my grandparents, thanks to David Fisher, Bob Fisher, and Larry Fisher (whose birth certificate really does read P.O. Box 1663). My brothers, Ben and Gabe Slotnick, for their support and guidance. My mother, Carol Slotnick, played an enormous part in hashing together my depleted memories of my grandfather's final years. From my grandfather kicking her date's car tires, to the specific top-secret contents of his security deposit box, this book couldn't have happened without her recollections. My father, Larry Slotnick, a history buff through and through, was the first person to read the manuscript. He researched the advent of vinyl floors and Pyrex beakers, fact-checking the stuff we could know for certain, and leaning into long debates about the stuff we couldn't.

My grandfather brought me closer to his oldest friends and colleagues in Los Alamos, six years after he left this earth. I had the pleasure of a Shabbat dinner with Murray and Frances Peshkin, and I visited with Ben and Betty Bederson in their walkup in Greenwich Village overlooking the roving Hudson River. Murray passed away in 2017 at the age of ninety-two, and Ben passed away only this past year at the ripe age of one hundred and one. Both are survived by loving children and grandchildren. To Ben and Murray, thank you for being such cherished and loving friends of my grandparents through a difficult time in their lives, and for all the years that followed. I'm so grateful that because of this book I had the opportunity to know you. You helped me understand my grandfather in a way that I never had.

To any others not mentioned here who helped me along my journey, who dusted off old memories, risked violating classified documents, who simply asked me how the book was coming, or what it was about, you did more for this writing process than you know.

Thank you to everyone who taught me to remember.